Harold
and
the Angel of Death

Gary McPherson

Dedication

First, to my wife. Thank you for encouraging me to write.

Dream Raven Editing. Thank you for an incredible journey together with this novel. You always seem to understand exactly where my characters and stories are headed and help me get there in one piece.

Ebook Launch. Thank you for your amazing cover designs and wonderful work on the interior designs

My beta readers. Your fresh perspectives and insights take my stories to the next level.

My parents. Thank you for adopting me and giving me such an amazing childhood.

CHAPTER 1

Harold stood over his father's casket. The heavy mahogany coffin's top was propped open. Tears flowed freely from Harold's eyes and continued down his cheeks to his collar. Allowing himself to lose control, he bent over and wrapped his arms around his father's lifeless body. Richard's cold, dead cheek pressed against his own.

Harold blubbered and stammered, "I'm sorry, Dad."

"That's okay, Son."

Harold released his grip and stumbled backwards. Something wet covered his hands. Lifting them up, he was horrified to see blood dripping from them. His shirt felt wet, and he found his chest covered in blood. When he looked around, the entertainment room no longer appeared warm and inviting with its tongue-and-groove pine walls and ceilings. Instead, it all looked pale, gray, cracked, and decaying. The glasses hanging from the bar began to vibrate and create a minor harmonic that sent chills through his body.

Harold turned and ran towards the dark doorway. He stumbled and bumped against the walls of the hallway. Maria's bedroom was locked as was his childhood bedroom. He looked back and saw the gray room beginning to fade. Forced by fear, he pushed forward and began to beat on the walls and windows, hoping to burst through somewhere, but they held fast. When he reached the front door, Harold beat and pulled on the door. He roared, but his voice seemed to die out rather than reverberate.

A familiar creaking caught Harold's attention further down the hall in the darkness. An odd thought crossed his mind. *Are Joshua and Maria back from their honeymoon already?* He stumbled forward and found Joshua's office door closed. The door latch gently lowered beneath his thumb. Peeking into Joshua's office, he found the lights off and the room dark. Dust and cobwebs hung from the corners of the ceiling and the sides of the computer monitors on his large desk. Another creak came from further down the dark hall. He turned and saw a light glowing from under his father's office door. Harold rubbed his face, hoping to wake up, but the darkness remained. Another thought pierced his mind as he looked towards his father's office. *No, Dad's gone. That's my office.* His fists clenched, and he stealthily made his way towards the end of the hallway. His large hand enveloped the handle on the office door, and he gently pushed it down.

As soon as he felt the handle click open, Harold burst into the room. He stopped short of his second step. Richard sat in his chair, and the office appeared as it once had. White oak wooden shelves lined the walls. Awards from his father's life and trinkets from past adventures filled the room. A grotesque pink and maroon texture was spattered against the adobe-colored wall behind his dad, and his dad's head appeared stuck to his chair.

"D…D…Dad?" Harold sputtered.

"Why did you fail me, Son? I trusted you to save the company."

From behind him, John's familiar whispered voice floated through the air, "What's the matter, brat? Seen a ghost?"

Harold screamed and found himself looking up at the dark ceiling of his master bedroom. His large hands gripped the sheet and blankets. He jerked his head to the right to check the alarm clock on the stand next to the bed. Three in the morning clicked over as the grandfather clock began to toll. He held his breath, but the house remained silent. As he sat up, he turned on the lamp next to the bed.

He patted his cheeks to make sure he was awake this time and then looked around the lit room. Everything was as it should be. His large four-poster bed was covered in a blue wool blanket that had once resided in his childhood room. The floral chairs faced the fireplace, but his favorite bear rug had replaced his parents' ornate red floor covering. The black of night painted the windows. Melancholy and relief filled his heart and mind. He missed his parents, but he was relieved the nightmare had been just that.

Joshua and Maria were still in Hawaii on their honeymoon, a wedding gift Harold had been more than happy to give them. After all, Joshua was like his second father. There was nothing he would not do for him. Harold imagined his mentor trying to bodysurf in the Hawaiian Pacific. A memory of Joshua, his father, and himself body surfing in Newport Beach brought a smile to his face.

Thanks to the time zones, Hawaii was three hours behind California. He entertained calling Joshua for a moment, but then a smile crept across his face. *Either they are asleep, or I don't want to interrupt.* Then another idea popped into his head.

CHAPTER 2

Harold could hear the phone ringing on the other end of the line. It was early, but at least it was not the middle of the night in North Carolina. A groggy voice with a soft Carolina accent picked up on the third ring. "Hey, this is Adam."

He felt his shoulders relax. "Doctor Murray, this is Harold. I hope I didn't wake you up."

He heard Adam clear his throat and then reply, "Oh, Harold, of course not, and call me Adam. It's good to hear from you again."

Harold stood up and walked over to a chair by the rock fireplace. He started to sit down but changed his mind and began to pace between the bed and the chair as he spoke. "Doc said I could call you if I needed help while he was gone. I started to call him first, but it's midnight in Hawaii."

He could hear Adam moving around and what sounded like a coffee maker just finishing in the background. "Did I interrupt your morning coffee?"

"Don't worry about that. I've been making my morning coffee and talking with people for years. You're no bother at all. So, tell me, what is happening with you?"

Harold walked out his bedroom door and made a right towards his office. The door was open, and the room was dark. "I've been having nightmares again. Did Joshua mention them to you?"

He turned on the light and relaxed as the office lit up, and his familiar furniture was all sitting in place. His new, oversized office chair sat behind his father's old desk. He had replaced the textured yellow and brown walls with a soft blue, and the tan Spanish tiles were replaced with an off-white. Although he had one shelf with trinkets and mementos from his childhood, the walls remained mostly bare. There was one sixteen by twenty photo of the family that hung on the wall next to the door, a reminder of happier times he could look up and see when he was working at his father's desk.

"Yes, we have talked about your dreams. We've both been trying to figure out if they're related to Joshua's hypnotherapy treatments. I'll be honest; I don't think that's the case. I think this has more to do with the trauma of losing your parents."

Harold walked around the desk, and his fingers traced the bloodstained wood that could not be cleaned. He had considered stripping the wood down or possibly replacing the boards, but he wanted to remember the day his father died. His dad set him on a mission to stop the men who caused his death and to save the family's defense company. So far, he had only succeeded in stopping the people responsible.

Sitting down in the chair, he finally responded to Adam. "Maybe it is about my parents, but I feel like I've dealt with that. Besides, it's the killer that's causing me to lose the most sleep. John's plan to take over

Dad's company succeeded in partially destroying it. When it comes to new contracts, nobody will touch us. There are multiple congressional investigations, and all our existing contracts are temporarily frozen. It may not matter when they finally find the company is above board because we'll be bankrupt long before then."

Harold could hear Adam trying to quietly sip his freshly brewed java before speaking. "I saw your testimony on Capitol Hill. I'm not a big C-SPAN fan, but I found your performance riveting. I'm not sure I could have controlled myself as well as you did."

"Well, it's like I tell Doc, I have my temper under control now. I'm not a kid anymore."

There was a quiet pause, and Harold wondered what Adam was doing. He was about to ask Adam if he was still there when Adam's voice came through the receiver. "You do know your problem isn't a temper issue? When you get angry, you have the ability to drive it up a few notches past a bad temper."

Harold exhaled slowly and leaned back in his office chair. The cool air flowing over his pajamas was starting to make him sleepy now that he had somebody to talk to. "I know, but it isn't like I turn green and become a CGI character. When I get that angry, it's because I foresee a threat that's serious enough that it has to be dealt with. I can't help it if my size and strength intimidate people."

Adam chuckled. "Well, you're certainly no barbarian. In fact, I would say your parents and Joshua have turned you into quite the gentleman. If you heard what I was yelling at my television during the congressional hearing, you might be counseling me. Who were those house members to question you on your efforts to get Maria legal US residency? It isn't as though she had a choice as a small child."

"I didn't take it as a slight against Maria or myself. All three congresspeople are up for re-election. One is in a liberal district that's full of peaceniks. Questioning my integrity scores her some political points with the groups that hate weapon's manufacturers. The other two are in tight races right now. Their districts are normally red but are changing to purple. If they can score political points with a perceived immigration issue, they will. I tried not to take it personally."

An audible *humph* emitted from the phone. "Well, I can't fault you there. I'm afraid my own temper would have gotten the better of me in that situation. I may need to seek Joshua's advice if he has taught you that much self-control."

"Joshua taught me to control my temper, but Dad taught me how to deal with politicians during my high school years. He told me if I wanted to work in the family business, I needed to learn those skills sooner rather than later."

Harold thought he heard Adam rifling through papers and the scratching of a pencil. "Tell me, if your father was alive today, what advice do you think he would give you?"

He sat there for a moment contemplating the question. He hadn't thought about what his dad would say. All he thought about was not failing and losing the company his late father had placed into his strong but inexperienced hands. "I'm not sure what Dad would say to me now. I know he wanted me to save his company.

At least, that was what he had hoped for and was one of the reasons he took his life. He assumed I could stop John and keep everything going."

Adam's voice grew somber. "Your father's plan didn't work out the way he had hoped though. I don't doubt he would still be alive if he had known the fallout from his decision."

Harold sat and stared at the family photo for several seconds. He put his elbows on his desk and rested his head on his left palm. "I suppose that's true. I guess that's my problem. I don't want his death to be in vain. Dad loved us, and he loved the company. He loved everyone who worked with him. If I fail, everything he tried to accomplish will be wiped out."

Adam's soft Southern drawl grew slower as he spoke, "Harold, your father didn't expect you to take on saving the company alone. You have Tom, Joshua, Maria, and I would think all of the employees at Parabolic Defense Systems, backing your efforts. Besides, I'm sure your dad would be proud of the way you brought the men to justice that tried to destroy your family."

"But they succeeded, don't you see? Dad's dead, and so is Mom. I'm an orphan again."

"As I said, you still have Joshua and Maria."

Harold stood up out of his chair, walked around his desk and began to pace. His left hand fluttered through the air as he voiced his frustration. "Yea, but I had Joshua when I was a little kid there at the orphanage in North Carolina. I mean, I sort of remember that. It's more like an impression that Joshua has just always been in my life. This is just a problem

I've never been able to shake since I was a kid. Everything I associate with the orphanage reminds me I'm an orphan. Now I feel like I've lost everything, and I'm back where I started. I'm alone in the world. There is Joshua, but one day he'll be gone too."

"But you're not where you started. Look around you. Your parents left you with a nice place to live. Joshua has told me he and Maria love living across the road from you. You're not alone, not really. I know you miss your parents, but we all outlive our parents, if God has mercy on them. No parent wants to outlive their child."

Harold stopped pacing and stared at the large photo on the wall. Of course, Adam was right, but he wished he could be a kid again. Just a kid wrestling in the yard with his dad while Joshua and Barbara leaned against the old stucco walls of the house watching them and laughing. Tears pooled in his eyes, and his vision blurred as the salty liquid trailed down his cheeks. "Doc...I mean Adam, I just don't know if I can do this."

Adam's voice increased slightly in volume and tone. "You don't have to do anything. Just try your hardest and make the decisions you think are best for you and the business."

"But what if I fail my dad?"

"With all due respect to your late father, he gave up the right to expect anything of you when he took his own life. I know his suicide was more complicated than a simple gunshot, but I don't believe he expected you to carry all of this burden. From what Joshua tells me, he loved you very much, and no father who loves his son would do such a thing."

Harold felt weak and a bit dizzy. He walked over and dropped down into his office chair. "I suppose you're right. I guess I'm just tired of waking up alone in this big house. If I lose the company, I might lose a lot of friends and maybe even my standing in the community. Right now, it feels like that's all I have left in this world."

"That isn't true. Joshua and Maria are still a part of your family, and of course, you have my friendship. Nobody is alone unless they choose to be."

Adam's concerned voice spoke up after several seconds of awkward silence. "Are you still there?"

"Yea, sorry, I was just thinking about what you said. You may be oversimplifying my situation, but you're right. I'm not alone. Still, I need to try and do what I can to save this company. Many families' livelihoods are on the line. I understand I may not owe anyone anything for my father's mistake, but that doesn't change my responsibilities. If the board decides to trust me enough to run the company, I need to live up to their trust."

"Fair enough," said Adam.

"I appreciate our talk. I have a board meeting this morning, and you have helped make things a bit clearer."

"Anytime, Harold. I think I'll go grab myself a second cup of coffee and start my day."

Harold looked at the metallic star-shaped clock on the side wall of his office. He had picked it up from a trinket shop in the middle of the desert on a college road trip to Palm Springs. It was 4:30 a.m. How had the time gone by so quickly? Harold said his goodbyes and hung up the phone. The fear of the nightmare had left him, but his mind now raced with his to-do list for the board meeting in a few hours. The board would certify him as CEO today. Once that was decided, it would be up to him to encourage the best minds to come up with suggestions to pull the company out of its tailspin.

He left his office and made himself some coffee. He sat down at the kitchen table and wished Joshua was there to bounce ideas off. His eyes trailed over to the kitchen island and to the bullet hole that remained in the wooden cabinet. A dark thought crossed his mind, *John, I hope you're burning in hell. If you were alive, I'd kill you all over again.*

He frowned and took a sip of his coffee. This was not helping. He needed to let go of the past, but everywhere he looked something seemed to haunt him. When Joshua and Maria returned, he would get them to help redecorate the kitchen. Harold got up and strolled through the dark family room. Stepping out the French doors, he could barely see the Pacific, which looked as black as his world. As he watched, the stars in the sky above slowly surrendered to the early morning gray of the sun that hid below the mountains on the eastern horizon behind him.

CHAPTER 3

Parabolic Defense Systems sent a car and driver to pick up Harold at nine o'clock. Harold was not a fan of being driven around in a black town car with tinted windows. His father had been a man who preferred to take care of things himself, including his driving, but the board insisted. It seemed pretentious, but he went along with the request.

Other than a cordial *good morning*, neither the driver nor Harold spoke much to each other. The driver's dark sunglasses and broad shoulders led him to believe the driver was more than simply a courier, but he could not imagine why the board felt he needed such protection. After all, most people moved out of the way of his broad six-foot-five-inch frame.

The company car wound its way through the hills to the entrance of the Parabolic Defense Systems. The large logo hung proudly at the private road's entrance to the company. Harold beamed with pride. What was it his father had said to him as a child?

"Harold, do you see the angel with her wings sheltering the globe? That's what we do. We guard God's creation from those who would harm all free men and women. The sword in her right hand and the missile rising up between the globe and the angel represent the weapons of the past and the present that we use to protect mankind from evil."

A mournful thought passed through his mind, *Dad, why did you use a weapon to take your own life? That didn't protect us. It exposed us.* His eyes misted up, and he turned to look out the tinted window at the surrounding hills to clear his mind.

The car pulled up to the gated entrance. To his surprise, the guard checked the driver's ID instead of his own and then waved them past. He noticed two extra men in suits at the guard shack and wondered why security had increased. The driver pulled him up to the main entrance then opened his door. Harold closed the laptop he had absently left opened on his lap the last few minutes of the ride. He walked up to the door to find a doorwoman with her blond hair tied into a bun. She wore dark sunglasses and a navy-blue dress suit.

"When did you get hired?" inquired Harold.

"Good morning," she replied with a broad smile.

Harold guessed she was in her early forties, but based on the tight clothing, she appeared to work out often. As he walked through the door, everything appeared to be business as usual. Photos of politicians and generals lined the walls with pictures of his father and other company members. He had expected the images to evoke more emotions than he felt, but the thought of the boardroom just beyond the security desk was forefront in his mind. It was time to put his game face on.

"Mr. Brown, it's so good to see you." Isabel's voice broke through his thoughts. She was a sight for sore eyes. Isabel had been a long-time family friend. She had been among the throng at his father's funeral when his mother collapsed, and her sympathy card arrived with tear stains. Although she was in her late fifties and had strands of gray hair among her black mane, she was still a stunning woman. Isabel and his mother often met with other women from the company for tea once a month to discuss working conditions and areas for improvement.

"Thank you. I assume the board is already waiting on me."

Isabel's face took on a solemn expression, and she spoke softly, "Yes. Don't let them bully you in there."

Harold rolled his eyes and then whispered back, "Nobody bullies me."

She grinned at his wink, and he walked across the marble flooring to the elevator. After passing his card key over the reader, he hit the elevator button and the doors slid open. He entered the familiar wood and chrome lift and placed his thumb on the fingerprint reader to access the restricted level. The doors slid shut, and he headed for the second floor.

The elevator doors opened, and Harold stepped out. He had never been a fan of the second floor. The mahogany paneling and red carpet made everything feel stuffy, dark, and antiquated. Although the executives' offices were on the fourth floor, the boardroom and the accountants' offices were on the second, and they liked the throwback office décor. He turned right and headed to the boardroom, which took up the center back of the floor. The glass exterior wall gave everyone a nice view of the mostly sunny weather and surrounding hills. The glass interior wall was supposed to show transparency, but nobody ever really knew what silent conversations were going on behind the glass.

Walking towards the room, Harold could see the board of directors. Abigail Perez was among his father's first ten hires and the only board member to have risen internally to her position. She was not only an exceptional engineer but had shown the rare ability to manage people and costs effectively. Her insight into keeping a diverse workforce content while keeping company costs down had been invaluable.

Cameron Green and Samantha Torres both helped fund the company at its founding. Their business savvy had aided his father and enabled him to create government contracts at costs lower than his competitors.

Fred Powell was the outsider. He had joined the board from John Richmond's company two years ago. Harold had him investigated in the aftermath of his father's suicide as a possible corporate mole. Fortunately, the investigation found no link to his old company.

Harold walked into the meeting room, and all the conversations stopped. Although the large table could easily accommodate at least twelve people, all the chairs had been removed except those the board members sat in, his father's chair at the head of the table, and two more chairs at the far end that sat empty. Samantha pointed to Richard's seat. Harold hesitated for a moment. The thought of replacing his father sent a wave of unexpected grief through his body. For a second, he was unsure he could take the next step.

At that moment, the door opened behind him, and Tom stepped in. He put his hand on Harold's shoulder. "Hi, buddy. I'm glad you're ready to take the reins. Let's get this party started."

Harold mumbled, "Yea."

He took his father's seat, and Tom took the other seat at the far end of the table. Harold looked around the room. Everyone appeared to wear the same dark suits or dress suits. Ties and other accessories were used in a desperate attempt to exert some sort of individuality. Harold's own suit included a suicide prevention ribbon lapel pin in memory of his father.

Harold made a point of projecting his voice around the room. "Ladies and Gentlemen, we all know the company is in trouble, but we need to get our house in order before we can address the elephant in the room. I do hope you have come up with a solution for the large void left by my father's sudden absence from this world."

Everyone turned their attention to Abigail. Harold took their cue and also looked to the company's resident management genius. Abigail rose and walked over to the whiteboard behind Tom, who slid to his left so he could watch her.

Abigail cleared her throat and began. "Harold, as you know, your father held two roles in PDS, that of chairman and CEO."

Abigail turned around and wrote the two roles side by side on the whiteboard and drew a short vertical line under each. "The board has looked at the challenges ahead for the company and has decided to split these two roles. The CEO needs to work closely with the chief operating officer to ensure our production costs remain low and employee morale high. In addition, the CEO will need to make sure that daily interactions with our clients are occurring without hiccups. Our chairman's role will take on a more strategic focus. That person will work closely with the board to direct the company's future business and help us bring the new clients we desperately need to maintain our operating capital. In other words, the chairman is going to be key to saving your father's company."

Harold doodled on the pad in front of him as he listened and began to think through how he would talk the workers into doing more with less. Abigail turned back to the board and wrote in two names. Under chairman, she wrote *Harold Brown*, and under CEO she wrote *Tom Hudson*. Harold's eyes grew wide. Abigail finished writing and turned around. Everyone looked at Harold. The room was uncomfortably still for thirty seconds.

"I'm not sure I understand. I have the business background, but I don't have my father's vision for defensive systems. I would have thought you'd want me as CEO."

Harold noticed Tom's eyes glance towards the door, and his head gave ever so slight a nod. The boardroom door opened, and Harold turned to see who was coming in.

"Hi, everybody, has our boy been filled in?" It was sunglass-clad CIA agent Garcia Hernandez.

"We are just getting started," Tom said. "Why don't you have a seat over here near me, Agent Hernandez?"

"Please, call me Garcia. Harry, good to see you."

With that, Garcia slapped a piece of paper in front of him.

"Sign this," said the agent.

Abigail cleared her throat. "Harold, it's a nondisclosure agreement. We have all signed one promising not to reveal anything discussed with Agent Garcia, as it is considered confidential."

Garcia stood there tapping his leg with one hand and pointing at the paper with the other. Harold looked down and scanned the contract. He saw he could go to jail if anything were leaked, and surrounding the threat was a lot of legalese. He tapped the table with his index finger, picked up his pen, and then signed his name at the bottom. Garcia snatched up the paper and slid it into an unseen pocket inside his jacket.

Harold crossed his arms. He had a feeling he knew where this was going. Garcia sat down next to Tom. Fred subtly tapped his face with his middle finger just below his right eye.

Garcia mouthed, "Oh" and removed his sunglasses.

"Harold, Agent Hernandez approached me with an offer to help the company," Tom said. "I brought him to the board, and they all agreed that his plan has the greatest chance to save PDS. Agent Hernandez, the floor is yours."

Garcia cleared his throat, stood, and stepped smoothly to the whiteboard. Harold could not help but notice Garcia's outfit blended in perfectly with the rest of the board members, although his frame was clearly in much better shape than the other men sitting around the table. He wondered if Agent Hernandez could always fit in that easily with a group of people or if office espionage was his forte.

Garcia erased what Abigail had written and began his presentation. "Harry—"

"Harold!" the board and Harold replied in unison.

"Please, I've known our new chairman since he was first brought home. My apologies though. Harold, as you know, the company is currently under several investigations by Congress. Although you managed to stop John, he was savvy enough to know that any hint of trouble would trigger the defense department slowing, or stopping, business with your company until their investigation was completed. Given the scope of corruption within the other two companies, and former Senator Jones—may he rest in peace, the investigations are going to drag on for a while. I'm afraid Parabolic is guilty by association for the time being."

Harold mindlessly rolled his pen around his fingers, and his shoulders slumped a bit. John's taunting from his nightmares murmured in the back of his mind.

Garcia continued, "But all is not lost. Fortunately for all of us, the CIA has its own budget, and we even managed to pull a few million dollars out of the black budget for top secret work. There's still political oversight, but as I told the board, everyone involved on that committee is a Parabolic Defense Systems supporter."

Harold raised a finger and Garcia stopped. He looked around at the board as he spoke, "So, are you all saying we're going into the spy weapons business?"

Garcia jumped in before anybody else had a chance to answer. "Forgive me, Harold. The CIA doesn't get involved in weapons creation. Sure, we still make top-of-the-line gizmos and gadgets to gather intelligence, but weapons are the responsibility of other acronyms. In fact, we prefer to allow the military, or mercs, handle that end of things. We may just borrow them from time to time. However, your company does offer us a unique opportunity. Several foreign terrorist organizations would kill for access to your equipment, if you'll pardon my choice of words."

A voice inside his mind spoke, *Your father never allowed his company to do anything illegal. What if they lose track of the weapons like the Fast and Furious operation?* Harold asked, "What if the weapons get away from the CIA? Then our company's weapons really will be in the hands of terrorists."

Garcia responded, "Please, we're the CIA. We don't give criminals real weapons. We plan to put trackers into anything we sell. We'll also render most of the weapons inoperable. The few that we need to make the sale with will be so small in number as to be insignificant."

"But what if they reverse engineer what they buy?"

"Harry…I mean Harold, you need to quit getting on the internet and reading anti-government propaganda. Besides, many US weapons are already in the hands of some of the terrorists. They found them on the battlefield or ISIS took them when they pushed their way into Iraq. If they had the capacity to reverse engineer equipment and mass produce them, they would already be doing it."

"If they already have some of our weapons, why do they need more?"

Garcia chuckled. "They have a hard time keeping any weaponry when a five-hundred-pound bomb is dropped on their heads from a drone. The opportunity here is not in the traditional theatre though. It's in northern Africa and some factions in the south Pacific. Much like the often-rumored Nazi reformation in South America after World War II, many of the terrorist leaders have abandoned the Middle East for other parts of the world. Unlike the Nazis who went into semi-retirement, these people are spreading their hate and fear and building new armies of terrorism. They need weapons, good weapons, to complete their vision."

Harold's eyes widened and he sat up. "So, you're going to pay us to create the bait to pull these groups into the open."

Garcia smacked the whiteboard, and everyone jumped. "You got it. Trust me when I tell you that there are plenty of fish in the sea, so we'll be buying plenty of bait."

Harold slid his chair back so he could give his legs more room and considered Garcia's proposal. It was certainly a good plan. The company could remain solvent between their few working contracts and the CIA's offer. He only had one question left. "Why me?"

"Excuse me?" responded Garcia.

"Why did you have me put in as chairman of the board?" Harold quickly held his hand up towards the murmuring board. "And please, nobody attempt to tell me that isn't the case. Tom has the military background, not me. He would be better suited for my role."

Garcia answered, "Okay, you caught me. Harold, I need somebody whose reputation precedes them. You have name recognition due to who your father was. If I have you involved with me when I meet with these scoundrels, they are more likely to believe the sting."

Harold leaned forward, and his chair squeaked under the strain of his weight. "I'm no spy. What if something goes wrong? Are you planning on using me for a human shield?"

"Please, Harold, we both know better. You're a big boy and can take care of yourself. That's why you're the perfect choice."

Harold leaned back into his seat, and the chair squeaked again in protest of its burden. "This sounds more like you want me with you to help take these guys out."

Garcia flipped the whiteboard pen back and forth in his hand. "Potato, potato. Either way works for me."

"That's not who I am, and I don't intend to become that person."

Garcia walked over and sat on the edge of the boardroom table between Harold and everyone else. He spoke barely above a whisper. "Harold, I don't want you to become that person either, but you are the best man for the job. I need your help. The people in charge won't give me the time of day if you aren't involved."

"Excuse me, Agent Hernandez," said Samantha. "The rest of the group would like to be involved in the conversation."

Garcia turned around. "Of course, please excuse my rudeness." He walked back and took his seat next to Tom.

Harold slid his chair forward and rested his large forearms on the boardroom table. He looked around the room until everyone focused on him once more. Pros and cons rolled through Harold's mind. What would his father do? Would he inadvertently pull the company into a real scandal? Handing over fake weapons was not the same as arming the world's enemies, and it would protect the homeland. "Okay, I'll do it. I expect to be informed on how operations are going. Tom, I know you can do the work, and Abigail, I expect you to make sure he does."

"That's the plan," responded Abigail.

"Good. Okay, let's move to the next steps."

Harold could not help but notice the smiles on Cameron and Samantha's faces.

"I'm forming a team who will manufacture dummy versions of advanced weapons," Tom said. "Abigail and I will handpick this group, and we are going to secure part of our warehouse to create a separate facility inside it."

"What sort of advanced weapons?" questioned Harold.

Tom raised his hand towards Harold as he spoke. "The CIA is giving us the specs. Our engineers will be researching how to improve them as a side benefit. The weapons we are producing for the CIA are well beyond the prototype stage, so there is little to no R&D for us to absorb."

"Excellent," said Harold. "What other business does the board have?"

"Money," responded Samantha. "Agent Hernandez, please explain our agreement to Harold."

Garcia stood up, faced the whiteboard, and began to scribble letters and numbers Harold had trouble reading. He turned and spoke to the group. "As you can see here, ninety percent of all money the CIA retrieves will be funneled back into PDS via a shell company I'll be setting up. Harold, I'll give you more details about this one-on-one later. In addition, we are going to pay you full price for both real and dummy weapons. We also will be giving you access to the patent on our GPS tracking technology. This will enable you to not only manufacture it for our purposes but implement that technology into products of your choice and sell them to a CIA-approved corporation list."

Harold jumped in with a question, "That's generous, but what about when you're done with us? What happens to my company when we're no longer useful?"

Garcia rolled his eyes. "Please. Harold, PDS has a long history with our country. You will always be useful, but you bring up a good question that was asked of me when I first approached the board. The head of the CIA is currently working with the FBI and others to fast-track the investigation into PDS. They have agreed to cooperate. So I expect your contracts will be rolling in again in the not too distant future."

Harold caught Garcia's redirection. "At what point would that be?"

"Real soon," was all Garcia would say, and then he took his seat again.

Harold looked around at the other board members. Their sullen looks told him there was no reason to push Garcia further. Yet, he could not let the conversation end there. His face hardened, and he glared into Garcia's eyes and spoke deliberately. "If you do anything to screw this company and the people here, I will come after you, and I think you know that you don't want me coming after you."

Garcia clucked his tongue. "Please, we're the CIA. Besides, how can you think that? If I hadn't showed up at John's death, you might very well be sitting in prison now."

"We both know that was self-defense."

Garcia gave a dismissive wave. "Yea, I know, but the local law enforcement didn't. You would have been cleared eventually, but that whole scene could have been much messier. Trust me, if I wanted to screw you, or your company, I would have done so a long time ago. In fact, my superiors originally wanted to buy John's old defense company and use it as a front, but I convinced them this was the better model. I'm not going through all this trouble to screw you. I'm trying to save you. Your father built a legacy that is about to be destroyed because of one bitter man, one greedy man, and another's poor life choices. Work with me, Harold, and we'll save what your father built."

Harold leaned back in his chair. "I already said you have our cooperation, but I want to be sure we have yours."

"Always," Garcia replied. With that, he put on his sunglasses and stood up. "If you will pardon me, ladies and gentlemen, I need to tell my superiors that operation Viking is a go." Without waiting for a response, Garcia briskly walked out of the room and was gone from sight.

"You're gonna have your hands full, my friend," Tom said.

Harold chuckled. He just hoped Garcia was a man of his word. Cameron passed out forms for everyone to sign acknowledging Harold as the new chairman of the board and Tom as CEO. Tom informed him he would be contacted by Garcia at home sometime in the next twenty-four hours. Harold decided to head back home once the meeting had adjourned. He had experienced more than enough drama with Garcia, and he wanted time to think through the company's agreement before their next encounter.

CHAPTER 4

Harold felt the snow crunching underneath his feet with each heavy footfall. The gray sky over the bare trees of the forest told him another snow storm was coming. He stopped to get his bearings. Looking over his shoulder, he could see his footprints leading into the woods and out of sight. Finding his way back to the village would not be difficult, as long as he started back before the snow began.

He loosely gripped his large bow in his left hand. His quiver of arrows hung off his bearskin-covered back. His battle axe sat securely in its leather sheath, crisscrossed over the quiver of arrows. He heard a noise and silently turned his head to his left. A large buck had walked out of the woods. Its ears flickered as it sensed danger somewhere beyond its vision.

Harold slowly withdrew his arrow and aimed his bow. He cringed as the bow creaked in protest to his mighty arms. Suddenly the animal's head jerked in his direction, and it scampered off. He closed his eyes in frustration. His arm still held the butt of the arrow to his cheek. The cold air filled his nostrils, and the smell of wolf filled his mind. Harold spun around and opened his eyes.

Three feet away stood a stranger dressed in a wolf skin. Although he was at least five inches shorter than Harold, his bare chest told him that the stranger had to be a berserker. "Friend or foe?" Harold asked in a deep and foreboding voice.

"Brother," answered the stranger.

Harold stared hard at him. The man's blue eyes flashed through him, and he could see his baby brother being held in Joshua's bare arms as the Browns took Harold by the hand and led him out of the queen's longhouse on the way to their village. Harold wept for Bill.

"I'm sorry, honey. We want your baby brother, but your mother won't let us have him," Queen Barbara said.

"But I don't want to leave. I want Bill," young Harold cried.

"We'll try to reunite you." Barbara held him close to her body. Her leather vest and skirt were rough. Harold reached up to touch the top of her sword's hilt. He felt safe in her arms. He looked at King Richard. His large battle axes peeked out from behind his battle gear, and Harold's eyes grew wide. His new mother was right. If anyone could reunite him with Bill, it was his new parents.

Harold's mind returned to the snow and the man in front of him. "Bill, how did you find me here?"

Bill's forehead wrinkled and his eyes looked skyward for a moment. "I don't know, but something tells me you're in danger."

The sound of snow crunching interrupted their reunion. John came strolling out of the forest. Harold raised his arrow at John, and Bill turned in his direction and raised his battle axe.

"Easy, boys," said John. "I come in peace."

"You're a liar," snarled Harold. "There's nothing peaceful about you."

John dropped his axe and lifted his palms to his shoulders. "See, I'm unarmed. I'm going to walk ten feet over to that log and sit down. Why don't you join me?"

"We'll stand, thanks," Harold growled.

"Who is he, Brother?"

"A thief, murderer, and liar."

John sat down on the log and looked at both men. "Brother? Oh, so you're this brat's long-lost brother Richard spoke about. Well, maybe you can help us out then."

"There is no us,"

"Hear me out. Garcia is a dangerous man. He's the reason I lost my company, and he's the real reason Richard is dead."

Harold tightened his bow further. The wood groaned under his strength, and the string tightened to the verge of breaking. His voice was guttural, "Mention my father one more time, and I'll loose this arrow into your skull."

John put up his hand. "Easy, brat. Besides, we both know that won't kill me. This is important. Listen to me and then shoot me."

Harold stood still as a stone.

John rolled his eyes. "Bull-headed runt. Listen to me. Garcia came to me when I was trying to get new defense contracts for my company. Contracts your dad seemed to always undercut. He promised me if I played ball he'd make everything right and help us with our future bids. All we had to do was play ball with him and provide our company as cover while he was embedded as an arms dealer in the Middle East during the latter half of the Iraq War."

Harold relaxed his bow and lowered his arrow. "What happened?"

"We played ball. The liar never intended on following through. After the war ended, Garcia got moved to some other project. His handler told me there was nothing they could do. The political winds were changing. Somehow your dad managed to navigate his way through it, but the CIA couldn't find time to help me out. It had all been a ruse, and I had taken my eye off the priorities of my company. That was the beginning of the end."

"Why are you even telling me this? You blamed my father for everything. You killed my parents and tried to kill the rest of us."

John's smile made Harold's blood run cold, and the darkness in his eyes seemed to suddenly flash with a fire behind them. "Because you are now the enemy of my enemy. You just don't know it yet. We'll always have our war between one another, and one day, I will drive you insane, but in the meantime, I want to make sure Garcia goes down for what he did."

Harold stood there and considered what he had heard. He spit to the side. "Forget it. I will never become your puppet. Even if Garcia did use your company, you were the one that blamed my father and pushed him to suicide."

John stood up, brushed off his butt, and walked towards his axe with his arm extended. Harold raised his bow again, and Bill stepped forward to stand atop John's weapon.

John stopped and pulled his hand away. "Okay, I can come back for it." He looked at Bill. "I would stay out of your brother's affairs. You'll only get yourself in trouble."

Bill stood silent, glaring towards John. John turned back to Harold. "Look, brat, you will help me with Garcia. If not for my sake, then for your own."

Harold stood like a statue. His bow fingers quivered as he fought the urge to release the string and drive the arrow into John's head.

"You think about what I said. It's time to wake up now."

A loud buzzing filled the sky and darkness filled his vision. He cracked his eyes open to find the morning sun shining over the beautiful Malibu hills and through his bedroom window. Harold slapped at the snooze bar to turn off the annoying buzzer and then turned off his alarm. He rolled over on his back. John's words were still echoing in his mind and he turned his thoughts towards his day to forget his nightmare. Joshua and Maria were coming home, and he needed to make sure he called the maid service to go through their house. John's warning about Garcia forced its way forward into Harold's mind. Harold pushed against his own subconscious to remind himself that Garcia was supposed to call.

John's words from his dream passed across his mind once more. He snorted and sat up in bed, rubbing his face in an attempt to remove the dream from his mind. Stumbling across the Spanish tile, he passed the wooden doors and walked into the arched entry of his shower. He stuck his head under the warm water and heard a voice say, "Don't forget, brat."

Harold pulled his body out from under the shower head and stepped out, dripping onto the tiled floor. *Am I still dreaming?* He slapped himself hard in the face. His right cheek lit up like fire. There was no doubt that he was awake. He spoke aloud to calm his nerves, "It was just a dream. Still, what harm will it do to chat with Garcia about what John said?"

Harold stood silently. The house was quiet aside from the hum of the HVAC pushing the morning chill from the air.

He let out a short laugh at his own fear and returned to the shower to start his day.

CHAPTER 5

The doorbell rang. Harold stretched and rose from behind his father's desk in the office. At first, he thought the maid service was done, but looking over at the wall clock he noticed they had only been across the street for a short time. The doorbell rang again, and he realized how much he missed having Maria around to answer the door. Harold plodded his way down the hall to the entryway. The doorbell rang a third time as he reached for the doorknob and jerked the door open.

Before him stood Garcia. Harold's scowl reflected off Garcia's large sunglasses. Garcia wore a broad smile, a T-shirt, shorts, and a pair of Van's denim slip-ons.

Garcia said, "Sorry about that. I thought maybe you didn't hear me."

"It's a big house," responded Harold.

"I guess Joshua and Maria are still gone, huh?"

"They return later this afternoon. Besides, that's not her job anymore. I thought you were going to call."

For once, Garcia removed his sunglasses without prompting. "I was in the neighborhood. I thought I would drop by."

"Come on in." Harold stepped to the side, and Garcia strolled in. "Let's go out on the back deck. I've been inside all morning and could use the fresh air."

"I could use the sunshine myself."

The two men walked through the living room, out the French doors, and took a seat at Harold's favorite table. When he realized he had not offered Garcia any refreshments, he slapped the white painted surface of the table. Garcia jumped.

"What am I thinking?" said Harold. "I'm sorry. Do you want a beer? I'm just used to having Maria here, and she used to take care of this stuff."

Garcia composed himself. "No worries. I'd love a beer, if you're going to have one."

"I'll be right back."

Harold returned with a couple Sierra Nevada Pale Ales. "I do hope you don't mind the more local stuff."

Garcia took out his pocket knife, pulled out his bottle opener, and popped off the top of the bottle. He took a long swig, put the bottle down, and let out a long belch. "I'm a big fan of this, but after you've had fresh German beer, the rest is just second place." Garcia reached over and opened Harold's beer for him.

Harold finished his bottle in one swallow. "To each their own. Let me know when you're ready for another one. Like I said, I'm afraid Maria has spoiled me. I should've brought out more beers."

Garcia quipped, "It sounds like you could use a wife to keep you in line."

Harold's mouth curled downward. "I don't think so. I don't want a woman who serves our guests beers. I want a woman who can drink me under the table or take me on in a fair fight."

"Sounds like somebody misses Darla."

Harold looked out over the hills and down to the ocean as he thought about his missing girlfriend and then decided he preferred to change the subject. "You know, Joshua really taught me to appreciate this view. We've probably spent years out here together thinking, talking, and remembering."

"It's beautiful," responded Garcia.

Harold turned to Garcia and pointed up and down at his outfit. "Before we get down to business, I just need to know, is it casual Tuesday at the company?"

Garcia ignored the quip and finished off his beer. After another burp, he answered, "No, but when I'm in the field, I'm free to dress as I see fit. This is my preferred attire, and it seemed appropriate on a day like today."

Harold rose. "Be right back." He left and returned with four more beers.

"Easy, big guy. We're not all six feet five."

Harold reached over and patted Garcia on the shoulder before sitting down. "Well, I don't know how long this will take, and I didn't feel like making another beer run inside."

"Fair enough."

The two men popped their beers. Garcia took a slow sip of his, and Harold finished off a third of his bottle in one swallow. "Alright, Agent Garcia, let's get to work. What's going on?"

Garcia took a short sip of his beer and then sat up and put his arms on the table. He leaned forward towards Harold and looked hard into his eyes. Harold's body stiffened, and he wondered why he suddenly felt like he was going to be interrogated. Garcia asked, "I'm curious. In our meeting yesterday, you shifted gears awfully fast when I said I needed your help. Why?"

Harold's finger wiped the sweat from his beer bottle. He stretched out his legs and took a slow sip from his bottle as he thought about Garcia's question. He put down his brew. "I don't know. I was sitting in Dad's old chair and asked myself what he would do. He was able to live with the bloodshed our weapons caused because he was convinced we were always on the right side. I just felt like helping you was the right side."

Garcia took another sip of his beer and stared out towards the ocean. Harold wondered what he was thinking about. Now seemed like a good time to bring up his concerns.

Harold cleared his throat, and Garcia glanced over at him. Harold said, "I do have a couple of questions, more like concerns really."

"Fire away," responded Garcia.

"Well, John told me a couple of things before he died."

Garcia pushed his beer bottle to the side. "What do you mean he told you things? I thought you snapped his neck?"

"Yea, well, I did. He said this stuff when Joshua was talking to him. I was listening in the hallway, trying to figure out when to make my move."

Garcia's brow wrinkled. "What did John say?"

"He was rambling on about the CIA and my dad. He claimed the two of you colluded to destroy JR Aerospace. John said a guy named Garcia had worked his way into his company and then double-crossed him.

I woke up this morning and the memory popped back into my head. I'm just wondering if that's you?"

"Why didn't Joshua mention this to me?"

Harold leaned back into his chair. "Doc was busy trying to save Maria. I doubt he was even listening to that part."

Garcia began to drum his fingers on the surface of the table while he looked down at them. Harold wondered if he was trying to think of a lie to tell him, or if he was debating telling him the truth. Garcia's drumming ceased, and he grabbed his bottle and finished off the remaining three-fourths.

After an extended belch, he sat up. "I suppose you deserve to know. First, the CIA and your father never colluded together. That was John's twisted mind trying to justify his actions. He was right about the CIA and his company having a relationship, and I was involved. My cover in Iraq was as an employee of JR Aerospace. My job at that time was to ferret out insurgents that had tried to infiltrate the ranks of the contractors. John was paid a modest stipend to ensure my cover was well documented in the company computers should anyone try to check up on me. In addition, I promised when I returned I'd try and help him win some defense contracts. It was pretty standard stuff really.

"I had assumed my handlers would throw a few contracts John's way. However, as Iraq wrapped up, I was asked to go dark and head into Syria to gather as much intel as I could on ISIS and other newly forming terrorist groups. Because of the danger, all communication was cut, and all the records inside of JR Aerospace that could identify me were mysteriously destroyed by a hacker attack."

"So why didn't you follow up when you came back?" asked Harold.

Garcia popped open another beer bottle and took a sip. He put it on the table and then rolled it back and forth between his palms. He continued to watch the bottle as he spoke. "I tried. Everything had changed by then. My handlers had all moved on to other jobs. The politics around the Middle East, and defense, were turning. Cuts were happening everywhere. Even your father's company saw two of their newest contracts cancelled before they had finished with their first production model. There was nothing I could do for John, and unfortunately, he couldn't accept it. John was sure Richard had somehow found out about our deal and had turned someone against him. The man had issues."

"Yea."

"The whole thing's a shame," mumbled Garcia.

"So, how do I know something like that won't happen to PDS? It doesn't sound to me like there are any guarantees in this little arrangement."

Garcia stopped focusing on his beer bottle and leaned back into his chair. His eyes seem to look past Harold as he spoke. "I can't tell you it won't go down that way. Maybe your dad didn't teach you everything about this industry, or maybe the truth is what killed him. Making weapons for national defense can be a nasty business. It's all tied to the boys in Washington, DC. Everyone from the Pentagon to Pennsylvania Avenue has their opinion on how the world should work and who should defend it. Those opinions change with each election."

"I thought this arrangement would help stabilize things. But it's sounding more like I just dug a deep hole, and a ladder may or may not be sent down to help me back out."

Harold looked back up to see that Garcia had put his sunglasses back on. He could no longer see Garcia's eyes, but his mouth formed a frown.

"Look, I understand if you don't want to play along. Here's the truth. If you back out, then the CIA will back out. That leaves your company in desperate straits. The board will likely vote to remove you because of your decision. I have no idea what Tom will do. Frankly, the board placed him in that position as a favor to you and our operation. Tom understands the military side of things, and he's worked in the company, but he isn't really CEO material. The two of you together make a great team, but with one of you gone, he's a weak link. I'm not trying to threaten you here, but I want you to understand what may happen if you just walk away. At least going with my plan, you and your company have a chance to survive."

Harold gazed down at the table and did not say a word. He turned his attention to the reflective ocean waters below. As he watched the waves racing towards the shoreline, thoughts raced around inside his head. Why had he allowed himself to be talked into this? After all, his personal financial future was assured. Garcia was a cagey individual at best. Harold had a feeling Garcia could take away his company and financial security with a simple phone call if he was crossed. Besides, it was not just his future in the balance, but all the employees and their families. Quitting now was not really an option.

"Earth to Harold, what are you thinking about?"

Harold looked up to see a smile across Garcia's face that disappeared behind his sunglasses. He finished off his beer. "Tell me what I need to do."

"How would you like to move away from the left coast lunacy and relax down in the Caribbean?"

Harold doubled over with laughter. He gripped the table and took deep breaths to get himself under control. Finally, he was able to sit up and face Garcia again, and Garcia's bland expression from beneath his sunglasses told Harold he was not kidding.

"You're serious," Harold said. "You expect me to walk away from one of the most beautiful pieces of real estate on the planet and move to some island or country with hot humid days that are cooled by tropical storms? And let's not even get started on the hurricanes."

Garcia finished off his beer and sat there. Harold was getting more annoyed by Garcia's sunglasses with every passing moment. He could not tell if the man was looking at him, looking away, or simply taking a nap.

Garcia finally spoke up. "Well, should we talk about fires, mudslides, and earthquakes around this coastal paradise?"

"Say what you want, our estate has survived them all."

"And where I'm taking you has done the same."

Harold felt cornered. Garcia seemed to be controlling everything—his job, his company, and now his home. Garcia was at least two steps ahead of him. Maybe he was smarter than he looked. Harold needed time to think things through. He stood up and extended his hand out to Garcia. Garcia looked up, and despite the sunglasses, Harold could see the wrinkles in his forehead from the surprised look on his face.

Harold waited for Garcia to stand. Even with the two men out of their seats, Garcia still had to look up to attempt to meet Harold's eyes. Harold said, "I appreciate our talk. I have a lot to think about. I'll call you in a couple of days."

Garcia tilted his head to the side. "You're planning on talking with Joshua?"

Harold worked to keep his deadpan expression, although inside he was surprised Garcia would guess that. "Doc is returning home today. My decisions impact him too. Do you think he'll have a reason to stay in Malibu if I move away? I'll be in touch."

Garcia released his hand. Harold stepped towards the French doors to let him out through the house. When he had opened them and turned back to Garcia, Garcia had disappeared. Although Garcia had obviously used the side path, his speed and stealth surprised Harold. He pondered whether Garcia was simply showing off or letting Harold know he could be anywhere nearby.

Harold went inside to grab a trash bag for the beers. He did not like feeling threatened. Insinuating the board would turn on him simply because he did not want to play in any spy games seemed a bit of a stretch. Still, he had not thought up any better plans in the months since his father's death. Perhaps Garcia was trying to help. Maybe the nightmares about John were playing games in his head. Joshua could help him sort through his concerns. He was happy his lifelong friend was away in paradise with the love of his life, but he would be happier when he returned.

CHAPTER 6

Harold sat in the oversized wooden rocker and stared out past his estate to the ocean below. Joshua's wooden deck creaked beneath his chair as he slowly rocked and waited for the driver to arrive. He had sent his car to pick up the newlyweds to ensure they would arrive back home promptly by six in the evening. There was a lot to discuss with Joshua, and Harold did not intend on waiting. Maria would forgive him for inviting himself into their home after a five-hour flight. After all, she was impacted by what was going on as well, and she should be included in their discussion.

The black Lincoln sedan eased into Joshua and Maria's driveway. Harold rose up, and a very tan Maria and a somewhat red Joshua emerged from the vehicle. Joshua walked around the car wearing khaki shorts, a Hawaiian flower shirt, and a straw fedora. Harold worked to hold in his snicker. Maria looked stunning in her white sundress. *Doc married up.*

Maria walked over to meet him at the edge of her porch and gave him a hug. "Harold, we didn't expect to find you here. Thank you for the car ride. Joshua was planning on grabbing a cab. The town car was much nicer."

Joshua walked up, hugged him, and gave him a friendly slap on the back. "How have things been going?"

"I'm the new chairman of PDS, so I've had a lot on my mind."

Joshua glanced up. "Chairman, congratulations are in order."

Harold smiled. "Thanks."

"Adam told me he's been talking to you."

Harold's eyebrow rose slightly. "We've had some interesting discussions."

"I hope that isn't why you're here. We would like to settle into our love nest before I hang my shingle out."

Maria giggled, and Joshua winked at her.

Harold felt an awkward shiver pass through him. "No, Doc. I wish that was it. I need to talk to both of you. Why don't I help you with your bags and then the three of us can chat for a bit?"

"Okay. I really would like one of my beers. Would you like one as well? I stocked my fridge with my favorite before we left."

Harold put a shoulder bag on each shoulder then lifted the two remaining suitcases, one in each hand. "None for me. I had some earlier today."

"Are you sure you have that?" asked Joshua.

"Doc, please,"

Joshua joked, "It sounds like somebody's been talking to agent Garcia."

Harold did not respond. Maria held the door open, and he walked into the house and gently put the luggage down in the living room. The maid service had done an excellent job on the home. The wood parquet was shining and flawless. Everything smelled fresh, unlike the musty odor that would sometimes linger when Joshua was living alone and was busy with his work.

Joshua appeared to have given Maria the run of the living room. Instead of staged antiques, Maria had covered the velvet couch in a beautiful Mexican blanket. The spinning wheel was missing, and the book *A Prescription for the Doctor's Wife* by Debby Read sat in one of the two empty chairs.

Joshua walked in and stopped between him and Maria. "Why don't you two go relax outside? I'll get a couple beers."

"I don't mind getting them, Doc. You two need to relax after your trip."

"They're hidden," Maria said.

"What's hidden?" asked Harold.

"His beers." Maria stuck out her lip in disapproval.

Harold's eyebrows went up. "You hide your beer from Maria? Where is it, an in-ground refrigerator?"

Joshua grinned. "I don't hide them from her. I just keep them in a safe place. Not all refrigerators are large after all. I told her I'll take care of my beer stock. She does enough around here, and I don't want to put the blame on her if I run out of my OMB Copper."

Harold leaned his shoulder up against the wall. "I don't know, Doc. It sounds to me like you're trying to hide your beer. Maybe you should see a psychiatrist about your obsession. It could be serious."

Joshua smirked at him and went out through the sliding glass door.

"Seriously, you don't know where he keeps his beer stock?"

Maria tossed her hair off her shoulder. "He would tell me if I ask, but this is more fun."

With a smile on her face, Maria strolled out the front door, and Harold followed. She sat in one of two chairs that were placed on either side of a small table. Harold resumed sitting in his oversized rocking chair.

Before he had a chance to turn his head, Maria asked, "What is it, Harold?"

He looked over, and Maria's large black eyes appeared to almost pool up amid the anxious look on her face.

He replied, "Something tells me you can get Doc to tell you anything."

Maria cocked her head to the right. "Is that such a horrible thing?"

"I suppose not. For a man who tells people to talk about their problems, Doc isn't always much of a talker."

"What about you?"

Harold squirmed slightly. "I see you're already learning his ways."

"I've studied my husband's 'ways' for many years. I have also studied you, and I can tell there is something wrong, and it has nothing to do with your father or some dreams."

The front door opened, and Joshua walked out holding the glass necks of two beers in one hand and a bottled water in the other. He handed Maria a beer and Harold the water.

The three of them popped opened their drinks, toasted one another, and took slow sips.

Joshua asked, "Okay, Harry, what's up?"

Harold took another sip of water and let it sit in the large palm of his hand on the armrest. He took a long slow breath and began to tell Joshua and Maria about Garcia's offer to save the company and the need to move.

"What about us?" asked Maria.

Harry made eye contact with each of his friends before responding, "I honestly hoped you would join me. I'm not sure I can do this alone."

When he finished, Maria and Joshua sat there staring at him. Maria reached over and took Joshua's hand. Harold finished off his water. Several seconds of silence passed between them before Joshua finally spoke.

"Harry, I honestly don't want to move. I made my peace with living here a long time ago. This is home to me now, and this is Maria's home, and it's your home. I can't imagine walking away from here."

Harold shifted his weight in the chair. "I know, Doc. I guess you technically don't have to go. I mean, Garcia needs me, but I really need you, and Maria."

Joshua's fatherly eyes rested upon him. "Harry, how important is this to you? Is it worth gambling away everything you have? Yes, your father wanted his company saved, but he would have never sacrificed your well-being to do it. He was wrong to shoot himself, but he did it in hopes of protecting you, not throwing you into more danger."

Harold looked down at the porch and back out over the estate. "I don't know what to do, Doc. I don't want to move either, although I would like a break from the ghosts."

"Ghosts!" Maria jumped in her seat. "I had enough of them as a little girl. If there are ghosts here now, we need to leave."

"Don't worry, honey. Ghosts aren't real. It's a trick the mind sometimes plays. Let's say you can't say goodbye to someone you love. When you're asleep, or possibly just tired, your mind will bring that person into your consciousness from your subconscious. That may cause you to see someone who isn't there. Like a mirage in the desert to somebody needing water."

Maria released Joshua's hand, leaned in towards Joshua, and waved her arm between them as she spoke. "You're wrong, honey. I saw ghosts as a little girl in Mexico, and they were not friends or family." She stopped, took a long breath, and got control over her emotions before continuing. "I had never heard of such things until after I came upon one. A little girl by a river. We would play every day. I told my mother about my new friend, and she thought it was another girl in the village. One day we were playing, and my friend fell into the river. I screamed and got my mother. When I brought her to where we were playing, she turned pale and asked me my friend's name. I told her it was Olivia. My mother picked me up and ran to the church. When she told the priest what happened, he put his hands on me and prayed over me in Latin. Once my mother calmed down, I asked her if we were going to try and find Olivia. She explained Olivia had drowned twenty years earlier in the spot where we were playing. She sometimes showed up and played with children and tried to get them to go into the river with her."

A shiver traveled down Harold's body as he recalled his most recent dream. "Well, Doc. What do you have to say to that?"

Joshua sat there silently. Maria looked over at Harold, and he tipped his head and water bottle towards her.

Joshua turned to Harold. "Are these ghosts in your dreams?"

Harold leaned closer to Joshua. "Yea." He turned towards Maria. "Don't worry, Maria. These ghosts live in my dreams. I think Doc may be onto something in my case. The only thing that could have held Dad to earth was Mom, and she's gone too. Besides, it isn't Dad who's the problem. John keeps showing up. He seems to be everywhere."

Maria's voice rose an octave with her question, "John died in the house. Do you think he will try to come over here?"

Harold looked over at Maria. "So far he hasn't walked the halls beyond my mind. If his spirit is around the house, he seems content to harass me in my head."

Maria scowled and began rocking furiously. "I don't like it."

"Neither do I." Joshua shot Harold a look that let him know he did not approve of his wife being frightened.

He knew everyone needed a break. He stood up and stretched. Maria raised a finger towards the empty water bottle in his hands, and he gave it over. "I think

I've caused enough worry for you both. I'm sorry, Maria, if I upset you. All I wanted to do was talk about the possible move. I'm sorry I brought up my dreams. I guess they are bothering me more than I thought. I've tried to keep the details between Joshua and me."

Joshua looked up at him. "It's okay, Harry. It sounds like a lot has gone on. I guess the world can't wait on the two of us." He turned and gazed at Maria. Their eyes sparkled as they gazed at one another.

Joshua turned back to Harold. "Let me drop by in a few minutes after we get ourselves settled in and we can talk details. I think the three of us probably need to speak with agent Garcia. I'm not saying we will join you, but if we do, I want to make sure Agent Garcia is on board so we don't show up unannounced."

"That's a great idea, Doc. I'll see you soon. I'm sorry to bring things down so quickly after you got home."

"Don't worry. You didn't. This is important. I'll be over soon."

Harold walked over, bent down, and hugged Maria. He turned and shook Joshua's hand. "I'll see you soon."

The walk back over to the estate felt longer than usual. He wished he had been more patient, but he felt like Garcia was pressing hard. If he had said nothing to Joshua and Maria now, Garcia could have shown up on their doorstep and told them himself, and that would have been worse.

Harold sat at his office desk for the next hour looking up information about the Florida Keys. When he heard footsteps coming down the hall, he let go of his mouse and clenched his fists, half-expecting John's specter to appear. Joshua came walking into view with a contented smile on his face.

Harold's hands relaxed, and he pointed to the chair in front of his desk. "Have a seat, Doc."

"I hope you don't mind me letting myself in."

"Nope. In fact, I'm relieved. I'm tired of having to walk that long hall to answer the door."

Joshua chuckled. "Well, I know you missed Maria."

"I missed both of you. We're a family."

"Yes, we are. Okay, let's talk shop for a few minutes. Adam told me about your nightmares. Those didn't sound any different from what you were dealing with when I left."

Harold sat up and put his arms on his desk. He leaned in towards Joshua. "They weren't, but, Doc, something else happened. John showed up the other morning, and I can't tell you if I was awake or asleep, but that wasn't the really weird part. Okay, maybe that sounds weird, but you know how confusing those nightmares can get."

Joshua moved himself to the edge of his seat. "What happened?"

"John showed up in the Viking setting we used to use in our therapy sessions and warned me about Garcia. He said Garcia had made him a similar deal and then backed out of it. He told me it was because of Garcia's broken promise that he started to suspect my dad of conspiring against him."

"Harry, that isn't really surprising. You're still trying to find a reason why John would target your family like he did."

Harold's hands started to slap his desk, and then he stopped. "Listen to me, Doc. I asked Garcia, and he confirmed the whole story."

"You told Garcia that Richard's ghost said Garcia had cheated his company and that your dad was involved?"

Harold took a long breath to slow himself down. "No. I made up some excuse about overhearing him telling you right before he tried to kill you and Maria."

"Perhaps you did."

"I did what?"

Joshua reached over and put both his hands around Harold's large fists like he had when Harold was still a boy. "Perhaps you did hear John say that. I can't tell you what John said to me there in the kitchen. I was too busy trying to think of a way to save Maria and myself. I saw your shadow in the hallway when I lunged towards John. I don't know how long you stood there, but maybe he did say something and we both don't remember it." Joshua let go of Harold's hands.

Harold relaxed his fists, rubbed his face with both his hands, and let out a sigh. "Maybe, Doc. Maybe it's all rolling around in my head. No matter how it got there, I think we should be leery of Agent Garcia."

"Agreed. Tell me, have you had any berserk episodes either in your dreams or when you're awake?"

Harold thought for a moment. "Amazingly, no. You'd think these nightmares would trigger something. So far, no furniture has been shattered, the walls are still standing, and I haven't found any couches at the bottom of the swimming pool. Even in my dreams, I manage to keep my cool. Well, if you call waking up in the middle of the night screaming keeping your cool."

Joshua patted the top of Harold's hand. "That's perfectly normal. You have gone through a lot, and many people never recover from things half as traumatic as you've been through. You and your brain are still healing. I have a feeling that your heart is still coming to terms with killing John as well."

"I would say I'm not a killer, but I know I am. I know I saved your life and all that, Doc, but I'm still trying to wrap my head around the kind of man I can become if I'm pushed too far."

Joshua looked him in the eye. For a moment, he thought he was looking again at his late father, and his breath stuttered in grief.

Joshua broke his gaze. "Harry, you saved our lives. If that's the kind of man the berserker is, I'll take him with me everywhere I go. I know you wanted to do more, to kill more. I saw death in your eyes. But you didn't follow through. You controlled your rage. Never forget the kind of man you are despite what you may have felt at the time."

Harold wiped a tear from his cheek. "Okay, Doc. I don't really want to talk anymore about that now. Can we talk about Garcia? He's wanting me to move, and I want you with me. Maybe we can come up with a plan to avoid this mess."

Joshua leaned back in the chair. "Why are you saying *we?*"

Harold felt his heart flutter. "Doc, I just assumed…I mean, I thought you'd be going along too. You mean, you'll stay here? But I need you."

Joshua chuckled. "Don't worry. I couldn't stand the thought of looking at your empty estate, or worse, someone else living here. I've been here all of these years because of you and then because we all became a family. I can't abandon you in your time of need. One day, you'll need to stand alone, but not right now."

Harold scowled. "Doc, that was mean. I'm here with my heart opened and wounded, and you pull a joke?"

"I'm sorry, Harry. I wanted to see what you would do. Garcia keeps everybody off balance, and the men he deals with are ruthless. If you couldn't take an out-of-place jab, I would call Garcia myself and tell him the deal is off for your own good."

Harold's thumbs tapped the top of the desk. "Okay, I guess. I'm not sure it's your place to decide the fate of Dad's company, but I get your intention."

"You do know you're more important than your father's corporation?" asked Joshua. "Richard would never have sacrificed your well-being for his company."

"Yea, I'm glad you're around to keep reminding me. Still, what do we do about Garcia's proposal?"

"I don't have a clue. I've been thinking about it, and I can't see a way around moving away if Garcia says that's what it'll take. From what you told me of your conversation, he is not leaving you too many choices."

Joshua looked down at Harold's desk, and Harold did the same. There was no reason to feel defeated, and yet he did. He was going to lose his house. He was going to lose everything his father built, just like John predicted. A still voice inside reminded him that Garcia never said the move was permanent.

"I have a question." Joshua's voice jerked him from his downward spiral. "What about Tom? He isn't any older than you. Why would they make him the CEO?"

"I argued with them about that. He has a military background and would be a great visionary for the company, but he's no CEO. Garcia told me today that it was his idea because the two of us complement each other's skill set."

Joshua's brow wrinkled. "Would you say Tom would be open to suggestions from others since he is inexperienced?"

"I had never considered that. Do you think the board is running the company by proxy through Tom?"

"Or Garcia," suggested Joshua.

Both men sat back in their chairs.

"What'd I do?" asked Harold.

"Nothing. At least not for the moment. If Garcia is really trying to help your company, it may be for the best, but let's keep our eyes and minds open."

Harold sat back up and typed a couple of keys on his laptop. A picture of Tranquility Bay Beach House Resort popped up on his screen. A smile crept over his face as he watched the live feed of the small swimming lagoon at the resort. "You know, Doc, this might not be half bad."

"What are you looking at?"

"Some resort's live camera feed on Marathon Key."

"Yea, it is beautiful there, but it's beautiful here too."

Harold closed his laptop. "What if we make Garcia arrange for tenants to stay in our homes? I mean, I don't know how long we're going to be gone, but the thought of leaving both homes empty for any extended period concerns me. After all, we hear about squatters all the time on the news."

"I'm not sure Maria will go for that. She is very picky about her house, and she takes a lot of pride in your home. I'm not sure how she will feel about strangers living in either place."

"Why don't we get together with Garcia tomorrow and see what we can come up with?"

"What about Maria?"

Harold's face allowed a broad smile to stretch across it. "Bring her. In fact, ask her to call the caterer and have them bring us a spread of fresh fruit and some burgers. Nothing helps bring out the truth in people like an intimate pool party among friends."

Joshua rose. "I could ask Maria if she'll prepare the food."

Harold rose with him. "No, Doc. She isn't our housekeeper anymore, and I don't want to start making her feel like she is."

"Maria isn't a woman who likes to be pampered. Your idea may backfire."

Harold grabbed the back of his chair and thought for a moment. "You're the doc. Arrange things with Maria however you think is best."

"If you'll excuse me, I'll go let Maria know. We don't have much time. So, noon tomorrow?"

Harold moved from behind his desk. "I'm telling Garcia to be here at 1 p.m., but you both can come over anytime you feel like before then."

The two men headed towards the front door.

Chapter 7

Joshua glared at the Hyatt Regency valet. "What do you mean I have to pay you to park? We're just going in for a drink at the Watertable."

The young man placed his hands on Joshua's door. "Look, I'm trying to do you a solid. I just ask you do me one back."

"What are you talking about?"

The young man leaned closer to the driver's window. "Let me spell it out for you. You give me a decent tip, and I park your vehicle so all you have to do is walk out of the bar and go straight to your car."

"I never," protested Joshua.

The young valet reached for the door handle, and Harold's large hand slid between Joshua's seat and the window. He laid it on top of the valet's hand that still gripped the window frame of the door, encompassing the young man's hand as well as his wrist and part of his arm. The young man froze and looked closely at the rear passenger window. His eyes grew wide, and he jerked his hand free of the door and back away.

Annoyed, Joshua cruised away from the hotel, fussing as they went. "Who ever heard of such a thing?

Valet-only parking for a restaurant. We live in Malibu and aren't this pretentious. Why did Garcia insist we meet him down here anyway?"

"He said he had business down here today," offered Maria.

"Doc, you've driven us down PCH and passed a plethora of restaurants along the way. Let's just pick one."

"I don't think Agent Garcia will approve of a sudden change in venue."

Joshua turned north on the Pacific Coast Highway and Harold pulled up a map on his iPhone. "Doc, I found a place, Ola Mexican Kitchen. It looks good, and it's only a few blocks north of here."

"Look," Joshua pulled over to some metered parking spaces just outside the restaurant, "it's just as I thought."

They stopped, and Joshua slid the console gear lever into park. Harold reached between the seats and pulled it into drive. The car lurched and Joshua hit the brakes. "Are you crazy?"

"Are you allowed to say that?" he made sure Joshua saw his sarcastic smile in his review mirror.

"Boys, am I going to have to drive?" Maria asked, clearly annoyed.

Harold responded, "Look, you don't know where that guy works. For all we know, he could park cars and pour drinks. You don't want to end up with something special added to your beer, do you?"

"I think you're being a little paranoid, Harry."

"Whatever, I'm in the mood for Mexican anyway."

"I don't think Garcia will like the sudden change in location."

Harold humphed in frustration. "Maria, what do you want?"

"I'm always in the mood for good Mexican food, but it better be good."

"I'll text Garcia," volunteered Harold.

"Fine," said Joshua. "But don't be surprised when Garcia calls to yell in your ear."

Joshua pulled back onto PCH and made his way towards the intersection Harold's smartphone had showed on its GPS.

"Ha! See, Doc. No worries. Garcia says he's looking forward to seeing us there."

"Hmm," said Joshua, "it's almost like he expected that."

"Now who's paranoid, Doc?"

"I think both of you are paranoid, and I'm hungry," Maria said.

Joshua found the underground parking lot and parked his car.

The group sat in the covered patio of Ola Mexican Kitchen overlooking the Pacific Coast Highway with a perfect view of the more touristy area of Huntington Beach. The sun poured in from the patio windows facing the beach. Tourists, surfers, and locals just enjoying the beach played and relaxed in the white sands across the street from the restaurant. Inside there was a large dark wooden bar, and tall tables and chairs were scattered about the eatery. Their table was near the far corner where they had a clear view of the surfers and the Huntington Beach Pier. Harold closed his eyes and enjoyed the sounds of people talking, laughing, and the calm feeling of the cool Pacific breeze.

Maria's voice rose slightly above the music and interrupted his Zen moment. "Harry, are you okay?"

Harold grinned and opened his eyes. "Yes, I wanted to soak in the moment."

"I know what you mean," said Joshua. "Yesterday I thought I could leave here, and now I'm not sure."

A waiter came up to get their drink orders.

"Give me a Sierra Nevada," said Harold with a hint of sorrow in his voice.

Joshua responded, "The lady and I would like rum runners."

Harold jumped back in, "And a round of waters and *queso fundido* for the group."

The waiter left, and Harold turned to Joshua and raised his eyebrow. "Rum runners? Did you guys turn into heavy hitters on your honeymoon?"

"Oh, yes," said Maria with a smile on her face.

Joshua jumped in quickly behind her. "It's a drink I had while I was in the Keys. It grows on you. Imagine multiple rums, some liqueurs, and incredible fruit juices. It's delicious."

"That does sound good, Doc. Maybe I'll give it a shot if we go to the Keys. New places and new habits."

"That's the spirit," said Joshua. "Now, if I can just grab hold of that same attitude."

Harold gazed out at the late afternoon sun that was beginning to head towards the ocean. He heard a chair being dragged across the ground behind him. Garcia sat down between him and Joshua.

"Good afternoon, everyone."

Harold asked, "How can you not remember your sunglasses? It isn't that bright in here."

"Oh, yea." Garcia removed them and slid one arm of the sunglasses inside his shirt above the last closed button. He was dressed more like a tourist than a native. He wore a tan panama hat and a button-up two-tone blue shirt with orchids on it. A pair of tan khaki shorts and sandals wrapped around his white-sock-clad feet completed the outfit. For the first time, Harold thought Garcia stuck out from part of the crowd, but the crowd seemed to take no notice. To them he must look like another Easterner they prayed would not move to the over-populated coast. Garcia flicked his hand at the first waiter he made eye contact with and ordered a beer.

Harold threw out the sarcastic question to Garcia. "So, are you on vacation or just an undercover tourist?"

Garcia ignored the quip. "Something like that. Like I told you, I'm heading out on assignment for a few days. So, are you guys joining me in the Keys?"

Harold, Joshua, and Maria all looked at one another, and Garcia slowly made eye contact with everyone. "Well?"

Harold cleared his throat. He needed to talk above the thumping of the bar music, but he did not want the rest of the room listening to their conversation. He leaned in closer to Garcia. "We have a couple of questions. Well, they're more like favors."

"Demands." Joshua leaned towards the two men. "They're demands."

Garcia looked over at Joshua. "I see. I suppose you coming along is one of those demands."

"Yes," responded Harold.

Garcia looked up at Harold and then back at Joshua and Maria. "It's already taken care of."

"What?" asked Joshua and Maria together.

"Please, we're CIA."

Joshua and Maria rolled their eyes.

Harold interjected, "There's more. None of us plan on staying in the Keys forever. All of us agree that if we move to the Caribbean, we'll return once the company is back on solid footing."

"How do you know you'll want to return?" asked Garcia.

Harold leaned over so his broad shoulder was touching Garcia's. In a low rumbling voice, he answered, "Because we don't want to leave in the first place." His voice relaxed, "So, our homes need renters. None of us want to return and find squatters." He sat back. "So, do we have a deal?"

Garcia seemed unintimidated and looked around at the group. "How do you propose we handle this? You three don't have time to interview prospective renters. Is the CIA supposed to house sit for a few years?"

"Years?" asked Maria.

"Months, years, I can't say. I've learned never to give promises or timelines on these sorts of projects. Parabolic Defense Systems is going to be making money because of the CIA. We can control that. However, getting back into DOD's good graces is outside even the purview of the CIA."

"Then what are we doing here?" asked Harold.

"Patience," replied Garcia. "I can't make promises about the DOD's timeline, but I can promise it will happen."

One server walked over with a platter full of drinks and another followed with the appetizer. Everyone grabbed their glasses after the staff left and toasted one another. Maria took a quick sip and grabbed one of the appetizers with Garcia following suit.

Harold sipped on his beer and stared at Agent Garcia Hernandez. Garcia pretended not to notice and turned his attention towards Joshua.

"Doctor, I trust you enjoyed your honeymoon in paradise?"

"We did indeed," Joshua said with a smile.

Maria leaned across the table. "We spent most of our time at the beach or in the water. Joshua took me snorkeling. The fish were beautiful."

"If you liked snorkeling in Hawaii, you'll love the Caribbean. The waters are crystal clear, and you'll be close to the third largest reef in the world."

"That does sound like it could be exciting."

Joshua broke in, "I've learned that if every day is a holiday, then no days are a vacation."

"So, you're saying we'll get bored?" Maria asked.

Garcia interjected, "I doubt you'll be bored. There's more than fishing. There are lots of things to explore around the island, and the estate is beautiful. I'm sure you can find something to keep you busy. As for your husband, Harold and I will keep him from getting bored."

Harold redirected Garcia's attention. "So, how about we have Tom stay at the estate? He's renting an overpriced one bedroom down by the beach. I feel certain he'll agree to living in a large estate for free. Besides, he spent a lot of time hanging out there with me as we were growing up. It should be easy enough for you to arrange that. While he's at it, he can keep an eye on Joshua's house for him."

"What makes you think I have any say so over Tom? What happens between you two, and your houses, is your business."

Harold looked at Joshua and then back to Garcia. "Come on, Tom the CEO. We both know there were better men and women. Abigail should have gotten the post if I didn't. Tom can handle himself well enough, but he's your figurehead. He's about the only man you can trust with the company's secret, besides me. Not to mention, Tom and I are friends. Our relationship will work in your favor when you have me out in the field with you and you need something from PDS. It wasn't that hard to figure out your plan."

Garcia turned to Joshua. "Did you teach him this?"

"He is a very capable young man. I hope you're not underestimating him because I think his intellect exceeds that of his late father."

"Thanks, Doc," Harold said in reply.

Garcia sat back in his chair, slowly picked up his beer and took a long swallow. He spoke just loud enough to be heard amid the noisy din of the music. "I can see I'm outnumbered here." He turned his attention back to Joshua. "Would you mind if I assign an agent or two to live in your house? That will make security around the estate easier."

"Why does my house need added security?" asked Harold.

Garcia placed his beer on the table. "The people we are dealing with will not only know who you are but where you live. They may try and send some people to snoop around the place after you leave. I don't want anyone stumbling onto Tom and catching him unawares. He may be ex-military, but so are these men. Besides, it stops Joshua and Maria's house from appearing abandoned."

"We aren't abandoning our home," said Maria in a distinctly annoyed tone.

Garcia stumbled over his words, "Of course not, that isn't what I meant."

Joshua cut off Garcia, "Having agents in the house is okay, but if they mess up Maria's home, there'll be hell to pay."

Maria held Joshua's forearm and glared at Garcia.

Garcia replied, "I can assure you our agents are professionals and won't do anything to disturb your lovely home."

"They better not." Maria scowled.

Garcia took another sip of his beer and let out a sigh. "Okay, I think we have a quorum. The next time I see you guys, we'll be on Salvation Key."

Harold jumped in, "Who said we have agreed?"

Garcia's face broke into a grin. "Please, you don't think I wasn't anticipating something like this? I'll admit, the request around Tom is a bit of a surprise. I had planned to put agents in both homes, but this works out too. Assuming, of course, that Tom agrees with your request." Garcia turned towards Joshua.

"Doctor, I knew you would not allow our boy to be pulled into some CIA scheme alone." Garcia's gaze panned around the table. "Believe me, I'm on your side, and you guys are going to love what we've done with John's old island."

"I didn't know that's where we're going. I don't believe it was called Salvation Key," Joshua said.

Garcia turned to Joshua and paused to swallow down his final bit of beer. "It wasn't, but I renamed it in honor of our mission. We're out to save PDS, and we're out to stop some terrorist. I think you'll be pleased with the changes when you see it, Doctor."

"That would be a pleasant surprise."

Garcia looked each person in the eye as he spoke. "I think we have the makings of a good team. Harold, you make a great front man for our mission, and, Joshua, your insight into human behavior will be invaluable. Maria, you brought Joshua out of his shell and into the light. Your love and compassion will keep these two in line."

Harold responded, "I believe we're missing someone."

Garcia looked over at him, surprised. "Who do you think we're missing?"

"Darla," Harold said. "Why isn't Darla part of the group? She said she was going back to work for you guys, but we've not heard a word from her or anyone else about where she might be."

"Well, people do call us spies for a reason. If you knew where she was, it could compromise her mission."

Harold could not hide his excitement. "You know where she is?"

Garcia winked.

Harold put his large arm around Garcia and pulled him close. "Is she okay? Does she ask about me?"

Garcia worked for a moment to free himself from Harold's impassioned grip. "She does, and she wants you to know that she's thinking about you. I can tell you that Darla is perfectly safe, but her mission is top secret. I'm afraid I can't say anything more than that."

A broad smile broke across Harold's face. He had been missing Darla since she left before Joshua and Maria's wedding. All she had said was that she needed to go back to the CIA and complete one last mission, but Darla had refused to tell Harold what her mission was. He wished he could understand what was driving her back to the CIA. The lack of communication had been eating at him. Hearing Garcia's news made Harold forget about some of the homesickness that had already started to creep in even though they had not left yet.

"If everyone is good," Garcia said, "I'm starving, and I'm on the clock. Let's order some more food."

Garcia waved the waiter over, and they ordered their food. Garcia made short work of his plate of tacos and then slid on his sunglasses, said his goodbyes, and was gone so quickly Harold wasn't sure he could say which way he exited.

Joshua looked out towards the last gasps of sunlight on the Pacific horizon and grinned.

"What's so amusing, Doc?" asked Harold.

"I wonder if he realizes it's almost dark."

Harold chuckled. "He might figure it out once he gets out from under all the lights."

Maria took a sip of water and then combed her hand through her hair. "That man needs a good woman."

The three of them slowly made their way from the restaurant, crossed the Pacific Coast Highway, and enjoyed a long stroll on the beach. Nobody said a word. Harold knew they all were wondering when they would see the calm Pacific Ocean on a cool clear evening again.

Maria spoke softly, "Joshua, what was the Caribbean like?"

Joshua silently watched the sand for several steps. "Do you want to know about what happened on John's island or just what the Key itself was like?"

Maria slid her hand into Joshua's. "Just the Key. Was it beautiful like it is here?"

Harold turned to Joshua. "Yea, Doc. You're the only person here that has been where we're going. What's it like?"

Joshua glanced at him and then let his eyes linger on his wife. "It's beautiful. The weather is somewhat like here. It's very mild, but it can be breezy. The water is calm most of the time, and it's so clear you can see the reef below. Even from shore, you can see barracuda, tuna, sea snails, rays, and all sorts of sea life."

"Are there sharks?" asked Maria.

"Oh, yes. Bull sharks, nurse sharks, and probably others. You have to know what you're doing or be with someone who does if you want to go snorkeling."

"It sounds interesting," Harold said. "Maybe this change of pace won't be so bad after all. I guess we have a lot of work ahead of us. I'll talk to my administrator to get some movers to help us pack. Maria, we haven't really talked about what you plan on doing now that you and Joshua are married."

"What do you mean?"

"Well, you used to help around the house, but now you're Joshua's wife. You're not my housekeeper anymore."

Maria smacked his large chest and then rubbed her sore hand. "Don't you ever say that. You're my *hijo*. I don't take care of you because you pay me. I take care of you because you're family."

Harold took a step towards them and wrapped one arm around each. They buried their faces into his shoulder, and he held them tightly.

Joshua began to wiggle and managed to push loose of his grip. "Easy, Harry. We still need to breathe."

"I'm sorry, Doc. You two mean the world to me. I guess I got a little carried away."

Joshua took back Maria's hand. "I know these are trying times for us, but we'll face them together."

The three of them began heading back towards the parking lot. There was a lot to do before moving day.

Chapter 8

Harold stared up at the white oak tongue-and-groove ceiling above his bed. He had never considered the workmanship that went into building the home he had grown up in. As he lay there, he wondered what the workers had been like. Did they envision his family living there? Harold felt a tap on his shoulder and startled slightly. He turned his head, expecting to see his mother standing next to the bed calling him to breakfast with the family. Instead, John's familiar sarcastic smile met his eyes.

Harold stared back up at the ceiling. "So, I'm dreaming again."

The bed creaked as John sat on the edge. He felt his body tilt in John's direction as the mattress dipped. "What is it, John? I'm busy."

"What's wrong, brat? Are you going to miss mommy and daddy's bedroom? I bet I could tell you some stories about the two of them in bed."

Harold laid his large arm across his eyes. "Please, don't. Do you have a reason for haunting my dreams again? I was hoping God had dragged you down to hell by now."

"Not a chance. Even the devil doesn't want to take me on."

Harold let out a long yawn. If this was a dream, it was one of the most annoying dreams he had experienced in a while.

John put his elbow into Harold's stomach and leaned down towards him. "I know you think I'm here in the house, but I have a secret, brat. I'm not attached to the house. I'm attached to you."

Harold dropped his arm, knocking John out of the way, and he sat up on the edge of the bed. Blankets and sheets sat jumbled, partially exposing his naked legs. He turned to John. "What are you talking about?"

John's laugh cut a cold chill through Harold's body. "You're going to my island. Why would I pass up that opportunity? I'm hopping a ride on the *H* bus."

Harold gripped the linen in his left hand and pulled it up into a massive ball. "I won't let you. You don't have permission to do that."

John cackled once more. "You really are a stupid kid. Do you think you can just say no? Why would I listen to you?"

Harold reared back his long arm and swung his huge fist towards John as hard as he could. His flesh connected only with air, and the momentum pulled him out of bed. He woke up groaning on the floor next to the bed. He had not fallen out of bed since he was a small boy, and he did not remember it being so painful. His face had taken most of the impact of his fist and the floor. Forcing himself up, he stumbled into the bathroom. He turned on the light and collapsed into a red-cushioned chair that sat between the sink and garden tub.

His right cheek throbbed just below his eye. He winced when he touched it with his fingertips. As he stood up, a cramp tightened in his right shoulder. Rubbing his shoulder, he looked over at the mirror in front of the sink. A bright red fist mark lay just below his eye. Judging from the puffiness, it would probably leave a mark.

Harold muttered to himself, "I can't wait to get out of here."

The words shocked him. This was his home. He had grown up here. There were so many good memories before John interjected himself into the family's life and took his parent's lives. His large fist slammed into the granite countertop. Deodorant and shaving cream bounced and fell over.

He looked at his reflection in the mirror. "Don't let John win. He's gone. You killed him. Don't let him beat you from the grave."

He held his breath, waiting to see if John would respond. Nothing happened, and he breathed a sigh of relief. His alarm buzzed in the bedroom, and Harold went in to cut off the annoying sound. *Six o'clock on the big day. At least I didn't wake up too early.* He walked across the Spanish tile to the shower. Looking down, Harold counted each tile, unsure if he would ever see them again.

***

The clock in the kitchen read nine o'clock when the doorbell rang. Harold put down the dishrag he was using to wipe the countertops and made his way to the front door. Joshua and Maria stood there. Although Joshua had a distant look, Maria wore her usual friendly smile.

"Good morning. I trust you're both ready to start our new adventure?" said Harold.

"Oh my! What happened to your eye?" asked Maria.

"I fell out of bed."

Joshua raised his right eyebrow slightly, and his forehead crinkled between his eyes. "I don't believe any of the beds are tall enough to give you a black eye."

"I'll tell you about it on the plane, Doc. Are you guys ready for the movers?"

"I suppose so," responded Joshua. "I feel a bit melancholy this morning. I'm going to miss my house."

"As am I," said Maria.

"We'll come back. Why don't you guys come on inside?"

The trio went back to the kitchen and sat in the familiar chairs that they had spent so much time in together. "Do either of you want any coffee?" asked Harold.

"No thanks," said Joshua. "We already had our fill earlier this morning. What time are the movers coming?"

"They should be here anytime."

Maria traced her fingers up and down Joshua's arm as she spoke. "I've heard it's very beautiful in the Caribbean."

Harold relaxed a little and let himself smile. "The photos I found on the internet of the area look nice. I guess we'll find out soon."

Maria stopped tracing Joshua's arm. He fidgeted a bit and said, "It's pretty enough, but I wish we were going somewhere else."

Maria placed her head on his shoulder. "I'm sorry. I always forget you were there and saw those terrible things John and his friends were doing, but they're gone now. We're going to make it our island."

"Well, for now it's the government's island," responded Harold.

He heard the sound of semi-trucks climbing the grade towards the house. A few moments later, the squeal of air brakes being set got the group's attention. Through the kitchen window, Harold noticed the front nose of a semi in the driveway. He started towards the front door when the doorbell rang. When he opened the door, he saw semi-trucks parked in front of each house. He greeted the movers and directed one team at his house while Joshua and Maria left to direct the other team on where to start at their house.

After the movers had their instructions, Harold called the company car to take them to the airport. Joshua and Maria wandered back inside through the open front door a few minutes later.

"Where should we wait for the car?" asked Joshua.

"Let's go down to our spot before we have to leave, Doc."

Joshua pointed towards the rear of the house, and the two men headed out the back through the French doors. Harold heard the doors open behind them as Maria followed their path.

"Am I not invited?" she asked.

Joshua stopped. "Of course, honey. You're a part of us now." Joshua walked to Maria, and the two of them caught up to Harold who was already sitting down by the infinity pool.

"Do you still remember that day, Doc?"

Joshua looked at Maria and then back to Harold smiling. "Oh, yes. You gave me quite a surprise."

Both men chuckled. "It all started here, Doc. I didn't know what was going on before I threw you in the pool. You were some strange guy that showed up, would put me to sleep, and then I would end up in all sorts of weird places around the house. To be honest, you sort of scared me."

"I didn't think anything could scare you."

"I was just a kid."

"Yes, you were, but a very disturbed child. I know your parents would be proud of who you've become."

A brief moment of grief swept over him as he thought about having to leave his parent's alone in the cemetery without anyone to tend their graves. "Hey, Doc, do you think my parents will care that I'm not around to visit their graves?"

Joshua reached over and took Harold's hand. "They won't mind. I'm sure they're in heaven. Whatever is in the ground are just husks now."

Maria scooted her chair closer to Harold and held his other hand. "Your parents were like my aunt and uncle. I know they would be proud of your decisions. This is my home too, and it's hard to leave. But you aren't doing it for yourself. You're doing it for others. Your dad would make the same decisions. In a way, he is still living in you."

Harold let out a long breath. He wanted to believe that, and some part of him still believed in a heaven. Unfortunately, whatever faith he had left was threadbare and worn. He decided to push the topic out of his mind. "Maria, I never did say thank you for keeping me out of trouble with my mom the day Joshua and I took our first swim together."

Maria laughed and rolled her eyes. "Oh, it was my mother that saved you both. If she hadn't kept Barbara occupied, I would have never been able to get your clothes in the laundry before your mom found them soaking in the bathroom."

"Hey, Doc, does the new place have a pool?"

"Yes, but it doesn't have this view."

"Ahh," sighed Harold and Maria in unison. Harold's cell phone rang from his pocket. The driver was out front waiting for them. "Time to go."

They all stood up and stared out over the Pacific one last time. Harold closed his eyes and breathed in the sea air that wafted up the hillside. A part of him prayed he would be back one day. The other part felt as though he could burst into tears like a homesick child. The three of them walked silently back up to the hill and into the waiting car. Nobody said a word as it pulled out onto the road. They passed between the estate and Joshua's house before the car made its way down the hill and towards LAX.

Chapter 9

Harold, Joshua, and Maria enjoyed their rum runners as the chartered Gulfstream G650 flew across the Gulf of Mexico. Harold was not one to splurge, but a man his size did not enjoy traveling by plane unless he absolutely had to. Even a first-class domestic flight was cramped, and he had never cared for crowds of strangers. Although their chartered jet was luxurious and spacious, he had to dip his head to keep from touching the ceiling, and its cramped bathroom would have been the stuff of nightmares if he were claustrophobic. He allowed his long legs to stretch out into the aisle. Joshua and Maria sat across from him.

Joshua raised his voice above the noise of the engines as he spoke to Harold. "So, you're telling me you got a black eye by punching the air in your sleep?"

Harold's fingers rapped against the foldout table that sat between them. "Doc, it wasn't air—it was John. At least that is what I was dreaming."

Joshua reached across and gently laid his hands on top of Harold's to stop his tapping. "That's very interesting. The human body normally puts us in a semi-paralyzed state when we sleep so we don't physically react to our dreams. It isn't unheard of, of course. People sleepwalk and have done all sorts of things in their sleep. That sort of thing normally happens when the brain is under a lot of stress."

Harold felt a little frustrated with his friend. He knew everything Joshua was telling him. He took another sip of his drink to try and relax. "Hey, Doc, on a totally different topic, I like the rum runner. You may make a liquor man out of me yet."

"Yes, they're wonderful, aren't they?" Maria said. "Harry, may I say something about your dream?"

Harold looked over at Joshua, who tilted his head. Harold looked back at Maria. "Fire away."

"Perhaps it is John's ghost. I told you about the little girl who drowned. We had other spirits that would show up in our village as well."

Harold leaned in closer to Maria. "How did you get rid of them?"

"We would get our village priest, and he would chase them away."

Harold gave Joshua a sideways glance and caught the twinge of a smile on his friend's lips. "I appreciate the idea, but I don't think I'm ready for an exorcism just yet."

Maria straightened up in her seat. "Suit yourself. I would suggest you don't provoke it. If it is John's ghost, he probably likes when you get mad. You should try and ignore him."

Harold's grunt was hidden beneath the drone of the jet engines. "I wish I could. He's very hard to ignore."

"Well, just try not to hit him. The next time you might break your own nose."

Harold heard a quick burst of laughter from Joshua. "Is something funny there, Doc?"

"I'm sorry. I just had this image of you with a broken nose saying, 'You should have seen the other guy.'" Joshua attempted to become more serious. "Truthfully, I think Maria is giving you some pretty good advice. If you don't escalate things with this image of John, perhaps your mind will start to let go of whatever it is that's haunting you."

"Wait, do you really think I'm being haunted?"

"It's just an expression. Frankly, I'm a bit concerned. There are cases where hypnotherapy has caused unwanted reactions, or side effects if you will."

Harold's eyes grew wide. "Keep going."

Joshua leaned closer to Harold. "There are cases of people's emotional trauma being put into compartmentalized rooms within the brain, for lack of a better way of saying it. Something triggers the brain, and it instinctively releases the memories as a defense mechanism. That can result in nightmares, nervous breakdowns, and other things."

Harold sucked on his lip for a moment, and then he responded, "That sounds pretty dangerous, Doc."

Joshua stared down at the floor for a moment and then sat up and looked into Harold's eyes. "It can be. Although, I don't think that is your problem. Ever since your teenage years, we have dealt with your berserker out in the open. Yes, the Viking village is fake, but your subconscious never locked away your rage."

"Then how can John suddenly appear, and what about Bill? Could he be having the same issues?"

"Adam assured me some time ago that Bill's demon was still safely locked away. That is how we referred to his berserker side. Although, I've started to have some concerns about him given your recent events. If he and John can appear in your dreams on a stage we set during hypnosis, I do wonder might happen to Bill's subconscious if he is ever confronted with real danger."

"Can you or Adam track down my half-brother and warn him? I can tell you that these dreams, or whatever they are, frighten me, and I understand some of what's going on. I can't imagine what would happen if I didn't have a clue."

Joshua reached over and patted Harold's hand for a moment. "I wouldn't worry about your brother. You need to focus on where this dead man's memory is coming from."

Harold let his body relax into the seat. "It has its origins from somewhere, but I have no clue as to why he's showing up. I'll try to not get angry, but I'd rather throw that ghost back through the gates of hell where he came from."

"I know, Harry. Just try and remind yourself that not every battle is physical. This is a battle of wits."

Harold leaned towards the window and looked out over the clear teal waters. The jet had begun to descend. *Beautiful*, he thought. *Maybe this won't be so bad after all.* The flight attendant walked up to the trio. "We are beginning our descent into Key West. You'll need to finish up your drinks and prepare for landing."

The group made short work of their remaining sips. Harold noticed Joshua's hands tightening their grip on his armrest as the plane gently touched the runway. They taxied to a parking spot, and the flight attendant opened the door. Harold stepped out and was hit in the face with the higher humidity. It was warm for an early fall day, even by California standards. The late afternoon sun was slowly making its way towards the horizon. Harold gazed around the palm trees and a terminal sign that read, *Welcome to the Conch Republic.* The scene reminded him more of some old classified photos his dad once showed him of Cuba than anyplace he had been in the US.

From over Harold's shoulder, a faint, familiar voice cried out, "Glad to see you finally made it."

The entire group turned to see Agent Garcia's familiar form briskly walking across the asphalt. He wore a teal Hawaiian shirt, white shorts, and white tennis shoes with white socks. A tan-colored hat, and of course, his sunglasses finished his fashion statement.

"Wow," mumbled Harold to Joshua as Garcia approached.

"How does that man see?" asked Joshua.

"I have no idea, Doc," responded Harold.

"Ay-ay-ay," Maria said softly.

Garcia walked up and shook everyone's hand. "I'm so glad you all arrived safely. If you'll follow me to my car, I've taken care of your hotel and bags. I wanted you to see your new home in the daylight, so we'll enjoy a night in Key West before we head to our destination tomorrow."

Harold rubbed his hands together. "Where are we headed?"

"What got into you?" asked Joshua.

"Well, Doc, when in Rome, do as the Romans do. I don't know what is going on at this mysterious island we are heading for, but I know what goes on in Key West, and I intend to enjoy myself on this adventure. Besides, this is a business expense, right?"

Garcia's eyebrows rose slightly above the rim of his sunglasses. "Absolutely. Just remember, those who receive much are expected to do a lot. So, take advantage of the hospitality. I have a feeling you're going to earn it. By the way, what's with your eye? Did you and Joshua get into a disagreement?"

Joshua chuckled, and Harold crinkled his forehead. "No, I fell down and hit my head."

"I'd hate to see the furniture or floor even if it did only give you a small bruise," Garcia continued. "The good news is that it helps you blend in with some of the bar crawlers. Black eyes around here are just another Friday night depending on where you like to grab your drinks. Speaking of drinks, why don't we get out of here and get settled into our digs before we hit the nightlife."

The three followed Garcia to his black GMC Yukon with tinted windows.

"I thought these things only existed in the movies," quipped Harold.

Garcia remotely unlocked the door and hollered back to Harold from the driver's side door. "They exist in movies because we like to use them in real life."

The drive from the airport was short. Garcia navigated the large Yukon through the narrow gates of the Coco Plum Inn. The small bed and breakfast was near the nightlife of Duvall Street. The group remained with the SUV while Garcia went inside and got them checked in.

"What do you think, Doc?" asked Harold. "Key West definitely has personality."

"Yes," replied Joshua. "I only got to spend an afternoon here on my last trip. It was a welcomed relief after spending the time with John and his gang on their island."

"Do you think you're going to be okay? You know, going back to the island?"

Joshua blankly stared at some of the dense foliage near the parking lot. "I hope Agent Garcia and his people have cleaned the place up. One thing is for sure, you can have the master bedroom. If I were you, I would ask Garcia if they burned the mattresses. If they haven't, I would insist on it."

Harold crossed his arms. "Good to know."

Maria stepped up and took Joshua's arm. "He won't tell me everything that happened. If I were you, I wouldn't ask Garcia too many details. I know John was a horrid man. Such men only use people, especially women, for their own twisted pleasures. I will know immediately if John's stench remains in the house. If it does, we won't take a step inside until they scrub it floor to ceiling."

Garcia came walking up wearing his sunglasses. Harold started to mention the quickly darkening sky but decided he would wait and see how long it took Garcia to figure out the sunglasses were still on.

Garcia handed out keys. "Good news, gang. I arranged for us to bunk up in one of the few three-bedroom suites. It's basically three rooms with a common connected room. That will give us a bit more privacy and security."

"Security?" asked Joshua.

"Don't worry, Doctor. The people we are dealing with are professionals. They have no reason to threaten us at the moment, but it's always best to be prepared."

Joshua looked wide-eyed at Maria and then Harold.

"Let's go." Garcia opened the back of the SUV, and they all grabbed their bag. "You have ten minutes to settle in, and then meet me here."

Harold appreciated Garcia's authoritative tone. He knew that meant the agent was on the clock. Whatever they had stepped into, things had already started. The sooner he could get this whole affair out the way, the sooner he could go home and the sooner his father's company could be free of its commitment.

Garcia had taken the deluxe room and left the other three with standard rooms. Harold did not mind the smaller room. After all, it was just for the night. After freshening up, he wandered back out by the SUV. When he walked up, Joshua and Maria were already there and engaging in small talk.

Before Harold could join in, Garcia's voice came from directly behind him, causing him to jump. "Let's go gang."

"Where did you come from?" asked Harold. "Did you see him walk up, Doc?"

Joshua raised his palms up and shook his head.

Harold turned to Garcia. "You and Maria should get together. She's very good at making sudden appearances."

Maria responded, "I'm just naturally quiet."

"That's a good quality," Garcia said. "Don't ever lose it."

The small gathering walked out of the bed and breakfast's entrance and turned right. Next door stood the Green Parrot Bar. "This place is an institution," quipped Garcia as he walked inside the bar. Joshua paused to look around and pointed across the street. "Look," he said, "Monroe County."

"What's that?" asked Harold.

"Oh, it's just the name of a town not too far from where I used to live in North Carolina. I guess I just realized how much closer I am to my old hometown."

"We have to go there sometime," said Maria.

Joshua turned and pointed at the door, and the crew went inside to find Garcia.

The Green Parrot's interior had a fresh coat of paint, but it still retained the feel of an old Caribbean bar. Garcia pointed towards a counter on one side of the room. The team walked over and grabbed some bar stools while Garcia headed for the bar.

"This feels like a bit of a dive, even by West Coast standards," commented Harold.

Joshua's face beamed, and his mouth held a broad smile as he admired the interior. "I don't know. I kind of like it."

Maria scowled and shook her head in disapproval. "In Mexico, nothing good ever happened in a place like this. He didn't even ask us what we wanted to drink."

"I'd settle for a cold beer," mumbled Harold. He put his elbow down on the counter and let his weight rest against it. The wood groaned against the burden.

Two friends sitting a few feet down from Harold looked over and then quickly turned away.

Joshua quickly nodded towards the pair and then slapped Harold on the back. "I don't think we'll have any trouble tonight."

Garcia walked up for four tall glasses of yellow liquid. "Rum and pineapple."

Maria scowled. Harold and Joshua looked at one another. Each person said thank you as Garcia handed out the drinks. He studied their faces as the team took them from him. "Why so disappointed? You haven't even tried these yet."

Joshua spoke up first, "I know we had rum runners on the jet, but the Florida Keys is the birthplace of the drink. I was looking forward to sharing the experience of drinking real rum runners with my family in the Keys."

Garcia placed his drink on the counter and turned to face the group. "I understand. Don't worry. This is just a quick stop off to wet our whistles and chat a little. You can't visit Key West and not experience some sort of bar crawl. Enjoy the fun, I can promise you there won't be too many times you'll be able to relax."

Maria raised her glass, and the men followed suit. They toasted and sucked down the wonderful flavor of Sailor Jerry Spiced Rum and pineapple.

After a couple of minutes of silence, the crew took a breather from their cold libation. Harold put his empty glass on the bar. The others held their half-filled drinks in their hands. "I guess I was thirstier than I thought," Harold said as his face turned slightly crimson.

"I think you're good for it," responded Garcia. "Okay, what questions do you have for me?"

Joshua looked over at Maria. They both turned their gaze towards Garcia without saying a word.

"Come on, Doctor. You've been there. You don't have any concerns about tomorrow?" asked Garcia.

Joshua took a short sip of his drink. "I guess I'm just in a wait and see mindset."

"Doc said I should ask if you guys burned John's mattresses."

Garcia attempted to catch the drink escaping his mouth back into the glass. He coughed and drew in a deep breath as he got himself under control. "We removed more than the mattresses. Let's just say after we went through his place with an ultraviolet light, most of our techs refused to go back inside without hazmat suits."

Maria crossed her arms. "Disgusting. I better not find anything that was missed when I get there."

Harold noticed Joshua shudder. "Are you okay, Doc?"

"Just something I hope I'll eventually forget."

"You used to tell me it's better to talk about it."

"This is hardly the time or place."

Maria put her arm through Joshua's. "If he needs to talk to anybody, he can talk to me."

Harold turned back towards the bar. He felt a little displaced by Maria's words. He did not blame Maria for the change between Joshua and him. His relationship with Joshua had begun to change from the moment his father had killed himself. He immediately saw Joshua as a second father figured rather than just an uncle or family friend. It was not anything he would admit out loud, and he knew it was not fair to put that sort of responsibility on Joshua. Still, it did sting a little to think Joshua would go to Maria before coming to him, even though Harold knew that was how things should work. He scanned the brown- and green-painted bar. A stage sat empty of performers, but their instruments were set up in their respective stands.

Harold asked, "Hey, Garcia, are we staying for the music?"

Garcia glanced Harold's direction. "No, we're leaving before they start up. I just wanted a cool drink and to see who might be staying on the island with us."

Harold leaned in towards Garcia. "What does that mean?"

Joshua and Maria closed in around Garcia as well. Harold saw their reflections in the tinted sunglasses that gazed at each of them. "Did you see the two guys that were checking out Harold earlier?"

Everyone looked wide-eyed at one another.

Garcia continued, "Those are Chuck's men. You can expect to be watched the entire time we're on the island tonight."

"This feels familiar," Joshua said.

Maria took his hand. "Is this what happened when you were here?"

Joshua closed his eyes and nodded his head once.

"You were at the Green Parrot?" asked Harold.

"No, I was just in Key West. One of John's men approached me and escorted me around for the day." The group loosened the tightly knit ball that had formed, and Joshua continued, "I made the most of it and had him take me to all the usual tourist spots. It made me pretty paranoid though. I spent a few extra days near LAX before coming back to the estate. I was sure I was still being watched."

"John didn't have those kinds of resources," said Garcia. "Still, you will stay alive longer if you assume somebody is watching you."

"That sounds a little paranoid," responded Harold.

"Harold, please. I'm CIA. There is nothing paranoid about thinking you're being followed when you probably are."

"Maybe, but if every stranger is possibly out to kill you, how do you know who you can trust?"

Maria slid her arm around Joshua's. "You can trust the people who love you."

Harold looked over at Garcia, "How do you do it?"

"What?" asked Garcia.

"Not go crazy," responded Harold. "Why aren't you paranoid? From the sounds of it, I know I would be."

Garcia leaned against the bar with his elbow. "I'm a funny guy. I like to keep things light. Otherwise, yea, this life can make you crazy. In fact, you guys may want to keep that in mind. Like it or not, from this point forward, you're part of my world. Things will be very serious when we're around Chuck. So enjoy your downtime. It will help keep you sharp."

"Is that why you always wear them? It amuses you to see people's reaction?" asked Harold.

Garcia raised an eyebrow. "What are you talking about?"

Harold raised his massive arms over his head and stretched. He was going to enjoy this. "The sunglasses."

"What about them?"

"Do you think people's reaction to you wearing them all the time is funny? If you think you're being followed, you are pretty bad at hiding. I mean, look at you. It's getting dark outside, and we're in a dive bar. Here you are with your mirrored sunglasses on. You stick out like a sore thumb. If somebody is following you, you're an easy target."

Garcia spun partway around on the barstool and rested his elbows behind him on the counter. He turned and looked at Harold, who smoothed down a hair he noticed sticking out in the reflection of Garcia's sunglasses. "It's true. I do wear these beauties more often than I should, but now is the proper time to be sporting these."

"You want to be seen?" Harold asked.

"For the moment. I've met Chuck. He assumes he's helping the company sow discord in northern Africa. He has no idea what's going to happen to him."

"And what exactly is that?" asked Harold.

Garcia answered with a half-smile. "It's need to know. You'll find out at the right time."

Harold decided to get back to his original discussion. "Nice try, Agent Garcia. Let's get back on topic. Why would you want to wear the sunglasses in areas that make you easier to spot?"

Garcia's face was expressionless, and he appeared to be looking at Joshua and Maria. Harold followed Garcia's lead and thought Joshua and Maria looked as enamored by the discussion as he felt.

Garcia finally spoke up. "Well, do you see the two pretty women in the corner forty-five degrees to your left? The redhead that is twenty and trying to pass as twenty-five? Her raven-haired friend is probably twenty-three. I would guess they are both University of Miami coeds."

Harold let his eyes dart over to the two women. The brunette had on a thin, tight, white T-shirt with the familiar green and orange *U*. The redhead wore an equally form-fitting purple T-shirt. Their short-shorts did not reveal any tan lines on their thighs. Harold assumed they must have been sunbathing most of the day. He looked back over to Garcia. "They're pretty tough to miss."

"And yet, you did," Garcia said with a smirk.

Harold waved off his comment. "I'm not here to trawl for women in bars."

Garcia's forehead wrinkled slightly. "Well, if you had been, you would have failed. Those ladies have been watching you ever since we walked in here. My eyes have been glued that direction during most of our discussion, but you couldn't tell. That's why I keep this pair of honeys over my eyes."

Harold let himself slide off his barstool. "How do you know they don't work for Chuck?"

Garcia followed suit and stood up and stretched his legs. "Chuck's a pig. He doesn't let women into his organization unless it's for his personal pleasure, or they are used to seduce a client or enemy. College girls are not his style."

Harold pointed towards the front door. "Are we going to stay here all night and talk, or are we going to get something to eat?"

"I'm famished," Joshua and Maria said in unison.

"Food it is," replied Garcia.

As they exited the Green Parrot, Garcia removed his sunglasses.

Harold asked, "What's wrong, Agent? Are you done hiding your peepers from the world?"

Garcia looked up at Harold. "Something like that. When it's dark enough, and crowded enough, you can look around and normally nobody will notice."

"Fair enough."

Garcia gave Harold a friendly punch on the shoulder. "Harold, I may make a company man out of you yet."

"You'll do no such thing," Joshua said.

Harold held up his hand, "Easy, Doc. I have this. I may have lots of questions about Garcia's tradecraft, but that's just to keep myself, and the rest of us, alive."

After a few hours of drinking and eating, the small band was exhausted and stumbled their way back to the bed and breakfast for a well-deserved rest.

CHAPTER 10

"Doc, we're all waiting on you two," Harold chided.

Joshua and Maria came meandering out to the SUV. This morning Joshua had joined Garcia in wearing sunglasses. Garcia and Harold stood waiting in front of the vehicle's grille with their arms crossed.

Garcia spoke up, "The plane is waiting."

"I thought we had a private plane," said Maria.

"We do," answered Garcia, "but we're still on a clock. I have people standing by for our arrival on the island, and they have work to do."

"I'm sorry," said Joshua. "I'm afraid it's my fault. It appears I'm not as young as I used to be."

Harold raised his voice as Joshua walked by. "Oh, I thought you were practicing your secret agent look."

Joshua winced.

Garcia leaned over to Harold. "I know you're joking, but go easy with the spy jokes. Your voice carries. Remember Chuck's people last night?"

Harold nodded and looked around, afraid he might find someone standing nearby, but thankfully nobody was in earshot. The crew finished loading up and headed to the airport. Harold kept a wary eye out the window as they left the complex. Except for a few pedestrians, the street was quiet compared to the night before.

The small company walked through the same terminal they arrived at less than twenty-four hours earlier and continued on their way out to the aircraft parking area then up to a blue and white Cessna Grand Caravan.

Harold noticed Joshua's shoulders slump. "What's the matter, Doc?"

"I've flown in this airplane before."

"Are you worried you'll get airsick?"

Joshua looked towards Harold, but all Harold saw was his reflection in Joshua's wraparound sunglasses. "No, my stomach is fine. Well, fine enough. I don't like small planes."

"How bad can it be? Fewer seats means fewer people. At least I should be able to squeeze in somewhere."

A man walked around from the other side of the airplane. "Everyone, this is our pilot, Frank," Garcia said. "Frank, this is everyone."

Frank gave everybody a broad smile and stuck out his hand. "Welcome aboard." After he finished shaking everybody's hands, he looked over at Harold. "You'll get the privilege of sitting up front with me in the right seat."

Harold raised his eyebrows. "Me? I don't know anything about flying."

Frank gave a sideways grin and reached up to give Harold's shoulder a friendly slap. "Oh, you're not helping me fly, big boy. We need to balance the weight of the plane. We're putting you up front to help balance your bags."

"See what I mean?" Joshua said.

Harold gave both men a slow nod. Frank directed the loading of the luggage, and everybody climbed aboard. The takeoff was smooth, and soon they were flying above the beautiful Caribbean. Harold looked out the co-pilot's window and enjoyed the view of the Great Florida Reef. The plane was only three thousand feet in the air, and Harold had a good view of the sharks and other large fish swimming below along the shallow reef in search of food. The view reminded him of a giant aquarium.

After a short flight, and several small keys later, Frank dropped the altitude of the plane to twelve hundred feet. Harold heard Garcia yell from behind him. "We're coming up on Salvation Key."

Harold's voice easily projected over the plane's engine, "May we never need her safety."

"If we do, this is the one place I can guarantee you that you'll be safe from danger." Garcia looked over at Joshua sitting across from him. "Doctor, I think you'll approve of the improvements we've made since you last came here."

Harold noticed Joshua's fingers dug into the armrest. He glanced to Maria who was smiling and looking out the windows.

Harold joked, "Doc, I thought you liked to fly."

"Not small planes!" Joshua answered emphatically.

Harold laughed and looked out the front window. Frank navigated the plane around the large key. Below Harold saw a new airstrip that appeared to extend off the key by about two hundred feet. On the other end sat a guard tower. A white-colored road led from the airstrip to a compound of large buildings. Harold heard Garcia's voice from behind, "Welcome to your new home everyone. Harold, that large mansion is yours. Doctor, you'll notice when we fly back over on your side of the plane there is a new two-story house. That's for you and Maria. The remaining cottages are for any agents that need to be assigned to the island, and for me."

From the air, Harold saw a large house with Spanish tile. It appeared to have a plaza, a swimming pool, and exterior stairs leading up to a large room and breezeway. Palm trees and sawgrass lined the white driveway and paths.

Harold turned in his seat to Garcia. "What's the road made out of? Concrete?"

"Crushed shells."

Harold turned back around and continued to gaze at the beautiful scene beneath him. The plane had cleared Salvation Key and was coming around for a pass from the other side. From over the top of the plane, Harold noted the more jungle-like conditions on the other end of the island. Looking out the side window, he saw large objects in the water that appeared to be manatees. On one side of the Key was a small cove with a modest cabin cruiser tied off next to a pier.

Malibu had its share of luxury. Richard had provided well for the family, but to Harold, this property felt more like a resort than a home. Harold reflected on John's obsession with wealth. How could John have thought his father had more wealth? Sure, his company was worth more on paper, but his family had always invested most of their wealth back into the company and its valuable employees. *Maybe this is why Dad did so much better than John. He never would have wasted his money on something like this.*

Harold barely heard Maria's voice attempting to yell over the drone of the plane. "Joshua, look at our house. It looks wonderful. It even has a front porch."

"I hope you like it," replied Garcia. "Real estate is premium, so we had to make it two stories. Your bedroom is upstairs, but I think you'll like the view. Occasionally a saltwater crocodile will wander out of the vegetation in the early part of the day. Don't worry. They don't get too close to the house. We have a fence set up a few feet from the back of the property. You just can't see it from the air."

"It looks very beautiful," Maria proclaimed. "Isn't this beautiful, Joshua?"

Joshua slowly nodded his head.

"Take us home, Frank," said Garcia.

The Cessna banked and extended diagonally past the island. After a few minutes, Frank did a U-turn and deftly landed the plane on the runway. The Grand Caravan barely stopped before four open-air jeeps filled with boxes showed up next to the parking area near the runway along with at least a dozen people. They all stood clear waiting for the prop to stop rotating. As soon as the motor quit, two people walked up and began to pull bags out from the belly of the plane.

"Everyone hold up until they get our gear," Garcia said.

Harold asked, "What's up with the welcoming committee?"

"As I said in Key West, we're on the clock. These people have been working non-stop for several months getting the island ready for your arrival. Most of them are finally getting to go home. There will be a few planes coming in and out today. Don't worry about the commotion. The airspace is normally kept clear."

Harold looked over his shoulder at Garcia. "You seem pretty sure of yourself."

Garcia tilted his head. "How so?"

"You started working on this long before I agreed to do anything."

Garcia tilted down his sunglasses and looked Harold in the eye. "You may not remember me from when you were a kid. You were busy doing what boys your age did, but I was around. Your dad and I did some work together. I knew your dad, and by extension, I know the type of man he raised. I had no doubt you'd make the right decision."

Harold turned back around and quietly gazed out the front window at the workers busily moving luggage and lock boxes around near the aircraft. After a few moments, the team was able to disembark.

Garcia walked ahead with quick strides. "Follow me."

The crew followed Garcia to an empty jeep and climbed aboard. "Hold on." Garcia threw the vehicle into first gear and made a U-turn that resembled more of a half donut before relaxing the gas pedal and cruising away from the airstrip. Within ten yards, they were clear of personnel. A short half mile later, they pulled into the compound, and Garcia pulled to a stop in front of a two-story house.

The house was covered in white stucco with gold trim along the top of the second story. A small front porch accented the home. The covered porch was decorated with four white wicker rocking chairs. One of the chairs was distinctly larger than the others. "Welcome home, Doctor, Maria," said Garcia. "We'll come back and take the grand tour, but I wanted to stop a moment and let you see it from the outside."

"It's nice," said Maria.

Garcia continued, "From here, you're within walking distance of the main house but far enough away that you can all have some breathing room."

"The doc was closer to me in Malibu," Harold said.

"True, but he could get away when he wanted to as well. Leaving the island is not always a simple affair. You'll appreciate the breathing room."

"Good thinking," said Joshua.

Harold turned around from the front seat with his eyes wide. "Doc, I didn't know I was smothering you."

Joshua patted the back of the headrest. "Take it easy. I was half joking. We all like to get away. I had the gym in Malibu, and you and Tom would disappear into the hills to do whatever it was you boys liked to do."

"Free climbing." Harold turned back and faced the front.

Garcia pointed ahead. Harold could make out the top of the Spanish-tiled roof of the main house. Palm trees graced the top edge of the wall of the Moroccan-styled structure.

"Onward," said Garcia with the enthusiasm of a small child showing his parents his latest school project.

He punched the gas, and the crew slid to a stop a few moments later in front of the entryway. The front door opened.

Harold gasped. A well-tanned brunette strolled out of the house. Her hair was in a ponytail to give her neck relief from the Caribbean warmth. Her khaki shorts and white T-shirt fit perfectly around her firm curves. Her dark eyes locked on to Harold, and he leaped out of the jeep. The vehicle rocked as it gave way to his escape. Time and space disappeared as he ran to her arms. He heard her grunt as he wrapped his arms around her and lifted her off the ground. Her firm, smooth neck felt like satin against his lips, and the distinct odor of coconut wafted into Harold's nostrils.

In his ear, he heard her gasp, "I can't breathe, darling."

Harold quickly lowered her down and released his bear hug. "Sorry."

Darla Johanson reached up, gently caressed his cheek, and gave him a long kiss.

He had forgotten how soft and silky her lips could feel. They finally released, and Harold asked, "What are you doing here? I thought you were on a secret assignment somewhere?"

"I was. Look around," said Darla. "This is it. Garcia asked me if I would rejoin the CIA and come help with this project. I'm sorry I didn't say anything, but we couldn't afford to risk any leaks, and we wanted to make sure that your motivation for being here was for the right reasons."

Harold winked and said, "You're all the reason I would need."

"Exactly," said Darla. "You need to be here first and foremost to help us capture some dangerous men and to help your company recover. Besides, I wanted to surprise you."

Joshua and Maria walked up, and Darla gave them both a hug.

"Doctor, I think you'll like your house."

"I think we will. I'm still adjusting to being back. It's definitely different, but very much the same."

Darla turned and let her gaze pan the front of the house. "Yes. Well, we didn't see the point in tearing everything down. It took a while to clean things up, but I can assure you it's all good as new."

"Is there still a path to the beach we walked on? It was one of the better places on the island. Aside from the senator's rendezvous."

"Yes. In fact, I widened the path and laid down fresh-crushed shells. It's easier to find and walk."

"Good," said Joshua.

"Shall we go inside?" asked Garcia.

Harold took a moment to look at the entrance. Despite the familiar Spanish tiles, the multiple sharp angles and rectangular dormers of the French, Italian, and Moroccan design was vastly different from the Spanish style he had grown up with. Although his estate was large, it maintained a semblance of humility. This home screamed money. John had wanted anyone coming to his private island to know he had a lot of wealth and to be intimidated by it.

Harold looked at the marble entryway through the opened mahogany doors and gawked in disbelief. A marble staircase with a wrought iron banister rose to the right. White marble walls encased the formal foyer. It was beautiful but cold and hard. A small mosaic was inlaid in the middle of the floor entrance. Harold wondered if they had entered a home or a mosque in the Middle East.

"What do you think?" asked Garcia.

Harold and Joshua were silent, but Maria responded, "It's so beautiful, but it is hard and cold. I see why John tried to kill me. He had no warmth in his heart."

"Well, according to the eggheads at the company, John spent well over a cool million just on the materials for this house," Garcia said. "I hope you like marble, because it's all over the place."

The crew continued through the house. They entered an outdoor living room with brown wicker furniture. The far wall opened to a beautiful ornate marble fountain sitting in the middle of the patio. On the other side of the room were the swimming pool lined in marble and a concrete deck.

Garcia turned to the group. "There's a lot of indoor and outdoor rooms in this place."

Harold had grown bored. Darla could show him the rest of the estate when the two of them felt like exploring. "Can we do the rest of the tour later? I'd just like to unwind."

Garcia stopped and answered, "I'm sorry. I am going on like a real estate agent. Of course. Let me just show you a couple more things first."

The crew walked to the pool area. Fountains flowed from the edge of the pool into its cool water. A small bar sat off in the corner of the pool deck. Glass walled archways faced a narrow strip of well-trimmed grass and a row of deciduous trees. Beyond them grew native vegetation.

"Everyone, I want us to meet here in a couple of hours. We'll start our first brief on Chuck McGill."

"Where's my room in this mausoleum?" quipped Harold.

Garcia paused and his sunglasses turned his direction. "You mean, you don't like it? I assumed you could appreciate the craftsmanship that went into John's old place. I mean, the man was a menace, but he did have good taste."

Harold took a glance back in towards the living room inside the house. "I guess I'm just homesick. I mean, yea, I grew up with money, but we had a home. This place is hard, cold. It doesn't feel like a home."

"Give it time." Darla gently laid her hand on his arm. "Take it from someone who has moved a lot; no place feels like home until you get settled into your routine. Garcia, let me show him to his room. Why don't you take Maria and Joshua to their house?"

"Agreed. Doctor, Maria, please follow me."

The three of them headed back out the way they had come in. A smile crossed Harold's face as he noticed Joshua reaching over to take Maria's hand. He hoped one day he and Darla could be a loving married couple.

Darla spoke with an edge of sarcasm in her voice, "I thought I'd never get you alone. Now you can tell me what you really think about your government housing."

"Yea, don't give me any grief," responded Harold. "I've just always lived in Malibu. I never considered leaving my family's estate. I miss the hills and my view of the ocean."

"Darling, you're sitting in the Gulf of Mexico. You're not seeing the scenery because you're in it. Let me take you up to your bedroom."

"I thought you'd never ask."

Darla slapped his shoulder. "Careful! You'll get us both in trouble."

"Oh, is there a rule about that?"

"You know what I mean. We agreed to wait."

He gave her a sideways grin. "I didn't say I wouldn't joke about it."

Darla gave him a light pop on his chest and walked towards the other side of the patio. They passed the fountain and walked up another set of marble steps that led up to a sundeck. Harold looked around.

"Finally, some sort of view," he muttered.

Darla stopped walking. "Oh, I see. You like seeing above everything."

He waved his hand apologetically between them. "No, I'm not like that."

"Relax, honey. If I thought you were that kind of man, you would have never gotten beyond a handshake after I first met you. I guess it's just this place. I've learned a lot about John since I came to this island. He really was a megalomaniac. Coming back here to clean up his mess, literally and figuratively, has been a real strain on me. You should feel honored. This is the first time I felt like joking with anyone since I got here."

"You can joke with me anytime."

Darla reached up and kissed him on the cheek. They walked along a covered walkway and passed by a beautiful mahogany porch swing and several other deck chairs before entering the master suite. Harold gasped. He was blown away by the beauty of the room. The walls were painted in sea mist, and the new white carpet and ceilings gave the room a happy, welcoming atmosphere. *This feels like a home.*

"I hoped you'd like it," said Darla. "I redesigned this room myself."

"I love it," he said.

"I couldn't do much with the bathroom. John was into all sorts of marble designs, and we couldn't justify tearing it out."

"It's okay."

The master bathroom they walked into was a beautiful combination of white and brown marble. A large garden tub framed by two large Roman columns sat next to the far wall. An antique brass chandelier hung from the ceiling. A corner shower sat next to the door.

"Now what?" asked Darla.

"Honestly, I'd be happy if we could just sit on the porch swing and talk."

"I'd like that, but I can't. I need to get things ready for our briefing. I promise we'll have time to catch up later. Why don't you grab some sun, and I'll see you down by the bar?"

Harold crossed his arms. "Business before pleasure, eh?"

She reached up and gave him a quick kiss on the lips. "I'm afraid it has to be that way if you want me around."

He sighed and dropped his head. "Okay, honey. Go to work. I'll try and be a good boy."

Darla turned on her heel and then looked over her shoulder. "You'd better be."

Harold did not try to hide his stare as she walked out of the room. He had forgotten how happy she could make him. Maybe he would have to wait to spend some real time with her, but so what? He was just glad they were in the same house. He raised his arms over his head and let out a loud groan as he stretched his sore muscles. That flight over in the small plane had made him stiffer than he realized. As he walked back through the bedroom, he decided he could get used to some of this.

Harold sat on the swing in the shade and slowly pushed the bench back and forth. The wood groaned at its newfound burden but held fast. He caught a glimpse of Darla from over the balcony, walking back towards the house with a folder in her hand. There was a lot to get used to, but having Darla around was going to make life around the mausoleum feel more like home.

CHAPTER 11

Joshua's voice seemed to penetrate Harold's mind, "Harry, Harry, wake up."

Harold could feel Joshua's hand pressed up against his shoulder as he attempted to rock him awake. His body began to sway back and forth. Harold opened his eyes to see what was causing the motion. As the world came into view, reality rushed in on him.

He had laid down for a moment on the wooden swing. In front of his face sat the arched, covered walkway of the new home. The unfamiliar smell of the Caribbean flooded his nostrils. The occasional call of an ibis or seagull could be heard as the fog began to clear from Harold's mind.

"Harry, it's time to wake up."

"Okay, Doc. I guess I just needed a quick break."

Harold sat up. The chains and wood groaned at his sudden movements. Harold rubbed his face, gave his head a quick shake, and blinked his eyes. Part of him hoped it was one of his ridiculous dreams with John and he would wake up back at home in Malibu, but he knew better. The world felt too real. He could smell the coconut suntan oil Joshua had put on. Harold was back in the land of the living, whether he wanted to be there or not.

"Harry, come on, everyone is waiting for you downstairs."

The meeting. Have I really been asleep for two hours?

"Sorry, Doc. I didn't realize the time."

Harold rose up and took deep, cleansing breaths on the way down to the pool bar. By the time they reached the group, his head had cleared out any remaining cobwebs. The rest of the team was already sitting in the wickered dining furniture between the pool and fountain. Most appeared to have fruit juice, which Harold assumed was the familiar rum runner that Joshua and Maria espoused so often. Harold was in no mood for alcohol, yet.

A man Harold had not met stood behind the bar. Harold approached it, hoping for something with a bit of caffeine rather than a cocktail.

"What's your name?" asked Harold.

"Frank," answered the bartender.

"Wow, that's the same name as our pilot."

"What will you have?"

"I don't suppose you can make a frap?"

"Yes, with or without alcohol?"

"The alcohol version sounds intriguing, but let's go without it. I'm still waking up."

Frank nodded and began working his magic.

"Frank will bring it over," Joshua said. "We need to join the meeting."

Harold and Joshua walked over to the table. Joshua sat down next to Maria. A seat at the head of the table had obviously been left open for Harold. His rear barely touched the cushion before Garcia began to speak.

"I hope you had a nice nap. Jet lag will come and go for the next few days. I'm giving everyone a week to settle in before the real work begins. That said, Darla and I need to fill you in on Chuck McGill now."

Darla jumped in, "Chuck is one of the most dangerous men I've ever met."

"You've already met him?" asked Harold.

Darla tossed an eight by ten photo onto the coffee table between the drinks. "He looks unassuming. He's five feet eight inches tall and weighs around two hundred pounds and can normally be found holding a cigar."

"He looks like a middle-aged tourist," said Joshua.

The photo showed a man in his forties with a white cotton button-down shirt like the ones worn by so many beachcombers in the Caribbean. He had on the usual tan khaki shorts. The photo ended at his knees, so Harold could only guess what shoes he wore, but he assumed they were probably the usual docksider styles seen around the marinas.

"Does he smoke cigars all the time?" asked Maria.

"Yes," answered Garcia. "He smokes his cigars like I wear my sunglasses. Sometimes he doesn't notice they've gone out or forgets to light them completely. We think it's his one vice. Chuck is meticulous in his business dealings, and his lifestyle, except for his cigars."

"I think they stink," answered Maria. "He should have a cleaner vice."

Joshua glanced over at Harold and tried to stifle a small smile that had crept across his face. Harold guessed that Joshua had not exposed Maria to his occasional cigar use.

"As I was saying," Darla said, "he is extremely dangerous. In addition to revamping Salvation Key, Garcia and myself have been working on a ruse to pull Chuck in close to us. It is rather complicated and involves most everyone seated here."

Maria tilted her head in and looked towards Garcia. "Most? Does that mean I'm not needed?"

Garcia leaned closer and looked back and forth at Maria and Joshua before he spoke. "Maria, not everyone who is needed works on the front lines. Take Frank for instance. His job may seem unimportant, but his support on the island is invaluable to the success of this mission because it frees us up to focus on our tasks. Your job is to support us as well. Believe me, I would not have gone through the trouble and expense of bringing you here if I didn't consider you important."

Frank walked over, and Maria stopped talking.

Harold took the cold coffee-infused drink and sucked in a long swallow from the straw. It was perfect. "That's excellent, thank you."

Frank gave a slight bow and a smile then walked back to the bar.

Harold turned to Garcia and asked, "What's with the two Franks?"

Garcia tapped his finger on the table for a moment and then answered. "Everyone who works here is Frank. Unless she's a woman, then it's Alice."

Harold's brow creased in confusion. "What? We can't know their real names, but they can know ours?"

Garcia reached over and picked up his drink. "Don't let their roles fool you. They are some of our best undercover and self-defense agents. They keep their aliases, so we never accidently slip up and give their real names to somebody."

Maria interjected, "Are we really in that much danger?"

Garcia stood and got everyone's attention. He bent over and pointed again at Chuck's photo. "I can't overemphasize how dangerous this man is. This island is not on any map, but if it were ever discovered by Chuck, it would take more than Darla and me to defeat his men. As for their names, that's for everyone's security. You aren't trained agents nor are you prisoners on the island. If you go to the Keys, or somewhere else, and Frank is with you, there is no chance you will accidently slip and use his real name. These agents maintain deep cover identities, and it's important we keep them anonymous even here on the island."

Garcia maintained eye contact with everyone as he sat down.

Harold asked, "What if two Franks are in the room with us?"

Garcia exhaled loudly and took a sip of his cocktail. "There won't be."

Harold leaned back and crossed his arms and legs, and Darla said, "There are protocols to who is where on the island. It's all need to know, and trust me, you don't want to know. It took Garcia and I a long time to come up with a security protocol that won't negatively impact our living conditions."

"It impacted mine," Maria quipped.

Harold looked over at Maria and noticed her lower lip slightly pouting outward. "What did they do?" asked Harold.

"They won't let me work! I came outside to sweep our front porch, and Frank, or whatever his name was, came over and took my broom. He said that he was more than happy to take care of any cleaning for me. When I started to argue with him, he said I should get Joshua and come up here for the meeting," exclaimed Maria. "They want me to sit around like some kept woman." She then began to speak in rapid Spanish. Harold knew Maria never slipped into her native tongue unless she was extremely upset.

Joshua reached over and took her waving hand into his. With his other hand, he gently rubbed and patted Maria's hand and told her it would be okay. Maria snatched her hand back and folded her arms. Several seconds of awkward silence followed.

Darla finally said, "Maria, what if I have you help me?

"Doing what?" responded Joshua.

Before he could complete a breath, Maria's folded arm shot out from her body and struck Joshua across his chest in a fast but restrained blow. Shock appeared on Joshua's face. He began to rub his chest and looked over at Harold, who quickly grabbed his drink and started sucking on his straw to restrain his laughter.

Darla and Maria looked at each other from across the table like two sisters with a secret shared between them. A smile crept across both their faces, and then Darla continued speaking, "You know Harold and Joshua better than anyone here."

"Hmph," responded Maria.

"I need somebody to make this island our home. The staff here is terrific, the best we've got, but they don't know what's needed to make our living conditions more like home. That's part of the reason everything feels more like a five-star resort than a residence."

"I don't understand," said Garcia. "You helped me put this together."

Darla turned her attention to Garcia. "And we did the best we could with the information we had. But Maria has grown up with Harold. She knows what he likes and dislikes, and she's known Joshua for over a decade."

Garcia protested, "But the expense. We hired a decorator to come through and change things just to make everyone feel at home."

"Boys, they just don't understand," Maria said.

Darla looked back at Maria. "You see what I had to work with? Will you help me make this a home?"

Maria nodded excitedly. "Yes. There are so many things I can do once our stuff arrives. May I remove some of the objects your decorator has put in?"

"Of course," answered Darla.

"Please," protested Garcia.

Darla looked over at Garcia. "You're CIA. This needs a mother's touch, and Maria is the closest thing Harold and Joshua have to a mother."

"It sounds good to me," said Harold.

"I'm not sure I'm comfortable with the mother analogy," Joshua said, "but I know Maria will do a great job."

Maria pursed her lips, reached over, and kissed Joshua's cheek. "Did I hurt you?"

Joshua gave a weak smile. "No, of course not."

The room grew silent, and everyone took the time to finish their drinks. Frank came over and got the empty glasses.

After he left again, Darla said, "Let's get back to Chuck, shall we?"

"Please continue," said Harold.

Garcia pointed back at Chuck's photo on the table. "As I was saying, we have created a ruse. This all started right before the memorial service."

"Chuck was in Malibu?" asked Harold.

Darla shook her head. "Not Chuck, but one of his men. His name is Nigel. He's a Brit who likes to sell arms to al-Shabab in northern Africa, along with some ISIS factions. He claimed at the time he was representing European mercenaries that needed more modern arms. When I spoke with him, he said he knew about you and me. He also told me he knew your company was struggling and thought he might be able to help out."

How could anyone know about him and Darla? They had not kept their relationship a secret, but only a few people had seen them together. Besides, they were still early in their relationship. Why would Nigel draw any conclusions from that? Harold looked at Darla wide-eyed. "How could he know about the company, and us?"

"Chuck," interrupted Garcia.

Harold turned to Garcia. His hands were clenched and his voice rose an octave, "But how? Darla and I weren't exactly going to parties together at the time."

"What about at the company?" asked Garcia.

Harold scowled. He could not remember her ever coming to his office. "I was hardly there. When I was, I was normally in my office."

Garcia's fingers tapped on the table. "Do you keep a picture of her on your desk?"

Harold's shoulders slumped, his fists unclenched, and he leaned back into his chair. "Yea. So, who could have seen it?"

"Cleaning crew, security doing their rounds, a co-worker, it's tough to say."

Harold pointed towards Darla. "Why go to her? Why didn't they come to me?"

Garcia answered, "You weren't officially in position yet. I'm guessing they checked out who Darla was and realized she not only had ties to you but to the CIA at one point. In fact, we counted on that, and so far, it's paying off."

Darla jumped back in, "This is where everyone needs to pay close attention."

"Right, this is where you all come in," Garcia said. "Darla reached out to me when she was contacted. At first, we weren't sure if Nigel had connections to John's old organization. When we realized he didn't, we dug deeper and discovered his link to Chuck McGill. Chuck helped broker thousands of illegal arms shipments to various dangerous factions around the world. Normally, the weapons are second rate because he can't get his hands on anything else. He's made it a good niche because those weapons are cheap, and the terrorist in developing countries are desperate to get their hands on what they can. However, Chuck is ambitious and always looking for ways to expand his reach. We assumed Chuck was hoping to get his hands on a fire sale when it came to Parabolic Defense Systems. Additionally, he was probably hoping Darla could give them intel on the CIA. He would love to know what we're up to."

Harold spun towards Darla. "Did they interrogate you? How much do they know about my company?"

Darla turned towards Harold and crossed her smooth, tan legs. Despite his best efforts, he was distracted by her. She had the look of a woman in total control as she answered, "No, Chuck assumed that I had joined the dark side since I was seen around John. Nigel mistakenly thought I had changed sides after you took down John. You know, all women are gold diggers, right?"

"Idiot," mumbled Harold.

Garcia took back over the conversation. "I explained to Darla this might be an opportunity to put away one of the most dangerous men in our lifetime, but I would need your help to pull it off. She agreed to let me pull you in if she was involved.

"So, we set up a backstory that Darla had changed sides once she realized you were planning on destroying John's company for what he did to your father. Additionally, we sent out leaks that there was a dirty agent in the CIA, and he was working with Harold to sell black box weapons to certain factions in Central America."

Harold interrupted, "I assume that would be you."

Garcia answered, "It is. Darla is working as the middleman, so to speak. Once Nigel checked out the rumors, he contacted Chuck. Chuck took the bait and is ready to meet."

"Where do we come in?" asked Joshua.

"Darla spoke with Chuck by phone and told him that Harold was not comfortable expanding beyond the Americas but that the company needed the money. Darla then communicated via Nigel that Harold had to meet Chuck face-to-face before he'd consider a deal with him and show Chuck some of the weapons he has to offer."

"Where does that put Doc?" asked Harold.

"I thought you might want Dr. Zeev joining us," said Garcia, "So, we told Chuck Dr. Zeev was helping you deal with your parents' death and may need to travel with you wherever you go."

Harold cleared his throat, and Joshua said, "That sounds uncomfortably close to the truth."

"That's not the only reason you're here," Garcia said. "Once you asked to join us, I called Darla to let her know you would be coming for sure and the house should be prepared. She pointed out that you bring us a unique dynamic that I hadn't thought of previously. You're a darn good psychiatrist. I want you to assess Chuck during our initial meetings. After we get back, you can report your findings to me."

"So, who was the house for if you weren't sure I was coming?"

Garcia looked at Darla, then Harold, and back at Joshua. "Do I have to say it?"

"If you don't, I will," said Darla.

Garcia turned to Joshua. "Honestly, that would have been my house if you both had stayed in California."

"That explains why the master bedroom has an extra-large shower and no tub," quipped Maria.

Garcia sheepishly replied, "I had hoped the front porch would make up for some of my design preferences."

Harold's mind was spinning. He could not decipher what was fact or fiction from Garcia and Darla's plan. He leaned forward in his chair. The creaking of the wicker got everyone's attention, and they turned his way. "Darla, please don't get mad at me for saying this, but I'm trying to figure out if this is a brilliant ruse or if I'm being played."

Darla's face looked concerned. "How so?"

"You both seem to know me, and Doc and Maria better than we know ourselves. How do I know you aren't using me and my company to get weapons to developing countries as some sort of CIA plot?" Harold's finger wagged back and forth between Darla and Garcia. "Maybe you guys want the bad guys to have these weapons. After all, the more unstable Africa and the Middle East are, the more money and manpower you need to fight them. It's job security."

Darla and Garcia looked at one another in shock. Garcia turned back at Harold with a confused expression. "I guess my ruse is a little too good. Harold, how can you even think that?"

Harold's large finger pointed at Garcia's nose. "You did it to John."

Garcia slapped the table. "I told you that wasn't what happened."

Harold waved off Garcia. "Yea, you told me. You also told me knowing I would be coming out here."

"What about me?" asked Darla.

Harold sat silent. He could not help loving Darla, and every fiber in his being prayed she loved him too. However, he could not help thinking, *what if.* Harold lifted his finger and then dropped it and said, "I hope I'm wrong, but what if I'm right? You're a beautiful, smart woman. You fooled John into thinking you liked him after all."

Darla's eyes narrowed. "I can't believe you would think that."

"Harold!" exclaimed Maria.

Joshua raised his hands up between everyone and jumped in. "Everyone, let's cool down. Harry and I are going to go for a walk. Darla, perhaps you and Garcia should think through this. I believe your assessment on who needs to know what may have some holes in it. Harry, come with me."

Harold was more than happy to follow Joshua out of the house. Things had gotten out of hand. He had not meant to hurt Darla, but sudden doubts swirled in his mind. He could not afford to make his father's mistake and trust the wrong people. Even if she was not involved, Garcia could be playing them all for fools. After all, Darla had been outside the agency for some time when she reached out to Garcia. Maybe he saw this whole disaster as a chance to further destabilize this region of the globe. It was not as if spy agencies had not done that in the past.

The two men walked in silence past the parking area, a short distance down the narrow two-lane road, and then onto a new walking path. "Where are we going, Doc?"

Joshua turned for just a moment. "Just follow me. I'll explain when we get there."

Harold estimated they had walked almost a third of a mile down the trail bordered on each side by overgrowth before emerging onto a narrow beach. The calm Gulf of Mexico gently lapped at the sugar-white sand, which was dotted with small rocks. The gently sloping sand descended beneath the water to a coral bottom. Small barracuda, blackfin tuna, and other fish swam near the relative safety of its shallows.

"This is beautiful," said Harold.

"Yes," replied Joshua. "This was the one spot on this end of the island that John had not touched and was still accessible even when I was here. Although, the trail was much narrower back then. Come with me. It's just a little further up the beach."

Harold stopped. "What is, Doc?"

Joshua gave Harold a quick, annoyed glanced over his shoulder. "Just follow me."

The two men walked several yards up the beach near some larger rocks. Joshua turned into the vegetation just shy of the coastline that curbed out of sight. Joshua stopped short of the bushes and pointed. Harold looked down to see several rocks sprawled about and a shallow hole.

Joshua pointed down at that hole. "Darla did that."

"What was there?" asked Harold.

"Everything," responded Joshua. "Everything we needed to stop John. She risked her life storing it here."

"I don't know. It looks pretty remote," said Harold.

Joshua spun around and smacked Harold in his shoulder. "Don't be an idiot, Harry. I was here. I know what happened. You think this is remote? John found me out here one morning while I thought I was alone enjoying the company of some manatees until his boat scared them away. That was the day Darla showed me this spot. If John knew I was hanging out here, he had to know Darla would walk along this beach." Joshua's eyes took on a blank stare as he pointed further up the beach. "We walked around the bend in the beach and happened upon Senator Jones and that teenager. It's a miracle this was never found."

Harold looked over Joshua at the shallow grave where the documents once lay. Was it a miracle? "Tell me, Doc. Why would she do that?"

Joshua scowled and looked straight into Harold's eyes. "Because she didn't want to see your father's work destroyed. Don't you get it? She felt partially responsible for Richard's death as well. If she had found the evidence sooner, maybe she could have stopped their extortion scheme."

Harold rubbed his chin. That is what he had assumed at the time. "What about now, Doc? Why is she still involved?"

"Maria is right," quipped Joshua. "Boys are stupid. She's in love with you, man. Can't you see that?"

"How do you know? Oh, because you're the doc." Harold did not mean for his comment to sound sarcastic. He meant it sincerely.

"Well, I don't know much, but what I do know I know pretty well. I saw Darla with John. Did she have him beguiled? Yes, but it wasn't because she acted like she was in love with him. She acted cold, cruel, self-centered—just like John. That isn't how she is with you. Nobody can fake the look of love. I've seen how she looks at you. Maria has looked at me the same way for years. I was a fool to ignore it. Don't be a fool and lose out on a woman who loves you."

Harold knew it was true. There was something about Darla. When they talked to each other, it was like the entire world disappeared. He could stare into her eyes and lose all track of time. There was nothing fake about that.

"Doc, what do you think about Garcia? Can we trust him?"

Joshua remained silent, and Harold was concerned that his friend did not have his mind made up already. After all, they had both been around Garcia enough to form some opinion at this point.

Joshua finally answered with a question. "Do you trust Tom?"

"Yea," Harold responded immediately. "What does that have to do with Garcia?"

Joshua crossed his arms and looked past him towards the still waters. "I think we should find a way to communicate with Tom outside of Garcia's influence. We should have a plan for extracting the company out of this if the need ever arises. Do you still have the funds your dad secured outside the country?"

"Yea, Doc. I haven't moved them. That won't be enough to help PDS though. I would burn through those funds in six months trying to keep the company running."

"True, but they could keep you and Darla comfortable for the rest of your lives. Keep those well-hidden. You may need that money one day if Garcia is tricking us."

"Okay, Doc."

Harold turned around and watched the still waters with Joshua. Harold hoped everything was as it appeared. One thing was for sure. He did not like being involved in espionage. The sound of footsteps grabbed both men's attention. Darla and Maria came walking into view.

Darla said, "Didn't I tell you?"

"This is where you hid everything?" Maria asked.

Darla nodded and then spoke to Harold. "Maria was wondering where you two wandered off. I guessed Joshua was bringing you here."

Harold walked over and held Darla. Her firm body felt good, and all his stress melted away in her strong arms. Harold whispered in her ear, "Can you ever forgive me?"

Darla released her grip, and Harold followed suit. She stepped back. "I was debating not forgiving you, but Maria keeps reminding me that boys are stupid. So, I guess I have to forgive you."

"I guess I had that coming."

Darla raised an eyebrow. "You guess?"

Everyone laughed.

Maria turned to Joshua. "Why don't you show me the rest of this beach?"

Joshua looked towards the bend. Harold thought Joshua had a sad look in his eyes.

Joshua replied, "There isn't much to see."

"Let me be the judge of that," Maria said.

With a sigh, Joshua took Maria's hand, and the two slowly disappeared around the bend.

Harold turned to Darla. "Alone at last."

Darla patted his chest with her hand. "Easy, big boy. We still have a lot to talk about."

Harold turned back towards the vegetation line and Darla's hiding place. "When you were helping us, who did you trust? I mean, the lies and intrigue. These gray areas that Garcia and you seem to be able to navigate through. I'm not sure I understand it."

Darla walked up next to Harold and put her arm around his waist. She rested her head against his bicep and said, "That's why I love you. I need somebody who can see black and white and not gray all the time. I trust you, and I hope you can trust me."

Harold considered Darla's words. "I loved you from the moment I saw you, and I do trust you."

Darla's hand slid into Harold's. "You didn't sound like you trusted me earlier."

Harold spoke quietly. "That was before Joshua explained things to me. He told me how you risked your life for us. You had nothing to gain by doing that."

Darla responded softly, "I did have something to gain. My life had been careening down a dark path. When I decided to come here and help your father, it gave me back my self-respect."

Harold looked down towards Darla. "What does that mean?"

Darla let go of Harold, and he turned and looked into her eyes as she spoke. "Maria told me you have been having nightmares about John. You're not the only one who gets visited by people they've killed. Some of my people were innocent. They were just in the wrong place at the wrong time. I left the CIA because I got tired of counting the innocent. Voices in my head said that I had become the very person I was fighting, so I left the CIA to find who I used to be. Your father was my first client after leaving the company. He gave me an opportunity to redeem my work, my talents. I had a chance to be involved in something that wasn't going to become gray. So, I did have something to gain by helping you. I gained my soul back."

"Is that why you rejoined the agency? You wanted to make sure Garcia didn't pull us into your gray world?"

Darla squeezed Harold's hand. "I don't know how much I trust Garcia. Although, I would say that's exactly why we can trust him. He's very good at his job. If he is on the side of right, Agent Garcia Hernandez is a powerful ally. If he's simply using us to transport arms to terrorist, then we're in a lot of danger."

Harold let go of her hand. "Which do you think it is?"

Darla pulled him close to her and put her head against his chest. "I hope he's on the side of good."

He wrapped his large arms around her body. "As long as I'm around, you won't need to worry."

She let out a ragged breath. "I wish that were true. Your size and strength mean little to a man who can kill you without lifting a finger."

Harold pushed her back away from his body. Her eyes looked fearful. "Are you really that afraid of him?" he asked.

"I'm only afraid of what he could do to us if he wanted to."

His voice took on a low growl. "If he does anything, he better hope I'm not alive to respond."

"Don't get angry, darling," she said. "I'm not saying he's our enemy. I'm just saying be careful."

"I intend to be."

CHAPTER 12

"Psst, hey, brat, wake up."

Harold groaned and swatted at the air.

"I said wake up!"

Harold jerked up from his stomach to his hands and knees when something smacked the back of his head, and the bedroom light came on. He looked over his shoulder and saw John standing there. John's hideous grin and sunken eyes no longer scared him. Whether this nightmare was simply his mind trying to think or John really sought revenge, he remembered it was only a dream. Harold let his body fall back to the mattress and slowly rolled over on his back.

"What are you doing here? I thought I left you in California."

"Come on, this is my island. I told you I was grabbing the bus. Besides, I really like the upgrades Garcia and Darla have done. I guess I did make an impression on that woman. She was really a tasty piece."

"Stop!" yelled Harold. "Don't say another word about Darla."

John cackled, "Or what, brat? What can you do to me now?"

"I'll figure out something," Harold growled.

John sat down on the bed next to him. "Okay, I'm calling a truce. I won't go there anymore. I'm not here about her anyway. I want Garcia, and you're going to help me get him."

Harold yelled into his arm and then pushed himself up so he could sit against the headboard. He looked around the bedroom. "I don't know if I'll ever get used to waking up here."

"What's wrong with it?" asked John.

"Nothing, it's just different."

"Ha," responded John. "What's the matter? Do you miss all those browns, yellows, and oranges?"

Harold pulled his knees up and wrapped his arms around them as he looked down towards the bed. "It's just not home."

John's ice-cold hand grabbed Harold's chin and turned Harold's face towards his ghastly specter. "Yea, I know the feeling. Now focus. I'm not here to talk home decorating."

"Why am I even listening to you?" asked Harold as he jerked away.

"Because deep down inside you know you owe me. Besides, I know your real secret."

Harold looked over at John's specter and rolled his eyes. "What big secret is that?"

"I know who you really wanted to kill the day you killed me."

Harold's eyebrows went up in surprise, and then he recovered. "I don't know what you're talking about."

John's laugh made Harold's blood run cold. "Yes, you do. You saw him cowering on the floor in fear. You wanted him dead. Inside that big chest of yours beats the heart of a murderer. In fact, you're going to kill again."

Harold dropped his arms and legs. His foot went through John's hip instead of kicking him. "No, I'm not. I'm no killer."

John gave another cackle. "I say different. If you don't start listening to me, Garcia is going to make you a killing machine."

The alarm clock next to the bed suddenly began to buzz. Harold looked over at it, and back to John, but John had disappeared. He hit the snooze button, but the clock kept buzzing.

Harold opened his eyes. He was no longer on Salvation Key. He drew in a deep breath of sea air and reached over to turn off the alarm clock. The time read six in the morning. He hated how disoriented he felt after his nightmares. It all seemed so real, and yet, it had only happened somewhere in his mind. After looking around the strange room, he remembered where he was.

The team had arrived at The Postcard Inn on Islamorada the previous day. Garcia had informed them last night that Chuck would be arriving shortly after lunch to meet with everyone. Harold stumbled towards the shower and attempted to wake up. After he finished with his shower, he walked across the slate tiled floor. The hard, cool surface reminded him of home. As he dressed, he took in the view of the room and the beach outside his picture window. He had never considered modern-style furniture to be particularly attractive, but somehow it fit this place. Although, the neutral grays and tans seemed a bit dull for the Florida Keys.

After making himself a cup of coffee, he went out on his front porch and looked out at the beach and the Atlantic Ocean. Garcia had set them up with one of the best views in the resort. Harold just wanted to enjoy the view and forget about the reasons he was there. A soft, soothing voice emitted from the other side of a latticed partition.

"Good morning. How are you doing?"

The empty chair next to Harold scraped against the concrete as he pulled it closer to him. "I'm good now that I hear your voice. Why don't you come over here and join me?"

He could not help grinning ear to ear as he watched Darla come into view. Her hair was pulled back in a ponytail. She had on a wrinkled T-shirt and shorts. Harold guessed she had not had a chance to prepare herself for the day.

Darla sat down in the chair next to his and cradled her coffee between her hands. "So, who were you yelling at so early this morning?"

"Oh, was I yelling?"

Darla raised an eyebrow. She released her coffee mug with one hand and grasped Harold's free hand. Her face relaxed. "Darling, you were having another nightmare about John, weren't you?"

Harold broke her gaze and stared over towards the beach. "Who said it was John?"

Darla leaned in a little closer and said just above a whisper, "You yelled his name."

"I don't remember yelling John's name."

"So you were having another nightmare about John."

"You tricked me," Harold complained.

Darla released his hand. "Not really. I heard you yell *no* and then you said something about my name. Your voice went up and down, and you sounded groggy. It didn't take me long to put things together."

"I had no idea the walls were so thin."

Darla took a sip of coffee. "I'm not sure how thin the walls are. Your voice does tend to carry. Darling, you can talk to me. You know, you're not the only person with ghosts."

Harold glanced over at Darla and then returned to staring blankly at the ocean. "I know, but Doc has always been the one I turned to for things like this. It's not that I don't trust you, but Doc has always been there."

"Should I be jealous?" Darla asked in a mocking tone.

Harold looked back at her and searched her eyes. "You will never have to be jealous of anybody. Doc says I need to give myself some time with everything. So, I'm giving us some time to get to know each other better."

"Perhaps," said Darla. She looked out towards the water and took another sip of coffee. "Let me ask you something." She turned back towards him. "What are you going to do when Joshua is gone? Maria wasn't exactly happy to be left behind on the island. Trust me, dear, Joshua's days here are numbered. Take it from a woman who knows. Maria will not simply sit around that island with nothing to do but decorate overpriced marble rooms. She'll tell Joshua she wants to get away, and he will listen to her."

Harold's eyes stretched wide. "What have you heard? Did she tell you she was leaving?"

Darla watched a tourist pass along the walkway. "Not in so many words."

"I'm not sure you know Maria as well as you think. I'm like a younger brother or son to her. Besides, Joshua wouldn't leave me on a whim. Doc has been like a second father to me. They both love me like a member of their own family. Neither of them would just abandon me."

Darla reached over and took Harold's hand again. "I'm not saying they will leave you, but every person has their limits, dear. At some point, Maria will want a break from isolation and boredom."

Harold's head drooped. "Well, then she and Joshua can take a vacation somewhere."

Darla raised an eyebrow. "Really? Where does one go to take a vacation from the Caribbean?"

Harold leaned back into his chair and glanced up towards the sky. "I don't know."

"Just promise me if they decide to leave that you'll come to me if you need somebody to talk to."

Harold crossed his legs and glanced over to Darla. "That's a silly thing to say. I'll always come to you, but it doesn't matter. Doc won't leave me."

"Did I hear my name?" Joshua appeared on the sidewalk from behind the partition.

Harold replied, "You did. Grab a chair and join us."

Joshua disappeared and reappeared in a few moments with a chair in hand. "I do hope whatever you were saying about me was good."

"Darla was just telling me how Maria will drag you away from the island never to return again."

"Oh?" replied Joshua.

Harold raised his eyebrows. "That's it, Doc? Just Oh? Is there something I should know?"

Joshua took several seconds longer than Harold thought he should to sip his coffee then finally put his mug down. "Well, Maria isn't happy. There is very little for her to do. The island and everything around it is on autopilot now that we have all settled in. She also hates the idea that our meeting with Chuck is too dangerous for her but not too dangerous for me. But don't be silly, Harry. Maria is here because she loves both of us. Even if she isn't happy, she'll see this through. I just recommend we don't take our time doing it."

Harold replied, "Well, maybe we should tell Garcia that he has to let her come along. She doesn't have to meet Chuck, but she could at least get off the island and hang around with us when we aren't talking to men who want to blow up the world."

"No, I agree with Garcia. I almost lost her to John. I won't risk losing her again."

"So, what are you saying, Doc?"

Joshua looked up at the sky and then down at his feet. "I don't know. It's not like you need a security blanket. Perhaps when things slow down, I could take her to North Carolina. She has never seen my native state or where you and I first met at the orphanage."

Harold reached over and gave Joshua's shoulder a friendly squeeze. "Well, Doc. Maybe a short visit would do you both some good, as soon as Garcia finishes with this Chuck business."

The corners of Joshua's mouth curved slightly, and he took another long sip of coffee.

Darla stood up. "Well, I need to go make myself presentable."

"I find you very presentable," said Harold.

"I agree," responded Joshua.

"Men are so easy. I'm not talking about for you. I'm talking about everyone else."

Darla strolled off the front porch towards her room. Harold made no attempt to hide his enjoyment of watching her walk away.

"So, Harry, I hear you had another nightmare."

Harold turned and looked over at Joshua. The doctor's compassionate eyes touched his heart as much as his own father's eyes once had. Harold thought for a moment, and then asked, "How long were you standing there, Doc?"

Joshua chuckled and paused. He turned and looked out over the water. "Oh, Harry, I wish I had been spying on you. The truth is, I could hear you through my wall."

"But your room is next to Darla's. You had an entire room between us and you still heard me? Did the entire hotel wake up?"

"I hope not. Nobody else has dropped by to check on you, have they?"

"No."

Joshua glanced at Harold and down at his feet. "Actually, I was already awake."

"What woke you up?"

Joshua took a sip of his coffee and paused. "It's nothing, Harry. I'm more concerned about your dream.

Things had settled down after we got to Salvation Key. I thought maybe your mind was finally coming to grips with everything that has happened. Do you think the upcoming meeting with Chuck today triggered something?"

Harold lifted himself up and adjusted his seat so he was facing the water. He gazed out over the ocean. "Doc, do you think I'm a killer?"

"Do you feel like a killer?" asked Joshua.

Harold scowled. "Come on, Doc. We're past answering my questions with questions. You know why I'm asking you. Tell me, do you think I'm a killer?"

Joshua put his mug down on the small table. "Harry, we all have the capacity to kill. The fact that most of us don't is a testimony to the existence of some sort of deity. I have spent my life trying to help people with their problems, and in the end, all of us really have the same core issue. We're all, at our heart, selfish, self-centered people. Even when we sacrifice for others, we do it because it makes us feel good. So, yes, you could be a killer, but it isn't because you're a berserker. It's because you're human."

Harold fidgeted in his chair. "But, Doc, if I hadn't been a berserker, would I have killed John? I'm not sure I could have taken him on if I hadn't felt the rage inside that I did."

"Harry, this condition of yours…you're not alone. Many people throughout history have gotten what is known as 'battle rage.' There are stories from every war of men walking through gunfire and even getting hit with shrapnel and not stopping until all the enemies had been killed. Even in everyday life, there are stories of mothers who have lifted automobiles off their injured children."

Harold turned back to the water. "But, Doc, do they have to deal with it all the time?"

"No, Harry, that does make you unique, but that doesn't make you a killer. Do you really think your problems are any different than the business executive who has a crush on a co-worker but has a wife and kids at home? He knows if he crosses the line his actions could devastate his family and the woman he is attracted to. Every day, he has to choose what is most important to his life and live with the consequences."

"Come on, Doc, I'm not saying I feel like I'm going to go berserk every day."

Joshua patted his arm, and Harold turned his head to look at his friend. "Exactly. There are people who must face their life-changing temptations daily. You only have to face yours when something endangers you or a loved one."

Harold looked back at the ocean. "It scares me, though, Doc. What if I can't control it one day?"

"Turn around and look at me."

When Harold turned his chair back around, Joshua's small hands attempted to wrap themselves around his. "Harry, you may not remember how bad you were when I first came to live with your family."

"I remember I felt pretty angry most of the time."

Joshua let go of Harold's hands. "Angry, my friend? You were positively demon possessed. Everything set you into a rage. Did you know I had suggested that you be put in an institution when you were younger?"

Harold's eyebrows went up. "Doc! I thought we were friends."

"We are. Even then I was your friend, but I was not sure if I could figure out how to cure you, and I was afraid you might hurt your parents, or me, and end up in prison."

Harold sat there quietly and tried to remember. In his mind, he could hear yelling and then see items thrown in the air. When the vision cleared, he could only see his father's dead body sitting in his office chair with the back of his head exploded on the wall behind him. Harold drew in a sharp breath, and he felt Joshua suddenly squeeze both his hands.

"Are you okay, Harry?"

Harold drew in a long breath and released it. "Yea, Doc. All I seem to remember is Dad's death."

Harold let Joshua take his hands and lift them to his lips. It was something Joshua had always done when Harold got hurt. The action made him feel like a child again, and he closed his eyes. He could see Joshua kneeling next to him at the beach, trying to comfort him after he almost drowned in a riptide. His dad lay next to him, still coughing up water. He had nearly drowned trying to save Harold, and Joshua had pulled them both the rest of the way to shore. Joshua had his lips on Harold's sandy hands praying as they expelled portions of the Pacific Ocean from their lungs.

When Harold opened his eyes, he saw Joshua had closed his. The doctor's facial expressions changed as he continued his unspoken conversation with the unseen God. Another minute went by, and Joshua opened his eyes. His eyes held a slight twinkle as he released Harold's hands. "I'm sorry, my friend. I let my emotions get the better of me. I felt like I needed to pray for you."

"There's no need to apologize, Doc. I noticed you're doing more of that these days. It's kind of nice. Did it give you any new insight?"

"I wasn't praying for insight. I was praying God would comfort your loss, but I know you will always carry it with you."

Harold let his head droop a little. "Yea. So, do you think these dreams about John could trigger something in me that would make me go berserk? I knocked myself out of the bed taking a swing at him."

"I really don't know. All my treatments were focused on your subconscious in the hopes of using it to help heal your consciousness. I started looking into some of this when your nightmares first started, but I stopped when things settled down after moving out here. I would like to think all those sessions will help you control your subconscious when these nightmares happen, but I really can't be sure. I am going to research this some more."

Harold drew in a ragged breath and let it out. He tried to let the tension out of his body. "I hope you find something soon, Doc. I'm not sure what I will do if I can't control myself when I'm asleep."

Both men sat in silence. Harold wondered if his life would ever return to normal. His dreams immediately after his father's death had been pleasant. He was in the Viking village hunting and living among their people, just like Joshua's hypno-therapeutic sessions. It wasn't until John's death that the nightmares had started. For a moment, Harold considered returning to Malibu and checking into Avalon, but he didn't want Garcia to know he was struggling with killing John. He feared

Garcia would pull the plug on the operation and abandon the plan to rescue Parabolic Defense Systems from its current financial crises.

Joshua's voice broke through Harold's thoughts, "I guess we should both prepare to meet with Chuck."

Harold gave Joshua a half-smile. "What do you mean, Doc? I've been ready. Haven't you showered yet?"

"No. I decided to grab some coffee and walk by your room to see if you were awake and found you and Darla out here."

"Oh," said Harold, "I thought that smell was the ocean."

Joshua rolled his eyes. "Yes, well, it could be the crust on your lip from you drooling when Darla was here."

Harold knew Joshua was kidding, but he still rubbed his lips.

Joshua laughed and stood up. "I'll see you soon, Harry."

"Make sure you shower before you do, Doc."

CHAPTER 13

Harold walked out of his hotel room and across the bustling resort. Patrons of every age hurried about to enjoy the attractions afforded by the luxury retreat. Many adults congregated around the tiki bar while others enjoyed the cool, clean water of the large swimming pool. Young children frolicked about the playground next to the small, private beach. Men and women zoomed along the calm Atlantic Ocean on their rented jet skis, and boats of every size cruised in and out of the resort's yacht club. Harold took a moment to soak in the atmosphere before heading over to the outdoor bar.

A brown-haired woman in a thong bikini strolled across his field of vision. He allowed his gaze to linger as she walked down the sidewalk.

"Uh-hum."

Harold winced at the sound of Darla's familiar voice.

Sarcasm dripped from her words, "Are you sure you don't want to take a picture for later?"

He turned to find Darla with her arms crossed and a smile on her face. She was obviously amused by her own comments and his red face.

"I, uh…didn't see you there," Harold replied guiltily.

Darla relaxed her arms and slipped her hand into his. "Obviously. I doubt you would have noticed a shark attack. Should I wear one of those?"

"No," he replied. "I would hate to have to beat down the first guy I caught gawking at you."

Darla released his hand. "What's good for the goose, dear. Anyway, let's head over to the bar. I'm sure Garcia and Chuck are waiting on us."

"Where's Doc?"

"Knowing the good doctor, he probably was there before anybody else."

"Why do you think that?" asked Harold curiously.

Darla began to walk, and he followed her cue. She answered him as they kept a steady pace. "I think Joshua is in a hurry to get back to Maria. They haven't been married that long after all. I was outside on my patio reading, and he passed by my room at least four times talking into his cell phone. Joshua is very good at keeping conversations private, but I could tell by the strain on his face he must have been talking with Maria. Only you and Maria really can cause him that level of consternation."

The bar was a sprawling affair. Surrounded by tables shaded by prawn roofs, the bar was a building without any exterior walls. Dark and faded wood housed a large U-shaped bar that encompassed every sort of liquor bottle one could ever imagine. They all sat nestled on wooden shelves that could be found on every side of the barkeeper's domain. Tap levers holding beers from big labels to small microbreweries nobody had ever heard about lined an entire side.

Harold spied Garcia and Joshua sitting at the bar at the same time Darla did. He had seen Garcia's sunglasses before he saw Garcia. Joshua sat next to him, and the two men appeared to be in an animated discussion at the bar. Four other patrons were scattered about the large multi-sided bar. A man and woman sat together. They were obviously a couple, and judging from her Valentino handbag, they were probably from the yacht club. The two other men sat on opposite ends of the bar from each other.

One of the lone men at the bar wore white khaki shorts, a pink polo, and white tennis shoes with white socks. The other man had short sandy hair parted on the side. He wore a short-sleeve blue plaid sports shirt and chewed on a cigar. The man appeared to be so involved in the soccer match playing on the television screen that he didn't notice his cigar had long since extinguished.

Harold noticed Garcia and Joshua stopped their conversation as the two of them drew close.

"You're late," said Garcia.

"No, you're early," responded Harold.

Harold and Darla slid onto a barstool. He looked over at Garcia. "Where's our new friend?"

Both Darla and Garcia nodded towards the far side of the bar. Harold looked over to find it empty. He turned back to see the stranger with the unlit cigar standing between Darla and Garcia.

Squeezing the stogie between his teeth and grinning lips, he stuck out his hand. "I'm Chuck, and you must be Harry."

Harold took Chuck's hand. "Harold."

"Gotcha," said Chuck. He reached over to Joshua and gave him a friendly pat on the back. "And you must be the famous psychiatrist Garcia has told me about. I looked you up on the internet, Doctor. You're quite the man."

Joshua gave Chuck a cursory glance. "Don't believe everything you read on the internet."

Chuck took out his cigar and spit bits of tobacco leaf on the ground. "Not even your blog?"

Joshua turned his attention back to Chuck. "Oh, of course you should believe everything you find there."

Chuck stuck the stogie back in his mouth. He waved his hand, and the bartender joined the group. "Rum runners for my friends. Put it on my tab."

"Yes, sir," responded the bartender, and he left to make the drinks.

"Why don't we move over to a table?" Garcia suggested.

The group made their way to a covered wooden table. Darla sat on one side of Harold, and Joshua on the other. Chuck and Garcia sat next to one another across from Harold.

Chuck pulled out a lighter. "Do you mind if I smoke?"

"Yes," Joshua, Darla, and Harold all answered in unison.

"Doctor, a little birdie told me you like an occasional cigar."

Joshua's eyes widened. "I'm surprised you know so much about me. I do indeed, but I loathe the smell of any brand but my own."

"What brand would that be?"

"I recently developed an affinity for Eiroa cigars, but the mood has to strike me, and frankly I'm not in the mood at the moment."

Chuck clamped down hard on his cigar as he spoke. "Fair enough."

He put away his lighter, pulled out his cigar, spit out a piece of tobacco leaf on the ground, and left the partial blunt between his fingers while he let his hand dangle by the chair. "So, you're Garcia's team."

Harold raised his eyebrow. "I don't know if we would call ourselves a team."

Chuck replied, "Yea, I guess you don't feel that way. I understand Agent Garcia has you by the short hairs."

He could feel his back tighten with stress. "What do you mean?"

Chuck stuck the unlit cigar in the corner of his mouth and bit down on it. Harold was surprised how adept the man was at speaking with gritted teeth. "He tells me your company is facing some pretty dire straits thanks to the late John Richmond. I had an opportunity to get to know that man. Good job dispatching him, by the way. He was a bad seed. I never trusted him."

"I see." Harold looked over at Garcia and back at Chuck. "It sounds like Garcia has let out all our little secrets."

Chuck pulled out his cigar and let out a short chuckle. He laid the burned stogie in the ashtray. "Garcia didn't tell me everything. I checked you all out. Do you think I'd take the word of a dirty CIA agent? For instance, I know you and Darla are an item. I appreciate you both keeping to business while we're meeting. I know the doctor is married to a woman who was an illegal immigrant. Nice job, Doctor. Given the current political climate, it's a miracle you and Harold were able to get a legal status for the marriage. It seems the politicians are more concerned with being reelected these days than they are with the sanctity of marriage and family."

Joshua gave a cautious nod. "Well, the Browns have done a lot for their community, and Harold is considered somewhat of a local hero. I doubt I had much pull in the matter."

Chuck slapped Joshua on the shoulder. "Garcia's right. You're a humble man. Humble and persuasive. That can make someone very trustworthy or dangerous, am I right?"

"Perhaps."

Chuck turned back to Harold. "Did you know your buddy Garcia is dirty? I have a feeling you didn't. He's been looking for a company he could source arms through. You see, my team checked him out too. I bet you didn't know he has a few offshore accounts with several million dollars in them."

Harold's hands clenched into fists, and he dropped them below the table so nobody could see. He turned towards Garcia and glared at him. "Is that true? You have a few million dollars offshore?" he asked in a low guttural voice.

Garcia's sunglasses looked in Harold's direction. "What difference does it make?"

"I didn't take on John to jump into bed with someone just as greedy and dirty."

Garcia was silent for a moment, and Harold wondered what was going through his mind, and where he was looking.

Garcia turned his sunglasses Chuck's direction. "I'm afraid Mr. Brown has some trust issues. You see, John tried to take everything from Harold, including his girlfriend."

Darla grimaced. "That man was a letch."

"So, Harold is concerned I might be pulling the same stunt," Garcia said.

Chuck laughed, reached over, and smacked Harold's large shoulder. "Is that true, big boy? I can't imagine that you have anything to worry about."

Harold felt Darla's foot slowly apply pressure on top of his own. He caught the hint. "I suppose I don't, but you can't be too careful."

Darla elbowed him. "Don't you trust me?"

Harold startled at the strength of her nudge and looked over into her eyes. "Of course, I do, but I'm not sure I trust our friend sitting across from us."

"Do I hear trouble in paradise?" Chuck asked mockingly.

"No, just youthful caution," Garcia said. "We're all good, right, Harold?"

Harold nodded and forced himself to smile. "Oh yea, I'm just having flashbacks I suppose."

Chuck played the table like the bongos for a moment with his hands. "Good. I would hate to have something mess with our plans."

Chuck picked up his cigar but appeared to change his mind and put it back down. A waiter walked over with their drinks. He placed the glasses in front of everybody and left them to silently enjoy their drinks. Harold stopped sipping when his glass was half empty.

"Thirsty?" asked Garcia.

"Yes."

Chuck took a second quick sip. "Back to business."

"Is that what this is?" Joshua asked. "I thought we were getting to know each other."

Chuck reached over and smacked Joshua in the arm. "It's all business, Doctor. For instance, I bet you're wondering what you're doing here. Garcia probably asked you to help with Harold, and you probably think it's a waste of time and miss your new bride, but Harold is your friend."

Joshua glanced over at Garcia. "I don't know what you mean."

Chuck answered Joshua, "The good agent has told me about Harold's temper. We don't want to upset him. After all, he's been through a lot." Chuck turned his attention to Harold. "No offense, I know you're sitting right there."

"None taken," said Harold.

Joshua fell silent. He just continued looking in the direction of Garcia and Chuck. Chuck returned his gaze for several seconds, and Harold wondered what both men were thinking.

Chuck broke away his gaze and returned his attention to Harold. "Don't worry. The good agent here doesn't know your medical records. He just shared with me some of the highlights from the local newspapers. Looks like you really got lucky."

Harold took a short sip of his drink and eyed Chuck in the process. He allowed himself to smile as he and Chuck continued their staring contest. Harold finally asked, "Lucky? How do you mean?"

Chuck looked both directions and then lowered his voice. "John falling and breaking his neck like that. The paper said an anonymous source from the police department claimed his gun was buried in his temple barrel first. Is that true?"

Harold waved off Chuck's question. "Well, it's an anonymous source, so you can't trust them."

Chuck leaned back and took a long swallow from his glass before putting it down and letting out a sigh. He leaned towards Harold. "Come on, big guy, you can tell me. Did you bury that gun in his head?"

"That sounds a little crazy if you ask me. I'm not a little guy, but I don't know anyone with that kind of strength."

Chuck rolled his eyes and then looked over at Garcia and spoke normally. "I like them. I believe they're trustworthy enough. I trust them more than I do you."

Garcia's sunglasses looked over at Chuck. "Good. When do we meet the rest of your team?"

"Oh, you already have." Chuck lifted his hand and gave two quick waves with his index and middle fingers. The waiter walked back over to the table, and the man in the pink polo left the bar and walked towards them. Both took their places behind Chuck.

"Everyone, let me introduce you to the most trusted members of my team. Darla, I believe you've met one of these men." Chuck pointed to the waiter on his right. He was a small man around five feet five inches. He had dark brown skin and short black hair.

His black eyes shot an icy streak through Harold's gut. The man's gaze appeared deader inside than John's did in Harold's dreams. "This is Haidar, a young man I rescued in northern Africa. I found him in the deserts of Libya. He was starving, thirsty, and nearly dead. He'd escaped from an ISIS offshoot."

"Kidnapped?" asked Darla.

"No, he was a soldier in their army, but he didn't see things their way, did you?"

Haidar's voice was hard and cold. "No, they were not true believers."

"And what do you believe?" asked Joshua.

Haidar stood silently.

"Well, answer the good doctor," said Chuck.

Haidar's voice hissed with hate as he pronounced each word, "I believe my people need to take their country back from those who have come in and tried to corrupt our people."

"Like America?" asked Joshua.

Haidar snarled as he answered, "Anyone who would ruin our beautiful country and steal our faith. We got rid of the brutal dictator Gaddafi, and now we have warlords who want nothing more than to enslave us, sell our oil, and make themselves rich. Our people deserve freedom and to live as Allah wills."

Chuck reached up and gently squeezed the young man's hand. "You see, none of us know what these small countries have to deal with. Haidar's parents were killed in a firefight between ISIS and the Shura Council of Benghazi Revolutionaries. They were caught in the crossfire before his family could get to safety. ISIS fighters offered Haidar food, shelter, and protection from the other factions, but things changed."

"They raped women and murdered small children for fun," Haidar said. "They claimed to be real believers, but they are just like the others."

"So, now he's with me," Chuck said.

Garcia turned and looked through his sunglasses at the two men standing behind Chuck. He looked back down at Chuck. "I thought you were selling arms to ISIS."

Chuck nodded. "A different faction in a different part of the country. Many of these militias identify with one group or another to recruit soldiers."

Joshua looked up at Haidar. "And you're okay with this?"

Haidar's voice softened a bit. "Yes. As Mr. Chuck has explained it to me, somebody has to win the civil war or the fighting will go on for generations. The men who buy our weapons are true believers. I have spoken to them myself."

Joshua said nothing else. Harold wondered if the young man trusted Chuck or was simply using him to find a faction of fellow believers who would one day kill Chuck and walk away with whatever bounty they could find. Harold looked over at Darla, but she appeared to be busy sizing up Chuck and his team.

"This other gentleman is Nigel," Chuck continued.

Nigel shook everyone's hand. "Pleasure."

"My British contact. How have you been?" asked Darla.

Nigel gave a slight bow of his head. "Fine. I never had the chance to ask you, have you made it over to my country?"

Darla clasped her hands in front of her. "I've been there a few times, although I believe you may be from somewhere in the southern part of the island. I have not had much time there."

"I am most impressed you picked up on my accent. I've worked very hard to hide it, although I'm not very successful in the attempt. The crown isn't always welcomed everywhere we go. That's why I like coming back to the colonies. Everyone here is so friendly to the crown."

Darla's lips curved slightly. "Well, this part of the US belonged to Spain, but I understand the sentiment. What parts of the world dislike your accent?"

Chuck jumped in, "Nigel is my middle man for my arms dealings with our ISIS friends in northern Africa. The British don't have a very good reputation over in Africa."

"But they still have all the connections," Garcia said. "Many of these militias see the British as a necessary evil, so they're tolerated."

"Sounds dangerous," said Joshua.

"It can be, but without me the warlords can't get their weapons," Nigel responded. "At least not the weapons they really want."

Chuck reached down and picked up his cigar. Haidar and Nigel stepped back, and Chuck stood up. He reached into his pocket and pulled out his lighter. After a flame and a few puffs, his dead cigar was alight once more. "It's been a pleasure. Agent Garcia, I'll call you when we're ready to meet again."

Garcia clumsily stood up and extended his hand. "I guess we're done."

"Yes," said Chuck.

The three men turned and walked towards the parking lot. Garcia sat back down.

"Is it over?" asked Harold.

Darla reached over and took his hand. "Yes, we can relax now."

"How do you know?"

Garcia interjected, "Well, we are not actually alone. I have people in the resort. They are watching a handful of Chuck's team. They're nothing to worry about. They're just here to ensure the CIA doesn't decide to suddenly arrest Chuck."

Harold turned to Darla. "Why don't you do that?"

"Do what?"

"Just arrest Chuck."

Garcia jumped back in, "We don't want just Chuck. We want his whole operation, and more importantly, who he is selling weapons to. Chuck is a dangerous man, but his customers are the ones who are doing the real damage to the world."

Joshua began to look around.

"You can relax, Doctor. We're safe," said Darla.

"I was just wondering where the fourth member of the team is."

"Fourth member, Doctor?" asked Garcia.

Joshua let a smile creep across his lips as he glanced over towards Harold.

"Doc has an affinity for eighties television shows."

"Oh?" replied Garcia.

"I love it when a plan comes together," said Darla.

Garcia slowly shook his head.

Harold looked over at Darla. "I'm impressed. Doc forced me to watch reruns with him when I wanted to talk and *The A-Team* was on."

Darla gave a short laugh and then said, "I binged watched it on Netflix." She turned to Garcia. "Seriously, you've never seen that show or the movie?"

"Nope, I prefer romantic comedies," Garcia said with a deadpan expression.

"Seriously?" asked Harold with a stifled snicker.

Garcia's brow wrinkled. "Harold, what was that whole episode between us in front of Chuck? If you have a problem with me, discuss it before we get in front of Chuck. We need to stay tight, understand?"

"Well, I do have trust issues when it comes to you, and that conversation didn't help anything."

"If you can't trust me, trust the woman beside you."

Harold turned to Darla, and she looked into his eyes. Her dark eyes danced and twinkled the longer he gazed into them. "Do you trust me?" she asked.

"Yes."

A different waiter appeared, took their empty glasses, and replaced them with another round of rum runners.

"We didn't order these," said Garcia.

"Courtesy of Chuck," responded the waiter, and he walked off.

Harold took a sip of his cool drink. Its cold, refreshing fruit juices soothed his warm pallet. He put down the glass and addressed Garcia again. "Just so we're clear, we're good for now. I'm not sure what your game is, but anytime I have a problem with it, I'll let you know."

Garcia sat for a moment and moved his head ever so slightly in both directions. "My game," responded Garcia with an edge in his quiet voice, "is to stop Chuck."

Harold and the others quietly sat and sipped their drinks, allowing the tension to cool down. Darla finally spoke up, "Did anyone else notice how pale Nigel is?"

"Well, he is British," responded Harold.

"True," answered Darla. "However, even the Brits get tanned or burned if they're out in the sun. How is Nigel running around northern Africa and the Mediterranean without picking up some sun?"

"So, what's your point?" asked Garcia.

Darla picked up her glass and appeared to stare into nothing. "Haidar was dark, even for a native North African. I just wonder who is Chuck's real right-hand man. Nigel strikes me more as an office boy than a man you send to the field to deal with warlords."

Harold noticed a gray Kodiak zooming in towards the marina. The craft slowed at the very last second before entering the shipping lane. He thought about how much fun he could have with a craft like that. Garcia's voice interrupted his mental getaway.

"Everyone, our ride is on its way. Please, come with me."

The team left the bar and walked towards the parking lot. However, instead of heading into the parking lot, Garcia had them veer left to the other side of the marina. As they walked down the ramp, Harold noticed the Kodiak pulling up to an empty slot on the dock.

Garcia stopped, turned, and spoke to the group. He pointed over his shoulder towards the Kodiak. "Everyone, this is Frank. He is going to be taking us out to Harold's new office. I think you'll be pleasantly surprised."

Harold raised his eyebrow. He had assumed he would be working at his mansion on the island. Frank greeted everyone and helped them carefully board the Kodiak. With deft hands, Frank backed out the boat and headed out towards the Atlantic Ocean.

CHAPTER 14

Frank expertly navigated between the reef markers and out towards the deeper waters of the ocean where the Kodiak skipped along the relatively smooth waters of the Atlantic. He slowed the craft slightly as the waves increased. At times it seemed as if they were simply taking a joy ride across some residual wakes, but they slowly made their way further from Islamorada. A ship that had been a small speck on the horizon when they left Islamorada grew closer.

Harold turned to Garcia. "Where is this office you want me to see? My butt is numb, and we're all getting sunburned."

Garcia said, "We're just making sure Chuck is bored watching us mess around in the water."

"I'm certainly tired of it," Joshua said.

Garcia looked over at Frank and spoke loudly above the droning of the engine and the splashing of the water. "Take us to the office."

The boat's direction changed, and soon the ship in the distance began to grow. Their direction left little doubt the yacht was their destination. The ship's lines came into view, and Harold found himself drawn towards her.

She had the classic V-lines coming up from her bow. Harold loved the way the ship's features became more modern towards her stern. A well-equipped array of radar, weather, and communication antennas sat midship above what he assumed was the bridge. Her white paint gleamed in the sunlight as Frank slowed the Kodiak.

"As you can see, she has four decks and is 190 feet long," Garcia said.

Harold raised his hand and then repeatedly pushed down against the air. "Shhh."

"Excuse me?"

"Let me just enjoy this."

The boat went silent as Harold soaked in the view of the ship. The dark windows on the decks contrasted perfectly against the bright-white painted steel. He had seen many yachts growing up. While he had enjoyed the times his father had taken him out on a friend's yacht, he had never understood the allure of these ships until now. This ship was more than a fashion statement. Harold could see himself exploring the world with her. The ship was not only large enough to accommodate a long voyage, but it had a casual classiness that felt like home.

The Kodiak made its way aft to the diver's deck. The name on the back of the yacht read *Sweet Revenge*.

"What's with the name?" asked Joshua.

"That's the name John registered. I'm sure he had laundry lists of reasons," responded Garcia.

Frank tied off the Kodiak, and the team disembarked. "Okay, if you all will follow me, I'll give you a tour."

"Later," said Harold. "Well, you can show everyone else. I want to walk around her by myself."

"I don't know if that's—"

Joshua interrupted Garcia, "Let Harold enjoy some time alone with his new love, Agent Garcia. I think it'll do him some good."

Garcia moved over, and Harold headed up the first set of short steps. He found himself standing among red wicker furniture and a beautiful teak decking. Obviously, it had been designed to relax in after spending some time swimming and playing in the water. He then followed the stairs up to the next deck. There he found two beautiful white couches framing modern black tables that sat between them. The deck opened to a dining area with a large round table. Just beyond the table was a small bar like he had at Salvation Key. *This is perfect for breakfast.* Rather than venturing inside, he climbed the spiral staircase to the next deck.

The view took his breath away. The floor just below the antenna array was lined with deck chairs on one end. In its center was a large dining table that could easily seat twelve, and an L-shaped bar was nestled into a corner just beyond the dining area. The aft section of the deck rose up and around a large Jacuzzi framed by a generous sunning area. Harold sat down on the steps of the Jacuzzi and admired the view of the ocean that gently rolled the ship. From his vantage point, he could see an occasional fish navigating through the clear waters around the yacht.

For the first time in a very long time, he felt happy. He heard footsteps and saw Joshua emerge from the staircase. Joshua rose up the steps with a sense of awe on his face as he looked around the yacht.

He walked up to sit down on the step just below Harold and looked up at him. "She's certainly a beautiful ship."

"You said it, Doc. Where's Darla?"

"She's below. I wanted us to share this moment together. I haven't seen you this happy in a long time. I never knew you were so excited about boating."

"Let's go have a seat at the table."

The two men walked over and sat at the large dining room table. Both of them ignored the other as they gawked at their surroundings.

"What do you think, Doc? Should we sail the seven seas with her?"

Joshua focused his gaze on Harold. "That does sound like an adventure. What has gotten into you? Up until now, I thought you wanted to get back to California as fast as possible."

Harold stared blankly towards the aft of the deck. "I don't know, Doc. Maybe it's because Darla is around and the four of us are together most of the time. I just don't feel as homesick as I did. I mean, I still miss home, but this ship… I think if Dad built a yacht, this would have been it. This isn't like John's house. This ship is welcoming. I could feel just as comfortable in shorts, a T-shirt, and bare feet on board as I could a tux. She's my kind of home."

"But you haven't seen the rest of it."

"It doesn't matter. I could just sit up here the rest of the day and soak in the ship, the ocean, all of it."

Joshua reached over and gave Harold's hand a friendly tap. "Do what you think is best, but Garcia has a surprise for you below deck."

Harold leaned back against the chair. "Tell him I'll be there in a little while, Doc."

"Okay."

Joshua got up and left. Harold lifted himself up and walked over to lay on the sundeck next to the Jacuzzi, letting the sun warm his growing sunburn as he felt the ship move beneath his body. He closed his eyes and took in the smell of the ocean far out from land. He had always loved the smell of the saltwater. It was in his blood.

He lay there deeply breathing, but then the warmth that baked his skin seemed to grow faint. Opening one eye, he saw the silhouette of a person above him. The flowing hair, beautiful curves, and smell of coconut butter told him who it was. His lips curled into a knowing grin and he closed his eye.

"I'm glad you're enjoying yourself, dear, but you know we're on the clock."

Harold chuckled. "No, you and Garcia are on the clock. Until our next meeting, or whatever Garcia thinks we need to know, I can just lay here for as long as my skin can take the sun."

The smell of coconut grew closer and then he felt Darla's body against his. She leaned over and whispered in his ear, "Don't make me throw you off this deck, dear."

He opened both his eyes and found her beautiful dark eyes staring into his. He quickly lifted his lips and kissed her. She returned his affection and then rolled him on top of her. Before he could think about what was happening, he was surprised to find her long legs wrapped around his waist.

"You know, dear…"

Before he could finish his sentence, Darla's legs clamped down tightly on his sides, and he struggled to catch his breath.

"What's that, honey? I didn't quite catch it."

Harold attempted to inhale. He flexed his core muscles, and her legs struggled to hold their lock on him until she squeezed them tighter. He nodded his head furiously and smacked the padded deck with his large hand.

"Tapping out, are we?" she asked in a mocking tone.

Harold gasped and gave one more loud slap against the padded sundeck.

With a quick roll to the left, she deposited Harold next to her. He tried to catch his breath, rub his sore sides, and laugh all at the same time.

Darla sat up. "Seriously, honey, what's the deal with you and this ship?"

He grunted as he moved his sore body into an upright position. "I don't know. I was raised around nice things, but I was taught never to get attached to them. Maybe it's because we are out away from land, and so I don't have anything to compare it to. I hate John's island because I compare it to home, but this ship… I've been on small schooner type yachts that cruised the coast but nothing like this. It's all new to me."

"Just promise me one thing."

"Anything," he replied.

"You won't leave me for this hunk of steel."

Harold reached over and gave Darla a long kiss. Their lips released, and she put her head on his chest.

He wrapped his arm around her. "Nothing can replace you. After all, you're the only woman I know that could take me in a fair fight."

Darla snuggled her head against his chest. "Size doesn't matter, dear. It's how you use your body."

"John might disagree with that."

Darla sat up and turned to him. "John told you size matters?"

Harold began to laugh. When he calmed down, he said, "No, that isn't what I meant."

Darla raised her eyebrow, and he felt himself melt inside at her mocking expression.

"I was talking about the fight. What are you talking about?" asked Darla.

His laughter stopped, but his lip remained curled up to the right side. "I can see I'm going to have to stay on my toes twenty-four seven when I'm around you."

Darla poked his chest. "Only when you keep me waiting. Now let's get below. Garcia has something to show you."

Harold raised both arms in surrender. "I'm defeated in the brains and brawn department."

He stood, and Darla raised her hand up to him. He reached down and helped her to her feet with little effort. The two walked down the spiral staircase to the second deck. They passed through a set of glass sliding doors and continued on through the living and dining areas and into a narrow hallway next to the galley. As they neared the stern, Harold could see an opened doorway to a large bedroom. A king-size bed with a built-in headboard greeted them as they entered the room.

Harold's face maintained a permanent grin due to the beauty of the ship. The outer wall was covered with windows, providing a clear view of the ocean. Dark mahogany flooring accented the white walls and bed frame, and a flat-screen television sat across from the bed. Harold heard a noise, and a door opened next to the bed. Garcia and Joshua entered the room.

"There you are," said Garcia, "I thought we had lost you overboard. Good job finding him, Darla."

Darla gave Garcia a quiet nod, and then she looked towards Harold and winked at him.

Garcia took off his sunglasses. "I wanted to look you in the eye for this part. I assume you've figured out this is your bedroom."

"I was hoping so," responded Harold.

Garcia motioned to Harold. "Come with me in here. This is your office, and I want to show you something."

Joshua stepped out of the way, and Garcia took Harold through the office door. Harold saw it immediately. His father's desk. The blood-stained droplets still lay near the center edge where they had been since that fateful day. Garcia had even had Harold's desk chair moved to the ship rather than simply use what was available locally.

"We wanted you to feel at home."

Harold turned to find Joshua standing close behind him.

"I should have known this was your doing, Doc," said Harold.

"No, this was Agent Garcia. He asked me how we could make you feel more at home, and I suggested your father's desk."

"The chair was my idea," interjected Garcia. "Besides, that size and style is expensive. It was cheaper to just bring it along for the ride."

"How did you know?" asked Harold.

Joshua reached up and took Harold by the shoulders. "I'm not just your psychiatrist. I'm your friend."

"I know that, Doc."

"Well, it was the only piece of furniture you left intact that terrible day. You've never asked to replace it when you redecorated the office. I assumed it was important to you."

Harold stepped forward and wrapped Joshua inside his arms. His old friend grunted under the sign of affection. "More than you can imagine, Doc." After a final quick squeeze, Harold released Joshua. The doctor drew in a breath and straightened his clothes.

"This is your sanctuary," Garcia said. "We sound-proofed the walls, and Darla installed encryption on your satellite connections for your computer and your phone. Even the CIA can't crack it."

Harold turned to Garcia and crossed his arms. "Do you mean you're spying on us too?"

Garcia reached in and put his sunglasses back on. "Please."

Harold rolled his eyes. "I know, CIA."

"No, this boat belongs to the CIA."

Harold reached over, turned his chair around, and sat down in it. He looked over towards Garcia. "It's yours for now."

"Glad you like it." He then turned to Joshua. "Doctor, why don't we finish our discussion outside and give these two some time together?"

Joshua nodded, and the two men left.

"You don't really think this room is free of listening devices, do you?" whispered Darla.

Harold glanced around the room. "I'm sure the good agent has thought of everything, but I do believe the phone is probably bug-free."

"Why?" asked Darla.

"Deniability. I'm sure Garcia knows I'll be talking with Tom in here. If anything goes wrong, he can claim he was unaware of the activity because I used the scrambled phone."

Darla leaned up against the wall and stared out the window. "You're cute but ignorant in the ways of intelligence. That would leave Garcia vulnerable to people claiming he was incompetent for leaving you an unmonitored line of communication."

Harold turned and looked out through the window in the same direction she stared. Far in the distance, one of the frequent gusts of wind lifted a parasailer ten feet into the air.

"So, you don't think the phone is scrambled?" asked Harold.

"Oh, it's scrambled," said Darla. "Garcia wouldn't want you talking shop on an open line, but I can guarantee you that he has a descrambler hidden somewhere on board, and he'll be recording your conversations. I wouldn't worry though."

Harold turned back to Darla. She looked down into his eyes, and he forgot what they were talking about. Darla walked over and gave him a kiss on his forehead. She stepped back and said, "I'm sorry. Did I distract you?"

Harold stared at her with a goofy grin and let the memory of her soft lips upon his forehead linger in his mind until a thought rushed back in. *The scrambled phone.* "Oh, I'm never distracted. So, what? Does Garcia just sit around in the evenings and listen to the conversations going on around the ship?"

"Only if he thinks there's a reason not to trust you."

"So, what if I want some real privacy between Tom and me?"

"Don't worry. I have a solution, but I need to give you your gift later."

Harold stood up. "Well, I suppose I should see the rest of my beautiful yacht."

"It belongs to the CIA," protested Darla.

"Whatever."

The two walked out of the office, and Darla showed Harold the expansive master bathroom. A freestanding tub sat next to a mirror wall. A separate shower covered in marble tile and divided by a glass door sat on the other end of the wall. Large double sinks rested inside a countertop across from the tub with mirrors covering the wall above them. Harold wondered if John had installed all the mirrors to make the bathroom seem bigger or so that he could admire himself. The idea that it was now his reflection and not John's in the mirrors brought a dark sense of joy.

The two of them walked back to the large living and dining rooms. "How many eating areas does this ship have?" asked Harold.

"Two main dining areas. This room and the top deck. The oceans are fickle. Some days you'll want to eat outside, and other days you'll be glad you're in here. John likely had the smaller areas designed for entertaining small groups."

"How many Franks work to keep the food going?" asked Harold.

Darla let out a short laugh. "We have two Franks that run the kitchen, one Frank that works as our bartender for any of the bars and one that helps keep the ship up. And finally, there is Captain Frank who works the bridge."

"How many Franks do we have for security?" asked Harold.

Darla held up two perfectly manicured fingers. "They pull double duty."

Harold's brow wrinkled. "What if something happens to the captain?"

Darla patted Harold's arm. "Not to worry, dear. Our Franks all have hidden talents that you will hopefully never have to discover."

Harold pointed towards the next door. "Please, continue."

Darla showed him the large galley. It had a griddle and gas grill, along with double ovens and refrigerators. Although the galley was tastefully done in stainless steel, teak, and mahogany, it was mostly covered by foodstuffs.

"Did the Franks forget to put away the food?" he asked.

"No, it's a big empty ocean. We will always be packed with food stores. You'll be surprised how quickly this kitchen will begin to empty out. Don't worry though, we have emergency stores below."

"Really? What are they?"

She chuckled. "You probably don't want to know. Let's just say the Marines didn't want to eat them during the Gulf War. They don't taste like much, but they would keep us alive in a pinch."

"Where to now?" asked Harold.

"That depends. Do you want to take the elevator or the stairs?"

His eyes grew wide. "This place has an elevator? That's awesome."

Her serious expression wiped the smile from Harold's face. "It's for the wounded. Sitting off the coast of the Keys today seems like fun and games, but our missions are dangerous."

Harold's expression became worried. "You guys do realize Joshua and I aren't trained for that sort of thing."

"I'm not saying you'll be involved, but it's here for the people that are."

His mood sobered. He loved the *Sweet Revenge*, but she really wasn't his. At least not yet. "I think we should take the stairs."

The two walked upstairs to the couches and black tables he had seen before. They passed through a small entertainment area and onto the bridge. Harold gaped at the sight of several flat-screen monitors that showed weather, radar, sonar, and a couple of screens he did not understand. He spoke in awe, "I feel like I'm on the starship *Enterprise*."

She laughed at his boyish words. "It's impressive. Everything here is automated."

"What if the computers go out?"

"Then we're all in trouble," replied Darla. "Don't worry. There are several redundancies built in. We do have some manual backups to ensure the engines and steering would be available so we aren't caught dead in the water during a storm, but hopefully we never have to use them."

Harold was enthralled. "So, do you think Frank will mind if I come up and keep him company sometime when he's piloting the ship?"

"I suppose it depends on how much of a pest you are."

"I can be a pretty big pest," joked Harold.

"Yes, you can."

He gave Darla's shoulder a friendly shove. "Hey, what does that mean?"

Darla poked him in the ribs and started to walk away. She looked over her shoulder. "I don't know. You said it. Come on, we're headed topside again."

He followed her back up the stairs to the top deck. Harold admired the sway of her hips as they climbed upwards. Darla stopped at the top of the stairs and looked down at him. "I hope you enjoyed what you were watching."

Harold's face flushed, and he did his best to look sorry, like he would with his mother when she found him doing something he shouldn't. She winked and strolled towards the mid-deck where the dining table rested. Garcia and Joshua sat near the head of the table with waters in front of them. Two more waters sat in front of empty chairs next to them.

Garcia waved them over. "Hurry up. I want to show you something we just discovered."

"Thanks, Frank," Harold said towards the bar on the far end.

Frank gave a cursory wave. Garcia was already turning his laptop around as Harold and Darla took their seats. The color video of the landscape reminded Harold of something out of *Call of Duty.*

"What am I looking at?" asked Harold.

"This is a high res video from a spy drone circling several thousand feet above us." Garcia picked up a walkie-talkie sitting in front of him. "Frank, move the image towards the *Sweet Revenge.* The camera on the screen began to zoom down until the image of the gleaming white ship appeared.

"Where are we?" asked Joshua.

"You can't see us. We're under the array, but watch this." Garcia keyed up his mic again. "Frank, turn on infrared." Several reddish ghosts appeared on the ship. Garcia hollered at the bartender, "Wave for us, Frank."

Frank raised his arm and moved it around for a few seconds. On the screen, Harold saw Frank's reddish silhouette waving to the camera.

Garcia hollered towards the bar, "Thanks, Frank."

He keyed the mic again. "Okay, Frank, show our guests their new fan club."

This time the camera zoomed back and then centered itself on the edge of Islamorada at the resort and infrared was turned off. They could see people with telescopes on the top balconies facing the water. There were at least two telescopes pointed out towards the water and four people manning them.

"Do you think they can see us?" asked Harold.

Garcia put down the transmitter. "How much they can see is anybody's guess. I expected Chuck to keep an eye on us. Except for our drone above, the airspace is clear, and sonar shows us clear below the water line as well. I didn't think Chuck would try a submergible in shallow clear water, but you can never be too careful."

Harold started tapping the table with his thumb. "So, that long ride out here, sore butts, and red skin were for nothing?"

"I wouldn't say it was for nothing. We are pretty far out here, and Frank did a good job bouncing us around the tourist route. Captain Frank has made sure to keep the registration facing away from the shoreline. Chuck will find out about this ship sooner or later, but nobody said I had to make it easy on him."

Joshua spoke up, "Did they know about the ship before we rode out here?"

Darla answered, "No. Chuck has been keeping his eye on the team and trying to gather intel on us. The ship was at the naval station at Key West getting her refit before she sailed. Chuck would have no reason to search for her."

"Until now," said Harold.

"It's time we get underway." Garcia picked the walkie-talkie back up. "Okay, Frank, we're good here. Let's head further out into the Atlantic and take her back into the Gulf close to Cuba." Garcia then pulled out an earpiece Harold had not noticed earlier.

Harold felt the engines engage for the first time. With a low hum, the ship glided over the water. Harold stood up and carefully walked over to the forward railing as he attempted to get his sea legs. Looking towards the small dot of Islamorada on the far horizon, he raised his large arm and waved goodbye.

"What are you doing?" asked Garcia.

Harold turned to face him. "I'm giving Chuck something to think about. He'll need to figure out if I'm waving goodbye to Islamorada or to them. If it was you instead of me, the answer would have been obvious."

"What good does that do?" asked Garcia.

"If I was him, I'd want to know what we know. Now he has to figure out if we knew they were watching us."

Garcia grimaced. "Got it. Do me a favor. Next time you want to try something clever, don't. Chuck is a murdering psychopath that has found a way to make money at killing. He's not somebody you can play with."

Harold's expression grew serious. He put down his arm and slowly walked back to the table.

Garcia's sunglasses panned around the group. "Okay, in ten minutes we are out of sight, and you're off the clock. We have an open bar, and Frank will be serving lionfish or BBQ, your choice. I also recommend the tomato salad. It's to kill for."

"Don't you mean to die for?" asked Harold.

"Please, we're CIA. We don't die for anything."

Harold chuckled. Darla and Joshua rolled their eyes and got up from the table.

Joshua spoke up first, "If you all will excuse me, I have a phone call to make to a certain wife who misses me."

"Meet me in the Jacuzzi later, Doc?" asked Harold.

"You got it."

"I suggest we all go below to freshen up before dinner," Darla said. "I don't know about the rest of you, but I'm tired of sweating in these same clothes."

"I'll escort you to your cabin," Harold volunteered.

Darla held up her hand. "I don't think so, big boy."

"Oh, you can come to my bedroom, but you don't trust me to go with you?" Harold said, mocking a wounded tone. His voice then became more sinister with a hint of sarcasm, "It's a small ship you know."

Darla dropped her hand. "That's true. Just remember, I know how to break your ribs."

"Are you guys going to be like this the whole trip?" asked Garcia.

They smiled at one another.

"If I'm lucky," responded Harold.

Garcia walked away shaking his head.

Harold hollered after him, "You're the guy who said to keep things loose."

Garcia stopped, turned around, and opened his mouth but closed it before saying a word. He headed down the stairs shaking his head again.

Darla walked over and locked her hands around Harold's waist. "Honey, I'm serious. We need to have some lines while we are on board. I don't want you in my cabin. Are you going to be okay with that?"

Harold felt disappointed, but he knew she was right. "Yea. I suppose now isn't the time anyway."

Darla released Harold. She put her hand on his chest and patted it. His eyes locked with hers.

Darla spoke softly, "That's the spirit, love. One day we will have our entire lives together, but not right now."

Harold mockingly stuck out his bottom lip and nodded. Darla dropped her arm and went to her cabin. Harold walked over to sit on the cushioned deck by the Jacuzzi and watched the clear waters of the Caribbean slip past the ship. The ship and Darla were beautiful, but he had never thought his life would end up where it was. The fact that the ship reminded him of home made him think about his childhood and how much he missed being around his old memories. He looked up at the sky and spoke, "Is saving the company really worth all of this?" No sounds returned except the lapping of the water against the hull and the humming of the engines.

CHAPTER 15

Harold grabbed a cup of coffee off the indoor dining room table. The bright sun sparkling across the blue water was too beautiful to look at from indoors. The ship gently rocked as he made his way through the sliding glass door. The yacht started a slow turn as he started towards the aft of the ship, and it sent him bumping into the bar. Hot coffee slushed over his mug and onto his shirt. Harold gasped from the sudden heat and murmured a string of words he preferred not to share with the rest of the world. He grabbed a towel from behind the bar and sat down on the sofa at the rear of the ship.

As he was attempted in vain to get the stain out of his shirt, Joshua walked through the door.

"Drinking problem."

He responded without looking up, "Yea, Doc, something like that."

Joshua sat down next to him and put his mug of the coffee table. "It looks like we both had the same idea."

Harold glanced over. "Where's your coffee stain?"

"I was speaking of the enjoying the beautiful morning."

"That's a shame. I'm willing to help you out if you care to join me."

Joshua grabbed his mug and took a long swallow. "Any dreams lately?"

Harold tossed the towel on the table in frustration and drank most of his mug. "Not last night. I sometimes wonder if my brain has developed a short circuit."

Joshua sat silently for a moment simply staring at his mug.

"Wow, Doc. I was expecting you to at least ask me a question. What's going on? Am I losing my mind?"

"I don't know, Harry. I don't think so, but this may be my doing. When I first started my hypnotherapy, I thought I was breaking new ground. I knew there were risks, like attaching my presence to whatever was going on inside of your mind, but we seemed to glide right past those. There is another risk though, and I don't know if I was wrong in my assessments about the progress we made."

"What risks, Doc? Please don't tell me you scrambled my brain."

Joshua put down his mug and turned to face Harold. "Nothing like that. There is a chance that we bottled up some of your anger, your rage, like coke in a bottle if you will. If something happens to shake it up, the cork could pop off."

"And all my rage comes pouring out."

Joshua tapped the back of the couch as he spoke, "Exactly. However, you haven't really exploded into any sort of uncontrollable rage. It's almost as if you have a slow leak. John could represent your hidden rage, and your brain may be trying to deal with it."

Harold finished off his coffee. "That doesn't sound so bad. They're just dreams after all."

"Yes, but I'm concerned about what could happen if you face another crisis before the pressure is released. What if Chuck or his men do something to set you off?"

Harold stood and stretched his back. "Well, Doc, we both know the only thing that sets me off is when somebody is in danger. Maybe it would be a good thing if the cork came off. It could save our lives."

Joshua stood. "Perhaps, but you're still dealing with killing John even though you saved our lives. What will happen to you if you kill again?"

"I keep asking myself that same question. I guess I don't know, but I do know I'll have you to help me through it."

Joshua started to walk away.

"Hang on, Doc. I do have you, right?"

Joshua turned around. "Of course. I just have a lot on my mind."

"That's nothing new."

"Yes, I know, but it concerns your half-brother."

"I'm usually the one to bring him up. What's going on?"

"I thought I had succeeded with Bill because I managed to completely shut down his rage. Now, I'm worried. What if I only bottled his berserker? What if the cork comes off, or it already has? You managed to take our sessions and blend what you learned with what was going on around you. I don't know how, but you found a way not to bottle up everything inside. Bill didn't. Everything was bottled up tight. At least for as long as he remained in the orphanage."

Harold sat down and looked up at Joshua. "What are you going to do?"

"I don't know yet. Adam doesn't know where Bill is. I'm thinking about going to North Carolina the first chance I get to look over my notes. I may need to find him for his own good, if I'm not too late."

"Do what you need to do, Doc. Just remember to tell him about me if you do have to find him."

"Of course." Joshua turned and went inside.

Harold looked back over the aft of the ship and the calm Caribbean waters. He hoped wherever Bill was that he was safe and doing well.

***

Harold sat on the lower deck, watching the sun's fiery ball rise above the watery horizon. He had quit counting the number of sunrises he had enjoyed at sea. His fishing pole gently bent back and forth against the drag of the lure.

"Good morning, Harry."

Harold jerked in surprise at Joshua's voice. "Oh, hey, Doc. I didn't hear you sneak up on me."

Joshua sat down next to him. "I was roaming the ship and saw you fishing. Have you caught anything?"

"Are you asking for a friend?"

"Is that pole being used?"

"Take your best shot."

Joshua baited the unused pole and casted aft from the other corner of the yacht. He took a seat next to Harold and let his legs dangle from the back of the boat. "So, you're the reason Frank slowed the boat."

"Ship, and yes. Evidently, we are on a slow boat that's not even going to China. Garcia told me this is a combined trip to save money. It's a shakedown cruise as well as a meetup with Chuck. So, we can slow down to fish or whatever will eat up time. Captain Frank told me we should get to where we are going soon, wherever that is."

"Well, at least it's beautiful."

"Yep, it keeps growing on me more and more. There's something about the salt life that just agrees with me. Maybe it's because I haven't seen this part of the world before. I know I'm feeling better about it, but what about you? I imagine you're missing a certain someone."

Joshua tapped the edge of the deck. "Maria. We've been talking by phone quite a lot since I've been gone. She keeps reminding me that I'm no longer a single man who can do as he pleases."

"Let me talk to Garcia. I can get her on board with us the next time we have to go out."

"I wish it was that easy," said Joshua with a sigh. "Maria isn't the type of woman who enjoys having others take care of her. That's one of the things I love about her. Don't get me wrong, she would enjoy fishing off the boat or riding one of the inflatables getting pulled along the back of the ship, but then she would want to do something she felt was useful. Be honest with me, if we didn't allow ourselves a few distractions, this ship would be pretty boring."

Harold looked concerned. "So, what are you thinking, Doc?"

Joshua took a sip of coffee and looked out over the water. "Leaving the ship is not an option. I know Maria isn't happy alone on the island either. I need to put her first, but I'm not sure how to do that at the moment."

Harold leaned in closer to Joshua. "What does that mean?"

Joshua grabbed Harold's hand in the same fatherly fashion he had always managed, no matter how large Harold's hand had gotten. "Harry, I don't know. I know we are a family, but one member of my family, the most important member, needs my time. No, she deserves my time, and she deserves to be happy."

"I agree, but how can you do that and this?" asked Harold as he slid his hand away.

Joshua went back to tapping the deck. "I don't know. To top it off, I'm still worried about Bill. I told Maria the situation, and she thinks we should go to North Carolina and try to find him before something happens to him. If nothing has happened already."

"Doc, I would never stand in the way of you and Maria, or Bill. I need you, but so do a lot of other people we love. You do what you think is best."

Joshua suddenly stood. "I think I'll go for a stroll around the ship."

"What about your pole?"

"Let me know if I catch anything."

Joshua turned and walked up the steps to the next deck. Harold looked over the water and wondered how he could help Joshua and Maria. A sudden sadness rushed through his chest, and before he could stop himself, tears began to fall from his eyes. Images of his mother's memorial service and father's funeral came rushing into the forefront of his mind. Harold took several deep breaths to regain control from his grief. *Why now? It's been weeks, months, why do I feel this way now?* Instinctively he started to go after Joshua but stopped.

Harold spoke to himself, "No, I can't keep running to Doc. I need to deal with this myself."

His glassy eyes looked aft. A small pod of dolphins broke the surface of the still water just behind his lures. They swam in a serpentine pattern and maintained a steady distance from the ship. Harold forgot his grief as he watched the pod for several minutes. He wondered what caused them to appear and how they managed to maintain such a consistent distance. After a few minutes, they disappeared below the surface. A moment later, they were to the port of the yacht. All three dolphins broke through the top of the calm seas and hurtled themselves vertically into the air, flipped over, and dove back under.

"Aren't dolphins amazing creatures?" Garcia's voice startled Harold.

"I didn't hear you walk up." Harold stood.

"Yea, I saw you were lost in thought, so I thought I'd give you a minute. Are you doing okay?"

Harold let out a jagged breath. "Yea. I don't know why, but something brought my parents to mind."

Both men focused their attention back to the sea as they heard a dolphin squeaking and saw it walking backwards on the water.

"It looks like they're going to give us a show," said Harold.

"Maybe they think you could use it." Garcia paused for several seconds and then continued, "I don't talk much about what I've experienced in my life, but I think this might help you. I lost my mother while I was in the field about five years ago. Nobody told me she had passed away. It wouldn't have done me any good to know since I was undercover. If I let myself think about the first time I walked up to her headstone and saw she was really dead, I could start crying like a baby." Garcia wiped a tear from his cheek. "I guess what I'm trying to tell you is that it's normal to feel the way you do. You didn't lose your parents that long ago, and the grief never goes away. You'll just get better at dealing with it."

"Dealing with it or burying it inside me?" asked Harold.

Garcia shrugged. "Some days I'm not sure there's a difference."

Both men continued watching as the dolphins danced through the still waters portside for another minute or two before they disappeared below the water.

Harold walked over and sat on the couch, and Garcia joined him. "I assume you didn't come up here just to check on me," said Harold. "What's up?"

"We should be arriving this afternoon at Crossroads Key to meet Chuck and iron out the business details for the buy. I wanted to see if you were ready for your debut."

Harold stretched his legs and arms and let out a grunt as he attempted to remove the stiffness from sitting on the deck. "I thought you guys were doing the deal. I'm just window dressing, right?"

Garcia leaned towards him. "It isn't quite that simple."

Here it comes.

"You are the face of PDS," said Garcia. "Chuck will expect you to cut the deal. I'm not sure he will even allow me to sit with you when it happens. Do you think you can handle the sale?"

"That's it?" smirked Harold. "You just want me to broker a business deal? That's not a problem."

Garcia sat back and picked up a white mug of coffee Harold had not noticed when he sat down. He looked over the rim at Harold as he drank. Garcia smacked his lips and slowly lowered his mug. "Frank sure does make a fine cup of coffee. So, what exactly did you think I wanted you for?"

"Beats me. I guess I had a crazy idea that you were going to try and recruit me. I assumed part of your interest in me was my berserker ability."

Garcia looked back at Harold with a blank expression. He finally spoke. "I didn't think you were the type."

"I'm not," said Harold.

"Then let me put your fears to rest. I'm not planning on making you some sort of secret agent. You and your company are assets. That means we can utilize you for our benefit for the greater good. There's nothing else I'm looking for."

"Good. I'm glad we got that cleared up. Now, what am I selling Chuck?" replied Harold.

"Rifles with smart rounds."

Harold worked to hide his shock. "I think I heard you wrong," said Harold. "You mentioned advanced weapons in the board meeting. We make missiles and rockets. Small arms has been a side business at best and a money loser at worst for PDS."

"Yep," Garcia shot back. "I knew you'd be surprised."

"That's putting it mildly. I had always assumed we'd be offering some sort of missile deal and go after some real psychos with real money."

"That's why I wanted to chat with you alone about this detail."

Harold leaned into Garcia until he could smell the coffee coming off Garcia's breath. "Don't you mean you have me alone on a ship in the middle of the ocean? You led me and the board members on."

Garcia held his ground, "My superiors and I thought about tempting Chuck with some of your more exotic weaponry, but we're concerned about what would happen if any real weapons managed to walk away. Besides, your company is being paid just as I promised. Nobody in California has complained."

Harold turned away and drummed the coffee table with his fingers as if he were playing the piano. He stared down at his hand and tried to form his question carefully. His tapping continued, and he looked back up and said, "I don't care what California is telling you. I don't think my company is the right fit. Many of my best people are rocket scientists, engineers, and physicists. Missiles and rockets are our specialties. I don't see them getting excited by the prospect of making rifles with no missile or rocket projects on the table. Not to mention, I have a contingent that are weapons averse and refuse to work on anything related to our missile work. I just don't see how this will fit."

"I understand your concern, but frankly I know your company better than you do."

"No, you think you know my company better than I do."

Garcia relaxed his posture and laid his arm across the back of the couch. "Smart weapons require a great amount of knowledge in physics. The armament uses a combination of microtechnology, the newest in laser-designation targeting systems that can fit on top of a rifle and air resistance to move the bullet where you want it to go. We need great minds that can build the targeting system into the rifles, and manufacture the guided bullets."

"That may be, but I know we are going to lose good people over this, and then what? How is any of this going to get us closer to the goal of gaining defense contracts, or NASA contracts for that matter?"

Garcia smiled and pulled his sunglasses out of his pocket. "Please, we're CIA."

Harold found himself looking at his reflection where Garcia's eyes once were. "I'm not sure this is the time to joke around."

"Who said I'm joking? The sun's reflection off the water has been killing me, but I wanted to look you in the eye before I put these things on. Seriously, it's not a problem. My people have been working with Tom. We already have prototype machinery in your factory. It's not much, just enough for small batch runs. The machines will create enough weaponry to convince Chuck we have access to these experimental weapons. Tom has some of your best people working to improve the prototypes. It's a win-win. Just like I told you in the boardroom."

"What about the rest of my employees?" asked Harold.

"There's going to be some attrition, but every company has that. Besides, you still have your existing projects once your contracts are unfrozen. I'm not reorganizing your company. I've just expanded its role."

Harold sat back, crossed his arms, and stared out over the calm waters. *Tom and I need to have a talk about what he is doing with my dad's company.*

Garcia broke his train of thought. "So, are you in or not?"

Harold knew Garcia thought he had him, and he did, at least for now. "I think we're probably past that question. So, how many weapons am I selling and for how much?"

"We are offering Chuck one hundred smart rifles with a thousand rounds of ammunition for twenty million dollars."

"Those are some expensive long guns," quipped Harold.

Garcia crossed his arms and grinned. "The advantages of the black market. So, can you do it?"

Harold let out a short laugh. "Please, I'm Parabolic Defense Systems. Making and selling weapons at a profit is what I do."

Garcia smacked the couch cushion with his hand. "Good. We'll be at the rendezvous point soon."

Harold scowled. "I thought you said we are meeting this afternoon. It's still morning."

Garcia stood and stretched. "I did, and we are, but we're taking the Kodiak. *Sweet Revenge* is our rest and recovery tool. I want her out of radar range long before Chuck arrives."

"But what about the defense systems and all the Franks?"

"Contingency. I'm sure you don't want to be stuck in the middle of the ocean defenseless if we're ever found."

Harold stood up. "I can get behind that."

"Good. Then it sounds like everything is clear. Be prepared to leave the ship at 11 a.m. The Kodiak ride is another thirty minutes on the water. One word of warning, it's going to be a bumpy ride. Bumpier than the first day we rode."

Harold looked past Garcia to the ocean. "She looks as calm as a lake."

"That's because she's not awake. Frank tells me a weak cold front is moving through, and the winds will pick up a little bit. It's nothing we can't handle, but the sea won't look this calm. Until then."

Harold walked to his office and locked the door. Unlocking his upper right-hand drawer, he pulled out Darla's welcome aboard gift. It was scrambled satellite phone she had smuggled on board. After the big tour, she had scanned the office for bugs, and Garcia was true to his word, there were no listening devices. Even so, Darla had told him not to use this phone for private conversations with Tom. The beauty of the large antennae phone in his hand was not just that it was scrambled, but it only worked on one channel and connected to a twin phone held by Tom.

The phone rang several times before Tom picked up.

"Is this my morning wake-up call?" asked a groggy Tom.

"Sorry, I thought you would be waking up by now."

Tom's voice slowly became clearer as he spoke. "It's not your fault. We had a late night at work. A few employees have left the company, and we're scrambling to get those roles filled. I don't understand why there isn't a pool of physicist with impeccable security credentials lined up for defense contractor jobs," Tom said sarcastically. "The attrition sort of surprised me. When word got around the rumor mill that we were focusing on smart rifles, several people quit in protest and said they didn't sign up to be involved in that kind of business. I guess they were able to talk themselves past the missiles since they are used so rarely and can only be owned by the government."

Harold's voice was filled with concern. "What's going on out there? I need to know if this whole thing is going to be a problem."

Tom yawned into the phone. "Sorry, no, nothing you need to worry about. I have everything handled for now. So, how's the Caribbean? Are you missing Malibu yet?"

"I miss it every day. It's beautiful out here though. Did you know Garcia has a yacht that we use to go meet people?"

Tom's low moan came across Harold's phone. He assumed Tom was stretching. "A yacht?" Tom asked. "No. When are you going to invite me out to cruise the seas with you?"

Harold laughed at the idea. "I don't think Garcia would approve, but don't worry. I plan on getting this ship one day. She's beautiful. You know me. I don't care about this stuff, so if I tell you she's beautiful then it's really special."

"Yea, now you have my curiosity peaked."

"Speaking of the few possessions I love, how's my home?"

Tom's voice sounded more alert. "Well, I appreciate you making me your tenant, but it's empty without you guys in it. I never realized how large your parent's place was until I moved in alone."

"What about Garcia's men?"

"You mean the Franks? They're around. There is one guy that sleeps in your old room on the other side of the house. There are two more over in Joshua's house. A lot of the time all three hang out there. Frank said it gives them a better view of the estate, but I think they're afraid of breaking something over here they can't afford to replace."

Harold looked down at his father's desk and ran his free hand across the bloodstains on the top of it. "Frank gets around. He's on the ship too."

Tom's laughter emanated from the phone, and Harold pulled the receiver away from his ear until he finished. "Sorry, I just think it's funny. It isn't like I care who these men are. But I am wondering why there aren't any women agents here. California, and the feds, are pretty particular about equal rights. It isn't like I need men guarding the place."

"Are you sure you're not just looking for a date?" joked Harold.

"You know better," Tom groused.

"Take it easy. I wasn't trying to infer anything, just making a joke. Besides, I'm wondering the same thing.

Garcia mentioned Alices, but I have yet to talk to any. Aliases, super-secret agents. There is something that doesn't pass the smell test with Agent Garcia Hernandez, but I can't put my finger on it. Darla tells me he isn't dirty, but I'm not sure. It's little things, like nothing but Franks, that get to me. Then there's this guy Chuck that we are trying to set up. He and Chuck know a lot about each other. Darla says it's normal to mix truth and lies, and that it's a sign of a good agent, but I'm not so sure. Finally, it's the company, Tom. How did Garcia get you and the board to agree to start manufacturing small arms?"

"I thought you knew."

Harold stood up and began to pace a couple of steps back and forth across the room. "Did he tell you I agreed?"

Tom's hesitated, and then he said, "No, not in so many words. He was so nonchalant about it when he first approached me that we thought you had already signed off on the idea. To be honest, I'm surprised to hear your reaction."

Harold stopped and looked out the window as he spoke. "My dad would have never agreed to this. I feel like I'm letting him down."

Tom's voice was soft and calming, "Harry, I don't want to hear that coming from you. I loved your dad like he was an uncle, and I can promise you that he would have done exactly what you're doing. You're trying to save the company."

Harold knew Tom was serious. Tom had learned of Harold's familiar name by observing Joshua when they were kids, and he only used it when he wanted

Harold to pay attention to him. Tom may be sincere, but that didn't make him right. "Rifles, Tom? Do you really think my dad would have agreed to rifles and working with the CIA?"

"You're keeping it between the lines, and that's what he would have done."

Harold plopped down in his chair, and it let out a loud groan from the sudden burden. "From out here, those lines are starting to look pretty blurry."

"Just stay between them."

Harold turned and faced the window. "That's what I plan to do. Now to the real reason for my phone call. I have an assignment for you and Abigail. I want you to find a way to get us out of this contract with Garcia."

"If we break that contract, the company will be ruined," protested Tom.

Harold tapped the heel of his foot. "That's why I'm asking you to find another way and to keep it between you and Abigail for now. The fewer people that know what you are doing, the less likely it is that Garcia will find out."

"You really think he's dirty, don't you?"

Harold looked out through the window at the sea. The crystal smooth glass had been replaced by small, choppy waves, and the ship began to rock a bit more than usual. "If I thought he was dirty, I would call the CIA, not talk to you. We just need a contingency plan."

"Okay, but what if you don't like what I come up with?" asked Tom.

"Make me like it."

Tom's long sigh was audible over the phone. "Is there anything else, boss? Should I work on world peace while I'm at it?"

A smile crept across Harold's face. "Nope. If you do that, we'll all be out of a job."

"Good point. I guess that's why you're the chairman."

"Something like that," said Harold. "I'll talk to you later. Don't forget your new project."

Tom's voice held an edge of sarcasm, "Yea, I'll get right on that after I finish Garcia's little weapons run."

"Try and do both."

Tom's voice was curt, "Goodbye."

The phone line went dead. Harold looked down at his receiver. "I do believe Tom hung up on me."

Harold put the phone back in the drawer, locked it, and looked back out over the water. "What am I doing, Dad?" Harold asked the empty room.

He knew leading was tough, but he never imagined he would be making these sorts of decisions. Tom already sounded strained, and he wondered if Tom would be able to keep their secret.

Chapter 16

"I haven't been spanked this hard since I broke Mom's vase," shouted Harold.

The Kodiak bounced along the surface of the water. Looking back at the yacht, Harold only saw a speck on the horizon. Captain Frank was taking her out of the area with all haste. Saltwater splashed on Harold's lips and stung his eyes.

Joshua's voice rose above the roar of the large outboard motor, "To be fair, Harry, that vase did have your grandfather's ashes in it."

Harold's lip curled up in the right corner, and he turned his head back to face the direction the boat was going. A small island had begun to come into view. He noticed two high-speed boats anchored just offshore and turned back to the group. "Are those boats Chuck's?"

"I hope not," answered Darla.

"They're friendlies," said Garcia. "I have it on good authority that Chuck is still an hour away from arriving."

"Aren't we meeting with Chuck's team alone?" asked Harold.

Garcia's face grimaced in the salty spray, and he answered above the cacophony of sea and outboard engine. "They'll be gone in under thirty."

Their boat continued its course, and Garcia beached them with barely a nudge on the small sandy shore. A woman in a tan business dress suit walked up.

"Everyone, this is Alice. She's handling our little project."

"You're late," exclaimed Alice.

Harold looked at this watch. According to Garcia, they were exactly on time.

"Couldn't be helped," said Garcia.

She makes one, thought Harold.

Alice walked them up a small hill and over to a group of chairs sitting under a pop-up awning. The awning was anchored to the sandy ground to avoid it blowing away in the wind. "We have a problem."

Garcia scowled. "What sort of problem?"

Alice pointed around them towards the sand. "Footprints, lots of footprints."

"Chuck won't count footprints."

Alice smacked her hands together like a school teacher. "Pay attention, everyone. When we arrived, there were several footprints. I was here yesterday, and the only footprints were my own. Chuck was here either last night or this morning."

Harold and Joshua looked wide-eyed at one another, but Darla appeared to remain calm.

Garcia's forehead creased and he faced Alice. "Do we have eyes on Chuck and his men?"

"We do, but be aware, Chuck has scouted the island. He probably understands this landscape as well as we do. We swept for bugs, and of course, we are running surveillance of the perimeter."

"Understood."

"You all will meet here," Alice said as her arm swooped around. "Our drone won't see you, but you'll be transmitting."

Garcia responded, "Chuck will expect bugs under the tent. I hope they aren't hidden in the awning frame."

"No."

Harold wondered why Garcia had not asked where the bugs were. His curiosity quickly got the better of him. "Where are the bugs?"

Alice shot him an icy look. "Need to know, and you don't need to know."

Now I know where Garcia gets it.

She waved over another woman who was dressed in a dark suit like Alice's. She rushed over with a tablet in her hand. Alice addressed the new woman, "Alice, share the video with the team please."

The tablet-toting Alice held up her device. Two small boats traveled at a fast pace along the sea. "They'll be here in less than an hour."

She shared a mutual nod with the other Alice then shut down her tablet and dropped it into a DeWalt ToughBox that held other equipment.

After Alice left, Garcia looked at everyone slowly. Harold felt like he was being sized up all over again. He wondered what Garcia expected to happen. Garcia looked over at Darla before she suddenly left to join the four people who were busy packing up.

"Follow me," said Garcia, and Harold and Joshua fell into line.

"Why isn't Darla joining us?" Harold asked as they followed the coastline around the tiny desert island. Although the other side was not in view yet, Harold guessed they would reach it in a matter of minutes.

"She knows the drill, and she was with me when we picked this place out."

"How long have you been planning this?" asked Harold.

"Since you took out John," answered Garcia flatly.

"When did Darla know?"

"Right before she left to come help me out."

Joshua interjected, "If I might interrupt."

"Please," Harold answered.

"Garcia, I think our concern is the secrets. It's easy to tell people they only need to know certain things if they trust you, but honestly, the more we hear, the less we trust you. You seemed very cozy with Chuck when we all met. Now you're saying that you started planning this the day Harold killed John. I think you can understand why we both wonder what other secrets you're keeping."

Garcia stopped walking, and he turned to look at Harold and Joshua. "Let me ask you a question. Do you trust Darla?"

"Of course," said Joshua.

"I already answered that before," said Harold.

"Good. Well, Darla trusts me. So, if you can't trust me, then trust Darla's judgement."

The three stood in silence for a few moments.

"Fair enough," responded Joshua finally.

"If that's good enough for Doc, it's good enough for me," said Harold.

"Good."

Garcia turned on his heel, and their pace quickened. They soon arrived at the other side of the island. Saw grass and sand sat above the waterline. Shallows and reef gently sloped down from the coastline. The shadows of two large fish could be seen just below the surface a few yards out.

Garcia finally spoke again. "I wanted you to see why you want to avoid this side of the island. Those fish out there are bull sharks. They were here the last time I was on the island. Well, I don't know if they are the same fish, but you get the idea. If we're ever in an emergency, this is not the location to retreat to. Chuck won't land on this side because I've already warned him. It's easier to defend one front instead of two, and this island only has one side that is favorable for boats."

Garcia looked at his watch. "Let's hurry back. If everything is going according to plan, the team has left, and Darla is by herself. Chuck should be here in thirty minutes or less."

The team found Darla sitting under the awning reading something on her cell phone. She looked up as she slid the phone in her pocket. "It's about time you all showed back up. I thought I'd have to talk with Chuck's goon squad on my own."

"Just giving a tour," said Garcia.

"How are Alice and Frank?" asked Darla.

"Swimming happily around looking for their next meal," said Garcia.

Harold chuckled. "You even named the sharks Frank and Alice?"

Darla stood up and walked over to Harold. "Why not? They look like a happy couple."

"How do you know they're male and female?" asked Joshua.

"We don't, but you're welcomed to check, Doctor."

"I'll pass."

The sound of boat engines grabbed the group's attention. Harold caught a glimpse of two boats speeding towards the beach. The crafts broke off from one another and began to circle the island. Harold noticed the two overly large outboard motors in the rear. A fifty-caliber machine gun sat mounted on the front. The guns were tied down, unmanned. Although Harold could still hear the muted motors, the boats disappeared as they circled the island. The noise increased as they appeared on both sides of the island, perfectly synced together. The two boats slowed and bit into the sand in the shallow water. Chuck hopped out of one boat by himself with a small splash. He quickly tied the boat off with a small anchor. Nigel and Haidar did the same in the other boat. All three men wore white shorts, tan shirts, and blue nylon shoes that windsurfers and others often used when out on the water.

Chuck walked up the short hill to the awning with the other two men behind him. He gritted a cigar in his teeth as he spoke, "Nice tent."

"Finally, a bit of bloody shade," said Nigel.

Haidar just glared at the group. Harold swore Haidar's dead eyes were drilling straight into his soul, and all he could feel was their anger.

Garcia swept his arm towards the chairs. "Gentlemen, please, have a seat."

Nigel and Chuck sat while Haidar stood behind Chuck.

Harold sat down. "Haidar, come take a load off."

Haidar glared at Harold.

What are you waiting for, brat? Kill him. Harold blinked. Was he awake? How was John's voice inside his head? *I'm telling you, kill him. If you don't, you'll regret it later.*

Harold mumbled, "No."

"What's that?" asked Chuck.

Harold glanced at Joshua who was watching Chuck and his men. He hoped the doctor would look at him and catch the concern in his eyes.

"Everything okay, Harry?"

He had hoped for cover, not a question. Harold thought quickly and said, "Yea, I was just saying there's no reason to stand."

Chuck removed his cigar and pointed it over his shoulder at Haidar. "Don't mind him. He doesn't like crowds."

"I didn't realize we constituted a crowd," said Joshua.

Chuck grinned and exposed bits of tobacco stuck to his teeth. "You got me, Doctor. He doesn't like people in general."

"I can assure you, Haidar, we're no threat," said Joshua in a soothing voice that Harold had heard many times. He had always found it comforting, but Haidar simply looked annoyed.

"Let's get started," interrupted Garcia. "Chuck, we will supply one hundred smart rifles and one thousand rounds of ammunition. Your payment to me will be twenty million dollars, just like we talked about."

Chuck stuck his cigar in the corner of his mouth and chewed on it for a moment. He pulled it out, spit, and said, "I don't think so. Your prices are much too steep. I want to pay half of that."

Garcia replied, "I'm not sure we can go that low."

Harold suddenly jumped in. "It's twenty million or nothing."

Garcia tore off his sunglasses and looked over at Harold. Harold glared back. Joshua finally cleared his throat.

"I'm sorry." Garcia turned back to Chuck. "I'm afraid my friend has forgotten who's in charge."

"No, I haven't," chimed Harold. "I think you are both forgetting who owns these weapons. They belong to me. Without me buying into the deal, you have no weapons. I want twenty million or you get nothing."

Garcia turned. "We'll discuss this later."

Chuck reached in his pocket, pulled out his lighter, and lit his cigar. "I like this kid. He's got moxie, Garcia. You could learn a few things from him. Harold, I accept your terms. They're steep, but you're right. You hold the cards this time, and if I was in your position, I'd do the same thing."

Garcia slid his sunglasses back on and let their reflection remain on Harold.

"So, when do we get a demo?" Chuck asked. "I want to see what it is we're buying if I'm putting up this kind of money."

Garcia turned back to Harold, and Harold said, "Don't look at me. That's Garcia or Darla's department. I'm just the supplier."

"We'll meet back here in a week for a small demonstration," Darla said. "If you're satisfied, we'll arrange for delivery."

Nigel whispered into Chuck's ear, and Chuck nodded. Nigel and Haidar suddenly pulled pistols out from behind their backs and pointed them at Garcia. "Nigel, why don't you share with the group what you just told me?"

"I was just saying that the CIA bloke seemed a bit useless. It's like you're excess baggage. Also, we never swept for bugs. You maneuvered us to these chairs and just started talkin' business. That doesn't feel very cricket."

Garcia drew in his breath and let it out slowly.

"Nervous?" asked Chuck.

Garcia pointed his sunglasses in Chuck's direction, but Harold was sure he wasn't looking at him. "Me, nervous? No. I'm just trying to restrain myself from killing your two boys."

"Nice try, but you can't get to your weapon that fast."

"He doesn't have to."

A click sounded, and everyone stared at Darla who had a silver revolver pointed towards Chuck's head. Harold guessed it was at least a forty-five based on the barrel size.

Chuck began to laugh. "I do believe we have what people used to call an old-fashion Mexican standoff."

Garcia calmly clasped his hands together. Harold's hands formed into fists and continued to clench tighter until his knuckles turned white. He looked over at Joshua, and the doctor gave his head a small shake while looking back at him.

Garcia finally spoke, "Well, we can all kill each other, or you can sweep for bugs. The choice is all yours."

Chuck took a long drag on his cigar and blew it towards Garcia's face. Garcia didn't flinch. Chuck's voice was flat, "Lower your weapons, boys."

Nigel immediately dropped his hand to his side, but Haidar kept his weapon trained on Garcia.

"Haidar, drop your pistol."

Haidar stood as still as a statue. Chuck moved swiftly and violently. Haidar's handgun went off right before it left his hand. The bullet tore a hole in the top of the awning. Chuck coiled back his same arm and released a fist into Haidar's diaphragm. The young man fell to the ground, struggling for air.

"Never disobey an order," Chuck said. He then pointed at Nigel who left towards the beach.

Darla lowered her weapon. "I think you need to screen your help better."

"He's still high strung. I should have never given him a weapon. We'll talk on the way home. I'm sure this won't happen again."

Harold could see fear replace the hate in Haidar's eyes. He was sure he didn't want to know what sort of conversation Chuck had in mind for his hate-filled compatriot. Haidar finally caught his breath and stood back up.

Chuck barked at Haidar, "Go help Nigel."

Haidar stepped towards his weapon lying in the sand.

"Touch that, and I'll kill you myself," said Chuck.

Haidar stopped, bowed his head, and ran towards the beach. Chuck stood up, picked the gun up off the sand, and wiped it clean. "Well played, Garcia. I believe you're the man I thought you were."

Chuck sat back down and turned to Harold. "Why didn't you take my boys down?"

"I considered it," answered Harold honestly.

"Considered it? I believe the doctor has made you soft," Chuck replied mockingly.

Harold could feel his anger begin to burn within his blood. His voice became deeper, despite his best effort to control it. "The doctor has probably saved your life today, and you don't even know it."

Chuck's eyes grew wide for a moment. Harold could feel the fear behind Chuck's façade, and everything inside urged him to set himself free and allow himself the joy of killing Chuck. After all, it would all be over then, and he could get his company back, but Harold resisted. He reminded himself again and again that killing Chuck would only enrage Garcia, and he might not be able to stop until he killed everyone.

"Why don't we all relax?" Joshua asked. "If we can't be friends here in this Caribbean paradise, we should just forget about the deal and all go home."

Chuck turned his attention back to the other three and quickly replied, "Oh, no, that isn't necessary. After all, why let one bad apple spoil the bunch? I'll deal with Haidar. It's just that I was curious as to what it takes for Harold to jump into action, in a manner of speaking."

Darla replied, "Pray you never have to find out."

"Let's just get your boys in here to sweep the awning," Garcia said. "I have places I need to be."

Chuck stood up, walked out towards the beach, and hollered, "You two, double time. Everyone is ready to sign off, but we're waiting on you."

Nigel and Haidar came running up the trail from the beach. The entire group evacuated the tent. Chuck's men both thoroughly swept the tent with a wand device. Next, they did a quick sweep of Garcia, Darla, Harold, and Joshua. They walked over to Chuck, who stepped away from everyone as soon as he saw they were done.

After looking at the readings, he stepped up to Garcia. "So, tell me, chief, which one of your people is transmitting?"

Garcia glanced back at his group and then Chuck. "Nobody."

"Then why are we picking up a faint signal?"

Garcia's mouth went flat and curled down at the edges. "Oh, I think I know." He pulled out his cell phone. He had left it on. Turning to his team he asked, "Who forgot to turn their cell phone off?"

Everyone on the team reached in, shook their heads, and turned off their phones. Garcia turned back to Chuck. "My apologies. I'm afraid it's an old habit in today's world. We probably all destroyed our batteries looking for towers."

Chuck responded, "You'll get used to life on the seas. That's why I only carry a satellite phone in the boat. I never use those little toys."

"What do you do on shore?" asked Joshua.

"I use Nigel's phone if we're in a town."

"Let's walk over and sign the papers, shall we?" asked Garcia.

Chuck and the group headed back under the tent. Harold signed his name, and Chuck signed his.

Chuck dropped the cigar from between his teeth and ground it into the sand. Nigel handed him a fresh stogie. Chuck lit the end up and drew in a long breath. Smoke escaped over the group, and then he spit a piece of tobacco leaf out. A knowing smile spread across Chuck's lips. "I love a business deal coming together," he said before sticking his cigar back in his mouth.

Joshua glanced over at Harold, and both men looked towards the sand to avoid laughing at Chuck's uncanny ability to channel Hannibal Smith. Chuck and Nigel said their goodbyes and left for their boats. Harold noticed Haidar's reluctance as he got into Chuck's gunboat. Chuck had Haidar sit across from where he stood as he backed the boat away from the island. The two boats made one more sweep around the island and then faded into the distance.

Garcia let out a long breath and turned to the group. "Time to head back to the ship."

"Isn't it coming here?" asked Joshua.

"No. She's in a secured location, so we go to her. Let's get moving. Alice and her team will take care of things here. It's time to get your butts numb again."

The group climbed aboard the Kodiak for another bumpy ride back to the yacht. This time Harold sat near the back of the raft with Garcia. Joshua was given point. He bounced like a ping-pong ball on some of the mistimed swells. Harold climbed forward to sit next to his friend to help flatten the ride while Darla sat in the center of the craft. Although the bumps were steady, they had reduced their ferocity. Harold was thankful when he saw the *Sweet Revenge* gleaming in the afternoon sun and cruising towards their position.

Harold was surprised how sore his body felt as he climbed aboard the yacht. While Frank cranked the Kodiak up to its tie-down, Harold reached the main deck and offered Darla his hand. "Care to join me in the hot tub?" he asked. "I'm afraid my body isn't used to this kind of abuse."

"You're not the only one. I'll grab my suit and meet you topside. I think I may try out the elevator."

"I'm with you," said Harold.

Joshua topped the steps.

"Hey, Doc, want to join Darla and me at the hot tub?"

Joshua gave Harold a nod. "That's just what the doctor ordered."

Garcia followed Joshua.

"Frank," said Garcia. "Tell the captain to take us home."

"Yes, sir."

"Slow down you three. Good job out there, especially with that drama around Haidar."

Darla turned to Joshua. "I hadn't expected you to be so calm with a gun pointed your direction."

"It isn't the first time, and you forget, my friend here was at one time a very angry berserker. Believe me, I have learned to face my fears."

"What about you Harold?" asked Garcia.

Harold's voice was flat, "I don't fear much."

"Good, I want to catch up with you in a little while."

"Is there a problem?" Harold asked.

Garcia seemed to be lost in the ocean behind the group for a moment. "I want to think through everything that happened and then talk about improvements."

Harold looked over his shoulder as the three friends began to walk away. "You know where to find me."

***

Harold stretched out in the oval hot tub and enjoyed the solitude for a few moments. The sun was pushing towards the horizon in the west. He felt torn inside. He loved the ship and the Caribbean. He loved Darla and was happy Joshua came with them, but he could not shake the feeling he was failing. Would his father really take the steps he had taken? The company would have been bankrupt in a few months without this arrangement.

Harold heard footsteps and turned to see who was arriving. "Oh, hi, Doc."

"Well, I guess we know who you prefer," chided Joshua.

Harold looked confused. "What do you mean?"

Joshua dropped his towel on the steps leading up to the padded deck. "You helped Darla out of the boat but not your old doctor."

Harold laughed. "She does have better legs."

"I can't argue with that."

Harold sat up and made room for his friend to join him. Joshua let out a verbal gasp as he entered the hot water. "I hope you aren't too disappointed," said Joshua. "I asked Darla to give us a few minutes to talk before she came up."

Harold's head drooped. "It's about today. I know. I almost screwed up."

Joshua settled onto the bench and closed his eyes for a moment. "On the contrary, my friend, I was very impressed with your self-control. Given what you've been through, it wouldn't have been unreasonable for you to attack Haidar. Your level of self-control is admirable."

Harold turned on the air jets and let his palms glide over the bubbles for a few seconds. "You know, Doc. I wanted to take him out. His eyes remind me of John's."

Joshua looked confused. "I don't remember John having eyes like that."

"Not when he was alive. I mean now, in my dreams, or nightmares. He looks at me just like Haidar does. The death and hatred inside Haidar are very real. I wanted to kill him. I felt like if I killed him, I'd be killing John, and I wanted to do it. More than anything, I wanted to kill Haidar."

Joshua gave Harold's shoulder a quick squeeze. "But you didn't kill him, Harry. That's what you were saying no to, wasn't it? You were telling yourself not to kill him."

"I don't know, Doc. The voice in my head sounded like John. Was that him or me?"

Joshua looked Harold in the eye with a firm and confident stare. "Harry, John is dead, and he isn't coming back. Your mind was playing tricks on you to help you deal with a very stressful situation, but I promise you, that was not John."

Harold reached over and gave Joshua an awkward hug. "Okay, Doc. You know more about this stuff than I do."

"That's why you pay me the big bucks."

"Wait, I'm still paying you?" joked Harold.

Both men were busy laughing when Darla appeared in front of them. They stopped their jovial outburst and stupidly stared at her. Harold thought his eyes were bulging out of his head. He wasn't sure what part of Darla's swimsuit he was gawking at, but he wasn't in any hurry to stop.

Darla gave them a wink and ran her hands up and down beside her body. "If you boys are done admiring all of this, I'd like to get in there. My butt is killing me from that boat ride."

Harold and Joshua bumped into each other moving to the far side of the hot tub so Darla could walk up and step in.

Harold gave Joshua an annoyed glare. "Doc, do you mind?"

Joshua's face turned beet-red. "Excuse me, Harry. I didn't see you there."

"Somebody misses his wife," joked Darla.

Joshua's face glowed almost purple from embarrassment.

Darla tried but failed to stifle her laughter. "I'm sorry, Doctor. I wouldn't call my swimsuit modest. Sometimes a girl needs to be reassured that she still has it."

"You have all of it," Harold said.

"Easy, boy," responded Darla.

Frank showed up a few moments later with ice-cold rum runners. Harold lifted himself out of the hot water and sat on the edge of the pool with his legs still in the water. The hum of the water jets replaced the small talk and laughter as the adrenaline rush of the day wore away. Harold let himself get lost in the bubbling water at his knees and Darla's calves below the water's surface. He nearly knocked his empty glass into the water when someone touched his shoulder. Harold looked up to find Garcia standing over him.

Garcia's voice was serious, "Harold, I need to speak to you alone."

"I'm done here anyway," said Joshua.

Harold reached out and touched Joshua's shoulder. "No, Doc. Garcia and I can go to the bar below."

"Okay," said Joshua. "I'm still heading to my cabin. I'm quite exhausted."

Darla waved her hand to Harold. "I'll meet you in a little while. I'm not done boiling yet."

Harold followed Garcia to the deck below. The two men sat down on the shaded couch by the coffee table. Frank brought two large ice waters and left.

Garcia started first, "Okay, do you mind telling me what the little episode with the price negotiations was about?"

Harold reached over and took a long swallow of cool water. He wanted to make Garcia sweat. He knew Garcia was about to tell him that he was not in charge, but it was time to exert what little authority he had.

Harold put down his glass and looked into Garcia's sunglasses. "It's pretty simple. You were going to undercut the price of the weapons."

"So what?" Garcia tore his sunglasses off so fast they flew out of his hands and bounced off the couch cushion. "I'm in charge here. I thought we were clear about that."

Harold sipped the cold water and took his time returning the glass to the table. "Oh, I'm clear you're in charge of the operations."

"Good," Garcia said as he fished for his sunglasses.

"But you're not in charge of my business deals."

Garcia stopped looking for his glasses, and his eyes shot up to glare at Harold. "What the hell does that mean?"

He knew he had Garcia exactly where he needed him. "It's pretty simple, Agent Garcia. If I'm going to sign my name to any contract, I'm going to make sure we get the most money possible."

Garcia looked confused. "Have you lost your mind, Harold? This is the black market; those contracts don't mean anything if Chuck decides to back out."

Harold took another drink of water. He wanted to keep Garcia off balance. "Sure they do. My father taught me a lot of things while I was growing up. One of those lessons was that the federal government will never bear the brunt of a financial downturn. The first thing it does is cut contracts and promises with the private sector."

Garcia rolled his eyes. "That's not true."

"Really? Tell that to the late John Richmond. Your actions with JR Aerospace started this whole fiasco. Maybe you really don't see it, so I'm going to give you a quick summary. If you undercut our weapon prices, the operation will cost more than is budgeted because I'm sure your accountants have not factored in shortfalls. That's fine if we have something to show for our effort. But if anything goes wrong, our operation will be on the chopping block."

Garcia scowled. "You could have cost us the whole operation if Chuck wasn't willing to pay that price."

"This is why government bureaucrats should stay out of business. Chuck knew our price when we arrived at the island. He was hoping to talk you down, but Chuck had already made up his mind to pay our original price when he spent the money to come to the island."

Garcia snarled. "I'm no government lackey. I'm CIA."

Harold turned sideways and crossed his large arms before he spoke. "That's still not business. From now on, I negotiate prices, and you handle the spook and security side of things."

"Don't change the rules again without clearing it with me first," said Garcia flatly.

"Deal," said Harold, and he stuck out his hand to shake Garcia's.

Garcia looked at his hand, grabbed his glasses as he stood, and walked inside.

Harold grabbed his drink, put his feet up on the coffee table, leaned back, and smiled. Frank stood over at the bar. Harold raised his glass towards him and said loudly, "Now that's how Dad would have done it."

"Yes, sir," said Frank.

CHAPTER 17

Harold and the team stood at the back of the yacht and watched the small cabin cruiser from Salvation Key come alongside the ship. The crew members tied off the boat, and everyone prepared to climb aboard.

"Maria!" shouted Joshua as he waved.

Harold saw Maria standing at the back of the cruiser with her arms crossed and a firm look on her face.

Harold leaned down into Joshua's ear, and whispered, "Hey, Doc, I think somebody's in trouble."

"So it would seem," said Joshua.

"Do you need any help, Doc?"

"No thank you. I believe I should handle this one alone."

Darla, Garcia, and Harold wisely held back and let Joshua board the cabin cruiser first. Maria tapped her foot as Joshua made his way on board. As soon as his feet hit the deck, Maria ran up to him and put him in a bear hug. Joshua looked over at Harold and feigned an inability to breathe. Maria released Joshua, and the two of them shared a lengthy kiss.

Harold leaned over towards Darla. "I guess Doc's out of the woods."

"I wouldn't be so sure."

Harold was confused. "How can you tell?"

"A woman just knows."

The remaining three team members boarded the cabin cruiser, and the small ship headed towards Salvation Key. Harold turned back and watched the yacht head out towards Islamorada. The ship looked as beautiful from the outside as it did on board. He felt Darla's hand slide into his.

Her lips brushed his ear, and she whispered, "If you leave me for that stupid ship, I will break every bone in your body."

Harold turned and looked down into her eyes. "I had no idea you loved me so much."

Darla gave him a half-smile. "Who said anything about love? I just won't be humiliated by a chunk of steel and wood."

Garcia grouped everyone together on the back of the boat. "Tonight you're on your own. There's no planned meal and no debriefing. I will be busy this next week getting weapons in place for a meeting with Chuck. For the next five days, you all can enjoy some downtime and do whatever you want. If you'd like to leave the island and go to the Keys, let me know ahead of time. I'm certain Chuck is still in the area, and you will probably run into him somewhere in Key West if you aren't careful."

The small cabin cruiser pulled up to the dock. Frank barely had time to tie off the craft before Maria and Joshua hopped onto the wooden pier and started heading towards the complex. Harold chuckled.

"What's so funny?" asked Darla.

"You know," said Harold. "The two of them. It looks like Doc isn't the only one who missed his spouse."

Darla rolled her eyes. "You men. It's always one thing with you. She isn't taking him home for that. They need to talk."

"Oh, another woman's intuition thing?" asked Harold.

Garcia walked up and jumped in, "Nope, CIA. I could tell by their body language that there was a lot of tension on the ride home."

Harold started to feel worried. "Do you think they'll be okay?"

Darla put her arm around him. "They'll be fine, but don't be surprised if your most trusted companion leaves for a few days."

"Doc won't abandon me."

"Don't be so sure that. We've been talking. There's more than his wife on his mind. I'm trying to work something out that will accommodate everyone," Garcia said.

"Is it Bill?"

"Bill, Maria, you. The doctor seems to carry a lot on his shoulders. You'd think the man would know better than to worry so much. I suppose it's true that doctors make the worst patients. Anyway, whatever happens, we'll make the best of it."

Harold mumbled more to himself than to Darla or Garcia. "I'll do anything to help Doc."

Everyone else departed the boat. Garcia went to his cabin while Darla went to her room in the main house, and Harold went upstairs to his master bedroom.

Harold decided to sit down in the lounge chair on his sundeck rather than going inside and taking a nap. He awoke to the sun beginning to set and his stomach beginning to growl. Downstairs he found Frank cleaning up around the kitchen.

"Any chance you can make a weary traveler a quick cheese sandwich?" asked Harold.

"Not a problem, sir. I hope your trip was successful."

"It was indeed."

Frank came over after a few minutes with a beautiful griddled cheese sandwich framed with fresh ripe tomatoes drizzled with a homemade Italian dressing. After Frank left, Harold wandered out of the house and walked down the path to the narrow beach as he ate from the plate. He set the plate down in the sand and climbed up on the familiar rock near Darla's old hiding place and sat down.

Harold admired the perfectly calm waters and the orange sky as the sun made its way towards the sea. Below the rock, he could see various fish taking advantage of the shallows and the darkening waters. A few feet out, the water increased in depth to about eight feet. The grass-covered sandy bottom looked dark even though the water was perfectly clear. A disturbance on the water's surface startled him.

The whiskers and nostril of a manatee broke through the water's tension. Soon, its squinted eyes pointed in his direction. Within moments, three more broke the surface. The group stared at Harold, and he stared back at them. Their large bodies floated just below the surface of the calm waters. He felt a light touch on his shoulder and almost jumped off the rock in surprise.

The touch quickly tightened and held him in place. A familiar voice whispered in his ear, "Aren't they beautiful?" asked Darla.

Harold turned and whispered, "I don't know if I would call them beautiful. A curiosity and a bit awe-inspiring. I'm surprised they are so calm and curious."

Darla slipped in beside him. "Do you wish you could be like them?"

"Are you saying I should be a large sea creature that can float on the water with my fat?"

She smacked him on the shoulder. "You know what I meant. Do you ever wish you could be as docile as they are?"

"No. At the moment I was just wondering if they can actually see me."

Darla slid her arm around his waist and sat closer. She put her head on his shoulder, and they both watched as the manatees slowly slipped just beneath the surface and casually swam to the bottom to graze on the grasses.

"I doubt they saw anything since manatees are nearsighted," she said. "They were probably just checking what was on the surface and may have noticed your shape."

Harold tilted his head over against Darla's and enjoyed the presence of her company. They were both silent as they watched the sun sink below the surface of the waters and then slipped off the rock. Harold picked up his plate, and they walked hand-in-hand back to the compound. They passed by Maria and Joshua's home, and Harold noticed the lights were out. "I guess Doc was more tired than I thought."

"You really don't get relationships sometimes."

"What do you mean?"

She raised her eyebrow. "Did your parents ever argue and then make up?"

Harold felt a shiver through his body. "I never liked to think about that stuff with my parents. I don't think any kids do. But yea, after they argued, they would always take a nap."

Darla laughed and released her hand as she stopped and doubled over. He waited for her to finish. She lifted her right hand, grabbed his arm, and gasped for air as she tried to compose herself.

After a couple of deep breaths, she finally stood up. "I'm sorry, dear. That was very cute. Sometimes you do sound just like a little boy."

Harold grunted, gently took Darla's hand back into his, and the two continue to the main house. They gave each other a kiss goodnight and headed to their respective bedrooms.

***

The rays of the morning sun warmed Harold's cheek like a friendly kiss. He opened his eyes and was surprised to see his digital clock on the nightstand read nine o'clock. Harold had showered and was on his way out of his bedroom door when Darla met him at the top of the stairs.

"Come with me," she said, "and hurry."

"Why, what's wrong?"

Darla didn't say a word as she hurried down the steps, and Harold struggled to keep up. They rushed across the patio, through the house, and out to a waiting jeep. Darla jumped in and started the engine. Harold climbed into the other side. Before he had time to ask her where they were going, shells and sand sprayed out behind the vehicle's tires. He hung on to the windshield's steel frame and wondered if Chuck's men had found them. He glanced around the vehicle looking for a weapon but saw nothing.

Darla slid the vehicle to a stop at the airstrip. Harold looked over to see several bags being loaded into the Cessna Grand Caravan. Joshua and Maria were talking with Garcia.

Harold hopped out of the jeep and bounded over to the three. "What's going on, Doc?"

"It's Bill. Adam found out he attended Columbia Business School. We're both sure we can find him, and I need to be there when we do," said Joshua.

Darla walked up beside Harold and gave a quick jerk of her head. Garcia followed her back to the jeep.

"You couldn't come up and say goodbye first?"

Tears began to form in Maria's eyes and drops begin to roll down her cheeks. Her voice cracked as she spoke, "I'm so sorry, Harold. Joshua thinks Bill could be in danger because of his hypnotherapy as a child. I asked Darla to go and get you."

Joshua interjected, "I need to see him as soon as possible. I also need my notes concerning Bill's treatment. The papers are in North Carolina, and Adam says he isn't sure which of the hundreds of boxes in the attic belong to me. I need to find those notes as well as your half-brother."

He reached over and took Harold's large hands into his, "We don't know when we're coming back."

"Is there something else going on?" asked Harold.

"Maria and I need time alone for our marriage. We came together during the tragedy of your parents' deaths. Maria was nearly killed; we went on our honeymoon and then came here. Our relationship needs some quiet time to develop. So far, our marriage has gone from one crisis to the next, and neither of us is sure we can continue as a couple at this pace. North Carolina is still my first home. Adam promised me that he would make sure Maria and I have some time together to just be a couple."

"I don't understand, Doc. How is that going to happen if you are chasing after Bill?"

"Adam is going to hold me accountable to focus on my marriage as much as my work. You've talked to Adam. He can be very persuasive."

Harold looked at Joshua and then Maria. "Yea, he's a good guy. I know you two will be in good hands."

Maria rushed over and put her arms around Harold. She laid her head on his chest and began to weep. All three held each other. To Harold, it felt like he was losing his family all over again.

The three released each other, and Joshua pulled out a handkerchief from his back pocket, dried his face, and returned the white piece of cloth. He stuck out his hand to Harold. "Until I return."

Harold shook his hand. "Come back soon, Doc. Without you and Maria, all I have left is Darla."

Joshua winked and said, "Don't do anything I wouldn't do."

Harold grimaced. "Doc, please, you're like my dad or uncle or something. Don't even joke like that."

Maria gave Harold a goodbye hug. "I will make sure Joshua comes back."

Harold looked down into her kind dark eyes. "You better, and keep him out of trouble."

Maria grabbed Joshua's hand. "Always."

She turned towards Joshua, and they both boarded the Cessna. Frank closed the door, and the pilot revved up the prop. Maria and Joshua waved from the windows as the small airplane made a quick turn to the runway and took off in under two minutes.

Darla walked up from the jeep and took Harold's arm and large hand. "We have a few days before we drop off the guns. What should we do to kill time?"

Harold looked down and saw Darla give him a sly smile and a wink.

Harold thought for a moment "I think we should go fishing."

Darla's mouth dropped open in surprise. "Fishing? Is that a euphemism?"

"No. Look, Mom and Dad loved each other very much. They always talked about how they had waited to, you know…get close, until their marriage. I know right now our decision seems old-fashioned, but my parents said they never regretted waiting. On the other hand, I had more than a few college friends who regretted not waiting. I want to be with you more than anything right now, but not because of this, and not like this."

Darla put her arms around him, kissed his shirt against his chest, and snuggled her head against his heart. "Harold Brown, you are the most romantic man I've ever known."

Harold stroked her soft hair. If he didn't change the subject soon, he might change his mind about waiting. Harold was relieved to hear Garcia's voice.

"Hey, you two, are you going to be okay meeting Chuck in a few days? Harold, you're not technically CIA, but we have rules about dating agents for a reason. I knew you two were a couple when I brought Darla back on, but then I had Joshua and Maria to divert your attention. Now that they're gone for a while, I need to know you won't do something stupid if you think Darla might be in trouble."

Darla let go of Harold. "Excuse me. I can take care of myself, thank you."

"I second that," Harold said, "and I take exception to your implications. Darla isn't some damsel in distress. I imagine if something goes wrong, she'll be the one protecting me."

"Uh-huh. Joshua told me something to that effect. I'm taking him and you at your word."

"We're all adults here. You don't have anything to worry about."

Frank cranked up the jeep behind Garcia, and he turned on his heel and hollered, "Frank, wait for me. I need a ride back!"

"So," said Harold, "about that fishing. Are you game?"

"I'm sorry, dear, I find bobbing in the ocean to catch large smelly sea creatures less fun than other ventures."

"What sounds fun to you?" asked Harold.

"Snorkeling comes to mind."

Harold remembered the fun he had scuba diving out in the Pacific. He also remembered a great white shark stumbling upon his dad and him one afternoon. The fifteen-foot shark circled above them for a short time and then went on its way. He and his dad got back to the small craft as quickly as they could swim. It was months before either of them ventured far beyond the Pacific shores.

"Any sharks around here?" asked Harold.

Darla reached up and stroked his broad shoulders. "Nurse and bull. Maybe some others out in deeper waters but nothing a big strong man like you can't handle."

Harold kissed her on the forehead. "Maybe we can snorkel some other time. I prefer to catch my fish inside a boat rather than have them catch me in the water."

Darla ran her fingers up and down his arm as she seemed to stare into nothing. She finally looked up into his eyes, "If you need me to come with you, I can. I'm here for you, but messing with fish guts and scales are not my idea of a good time."

"I can't argue with that. To be honest, I think some time alone would do me good. I need to process Doc, Maria, and Bill."

"What about me?"

"Are you leaving too?"

"Not unless you give me a reason."

Harold bent down and gave Darla a long kiss. "Not if I can help it. What are you going to do while I'm not around here to ogle at you all morning?"

Darla's lips curved upward, and she gave Harold a knowing wink. "I guess I'll just have to lie around the island and talk with Frank."

"Which one?" asked Harold.

"The cute one."

Harold rolled his eyes. "I guess I haven't met him yet."

"Hmm…" Darla swept her hair back over her shoulder and turned to stroll to the jeep. "Toodles," she hollered with a wave of her fingers and then cranked up the jeep, spun the vehicle around 180 degrees, and sped off to the compound.

Harold spoke to himself, "I guess I'm walking to the dock." He made the short hike to the boat dock. By the time he reached the fishing boat, his body was reminding him that he hadn't had any breakfast. Harold stuck his head inside the small dock shack to find Frank working on some paperwork on his laptop.

"Hey, Frank. I was planning on taking the boat out. Is she ready to go?"

Frank spun with a pistol in his hand at the sound of Harold's voice. "Sorry, I didn't hear you walk up. She's all gassed up. I just finished giving her the once-over yesterday after you returned."

Harold blinked for a moment. "I'll be sure and knock next time. I hate to be a bother, but things over at the house were pretty hectic this morning, and I didn't get any breakfast. Do you have any spare coffee?"

"Yea, I heard about Doctor Zeev leaving."

"How did you hear that already?" asked Harold.

Frank snapped the holster shut around his gun. "It's a small island. The pilot told us last night about his plans."

"Something wrong?" asked Frank.

"I'm just wondering why I'm the last to know about Doc," mumbled Harold.

"Oh, I wouldn't take it personally. We were all told not to discuss the topic near you. Garcia said it was a personal matter between you and Dr. Zeev. I hope he wasn't mistaken."

Harold shook his head. "No, he's right. It's personal. Anyway, how about that coffee?"

"I'll do you one better," said Frank. He pulled out a box of donuts from a shelf underneath the desk in front of him. He then pointed to the coffeemaker sitting on the shelf on the opposite wall. "Coffee is fresh. I'm full, and there are half a dozen donuts in here, all yours. Insulated mugs and a thermos are in the cabinet above the coffeemaker."

"Thanks. You just improved my morning."

"Glad I could help."

Harold gathered his quarry and boarded the fishing cruiser. Frank helped load the fishing gear as Harold got his much-needed food settled into the cabin. After a quick check of the GPS and sonar, he was ready to go. Frank hopped off, untied the craft, and tossed the rope on board. Harold quickly stowed the rope, climbed up the ladder to the bridge, and headed out into the calm gulf waters.

CHAPTER 18

The glassy waters parted before the small craft and then fanned out into ripples behind it. Harold stopped the fishing boat near a reef a few miles from their key. Looking back to where he came from, he only saw a barely perceivable spot on an endless sea of water that glistened in the morning sunlight. The warm air was calm and slightly humid.

After dropping anchor, he grabbed the remaining two doughnuts and what was left of his coffee before sitting on a bench at the rear of the boat. Harold found the quiet waters and the still air a bit unnerving. It was very different from the cold Pacific that he grew up with. He was used to having some sort of background noise emanating from the coast. It wasn't until this moment that his loneliness completely enveloped him. Suddenly, the reality of losing his parents, and that Joshua was really gone, hit him with brute force. Harold broke down and wept bitterly.

The hatred he had kept buried for John and his team poured out in a wave of grief from behind his tears. Shortly behind the anger came the regret of killing John with his bare hands. He hated the fact that he had not just killed a man but that he had enjoyed it.

Harold trembled in fear at the idea that there was a part of himself that had no regret for killing John.

He tossed the donuts and mug to the other side of the boat, crying and wailing until tears soaked the front of his shirt. The more he allowed himself to weep, the better he felt. After a while, grief gave way to exhaustion. Harold lay down and stretched his body out across the bench seat.

He closed his eyes, and the warmth of the sun and the mild air wrapped around his body. Although he had been nominal in his faith for many years, he felt as if God was wrapping around his body and holding him. He prayed the feeling would never leave him. Before long, Harold drifted off to sleep.

His body hit the deck of the ship with a thud, and a dull pain spread across his chest. He groggily opened his eyes. The light of the sun blinded him, and he raised his arm to guard his eyes, but then a shadow took the place of the light. His ribs felt like he'd been kicked by a mule. He moaned and rolled over on his back. As he got his bearings, he saw the silhouette of a man standing over him. Startled, Harold hastened to his feet. Looking down, he saw John's dead eyes staring up into his.

"Good morning, brat," John said with a crooked smile.

Harold wasn't sure, but it looked as if John's teeth had started to rot.

"John, what are you doing here?" Harold asked as he rubbed his arms and chest to remove the aching from the fall. "Don't tell me this is another dream."

"Does it feel like a dream?" John's face remained twisted in a macabre grin.

Harold grimaced as he attempted to take a cleansing breath to wake up. He was sore, tired, and annoyed. "What do you want?"

John went over and sat down on the bench. Harold noticed the open wound where the gun had been embedded flowed with a steady stream of blood. His clothes had a trail of rust and red that ran from his collar down to his chest. As he sat on the bench, a pool of blood began to form.

John's perverted smile finally disappeared. "I've missed this boat. I had a lot of good memories on this thing. Darla really likes a boat that rocks, if you know what I mean." John finished his statement with an exaggerated wink.

Harold's large hands quickly formed into fists, and his knuckles turned white and began to pop. "You better have a reason for being here."

"Or what? You stupid brat. You killed me. It's game over. You can't do anything to me, but I can ruin your days for the rest of your life."

"I refuse to listen to you," growled Harold.

John let out a sigh in faux disappointment. "You kids are so impatient. I only came by for a friendly chat. Joshua has flown the coop, and here you are all alone. I thought you could use some company."

"I don't need your kind of company."

John's horrid smile returned. "I would say we need to bury the hatchet, but, well, you know."

Harold unclenched his fist. "I don't know why you hate my family so much. I don't know what kind of man reaches out from the dead to give the only surviving member grief, and I don't know how, but one day I'm going to be rid of you."

230

"Brat, I wish you would, but I think you'll just keep on feeding the hate I've planted."

Harold's fists clenched and then released once more. "What is that supposed to mean?"

"It means I know how to press your buttons. I will destroy you. That is if Haidar or Chuck doesn't kill you first."

Harold could feel his annoyance turning to rage as John crossed his legs and leaned back against the portside wall. His top leg lazily swung up and down. His macabre smile stiffened Harold's back. He had seen enough of his dead enemy. "Get out of here. In Jesus' name, go away."

John started to laugh, and his cackling shot through Harold's body like ice. "What? Did you learn that in Sunday school or maybe on TV? That's not how this works. You really are as stupid as your old man." John's dead black eyes looked up towards the sun as if he was thinking. "I tell you, I really wish I could have been there." He looked back at Harold with his empty stare. "You know, to see when your dad killed himself. Tell me, what was it like?"

The rush began inside his body. It felt as though electricity was shocking every muscle. Harold replied in an unusually deep, foreboding voice, "Don't say another word."

John's laughter echoed over the still water, and then his voice seemed to bounce around inside Harold's brain. "Oh, is daddy's little boy going to go berserk? Oh my, get the doctor… Oh, wait, you can't. You know, brat, your old man was weak. He couldn't even take a little extortion. He's nothing like Darla. That woman loves a good spanking. Put her against a wall, and she really comes through for you, but your old man, he couldn't handle a little abuse. Tell me, what was his expression when he pulled the trigger? You were there, you lucky jerk. I wish I could have seen that sadness and fear on his face. Oh, boohoo, I can't do anything, so I'll blow my head off in front of my son. What a pathetic loser."

Harold's world turned red. Shapes blurred to become outlines, but Harold's mind knew exactly what each outline was. He could see John's silhouette sitting on the bench. Harold was going to end this nightmare once and for all. A feeling of joy and warmth crept through his soul as he reached for the ladder leading to the upstairs bridge. Metal screamed, and fiberglass exploded as he pulled the ladder free of its moorings. The screws slowly flew through the red sky before his eyes. Some of the maroon projectiles seemed to fly right through John.

Harold raised the steel remains of the ladder over his head. One handrail pointed crookedly towards the sky, and the remaining pieces hung on in a vain attempt to keep its identity. He spun the pole over his head and gave it a snap. Every loose piece broke free of the handrail in his hand with a cacophony of pops and metallic squawks. Despite his best efforts, John's wobbly red silhouette seemed unfazed. John's cackle filled Harold's ears and echoed inside his head. With a roar that reverberated through the boat under his feet, Harold swung his newly created metal club with all his might. He watched as the auburn pole split through the figure that should have been John.

In his berserker rage, Harold found himself carried forward by his momentum. His body passed through John and over the edge of the ship's rail, and then all went black.

Water began to fill Harold's lungs. His eyes shot open, and he found himself looking down towards the reef a few feet below. Instinctively, he moved his body vertically, and his mouth took in a mixture of saltwater and air as he broke the surface. He coughed and sputtered to clear his airways. Looking up, he found himself off the starboard side of the ship. He was sure he had been fighting John on the port side, and when he glanced towards the cabin cruiser, he saw the ladder to the open air bridge destroyed. Harold's body felt tired and heavy as he floated there for a moment. Gradually, he made his way towards the aft of the boat with slow gentle strokes. He watched the boat and waited as he moved. Was he still dreaming? Was John still there?

Harold felt something brush the bottom of his foot. A shadow larger than himself swam beneath and away. A twinge of fear shot through him. "Shark," he whispered to himself.

He turned over on his stomach and swam freestyle towards the boat with all his remaining strength. Harold beached himself like a seal onto the diving deck at the back of the small craft. After he pulled his legs in, he attempted to slow his breathing. A gray dorsal fin broke the surface and then dropped back down under the ripples as a seven-foot shark crossed sideways beneath the dive deck. A second shark, even larger, also crossed beneath the dive deck and ship. Harold had had enough of the curious fish. He grabbed hold of the step ladder and forced himself back inside the boat. He lay there for a moment on the deck, facing the sun and thanking God he was safe. Then he remembered John, and a sense of déjà vu hit. Harold leaped to his feet. It was just a nightmare, but he had to be sure it was over.

He hurried into the cabin, but there was no sign that anyone had been on board other than himself. After heading forward and below to the only berth, he confirmed he was alone on the boat. Harold came back up the steps and sat inside the cabin. He was sticky and a little cold in his wet clothes. He needed to return and get cleaned up and dried off.

Harold stood and stepped back out to the aft deck but then stopped himself. A few screws and scraps of metal pipes littered the deck floor. The missing ladder and damaged fiberglass reminded him that scraps of chrome and metal now sat at the shallow bottom of the sea. He attempted to reorient himself and spoke to the calm sea as he went to weigh anchor. "I have no idea what I'm going to tell Garcia about his boat. How can I even explain this to Darla?"

Harold went into the cabin and sat down at the small pilot section inside the fishing boat and started the motors. He decided to take his time getting back while he tried to think of a good explanation. Saltwater saturated clothes stuck to his cold, wet skin and the vinyl seat as he slowly slipped the ship into the small cove and next to the dock. Although he had turned a thirty-minute boat ride into a sixty-minute cruise, the island had come into view far too soon. Part of him cursed himself for not killing more time, but the other half just wanted off the boat and away from the remnants of his nightmarish fit. Harold maneuvered the boat to the dock and Frank helped him quickly tie off the craft.

Frank hollered to him as he was ducking back inside the cabin to grab the coffee mug he had retrieved from the deck on the way home. "Where's the ladder?"

Harold cringed and took his time getting the mug. He needed to stick to the story just as he planned. Emerging from the cabin, he found Darla standing next to Frank.

"Well?" asked Darla. "What happened out there?"

"You wouldn't believe me if I told you," responded Harold as he hopped from the boat to the wooden pier.

"Try me," Darla and Frank said in unison.

Harold had not anticipated Darla showing up before he had a chance to talk with Frank. He had hoped to convince Frank of his ruse and then Frank could have cleaned up the boat before anyone else saw it. Instead, he was cornered and outnumbered, but he would stick to his plan.

"A shark," he said with a straight face.

Darla crossed her arms. "Do you mean to tell us a shark jumped into the boat, tore the ladder from the wall, and then jumped back into the water?"

Harold needed to think of a response. The dull ache across his chest gave him an idea. He lifted his shirt. To his surprise, he found three bruises across his chest. He needed to stay focused on his story. "See? I got these when I was pulled over the side of the boat."

Harold could tell by the surprised look on Darla and Frank that they were buying part of his story, but then Darla scowled. "Wait, you really wrestled a shark? Where is it?"

Harold shook his head. "No, I never said that. I had him on the line. He nearly pulled me in twice, and I fell on the deck once. The second time he took me off my feet, I grabbed the ladder."

"Hold on a minute," Frank said. "That ladder is very stout. It should have held your weight without any issue."

"I was pretty upset by that point," quipped Harold, and he walked past the two inquisitors in hopes of getting them away from the boat.

"Stop right there," said Darla.

Harold stopped and turned around.

"Yea," followed up Frank. He looked over at the boat again. "Those screws were ripped out pretty violently. What gives?"

Darla responded before Harold could speak. "Don't worry about it, Frank. Harold's a big guy. With enough adrenaline, he could have ripped the ladder off. My question is why? Frank's right. If you were just falling, the ladder should have held."

Harold's eyes darted to the right towards the treetops and back to Darla and Frank as he attempted to come up with a good answer. "Well, the truth be told, the shark was pretty large. I would guess at least twelve feet. When I got him close to the boat, he started ramming the side."

"It's solid fiberglass," Frank said. "He couldn't sink that boat if he was twenty feet long."

"Yea, well, I'm afraid of sharks," answered Harold truthfully. "I guess my adrenaline was pumping pretty good because I grabbed the ladder and tried to yank off one of the side poles to use it as a club. The whole thing came off instead. I started swinging at the fish until it left."

Darla and Frank looked at each other with eyebrows raised. "Should you ask or should I?" said Darla.

"Ladies first," responded Frank.

"So, Harry, why are you wet?"

Harold knew he was in trouble. Darla never used his childhood name unless she was teasing him or very angry. He guessed this was not an affectionate moment.

"I fell in while I was swinging at him."

"I thought you were pulled over."

Harold cleared his throat. "Yea, well, I was trying to avoid the part about the ladder."

Frank interjected, "I still want to know how you did that."

"Don't worry about it," responded Darla and Harold together.

"Look, honey, you know I'm not fond of sharks. Things just got out of hand."

"Uh-huh. That must have been terrifying. Being in the water with an angry shark you've been hitting with a boat ladder."

Darla's glare was almost too much for him. He wanted to tell her the truth, but not with Frank standing there. Besides, he was in too deep now to stop. If he tried to step away with Darla, Frank would go straight to Garcia, and Garcia would go straight to Joshua before his plane barely had time to touch down in North Carolina. Besides, Darla would understand later.

"Oh, it swam away at some point. I guess I was so scared and agitated I didn't notice and just kept swinging at the water until I fell overboard."

Harold watched Frank board the craft and inspect the torn wall where the ladder once stood. He looked around the deck and gathered what few screws he could find, along with a cross piece still sitting in the aft starboard corner.

"One second," said Frank as he stepped back over on the pier. "I have one more question. What fishing pole did you use?"

Harold responded quickly, "The one you gave me."

"Huh?" said Frank.

"What's wrong?" asked Darla.

"Well, it's sitting in its stand with full tackle. Based on your story, I would have expected the line to break. Otherwise, the shark couldn't have gotten away."

"It did," said Harold. "I reset the line. I've gone fishing before. I know how to set up the tackle."

Frank scowled and mumbled loud enough for Harold to hear as he began walking towards the shack. "Those are my knots. What the heck happened out there?"

Harold looked back at Darla. She dropped her arms to her sides and a smile crossed her face, but it made Harold feel cold inside instead of the warmth he was used to experiencing. She strolled up to Harold until she was inches away. The coconut oil in her sunscreen made Harold wish the setting was different. He felt Darla's fingernails slowly glide up the outside of his arms. A thrill shot through his body. She put her hands behind his neck and pulled him down, so she could whisper in his ear.

"I don't know why you are lying to me, but I would suggest you tell me the truth when you're ready. I'll never be with a man I can't trust."

Harold's breath slowed and deepened as he felt Darla gently blowing against his eardrum and her lips gliding across his ear. Her hands released his neck. By the time he had recovered his senses, she had already cleared the pier and was moving at a quick pace past the boat shack. Harold stood up and took in a deep breath, trying to decide what to do.

"Hey," yelled Frank from the boat shack.

How long has he been watching me stand here?

"Are you going to stand there all day like an oaf? If I were you, I'd go after her."

Harold wanted to go to Darla and tell her the truth, but he could not make his feet move. He hoped Darla would not run to Joshua without all the facts, but he knew if he told her what really happened, she would call him immediately. He would not be the cause of marital strife between Joshua and Maria or hinder Joshua's search for his half-brother. Besides, the whole affair was not just about the people closest to him. If Garcia got wind of this, he could shut down the whole project. Workers could lose their jobs and families' lives would be turned upside down. John would win.

CHAPTER 19

It had been a long week, and Harold was thankful to be back aboard the *Sweet Revenge*. Darla had not spoken to him, except during their meetings with Garcia. He had attempted once to explain his actions at the pier, but she cut him off. "Tell me the truth or don't tell me anything," were the last words she had said to him when they were alone.

Harold looked at the moon's reflection on the glassy water. He knew the morning would bring another encounter with Chuck and his crew. He wished Darla could forgive him before they walked into the weapons demonstration.

Harold closed his eyes and tried to relax. After a while, he felt a tap on his shoulder. He scowled. "Leave me alone, John."

"Well," said Darla, "I guess the coconut oil isn't doing it for you now, huh?"

Harold jumped and opened his eyes, sending a wave of water over the hot tub. He spun his body around to find Darla standing over him with her bathing suit on. Her flawless skin seemed to give off a bronze glow in the moonlight, like an angel.

"Oh, I didn't hear you," said Harold. "Unfortunately, all I'm able to smell is the hot tub."

Darla slid down into the water next to him without saying a word. She leaned in and gave Harold one of the most passionate kisses he had ever experienced. Euphoria, excitement, and then confusion rushed through him.

She released her lips, and hopeful words poured from his mouth. "I'm sorry... Does this mean we're okay again?"

Darla's forehead crinkled, and she shook her head. "You men are all the same. That kiss is to tell you I forgive you for lying to me. That doesn't mean everything is okay, but I wanted to bury the hatchet before we meet with Chuck tomorrow."

"I'm so sorry, honey. It isn't that I don't trust you. It's more about my fear of your response. I just wish you could see inside my heart. It would all make sense."

Darla opened her mouth and then closed it. Harold waited, knowing better than to force a response from her.

She finally began again. "Darling, I want to see inside your heart, but you're hiding it from me. You're just lucky that I'm a good intelligence agent."

"Why is that?"

Darla reached under the water and pulled his hand up. She played with his large fingers as she spoke. "You called me John when I tapped you on the shoulder."

Harold had hoped she hadn't heard the name over the roar of the water jets. Darla lowered his hand back into the water and then took his chin and focused his face on her own. "I think I know what happened on the boat now. I'm not going to ask you if I'm right because I know you don't feel like you can tell me. I just want you to know that our hearts are not that different. Just promise me you will trust me when the time comes, and you finally want to talk to somebody."

Harold saw a look of sadness he hadn't noticed before. Pushing past the sadness, he could see her love for him behind her eyes, and it brought hope to his heart. All the coldness over the last few days had disappeared. Yet, for all the dancing her pupils did, somewhere deep inside her was an aching he had never noticed. Harold nearly cried as he felt her hidden pain push into his heart.

He worked to keep his composure. "I promise. I will always come to you," was all he could manage to get out.

Darla released his chin, turned, and rested her head on his shoulder. She sat there and rubbed his chest. "We're going be okay, dear. I promise."

Harold rested his cheek against her head. The two of them sat there and stared out at the moon on the water. Neither had noticed the water jets had long since cut off.

***

The glowing orange sun crested over the edge of the calm waters, reflecting fiery light off the mirrored Caribbean Sea. Harold sat locked in his office with his satellite phone on his desk near his steaming cup of coffee.

He gazed out the window at the beautiful morning. Harold believed that such beauty existed for a reason.

There was something about the dawn that made everything feel fresh. Maybe it was a reminder that there is a beginning and an end. Maybe it was to point mankind towards the beauty and awe in the world instead of the evil. Whatever the reason, it gave him hope.

Harold took a deep breath. It was early in California. He hated being awakened at three in the morning, and he was sure Tom was going to feel the same. He picked up the phone and hit the call button.

Tom's voice broke through on the second ring. "You must be psychic. How did you know I'm awake?"

"Sorry?" said Harold. "I was afraid I'd be waking you up. We have the weapons demo today, and I wanted to chat, you know, in case things go wrong out here."

"You won't believe this," said Tom, "but I was staring at the phone hoping you'd call. I have some news to tell you. I've looked at our problem from several directions, and I even managed to get the board together at the house to talk about it since I know where all the bugs are hidden here."

"How do you know that?"

"When the police returned your dad's belongings he had a device to detect hidden transmitters. We deal in nukes, remember?"

"Those seem like a distant memory these days."

Tom cleared his throat. "Yea, well, your dad was a careful man. So, when the agents went to hang out at Joshua's I swept through the house and was surprised to only find a couple bugs. One was in the old office phone, and there is one in the kitchen. I think the agents really are focused more on external threats than anything I'd be doing. Anyway, we met in a secure location here."

"What about the agents?"

Tom's voice was confident as he responded, "Oh, I told them we were getting together for a celebration of life party to remember your dad and we wanted privacy. They complied immediately. There were three Franks on an old wooden porch over at Joshua's place during our event. I had the board bring their swim trunks, and we actually met in the pool. You wouldn't believe what some of these people look like in swimsuits."

"I'd rather not think about it."

Tom chuckled. "Yea, you owe me." But then his voice turned serious. "I wish I could say it was good news. We have a solution, but you won't like it."

"Anything has to be better than where we are now. One slipup and I feel certain Garcia will leave us flapping in the wind. If we hope to survive this, we need to find a way out," said Harold.

"Maybe. The only way for the company to survive outside of our current game plan is to merge with JR Aerospace and Guilford Defense systems."

"So, John wins," growled Harold.

"Hold on a minute before you throw the phone into the ocean. I wouldn't say John wins. First, he's dead. Second, PDS would absorb the other two companies."

Harold silently focused on the rising sun and tried to relax.

After several seconds, Tom's voice broke in, "Are you still there?"

"Yea, I'm just trying to stay focused. How is this going to work? Are there enough contracts? And what about layoffs? How many people would we have to lose?"

"Believe it or not, we'd have to hire some people. Both JR and GDS lost a lot of employees due to the fallout of John's conspiracy. And as you know, we've had our fair share of walkouts as well."

Harold tapped the edge of his seat and said, "Okay, so let's say combining the companies is a good business move. We still have a huge problem named Garcia. Any move to do this will trigger meetings and reports to the FTC, the DOD, several congressional committees, and who knows how many other acronyms. Garcia is likely to kill it off before it gets started."

"Well, we thought about that as well, and you're right. He could. However, we don't think he will. The numbers are solid for the merger. If you removed the CIA contract, we only have a few months left. John's company is in the same boat. Jerry's company came out better because he provided state's evidence, and as part of the plea deal, took the brunt of the punishment for his company. However, a lot of good people have left. They still aren't getting a lot of new work as the DOD sees them as a high risk. So, all three companies are shy of manpower and long-term sources of income. If our companies close, it would be a big hit to the area economically. That isn't real popular with the politicians in Sacramento or our locals in DC. Garcia would have a hard time fighting this much public fallout without somebody leaking what's been going on."

Harold let out a sigh. Tom had always been a good salesman and an encourager. It all sounded doable. That was what worried Harold. "What's to stop Garcia from pulling the newly formed company into this mess or even stopping the DOD contracts from coming our way after the merger?"

Tom's voice sounded strained, "Here comes the part you may not be so thrilled about."

Harold paused and took a sip of his coffee. He was unsure he wanted to know whatever was left. He responded slowly, "Go ahead. I need to hear it all."

He could hear Tom take a deep breath and let it out slowly before speaking. "Well, there's a good chance you'll have to step down as chairman."

"Never," interrupted Harold. "This is Dad's company. If I step down, then I've failed. It's no longer his company."

Tom's voice was calm and steady as he continued, "Harold, your father is gone. His legacy isn't you working at Parabolic Defense Systems; it's the company's survival, and that's what I'm trying to help you accomplish."

Harold's voice rose in frustration, "Survival! Who's surviving, Tom? You're telling me people are leaving. Now you want to get rid of me too? What about the other companies? Are you planning on putting one of those executives in my place? We don't know what those people knew. You could be handing Dad's company right into John's hands! Besides, how do you know what Dad wanted?"

"Harold," Tom responded quietly, "both your dad and John are dead. The board isn't handing over anything to anyone. Our board will take over the new company. I may or may not stay on as CEO. If they do replace me, it will be with Abigail."

"Who's replacing me?" Harold snarled.

Tom's voice attempted to sound upbeat, but Harold could hear the strain, "The board is of the same mindset as you. Promoting somebody from within the newly formed company could land someone who secretly agreed with John into a powerful position. Our plan is to go outside the company. This is California. We have a plethora of technology, aerospace, and defense talent to choose from."

Harold was unable to hide the shock in his voice, "So, I'm replaceable then?"

"No, come on, man, give me a break here. You've been like a brother to me. I'm not saying that about you, but you know the drill. Everybody is replaceable. If that wasn't true, no company could continue once its founder died or retired. Besides, this is worst case."

Harold stood up and leaned against the window on the other side of the small office. "So then what, we tell Garcia it's over?"

"It's not like we can just call him and tell him to pack it up," Tom said. "We have a contract. Our plan is to renegotiate that contract during the merger. As you know, that's not an abnormal business practice during a merger."

Harold looked across the small room, shielding his eyes from the sun's full fury now shining across the water. "Keep talking."

Tom continued, "We'll agree to finish the project with Chuck. Garcia has told me Chuck and Nigel are selling our guns to three terror training camps. He wants to give Chuck three shipments of GPS-configured weapons to ensure they can tag all the training camps, and if they are lucky, maybe even their headquarters. The plan is to use drones and cruise missiles to take out those locations. Garcia is hoping Chuck and Nigel will be in Africa at one of the camps during the attack. If they are both there, Garcia plans on targeting them as well. We'll see that through, but then the contract is ended."

Harold leaned against his desk. He reached down and ran his fingers across the bloodstains on the desk. His voice was barely audible, "Is this really the only way, Tom?"

Tom's replied in a soothing voice, "Believe me, my friend, we looked at every angle in our brainstorming pool party. Everyone went away to pursue their idea. In the end, this is the only idea that would save PDS, and make us fiscally healthy again without Garcia, and even then, there are still some concerns. Garcia could go for broke and report this whole plan to a closed session of the intel committees, but he would only do that if he felt betrayed. We're hoping that pulling him into our offer as we rewrite the contracts will be enough to appease him."

"What if he wants more?" asked Harold.

"Well, we'll cross that bridge when we come to it. Whatever we negotiate, we'll let him know none of us will be joining him in the field any longer. Garcia's a creative guy. I'm sure he'll come up with another story for his next target."

Harold stopped tracing the bloodstains and stared out the window. "When can you start?"

"We already have."

Harold's free hand clenched into a large fist, and he began knocking on the top of the desk. His voice strained to maintain his composure, "What do you mean?"

"Don't get upset. It's just paperwork. I asked Abigail to start filling out the proposals for the other two companies and begin putting the paperwork together for the FTC, etc."

"So, you assumed I'd agree?"

"Harold, you're my friend. You're the most standup guy I know. I knew you'd understand."

A question popped into Harold's mind. "You're forgetting something. What about the investigation? Why would the DOD approve the merger of two defense companies under investigation?"

"Well, here's a bit of good news. The company has been cleared, but they are still looking into your dad. Even though he's gone, the estate could still be held liable for any civil fines if the investigation finds any wrongdoing on your father's part."

"That's a waste of time. Dad always kept things legal."

"I know. John's company didn't come out so well, and it's hanging by a thread. The board has been replaced, and they have a temporary CEO. The new guy had been a middle manager in the company. The investigators leaked to me that anyone who may have been complicit at JR has quit or retired. In any case, a lot of senior leadership suddenly left California, and in some cases, the country."

"So, you're sure we aren't merging someone into our company that's holding a secret grudge?"

"Believe me, Abigail and I went over this with a fine-tooth comb. This is our best bet, and we have you to thank. The board got in bed with black box contracts and threw you into danger. Everyone here feels like you're the one that was thrown under the bus, and they want to make things right. It's because of you that we came up with an alternative, and it will save the company's soul as well as our finances."

Harold released his fist and bowed his head. His voice cracked as he whispered into the phone, "Tom, I know you're right, but I feel like a failure. Dad trusted me to save his company and his reputation. Look at where we are. Dad's reputation is still being investigated, Parabolic as he knew it is gone, and I may not have any control over the company when this is over."

"You still own the majority shares of stock," Tom reminded Harold.

"That may be, but all I can do is dump them if I don't like what they're doing. Thanks to Dad's foresight, I can't replace the leadership."

Tom cleared his throat. "Harold, listen to me as a friend for a minute. You've been amazing through all of this. Your dad never acted as a lord over his family or the company. He built a solid corporation that helps protect the country he loved and provides good paying jobs for its employees. You're continuing that vision. In a way, you're expanding it. The employees from JR and Guildford didn't have good leaders, and now they will."

Harold plopped down in his chair, and it groaned to hold him. "But that's just it, Tom. What if the board replaces us with people who aren't good leaders? What if the worst case happens?"

Tom's voice was soothing but stern, "I think Abigail will make a great leader, and the rest of the board will hire the right person as chairman. Besides, you still have a say in those votes."

He was out of excuses. "You're right. I guess the idea of possibly letting go is harder than I thought. Of course, Abigail is more than capable, and the board is solid. Okay, I surrender. Keep pursuing your idea."

Tom's voice sounded more upbeat, "I'm glad you're okay with it."

Harold turned to put his feet up on his desk and leaned back. He stared at the ceiling and then moved his eyes down to stare at the ocean over his feet. A smile crept across his face. "Tom, I want to make one alteration to your plan."

"Okay," Tom answered hesitantly.

"When the time comes to discuss the CIA contract with Garcia, tell him he has to throw in the yacht for us to finish our agreement."

"Yacht?" asked Tom. "What yacht? Why does PDS need a yacht?"

Harold chuckled a little. "It's not for the company. It's for me."

Tom's voice became more inquisitive, "Why would Garcia do that?"

Harold's voice had a tinge of stress behind it, "For putting Joshua, Maria, and me in harm's way. This Chuck guy is no joke, and the two men he keeps with him would turn your blood cold."

Tom sounded concerned, "They must be bad if you're saying that. I've never known you to be afraid of anybody."

Harold's forehead formed small creases across his brow. "Trust me, buddy, you'd probably shoot these guys on sight. In a fair fight, I could take them out in a second, but these are the sort of men who never fight fair."

Tom's voice softened, "You be careful out there."

"Believe me, I plan to." Harold reached over and took a sip of cold coffee then put the mug back down.

"How is our favorite doctor?" asked Tom.

Harold paused and then responded, "Oh, he and Maria have gone to North Carolina. Doc is doing some research about my half-brother, and Maria and he needed to get away for a little while."

Tom's voice sounded concerned, "How are you doing without him around?"

"I'll survive."

"Is Darla keeping you in check?"

Harold chuckled. "I think she's more than capable of keeping me between the lines."

"You are hooked, my friend."

A lilt was in Harold's voice as he replied, "Hook, line, and sinker."

Both men laughed.

"Well, congratulations," Tom said. "Whenever you both decide to give up your independent ways, I expect to be at the wedding."

Harold sat up. "I expect you to be part of the wedding party."

"Good. Well, I need to try and get some shuteye," Tom responded through his yawn.

"Have a good night," said Harold.

"Good luck."

Harold hung up the phone and locked it back inside his desk. There was a knock on the door, and

Darla's voice hollered from the other side, "Are you decent?"

Harold's heart quickened with anticipation. "Well, I'm dressed, but the jury is out on decent."

The door opened, and Darla leaned in. Her white linen blouse, dark eyes, and black hair made Harold long for the day when they would be married, and he could make proper use of his cabin.

They gazed at each other for a moment, and Darla finally blinked. "It's time to meet up on deck. Hip-hop, dear. We have a meeting with the devil."

"No rest for the wicked," Harold responded.

Darla had disappeared by the time Harold got out of his chair and left his office. *How is anyone that nimble?*

CHAPTER 20

Harold and Darla sat mid-boat, and Garcia gunned the Kodiak's engine as they completed the short journey to the familiar Crossroads Key. As the crew prepared to disembark, Harold saw the top of the same tent sitting on the short hilltop, just as before. However, closer to shore sat a couple of boxes. Harold had been around weapons enough to recognize that rifles were packed within. Several canisters of ammunition had been placed under a table that was set up on the beach near the boxes.

Darla disembarked first. She turned her attention to Garcia. "Looks like we get to have some fun for once."

Garcia twitched with a slight smile as he responded, "Don't get too excited. Remember, this is business, but business can be fun."

Harold was about to ask where the targets were located when Alice appeared from the direction of the tent. She stopped at the base of the trail. "I'm glad to see everyone is here. We only have a few minutes. Gather around the table so we can review the weapons."

Without a word, Garcia walked up and stood between Harold and Darla. They all had their backs to the ocean and faced Alice. Harold wasn't sure why they chose the spot they had, but Alice's commanding presence seemed to go beyond verbal direction or need for questioning. Today Alice wore a khaki-colored short jumper. Although she was not unattractive, her features dimmed when near Darla in her white linen blouse and tight white shorts.

Alice's voice broke through Harold's rabbit trail of thoughts, "Everyone, pay attention. Before you are the latest prototypes of smart rifles." Alice lifted one of the weapons, opened its bolt, confirmed the empty chamber, and left the bolt open. She flipped the rifle around so everyone could see the bottom. "Here is where the magazine is loaded." She placed the butt of the rifle on the table and flipped it around. "This is the laser sight that guides the smart bullet to its target."

Harold raised his hand.

Alice turned in his direction. "Do you have a question, Mr. Brown?"

Harold lowered his hand. "Yes. I'm curious, why did Chuck agree to pay such an outrages amount for these guns? I mean, today we can use laser sights that are so accurate an eighty-year-old with poor eyesight can hit a target down range. What's so special about these?"

"I'm glad you asked." She reached, grabbed a loaded clip, and shoved it into place. She reached back down to a small control panel on the table and threw a switch. A humming could be heard drawing closer from the far side of the island. "I programmed some targets for today, and I made sure I included a few extras. Now watch."

The drone zoomed overhead and out over the water. Alice locked and loaded the weapon. "Before anyone asks, the patterns are programmed, but they are run in a random order, so I can't anticipate the moves. As you know, with a normal rifle, you need to lead a moving target. That makes laser targeting with dumb weapons useless in many situations. Now watch this."

Alice lifted the weapon and put the butt hard into her shoulder. The rifle followed the drone for approximately four seconds before the round went off. Even though it was expected, the entire group jumped when the bullet's sonic boom emitted from the front of the rifle. In less than a second, the traveling drone exploded in the air, and parts drifted to the sea below.

"That, my friends, is what makes these weapons so valuable. With a little training, you can hit moving targets with predictability. It not only ensures lethality with each round, but it helps avoid friendly fire, assuming someone does not insert themselves into the bullet's path."

Harold broke in without asking this time, "I thought I read that the fin technology slows the bullet down faster than the wind resistance of a regular bullet."

Alice replied, "There's decreased range. I wouldn't use one of these rifles for sniping, but at mid-range, they can be devastating, and before you ask, yes, we are working to improve things. In fact, your company is helping us research better propellant and more efficient fin technology."

Harold wondered why Tom had not mentioned the projectile work. These bullets were essentially miniature missiles, and the ammunition alone could be very lucrative down the road for PDS.

Alice seemed to notice his change in expression. "Mr. Brown, do you care to share your thoughts?"

She is good. "It's nothing important. I was just wondering what that technology will be worth to PDS in contracts once we help the government perfect the weapon."

Alice passed a knowing smile, as if amused by an inside joke. "I'm quite sure you'll find out. Any other questions?"

"I take it you have something more in mind for my company?"

Alice cocked her head to one side. "Well, Mr. Brown, aren't you observant. Let's just say the military is looking for a reliable contractor they can trust to produce cutting-edge technology that won't get our sons and daughters killed in theatre."

"Understood."

"Any other questions?"

Everyone remained silent.

"Good." She pointed her finger at Garcia. "You, with me. The rest of you feel free to look, but don't touch. I have things set up in a certain way, and I don't want them changed."

Alice turned on her heel towards the tent and Garcia fell in line like a puppy behind its master.

Harold leaned over to Darla. "She has him on a short leash. Do you think they're dating?"

She shoved his large shoulder. "What is it with men? She's his boss. In case you haven't noticed, all of us are on her short leash whenever she's around."

"Not me," he said confidently.

Darla let out a short laugh.

Harold turned and the two of them faced each other.

"What?" he asked.

"Really?"

"Really," retorted Harold smugly.

"When was the last time you raised your hand and asked for permission to speak?"

He crossed his arms with mock indignity. "Fine, you got me."

She looked around and then grabbed the back of his head with her hand, lifted herself up, and kissed him. Just as quickly, she released him and looked around again.

Harold just stood there for a moment, and finally said, "I don't understand you sometimes. I thought we're purely platonic on mission."

Darla playfully poked him in the chest. "We are, but I couldn't help myself. Sometimes you're too cute."

He shook his head. "Women."

Darla reached out and grabbed his left arm. "Don't worry, dear. You'll never understand us. That's why women secretly run the world. You boys just don't know it."

Harold stood there gazing into Darla's eyes and thinking how he would not mind her as his dictator.

Garcia's voice broke through their quiet moment. "Okay, you two, game faces only."

Harold broke away his gaze and turned towards the water. Off in the distance, he noticed a dot coming towards the island. Garcia walked up and stood between him and Darla.

Garcia said, "He's coming. One boat this time. That's a good sign. It means he trusts us a little bit."

"Where's Alice?" asked Darla.

Garcia maintained eye contact with the tiny vessel quickly coming towards the small island. "She managed to create a hiding place on the side of the island."

"How?" asked Darla. "There's nothing on either side but sawgrass, sand, dry coral, and some very nasty sea life."

"I would tell you if I knew. That's all she would tell me. I'm not even sure where she is. Alice said to tell you all that, as far as anyone knows, I have a dirty agent working for me nearby, and they are controlling the targets."

"I'm not sure Chuck will like that," said Harold.

"Well, none of us have a choice at the moment since she's the boss. I knew better than to question her directions," responded Garcia.

Chuck's boat wasn't much bigger than the Kodiak, and other than the guns Nigel and Haidar carried, there were no other arms. Harold noticed the craft had several antennas sticking up from the steering column. He assumed Chuck had at least one radio beneath the steering wheel. All three men stayed in the craft after it beached, not saying a word. Chuck moved towards the front of the boat but did not disembark. Haidar and Nigel began to fiddle with something underneath the steering column. Darla and Garcia did not lift a finger or even twitch their faces.

Chuck finally looked up. "What gives? I was all set for a fun day of shooting down targets, but now…" He pointed towards the group, and Nigel and Haidar stepped up to the bow of the shallow craft and leveled their weapons at them.

Harold noticed Haidar's two black eyes and the tan tape across the bridge of his nose. Dark blotches and circles could be barely seen around his bare arms.

Garcia raised his voice in reply, "Please, we're all friends here. What has you so spooked?"

"I'm detecting a drone signal."

Garcia started laughing, and Darla quickly followed suit. Harold stood there focused on all three men, wondering what they could possibly find funny.

Chuck hollered back, "Harold, why aren't you laughing, boy?"

"Evidently, I'm not in on their joke," Harold responded truthfully.

Garcia stopped his chortling, and his face became somber. "Forgive me, Chuck. Harold isn't in on a lot of what we're doing. He only needs to know his part. I'm sure you can understand. You have your lackeys too."

Lackey?

"I have an agent who has been helping me, but she can be trusted," Garcia said. "She's a bitter but great woman. Her name is Alice. She's somewhere on the island and will be handling our targets today."

"Somewhere on the island? What the heck does that even mean? I deal with people I know, and now you bring in somebody new that I can't even see? Speaking of not seeing, where is the good Dr. Joshua Zeev?"

Harold interrupted before Garcia could speak, "He had to leave, family business."

Chuck mockingly stuck out his bottom lip. "Oh, I'm sorry. It must be hard for you." Chuck's serious expression returned, and he stared at Garcia. "You better have a darn good reason for losing the doctor."

"It's actually like Harold says. Family business. His new bride is not one to sit around and sip out of coconuts all day. They needed some time away to work on their new marriage."

"Young love. Well, young-ish anyway." Chuck laughed at his own joke.

Harold noticed Darla's hands ball into a fist and then release.

Chuck continued, "I'm not stepping off this boat unless Miss Alice agrees to show herself at some point."

Garcia talked into his poorly concealed microphone that was wired into a wristband, paused, and said something else while nodding. He hollered back at Chuck. "She will join us after the demonstration."

"No tricks," responded Chuck.

"Please, I'm Garcia."

Harold found Garcia's ability to change his words around with ease a little disconcerting. Was there anything Agent Garcia had said to him that was the truth? Harold certainly was unable to tell by his demeanor or speech. If he found Garcia hard to trust, what was Chuck thinking?

Chuck's crew disembarked. Garcia motioned with a quick finger wiggle and flick of his wrist to the table. Everyone made their way across the white sandy surface to the weapons.

"I see Haidar is armed. I take it his confusion from the other day is cleared up," quipped Darla to Chuck when he got near.

"We had a talk, and I believe Haidar knows what I'm expecting of him. There won't be any more miscommunications, will there, my friend?" Chuck shot a glance at Haidar and then back to Darla.

Haidar's dead eyes remained locked in a distant stare. "No."

Harold thought Haidar looked and sounded like a wounded, angry child, and the dark blotches were clearly bruising and burn marks on his arms. There was a part of him that pitied the unfortunate man, but something inside Harold's gut felt a mix of fear and anger every time he looked into Haidar's eyes.

Garcia reached over to pick up the rifle Alice had demonstrated with earlier. He spoke into his mic. "Send me two."

Harold heard a distant hum that quickly grew louder. Everyone except Garcia looked up to see two small drones dropping from the sky. Their gray paint made them barely visible even in the clear sky. The small devices buzzed fifty feet above the group and looped out from the beach and over the sea. Garcia lifted the rifle and aimed at the drone on the left. He followed as it began tracking to the right. Harold noticed the drone on the right began tracking left.

A moment before the two would meet, Garcia fired, and then fired a second time and gave a slight twitch to the left. Both drones exploded in respective order. Everyone applauded. Harold noticed even Haidar seemed amazed at the marksmanship demonstration.

"Very impressive," said Chuck, "but how does it work for an inexperienced old horse like me?"

"Come find out," said Garcia.

Chuck walked over and spit out the cigar butt he had been ruminating on. Garcia handed him the weapon.

"It's just point and click?" asked Chuck.

"Yes. Just trust the optics. Aim your laser, fire, and keep the laser on target."

Chuck looked the weapon up and down, gave an approving nod, and shoved the rifle butt into his shoulder.

"Send one," said Garcia into the microphone.

The familiar buzz fell from the sky, but this time headed straight for the water instead of flying over the team. Chuck raised the weapon and tracked the drone for several seconds. He squeezed the trigger, and the drone continued flying its course.

"What gives?" asked Chuck. "I thought it was point and click."

Garcia let a knowing smile slip from his lips.

"I know how to shoot," said Chuck, anticipating Garcia's words.

"I completely agree, and that's part of the problem. You're leading the target, aren't you?"

A grin broke across Chuck's face. "Of course, you said keep the laser on the target."

"Let the tech do the work, my friend." He spoke once more into the mic.

Chuck raised the rifle, and the drone zipped across from left to right. Chuck raised the weapon and almost immediately fired. The drone exploded over the sea.

Chuck caressed the weapon's casing and rifle butt like an intimate girlfriend. "This is the most beautiful weapon I've ever had the pleasure of shooting." Chuck handed the weapon back to Garcia. "I was going to try and negotiate the price down again with Harold, but after getting to fire it, I think the price is fair."

Garcia carefully placed the rifle on the table. "I have more good news. Harold's company is working to improve the ammo. You'll soon be able to effectively take out any target within a mile as long as you have clear line of site."

Chuck slapped Garcia's back. "Aren't you full of good news."

Darla finally spoke up, "Gentlemen, we've arranged rum and fruit juice in the tent to celebrate. That is if we're moving forward as planned."

"Absolutely," said Chuck. He reached into his pocket and pulled out a fresh stogie.

Nigel was by his side with a lighter already lit before anyone else could think to offer him a light.

Chuck took three long puffs, turned, and spit out a couple of tobacco flakes before turning his attention to Haidar. "You stay down here and watch over the weapons."

Haidar bristled. "Why? There is nothing here but sand."

"Baby steps," shot back Chuck.

Chuck turned around and slapped Garcia's back again. "You, my friend, are a great ally. Never betray me. I'd hate to have to kill you."

Garcia returned the gesture. "The feeling's mutual."

Harold caught a quick sideways glance from Darla. He wondered if she was concerned about Chuck, Garcia, or both.

The group sat in the shade of the tent. Garcia poured a dark and light rum into the bottom of their cups, added ice and some tropical fruit juice, and swirled the mixture around in each cup.

Harold volunteered to take the first sip. His pursed his lips. "I think you may be doing that wrong."

Garcia smirked. "It's a desert island. We're roughing it."

Everyone looked back at Harold at the sound of him swirling the mixing straw inside the cup a few more times. He looked back at everyone as he took a sip, and then finished the contents of the cup.

With a smile on his lips, Harold said, "It grows on you."

Garcia served the rest of the team. He tried to refill Harold's cup, but Harold held up his hand and grabbed a nearby water bottle. "One is my limit at work."

Chuck lifted his red Solo cup, and everyone joined in. There was something about this that reminded Harold of his childhood and playing pirates with Tom down by the sea in Malibu.

Chuck's voice was deeper and louder than normal, "To successful contracts, more money, and the violence that makes it all possible."

"Here, here," said everyone.

Harold looked over his cup at Darla. Love and sadness met his eyes. Neither stopped drinking until their containers were empty.

"Chuck! Chuck!" Haidar yelled from the beach.

The entire group jumped to their feet, but Chuck put up his hand. "I think he just feels left out."

"Chuck, come quick!" Haidar screamed.

"I'll check it out," said Chuck.

"Darla, go with him," said Garcia.

The two walked out of the tent and began their way down the short path. Harold started to follow a few steps behind.

"Stay here," demanded Garcia.

Harold glared at him and continued to follow Chuck and Darla.

Chuck stopped halfway to the beach. Harold remained a few yards behind, but he could see Haidar with his rifle held across his body. Everything appeared in order.

"This better be important," said Chuck, clearly annoyed.

"I said come here!" demanded Haidar.

"Nobody orders me around, boy. Especially not you!"

By the time Chuck had finished his sentence, Haidar already had his Kalashnikov leveled at Chuck. A quick three-round burst exploded from the weapon. Harold heard the bullets whistle by, and he instinctively dove to the ground. Another round exploded before the first echoes had subsided, and Harold watched as a pink mist exploded from Chuck's right thigh. Chuck yelled and collapsed. Darla dove on top of Chuck to give him cover, and a pink mist shot out from her shoulder.

Harold did not hesitate. Anger and rage began to fill his body. His whole soul felt as though it wanted to burst forth and destroy Haidar. He welcomed the battle. His mind prayed he could feel the pain of a bullet. He wanted to envelop and destroy everyone around him. *Everything and everyone will learn to fear me,* resonated inside his mind.

Harold rose to his feet. The world took on a reddish hue. Harold felt his heart beating and his blood coursing through his veins. He wanted to burst forth into the chaos, and a roar exploded from his very soul and across his lips. He could see the people around him. Fear filled their eyes, and he felt energized by their terror. He began his deliberate walk towards Haidar. Haidar shook and let off another burst. The rifle recoiled wildly, and bullets whistled in all directions through the air. Harold let out a deep reverberating laugh that carried far out towards the sea. He stopped and slapped his chest. He dared Haidar to shoot him. He wanted to feel the joy of burning flesh.

A gunshot just behind him rang out, and Haidar fell to the ground. He was crying out and holding his leg. Harold turned and saw Garcia lowering his weapon. Harold growled at Garcia who raised his weapon at him.

"No," came Chuck's voice.

Harold could see Chuck's reddish body lying on the ground. He held his pistol directly at Garcia. "Let him be."

Garcia lowered his weapon. Electricity and power flowed through his veins—so much fear, so much panic. It felt good, exciting, pleasurable. Chuck averted his eyes when Harold glared at him. Then Haidar's whimpering caught his attention. Harold turned and bounded down to the beach. Haidar's leg was bleeding into the sand, and he was already too weak to lift his rifle. Harold's large hand grabbed nearly all of Haidar's hair and lifted him up and off the ground.

Haidar screamed, cried, and twitched in agony. Harold loved watching his enemy suffer. How dare he harm Darla? Then it dawned on him. He looked over his shoulder. Garcia's reddish hue was pressing a bandage onto Darla's shoulder. She looked Harold in the eyes with no fear or terror, only sadness and love.

"Please," she said only with her lips.

Harold looked back at Haidar's twitching body. His convulsions sent electric pulses of pleasure through Harold. He loved the power and had to finish what he started. Darla would understand. With Haidar dangling, Harold began to walk back up the trail. Haidar convulsed with each step. As he passed by the tent, he saw Nigel cowering behind a chair.

Harold knew where to take Haidar. His two friends in the sea would finish what he had started. Two-thirds of the way to the back of the island, a woman he barely remembered appeared. She stood two feet in front of him. Her pistol shook as she aimed at his chest. He swung Haidar's limp body in between them. She instinctively shot into Haidar's motionless body. Harold grabbed the pistol's hot barrel from the woman and threw the gun towards the sea. The woman took a deliberate step back and let him pass.

When he arrived at the rear beach, he waded knee-deep into the water. He could see the dark shadows of the bull sharks patrolling the water nearby. Harold roared. The sea vibrated, and the shadows darted away. He reached over and bit into Haidar's neck and swallowed. Blood barely trickled out of Haidar's artery. Harold tossed the body over his shoulder then spun around against the shallow waters like a macabre shot putter. Haidar's body flew end over end in the air and landed nearly ten yards out in the sea. His blood mixed with the water. Within moments, the familiar shadows of the bull sharks returned. Harold turned to walk back to the beach. Behind him, he could hear the sea roil with hungry fish devouring the empty shell that had been Haidar.

With his enemy destroyed, the rage seemed to evaporate and he collapsed. No matter how much oxygen he sucked in, it did not seem to be enough. The acrid flavor of blood, Haidar's blood, emanated inside Harold's mouth. He stuck his finger into the back of his throat and gagged, doing it again and again until Haidar's flesh was flung from his stomach and onto the beach in front of him.

"Harold!"

It was Darla, but he couldn't look up. He backed away from his vomit, repulsed by what he had given himself into. Ashamed and exhausted, he collapsed onto the sand and prayed for God to end his nightmare. He felt Darla's body collapse onto his and heard her let out a short muffled cry as she winced from her wound.

"Harold, please tell me you're okay. Are you okay?"

"I'm not hurt," mumbled Harold. He was glad Darla missed seeing him bite into Haidar's lifeless body. "Are you okay?" he asked through a dejected voice.

"Thanks to you."

"There he is!" yelled Chuck several yards away.

"Not now," bemoaned Harold.

"Please, honey," whispered Darla into his ear. "Don't show Chuck any regret. You're not done saving our lives yet."

Harold gave a slight nod. Darla slid off of him. Every muscle in Harold's body felt as though it had been punched by a large, powerful fist. Through sheer will, Harold forced his tightened muscles to give way, and he stood up.

Chuck's leg was tied off with a tourniquet. Although he should have been lying still, he hobbled towards Harold with his good leg and dragged Garcia along as his reluctant crutch. Blood still oozed from his wound due to his determination to get to Harold. "Boy, you saved my life." Chuck released Garcia, and he collapsed into Harold. Chuck's head turned up from Harold's chest. "Where's Haidar?"

Harold pointed over his shoulder with his thumb as the current washed up some blood and bits of flesh. Chuck pushed himself off Harold, balancing against his body to take a look with everyone else. The sharks still swam among the remnants of blood and flesh floating a few yards from shore.

Chuck grimaced. "I'd call that dead."

Harold only grunted in reply.

Chuck grabbed Harold's broad shoulders and steadied himself on one leg. He looked up directly into Harold's eyes. "I owe you my life. Do you understand? Not that you need protection, but if you ever do, I will gladly give my life for yours."

Harold brushed off some of the sand from his head that he had gathered while collapsed on the beach. That was when he felt the dried blood clinging to his red locks. He worked to push the shame from his heart and replied to Chuck, "I believe Garcia put Haidar down."

"So, you remember everything?" asked Garcia.

"Always," he replied flatly.

"You were the one who distracted Haidar," Chuck said. "As sure as I stand here, we'd probably all be dead if you hadn't dared him to shoot you. That reminds me, this hot girlfriend of yours was just as brave. My mind still can't decide if I'm turned on or relieved that you tried to shield my body with yours."

Darla gave Chuck a dismissive look. "It's nothing, just training."

"Pity."

"I don't think you want to try to compete with my boyfriend," said Darla, pointing to Harold.

"You have a point. Well, will you both do me one more favor?"

"What is it?" asked Darla.

"Please carry me back to my boat. I'm not as tough as I used to be."

"I have him," said Harold. He hoisted Chuck into a fireman's carry and began trudging back up the path. "Where's Nigel?" asked Harold.

Chuck's voice sounded like a low growl. "I have that coward prepping my boat."

Garcia pointed at Chuck's wounded leg. "You know, I have people who can fix that for you. The sooner the better."

"This isn't my first rodeo," responded Chuck. "Tell your drone friend I expect to meet her next time we all get together. Now, get me to my boat."

Everyone arrived at the other side of the island. Harold lowered Chuck into his small craft. Chuck lay down on the side bench, and Nigel placed two life preservers under Chuck's wounded leg. Nigel's hands shook as he turned back and started the engines.

"I'll be in touch!" yelled Chuck to the sky as he waved a fresh, unlit cigar. "Make sure you bring Harold. Until we meet again."

Harold pushed the light craft away from the beach as Nigel increased the reverse thrust on the outboard motor. With a quick change in direction, the boat headed back towards the sea and out of sight. As the boat shrank towards the edge of the horizon, shadows began to form around the edges of Harold's vision. He felt light and dizzy, and the darkness continued to overcome the light. His face felt warm, and a wave of light nausea swept over him as everything went black.

The sour taste of seawater choked Harold's throat and filled his nostrils. He coughed and sputtered. His world was still dark, and somewhere in his mind, he hoped it all was another bad dream. Harold tried to open his eyes, but the bright sunlight forced them closed again. He could feel the sand against his bare arms, and he feared his current memories were all too real. After he blinked several times, a shadow suddenly blocked the light from his face.

Harold opened his eyes, and Alice stood over him. She quickly stepped away, and Harold had to shield his eyes once more. Looking down, he could see Haidar's dried blood still stuck to his shorts, legs, and shirt. A shudder ran through his body, and a feeling of shame quickly followed.

From behind, Alice barked, "Agent Hernandez, with me."

Harold heard footsteps. He rose up on his left elbow and turned to see Garcia running from the Kodiak and up towards the trail to the meeting tent. Darla came down the path and past Alice and Garcia without saying a word. Her shoulder was bandaged, and her arm was in a sling. She walked over, sat down, and began to gently rub his blood-speckled arm with her free hand.

"How bad is your arm?" Harold asked.

Darla looked at Harold with a gentle smile. There was no anger, judgement, or sadness in her dark eyes, only love. "The bullet passed through without hitting any bone. The tissue damage will heal. It's nothing more than a flesh wound really. You don't need to worry about me."

Harold dropped onto his back. Darla took his other arm and slid her hand down it until she reached his hand. He gently grasped Darla's elegant, strong fingers. Despite focusing on Darla, he could feel tears begin to trickle from the corner of his eyes.

Harold whispered, "What have I become?"

Darla bent over and kissed his forehead. She sat back up and said, "Dear, I have seen far worse than what happened today. My hands aren't clean either. To be honest, I was afraid things would go far uglier than they did. You aren't trained for these sorts of situations."

"I ate a man's neck," bemoaned Harold. "He was wounded, unable to do anything, and I lifted him by the hair and carried him around like a rag doll, and then I fed him to the sharks."

"Yes, you did," said Darla. "In doing so you may have saved our lives and the mission."

Harold turned his head and looked at Darla. She stared back at him, almost like she was willing him to believe her.

"When the gunfire starts, it doesn't always stop once the target goes down," she continued. "People like Chuck are paranoid. They must be if they want to stay alive. If you had not been there, it could have ended up completely different. Garcia could have thought Chuck set us up, and the two sides would have sat there pointing pistols until somebody fired or Alice flew in a drone, and then all hell would have broken loose. When you went berserk, the entire dynamic changed. Chuck was so enthralled with your performance that he forgot all about the possible threats around him."

"It wasn't a performance."

Darla gently squeezed his hand. "You know that isn't what I meant. Nevertheless, you not only changed the dynamic, you won over Chuck. He thinks we're his new best friends. Maybe what happened was bad, but the outcome is good. Now that we have his trust, we have a good chance of capturing him. You've saved a lot of lives today."

Darla's last statement made Harold feel better. He had avoided hurting anyone else. If he had not killed Haidar, perhaps Chuck would have kept the dangerous man around. They had all survived, and Darla was not seriously wounded. To make matters better, he and Darla had saved Chuck, and now he trusted them implicitly. Then he looked down at his shirt. The blood from Haidar's neck wound was splattered about his chest. He still felt like he had taken things too far. Like an animal, he wanted to consume his prey. The thought made a chill shoot through his body. He sat up and pulled his knees to his chest then began to rock back and forth.

"What is it, honey?" asked Darla as she played with the hair at the base of his neck.

"I just need some time," said Harold.

They both turned at the sound of Garcia's feet stomping the sand. "We're leaving now," he said before continuing straight for the boat.

Harold rose and helped Darla to her feet. He helped her maintain her balance as she got into the small craft then shoved the nose off the beach, hopped in, and they headed back out to sea towards the yacht.

CHAPTER 21

Harold sat at the very front of the boat on their way back to the yacht. Nobody said a word on the thirty-minute ride. Thanks to calm waters and Harold's location on the bow, the ride was mostly smooth. They all boarded the *Sweet Revenge*, and Harold headed directly to his cabin. He dropped his bloody clothes in the middle of the floor and walked into the steaming shower. He scrubbed himself down three times, and then stood under the hot water until his entire body was as red as a lobster.

Feeling like his skin had finally been cleansed of the apostasy that clung to it, Harold got out, put on his swim trunks, and headed upstairs to the hot tub. He passed Frank the steward in the hallway. "Frank, burn the bloody clothes on the floor of my cabin. I never want to see them again."

Frank looked confused, but said, "Okay."

Harold continued his climb to the top deck. He made a beeline for the hot tub and eased his already warm body into the 104-degree water without bothering to turn on the jets. All he wanted was the water and the view. He drew in a breath as the hot water rose and fell against his chest. Stretching out his arms along the edges of the tub, he focused on slowing his breathing.

The sound of someone walking up the deck steps quickly broke his relaxed mood. Garcia appeared carrying two rum runners.

Harold laid his head back on the edge of the tub and closed his eyes. "Not now, I need some time to process what I've done."

Garcia appeared to ignore him. He kicked off his deck shoes and sank his legs into the water opposite of Harold. "Yea, that's what everyone tells himself. Take it from someone who's been where you are. This is not the time to be alone."

"Really? Then why didn't Darla come up? Maybe she knows I don't need the company right now."

"Darla didn't come up because I wanted to talk to you first."

Harold scowled at Garcia. "Come on, man. You've never taken a bite out of a man's neck. What can you possibly say to me?"

Garcia sat there for a moment and then spoke, "No, I haven't. The stuff I've done is so bad I won't talk about it. But I've been there. I know what it feels like to destroy a piece of your soul. To do things you thought you would never do, and before you ask, yes, it was necessary, and it saved lives too."

"So," said Harold, "you did some bad things, so what? Everyone tells me killing John saved lives, and you know what? I believe them. But this? What I did? You can't possibly know what that's like."

Garcia ignored his khaki shorts and linen shirt as he slid into the hot tub across from Harold. Garcia handed one of the drinks to him. "Drink this."

Harold took the drink. "Are you trying to dehydrate me?"

Garcia gave a half-smile. "That's ninety-nine percent fresh fruit juice."

Harold took a sip. Garcia must have been telling the truth because there was no perceivable rum flavor. Harold drank the rest of it down. The taste of the fresh fruit juice erased the horrible acrid flavor from his mouth. Garcia handed him the second glass, and Harold swallowed the juice and began to chomp on the ice.

Garcia rested his arms on the back of the hot tub. "I won't tell you what I've done, but let me tell you about my dad."

"Was he a spook too?" asked Harold.

"No, he was a mechanic. The kind that works on cars. He had a little shop he ran out of a small garage at the back of our property, but before all of that, he was a young kid fresh out of college when he got drafted and sent to Vietnam."

Harold rolled his eyes. "Oh please, don't give me one of the *Platoon*-style stories. If you don't have anything real to tell me, let it go."

Garcia frowned. "I'm not here to bs. Just hear me out."

Harold nodded.

"Dad was part of a platoon near the front. If you could say Vietnam had any fronts. Mostly, men would go take a point in the jungle, fight the Vietcong, fall back, and do it all over again. It was that way all over the country. His team was based out of a friendly village about five miles from the fighting. The men shared some of their rations with the locals to keep things amicable. A couple of guys in the platoon that grew up on farms helped the locals with their crops. It gave them a sense of normalcy before they'd return to fighting."

"Did they double cross them?" asked Harold.

Garcia held up his index finger. "Listen."

"Keep going."

"Dad's platoon came back after a nasty two days of jungle fighting. Instead of the village leaders greeting them, the place was dead silent, and when I say dead silent, I'm emphasizing *dead*. The Vietcong had flanked their position while they were fighting forward and destroyed everyone in the village to send a message about helping Americans. These guys were brutal and made ISIS look like amateurs. They had taken many of the young girls and then killed everyone else they didn't want along with the livestock. Dad said it was like something out of a nightmare. Then, just to emphasize their point, they raped a twelve-year-old girl and hung her on a makeshift cross in the middle of the village. Dad said they guessed at least eight men must have raped her. I didn't ask him why they thought that."

"That's inhuman," muttered Harold.

Garcia stared down into the water and then looked back up. "Dad said they buried the little girl and then went to hunt the Vietcong who did it. According to Dad, everyone from the lieutenant on down wanted revenge. They left their radios in the village and began the hunt. They never stopped to rest. He said their rage kept them going, and they felt superhuman, like nothing could stop them. By the second night, they had caught up to the group's camp. They saw one young woman dead on the ground and three men raping another. The rest were tied up to a tree. The lieutenant cut the women loose while the rest of the men came in firing. They laid waste to the entire camp of Vietcong."

"Good," said Harold.

Garcia raised his finger once more. "But they weren't done. Dad said they wanted to send their own message. They hung every dead man by his neck from the surrounding trees, castrated them, and cut off their hands. They boiled the hands until the flesh came off the bones then ground some of the bones into dust and mixed that with a pot of coffee that they passed around. Then they left the entire mess behind and headed back to the village. When the platoon returned to the village, the lieutenant picked up his radio and reported the village had been attacked while they were gone. The lieutenant claimed they had gotten lost, and the radio was out of range. He said they maintained radio silence while they were busy trying to find their way back and avoid Charlie. All the men backed his story."

Harold rubbed his face with one of his hands. "Wow, that's rough. How did they deal with it?"

"They didn't," said Garcia. "Most ended up putting themselves in front of bullets while fighting in the jungle. I guess they couldn't live with themselves. Those that could live with it in Vietnam ended up drunk, addicted to drugs, homeless, or all of the above once they came stateside."

"But your dad didn't, right?"

"He was a drunk most of my childhood. My mom was a good woman. Maria reminds me a little bit of her. She would keep us kids away from Dad on his bad days. Dad managed to support us working on cars. I guess hiding out in the garage and working on those vehicles kept his demons at bay, at least for a little while. I eventually went off to college to study criminal psychology. One Christmas I came home to find Dad clean and sober. To top it off, he dragged us all to church while I was home."

"He got religion?" asked Harold.

Garcia stretched his arms out along the edge of the hot tub. "And then some. He still liked working on cars, but he would take trips every couple of months to try and find anyone still living from his Vietnam days. He said he had to tell them the good news. I think he found a total of three guys. One guy liked what Dad had to say. The other two wanted nothing to do with it."

"What did your dad do?" asked Harold.

"Dad was relentless. Even with his old buddies that told him to stick his faith where the sun don't shine. He'd still go visit again and again. All three died before Dad, and he went to every funeral and mourned for every one of them."

"Wow, it sounds like your dad barely made it out alive."

"Not really. All the years of hard living and guilt took their toll. Dad was dead by the time he was sixty. Liver failure. Still, he was happier in those final years than all the years I knew him combined."

Harold cocked his head. "So what are you saying? I need to get religion and start preaching? Maybe I could start with the crew."

"Don't be obtuse," said Garcia. "The point is you need to forgive yourself. I thought you grew up in church, not to mention Joshua. Didn't you ever learn any of this stuff?"

"Yea. I've had large doses of it, but it's easier said than done. Hey, you won't tell me your story, but you'll tell me your dad's. Why is that? I can't imagine your stories are any worse, and so what if they are? Don't get me wrong; I appreciate you telling me about your dad, but I feel like maybe you're not practicing what you preach. Did your dad like to talk about what they did when you were growing up?"

Garcia's eyes appeared distant. "No. Dad never talked about it. Not until he was dying. He knew I was working to get into the CIA. He pulled me into his garage office and told me everything. He said I needed to be ready before my day came."

"What day?" asked Harold.

Garcia's eyes began to glisten. "The day I broke every rule I said I'd never break because in the moment I felt justified."

"Did it help?"

Garcia slapped the sides of the hot tub with both hands for a moment. "Honestly, eventually, yes. Do I still regret it? Yea, I regret some of my decisions, but I came to realize that my world of right and wrong was dependent on what other people told me were right and wrong. I had lost who I was and what I believed."

"And now?" asked Harold.

"I have a pretty good feel for what's going on. Regardless, I know I can't change the past. I can only impact today, right now, and hopefully do better tomorrow, if I have a tomorrow."

Harold dropped the last ice cube from the glass into his mouth and crunched down. "Did you get religion like your dad?"

"I'm not sure anyone had faith like my dad. You would have had to know him before to appreciate the turnaround. I guess you could say I have faith because if there isn't a God and a path for salvation then I think all of mankind is doomed to self-destruct. I'm not sure that's what your average Sunday school white middle-class family would call Christianity."

Harold put the empty cup on the deck behind him. "At least you're being honest. I guess I can be a little honest with you. I don't know how anything can cleanse away what I did today. I would say that wasn't me, but it was."

"Alice wants me to bring Joshua back to help you."

Harold leaned forward towards Garcia and sent a wave of water splashing against Garcia's chin. "No, don't you dare! I will not do that to Doc."

"What do you mean?" asked Garcia.

"Doc has helped me all my life. He just got his confidence back after Dad's suicide, and he and Maria are trying to adjust to married life together. On top of all of that, he's trying to find Bill. Doc thinks he may need help. I won't put any of those things at risk because of me."

Garcia's face looked back at Harold, confused. "How can bringing him back do all of that? Surely he can look for your brother online from here. As for him and Maria, I'm sure they won't mind returning to help you."

"Doc said he thinks I'm controlling this berserker thing. If he finds out I went full blown cannibal, it'll devastate him. I don't want him brooding around with that faraway look in his eyes again, and Maria doesn't need that either. The two of them need time alone, away from this zoo. Just give me some time to think through this."

"Okay. Well, we should be back to Salvation Key in a couple more hours. You can have more privacy there."

"No," pleaded Harold. "The sea, this ship, they calm me. Can we stay at sea and go back tomorrow evening? After all, we meandered all over the Gulf the first time we came out here."

"I don't see why not. I'll go inform the captain."

"Thanks."

Garcia climbed out of the tub.

"One more thing," said Harold. "Can you let Darla know I prefer to be left alone up here? I just need time to think."

"You got it." Garcia carefully made his way down the steps, leaving a trail of water from his drenched clothes as he disappeared.

Harold closed his eyes and listened to the ship's motors hum. He felt the gentle sway of the yacht and the hot tub's water against his body. He drew in the salt air, and slowly blew it out. After the second breath, he listened. The entire ship seemed at peace. It was almost like it knew Harold was in mourning, not just for his parents, but for his actions.

He opened his eyes and looked around the empty deck then up into the sky. A few puffy white clouds floated like cotton balls. Harold said, "I know I don't pray like I did as a kid, and I don't know if Mom and Dad can hear me. I'm sorry. Everything made so much sense as a kid. If I did something wrong, I got punished, and I didn't do it again. That isn't how my life is working out now. Dad, you left me here, sink or swim, and lately, it feels like I'm sinking. I could use the help down here." He stopped and listened, hearing nothing but the hum of the engines and the faint sound of water sloshing against the ship.

The ship started to shift direction slightly. Garcia must have requested the course change. Harold waited a couple more minutes, but the only thing he felt was lightheaded from being inside the hot tub for so long. He forced himself out of the tub and collapsed on the deck, exhausted from the day's events.

***

Darla had shown up at some point after the sun went down and got him to go to bed. He had protested when she put a sleeping pill in his hand, but she'd insisted he took it to avoid having nightmares. The next thing he knew, the sun was up again, and the sea's small waves slapped the sides of the ship. The yacht gently rocked as they made their way towards the tiny dot on the horizon outside his cabin's window.

Harold rolled out of bed and into the shower. He was not motivated to face the world. The day was new, but his memories of yesterday were still fresh. He forced himself to get dressed and then sat on the edge of his bed, unsure how he would face the day.

Darla's distinctive knock broke through his self-pity. "Are you decent, hon?" her muffled voice asked through the door.

He wanted to send her away, but he knew a *no* would bring her in as quickly as a yes. His voice was sullen as he responded, "Come in."

The door opened. Normally, Harold would have been happy, even excited, to see Darla in her tight white shorts and clinging red cotton V-neck T-shirt. Her black hair was pulled back into a ponytail, and her makeup highlighted her dark eyes. Darla had even managed to make her black sling look sexy resting against the right side of her chest. Although he felt self-absorbed in his pity, he could tell Darla had hoped to take his mind off his troubles. Despite his foul mood, he was still drawn to Darla as she gracefully walked into his cabin on the slope of three-inch pumps that barely tapped the floor as the ship gently rolled.

Before Harold could stop himself, he said, "I see you have your sea legs."

Darla walked over and sat down on the bed. "I'm glad you complimented something. You have no idea how uncomfortable it is to wear these tight clothes on a moving ship."

"A little beauty to make me forget my beast?"

Darla kissed his cheek. "You're not a beast, love."

Harold glanced in her direction. "Uh-huh."

Darla slid her left arm across his shoulders, leaned in, and kissed his neck. "We'll get through this together."

"I know, but I can't undo what I've done. Every time I start to relax, the scene begins to run through my mind again."

Darla played with his red curls around his ears. "Then why do you want to be alone?"

Harold turned and faced Darla. Her hand dropped away.

"I don't want to be alone. I need to be alone. I need to figure out how to even face this."

She took his hand into her own. "But that's what I keep trying to tell you, love. You don't have to do it alone. I'm here to help you through it."

Harold raised her hand to his lips and held it there for several seconds, feeling the strength of her fingers. Then he gently laid them back down. "I know you're trying to help. Even Garcia gave me a pep talk last night."

Darla's eyes widened slightly. "What did he say?"

"He basically said what you have. I shouldn't be alone, and he told me some story about his dad in Vietnam. Then he said he knew how I felt but couldn't tell me why. He lost me at that point."

"Do you want me to tell you?"

Harold's head drooped slightly. "I'm not ready to talk about anything this morning. I just want some coffee and to take in the sea. I'm hoping that will cheer me up. Then we can talk later."

"May I join you?" asked Darla.

"If you like, but I'm afraid I'm not much company at the moment."

Darla stood and took his hand, and he stood up next to her. She looked up into his eyes. "That's okay, love. We don't have to talk. You can just sit and admire me."

His lips curved upward slightly. The two headed to the top deck where Frank had coffee and donuts waiting. Harold sat down across from Darla. "I feel like I'm at the butt of a conspiracy. A very fattening and delicious conspiracy."

Darla put her finger to her donut-crumbed lips. "Shh, you said no talking."

Harold slid a donut into his mouth and bit down on half of it. Perhaps this sort of silence would help him feel a little better.

The morning lifted Harold's spirits. Frank's fresh donuts had really hit the spot. He felt warm, relaxed, maybe even a little happy. He was sure somebody had spiked his coffee. Two hours after breakfast, he lay sacked out on a couch at the aft of the ship. A hard shove against his shoulder awakened him.

"Go get your stuff together," Garcia said. "The cabin cruiser will be here in under thirty to pick us up."

Harold felt a little groggy headed as he made his way to his cabin. He grabbed what few clothes he wore both on the island and the yacht, and that was when he noticed some clothes were missing, the clothes he told Frank to burn. How Frank burned them on the ship he had no idea, but he was glad to be rid of them. He packed his satellite phone and headed out towards the dive deck in anticipation of being picked up. By the time he caught up with everybody, Darla and Garcia were chatting and the boat was pulling up.

Garcia and Darla stopped discussing whatever topic they had been engrossed in when he got within earshot. Garcia turned to him. "Glad you made it in time. I was afraid we'd have to send Frank to help you along. Let's get off this ship and put the past few days behind us."

"I'm all for that."

As they rode away on the cabin cruiser, Harold looked back at *Sweet Revenge*. He spoke to himself, "We should change the name."

Darla overheard him. "What are you talking about?"

Harold pointed towards the yacht. "The ship. There's nothing sweet about revenge."

"I agree, but Garcia didn't see any point in changing it."

"Did I hear my name?" asked Garcia.

Darla turned to him. "Go back to what you were doing. We're just talking about your poor choice in ship names."

"John did that."

"We know," replied Harold.

Darla slipped her hand into Harold's. "We'll be home soon, love."

"Is that what we're calling Salvation Key now?" asked Harold.

Darla pressed herself against Harold. "Anywhere we are is home."

Harold smiled and tightly wrapped his arm around Darla. No matter how much he hated himself, her love made him feel human, hopeful.

Chapter 22

"Wake up, brat!" John's annoying voice echoed from the back of Harold's mind.

"Leave me alone," Harold mumbled in reply.

"I said, wake up!" A sharp pain hit Harold in his ribs. His arm jerked, and another pain shot up from his wrist to his shoulder. He rolled over onto his back and started breathing heavily. A black shadow slid over his view of the moonlit room. Harold felt paralyzed.

"Now, don't move," John's sarcastic voice said.

Harold was pinned, unable to raise his shoulders.

"This is just a dream," said Harold. He blinked his eyes several times, but the darkness remained.

"Come on, Harry, you have nothing to fear. It isn't real," Harold said to himself in a shaky voice.

Harold heard John's cackle crack the still air. "Oh, poor Harry. Do you miss Joshua so much that you have to mimic him? Are you going to start talking like your daddy next? You're just a pathetic, weak gorilla."

The mention of his father and Joshua's name did something inside Harold. Why was he afraid of John, even if he was a ghost? He had already defeated him. Why was he letting him manipulate his life? "You know, John, I really think it's time for you to go."

John's laughter shot an icy fear up Harold's spine. "Oh, you silly brat. You're a little late with that request. I mean, sure, I'll go, but after I introduce you to our new friend. Of course, you may want me to hang around, just to keep things from getting out of hand. I believe he's coming now."

Harold heard the French doors leading to the sundeck begin to rattle. He turned his head in that direction, and the black mist surrounding the bed lifted a little, and he could see his room. The blackness approaching the door seemed to consume every moonbeam around it. The French doors simply vanished into darkness. Suddenly yellow flames shot out where the eyes would be, if the blackness had eyes.

Harold didn't know why, but he knew immediately who it was. "Haidar," he whispered.

The blackness floated between the door and the bed. He hissed out, "Harold."

Harold wanted to run, but he was frozen, held down.

John's voice spoke from above the bed, "Do you see what you've done? You've unleashed the worst kind of evil."

Harold spoke, his voice barely above a whisper, "I let nothing loose. He was pure evil when he was alive."

"True, but that's because he only knew evil. You saw the bruises. You know Chuck beat him. You saw his fear. He was abused by ISIS, and then when he thought Chuck was his salvation, he entered another nightmare. Now look at him. You used him as a snack."

Harold glared at the darkness above him. "You know it wasn't like that. I couldn't help myself."

"Wrong!" screamed a tenor voice from the pitch-black void floating in the room.

Harold began to plead, "But I couldn't." He turned to face the darkness now floating closer to the bed. "You hurt Darla. You wanted to kill us. I couldn't let that happen."

The mist drew closer to the bed, and Harold nearly gagged on the sulfur emanating from its very presence.

"You could have killed me quickly, but you wanted to torture me. You wanted me to suffer."

Tears began to flow down Harold's face, and he hollered, "Yes, yes, I wanted you to suffer. I wanted to make you suffer like you wanted us to suffer. You're evil, pure evil."

The two voices floated through his mind, "Who's the evil one?"

Harold yelled, and the bed vibrated. With a mighty shove, the sheets and blankets flew over the foot of his bed. The empty room was lit with moonbeams shooting their light streaks through the French doors and window. Out the window, Harold could see the early gray light of dawn start to crack on the dark horizon to the east. He turned on the light next to his bed. It was almost six o'clock, but his body really wanted a few more hours of shuteye. Even so, he had no desire to walk back into another nightmare.

After a quick shower, Harold dressed in a pair of blue shorts, a PCH T-shirt, and sandals. Coffee was begging to be made. He left his bedroom, stood, stretched, and groaned on the sundeck. He turned to make his way down the stairs when a figure stunted his progress. A very annoyed looking Darla stood at the bottom. Her hair was tied up but had not been brushed out. Her shorts looked wrinkled, and she had obviously slept in the rumpled oversized shirt. She had a mug of steaming coffee in each hand.

"Oh," Harold said, "I'm surprised to see you. I thought you would sleep in." He then proceeded to walk down to her.

"I'm surprised to see me this morning, yet here we are," responded Darla.

"Did I wake you up?" asked Harold.

"Gee, I don't know. I heard someone holler, and the painting on my wall vibrated. Was that you?" Darla's sarcastic look caused him to respond with a single nod. "Then you woke me up."

He had seen her annoyed before, but he was pretty sure he had broken some sort of personal record. Harold took the coffee from her hand restricted by the sling.

"We're going for a walk, and we're going to talk through this problem of yours." She turned and began to walk away.

Harold quickened his pace to catch up.

"Wait, I've told you I don't want to talk about it."

Darla stopped and turned to face Harold, shocking him with the intensity of her glare. She forced her mouth into a twisted, sarcastic smile that he found terrifying. She spoke slowly and deliberately, "Darling, I love you, but protest this one more time, or say another word until you're spoken to, and I'll punch your beautiful throat."

Something inside him told Harold she wouldn't do it, but the look on her face told him not to test her. He pointed forward with his coffee mug, and the two began walking. They left the house and headed towards the quiet seaside. The crunching of the seashells under their feet sounded like thunder to Harold's tired brain. He carefully sipped his coffee and wished he had never awoken Darla. With the sky's slow transference from black to gray to gold in the early morning, Harold's fear from his nightmare had long since melted away, and now exhaustion began to push its way back into his body.

He heard something out in the glassy sea and saw six rings emanating on the still waters. Darla stopped and put her finger to her lips. They arrived at their favorite rock, and she looked at him then tilted her head at it. He put his coffee on one side of the rock and gently lifted Darla onto its flat surface before grabbing his coffee and joining her on the other side.

She held up her hand to stop his ascent then spoke quietly, "Don't say anything. Just wait."

Harold stood and silently sipped his coffee while he struggled to stay awake. In a few moments, he heard the waters ripple again. Six manatees broke the surface.

Darla whispered, "They're here around this time every day."

One of the manatees slowly approached the shallows. The large sea cow floated just beyond the rock, a few inches from the sandy bottom.

"Go say hello," said Darla quietly.

Harold looked at her, and she stuck out her index finger towards the water. He wanted to avoid another tense exchange, so he put down his mug and slowly waded out until the water's surface began to lap at his shorts. Although the Caribbean was not cold, the early morning was chillier than he liked. The cool waters cleared his cloudy mind. He was contemplating turning around when the manatee navigated to within arm's reach.

Harold reached out, and the mammal nudged his hand with its nose. Its stiff whiskers poked at his hand. The moment was surreal. In an instant, Harold forgot everything. He stood in amazement at the large, gentle creature who saw him more as a friend than a threat. He didn't know how long he had stood there, but the manatee dropped its head just below the surface and slowly swam out to deeper waters and greener pastures.

The sun had cleared the horizon by the time he joined Darla. Although he felt a little chilled, the sleepiness had completely cleared from his mind.

He reached over and kissed Darla on the cheek. "Thank you."

"Don't thank me yet. That isn't why we're here. I just thought you could use a pick-me-up before we have our little chat."

Harold pulled his feet up close to his body, wrapped his arms around his knees, and let himself relax. "Okay, I give up. What do you want to know?"

Darla traced his strong right arm with her index finger and then pulled it away. He followed her hand and then gazed into her face. The sadness Harold had seen before looked back into his eyes.

"You're not the only one to see ghosts. I was haunted by my victims for many years."

Harold's eyebrows went up in surprise. "What do you mean victims?"

"Well, that's how I saw them. All of them deserved to die, or at least deserved to be stopped, and that was the only way I had been trained to stop them. Unfortunately, those people never had a chance once they were in my crosshairs. So yes, I would call them my victims."

Harold silently stared out over the water.

Darla's left hand passed along his face. "What are you thinking?"

He gave a slight shrug. "I don't know. I just never pictured you as a killer."

She rested her head on his shoulder. "Neither do I. Most of the work I did in intelligence involved identifying targets in the field."

"So what? You are one of those geeks that sat behind a desk looking at satellite images and then one day decided she wanted to be a field agent?"

"No. I was always in the field. Satellite images can only take you so far, especially in countries like Afghanistan. Being a woman with olive skin, dark eyes and hair, I could blend in when I needed to with the population. Besides, a burqa can conceal many things. I liked my job because I never had to pull the trigger directly. The people I identified had not just killed one or two innocents but whole families and villages. Many were planning, or had planned, attacks on our homeland. I felt like I was doing God's work protecting the country."

Harold raised his hand. "Wait a minute. When I met you, you told me you were an analyst and spent time in Northern Africa."

She patted his knee. "My missions were need to know, and you didn't need to know, yet."

Harold stroked her ponytail and spoke as he looked back out over the waters. "I'm not sure I understand what this has to do with me. Suddenly I need to know? I'm out here in the middle of the Caribbean with arms dealers and spies. This is not what I went to business school for. You were doing what you were trained to do, and what you wanted to do. I'm not."

Darla took her head off his shoulder and turned and looked at him. "Just because you're doing what you are trained to do, and doing it for the right reasons doesn't mean you don't face consequences. I know what your nightmares are like. I had them myself, and sometimes I still have them."

He looked deeply into her sad eyes. "I had no idea. Why are you still doing this work if you're going through what I'm going through?"

"Well, to be perfectly honest, Garcia and your dad are to thank for that. Garcia pulled me into the church, and your dad gave me a chance to redeem myself."

"Humph," said Harold. "Despite what he claims, Garcia doesn't seem to be the religious type to me, and if I'm being honest, neither do you."

Darla's forehead wrinkled up into a scowl. "I'm not sure what your beliefs are, but I can assure you there's a history over many millennia of warriors who believed in God."

"What, like the Knight Templars or something?"

"No, they were heretics. I was thinking David, Gideon, Sampson, and the modern-day Mista'arvim. These people have helped the innocent."

Harold gently clasped her strong hand. "I'm sorry. I didn't mean that the way it sounded. Garcia just surprises me; that's all. So, how does going to church work into your life as a spy?"

She allowed her hand to remain in his as she continued. "It isn't about church. It's about forgiveness. Once I allowed myself to believe in something greater than myself, it was not a hard leap for me to accept the fact that a God would provide a way for people like me to be redeemed. It wasn't just the death that was eating away at my soul, it was the nightmares. It got to the point where I was waking screaming on almost a nightly basis. I had to re-battle the very enemies I had already defeated. At first it seemed fun to defeat the ghosts of my enemies, but then everything changed. I honestly thought I might end up going nuts."

"So, what changed?"

Darla took back her hand, put her arm across her chest, and held her injured arm. She pulled her legs in close. "She was an eight-year-old girl or at least she looked eight years old. She was really a small angel. I had been tracking an al-Qaeda target for two days. He finally ended up in a village deep inside the mountains of Afghanistan. I radioed his location to my contact at the appointed time. By that point, the target had been in a house for two hours. Nobody else was seen coming in or going out. I painted the side of the house with the portable laser, and a drone strike was called in. It was a good clean hit with no civilians close by. Or so I thought. Before the dust had settled, a woman came screaming from another street. She ran into the rubble, and men joined her moving rocks. In a few minutes, they pulled the dead body of a small child out of the rubble. I had no idea that there had been a sleeping girl in the house the entire time."

Harold reached over to kiss her strained forehead and gave her a long, gentle hug. He leaned back, and Darla's face appeared to relax a little, and then she continued.

"It was one thing to fight the demons that were rolling around inside my head, but everything changed after that little girl. They pulled me out of the field until I was cleared of intentionally targeting a civilian. Then one night, she appeared to me. It was almost as if she had waited for the investigation to end."

Her eyes began to tear up. Harold reached up and wiped away the first couple drops that ran down her cheeks. Darla looked at him with tears pooling. "She wasn't like the other things that haunted me when I slept. From the moment she showed up, she told me she forgave me. She would say things like, 'It's peaceful here, much better than the place I left.' That just made me feel even more guilty. I thought my mind was just trying to justify killing a little girl.

"I guess other people noticed I was having issues because I was reassigned stateside. That's how I met Garcia. He had me keep a watch on your family. We had some idea that one of your dad's competitors was attempting to color outside the lines in an effort to take out your company."

"Wait," said Harold. "Do you mean to tell me that you were still part of the CIA when I met you?"

Darla took a slow breath. "I had quit over your dad's suicide. Garcia talked me into staying with the investigation as an asset."

"So, what happened? How does this little girl's death tie into everything?" he asked.

"Garcia introduced me to your father before the suicide. Both had struggled with what I was going through. Garcia had his own demons from the field, and your father carried the burden of knowing his weapons were used not only on the guilty but sometimes the innocent."

Harold's eyebrows went up in surprise. "Dad never told me about any of this. I guess he didn't want to worry me. So, what happened?"

"I had given up trying to figure out what was real, a dream, or a nightmare. I had just hoped the nightmares would end. I'll confess, I was ready to end them myself if something didn't change. I had been to church, so I knew the whole Jesus thing, but I didn't think it applied. Your dad took me to the church to talk with his minister to see if he could help. By that point, I decided I would much rather accept something on faith instead of always looking for a solution where there was none. Garcia was key in helping me apply what I learned and work through forgiving my enemies."

Harold scratched his head. "So what? You just forgive your enemies? They disappeared from your dreams, and your nightmares ended? I'm not sure I buy that. Dad drove me to church my whole life, and I have forgiven a lot of people. I even forgave John for the hell he put us through. He's dead. There isn't anything else he can do to me. Still, John seems intent on hanging around, and last night Haidar joined him."

"That's not the only enemy I'm talking about. You must forgive yourself as well. We both know that killing someone evil makes us feel just as evil. You see, you still need to forgive yourself. For me, I learned to accept the fact that, for whatever reason, this is who I'm supposed to be. I don't understand it, and there are days I don't like it, but for now, it's who I am."

Harold sat silently, trying to comprehend everything she had shared with him. A question formed in his mind, "Why do you call the little girl your angel?"

A slight smile formed on Darla's face. "Because she's the one who taught me the most about forgiveness. After I forgave myself for the other deaths, I would still have nightmares. At first, the demons from my past would try to taunt me and make me angry, but I had grown tired of the game and refused to give in. Over a period of days and weeks, they begin to drop off one by one. I guess my mind was so busy with them that I'd forgotten about the little girl. Then one night, she appeared in my dreams again. She told me she forgave me, and I should forgive myself too. I woke up crying and asking God to show me how to forgive myself for killing someone so beautiful."

Harold reached over and gently rubbed her left arm. "So, is she gone now? Are you finally at peace?"

"I'm at peace, but she's still around. I knew she was someone special when I saw her in my room one day when I wasn't asleep. It was here on the island while John was still alive. Just after Joshua left, John was trying to decide if he could trust Joshua or if he should have him killed. I talked him into trusting Joshua. When I was done, I locked myself in my room and cried."

"Why?" asked Harold.

She looked into his eyes once more. They were filled with regret. "Please don't ask me those questions," she said in a pleading voice.

Harold thought he could figure out the answer and decided he should let it go. After all, it was in the past.

Darla continued, "I was on the floor, my face in my hands, weeping. I felt something touch me, and I jumped. I looked up, assuming it was John or one of the other men. Instead, my little angel stood next to me. I was very confused and wasn't sure what to think. I was afraid I was losing my mind at a time that I needed my wits about me the most. She told me not to fear, that I was forgiven, and everything would be okay. She reached over and hugged me. I really can't explain it. When I reached out, she was gone, but I could still feel her near me. I sat there and thought about what I had learned about love and forgiveness when I was at the church with Garcia and your dad. I decided to keep going, and in the end, we succeeded."

Harold let out a long breath. For several seconds, neither said a word. He finally asked, "Have you seen her since then?"

Darla turned and looked out over the water. "A few times. I felt very guilty about you attacking Haidar. I know I didn't cause myself to get shot, but I'm the reason you went berserk. She appeared last night and reminded me I'm loved and that I should talk to you. I went to sleep, and a few hours later, here we are. You need to let go of your demons. It isn't your fault. You're not the one who went after them. They came after you.

I don't know why you're the way you are any more than I know why I am the way I am. But, if I can accept who I am, so can you."

Harold responded in a raspy voice. "But that's part of the problem. I don't know who I am. I know I'm not some sort of superspy or some superhero that stepped out of the comic books. This is real life. How do I incorporate what I can become with the way I want to live my life?"

Darla leaned over and kissed him on the cheek. "I don't know, honey. I just know you need to take things on faith and live one day at a time. We can figure it out together. I know your secret, and now you know mine. Just promise me one thing—you will forgive yourself for those two killings. If you do, you can make the nightmares stop. As for the rest of it, you may need to lean more on faith and less on questions you can't answer."

Harold wanted to believe her. He wanted to be the man that she was describing. "Okay, I'll try."

She maneuvered around to get her good arm around his waist and rested her head on his shoulder. "It'll be okay as long as we can be together."

He put his arm around her, pulled her in close, and whispered, "I hope so."

CHAPTER 23

Harold sat at his father's old desk inside his office on the *Sweet Revenge*. His fingers ran across its bloodstains. He looked out the window and wondered what his dad would think about where his old desk sat now.

"Missing daddy, brat?" John's familiar voice made Harold cringe.

Harold kept looking at the window. "You know, a friend of mine gave me some great advice. She said I should just forget about you. What's done is done after all. It's not doing me any good to let you inside my head just because I killed you. In fact, you might even argue that you killed yourself."

John's familiar cackle brought the same chill down Harold's spine. "I think you have me confused with your father," snarled John.

"That's not going to work anymore. We all make our decisions. Dad made his; Joshua made his, and you made yours. You could've gone into hiding. Heck, you could have even given yourself up."

John's deep laugh echoed around the room. Harold finally turned to face him. The familiar ashen face and hollow eyes stared back at Harold. The embedded gun had returned to the side of his head.

Harold ignored his repulsion and continued speaking, "I'm being serious. What did you think would happen when you came to our house? Did you really think you could kill all three of us? And then what was your plan? Face it; you were driven by your own rage. Your hate had eaten you alive, and you were dead long before you stepped through the door of my house. I know that, and you know that. You can hang around here and waste your time, but I'm done fighting you or worrying about you."

The lips of John's specter twisted into a smile. He hissed and said, "Fine. I'll leave you to my compatriot. Good luck. You're going to need it."

"You can take Haidar with you," Harold shot back. "I can't change what happened, but in the end, he wanted to die too. If anything, I was more merciful than Chuck would've been. Either way, the past is over, and I'm moving on."

Flames shot from John's eyes, and his words reverberated in Harold's mind, "Who said I was talking about Haidar?" With that, the specter disappeared.

Harold's world turned dark. The alarm clock seemed to echo in his head, and he opened his eyes. The familiar roll of the yacht reminded him that he was at sea. The clock showed 7:30 a.m. Harold sat up on the edge of the bed and looked around. The cabin was quiet, and the ocean outside the windows was calm and beautiful. Although the deserted key was only a day's trip by ship, Garcia kept everyone aboard the yacht for an extended period to keep the team focused on the important work at hand. He had left Darla and Harold aboard ship most of the first day while he joined Alice at Crossroads Key in preparation for the meeting with Chuck and Nigel. Darla repeatedly discussed with Harold how he would simply confirm the electronic transfer of funds into the CIA's offshore account, but he was left out of the loop about everyone else's role. He only knew that they were to deliver two boxes of weapons and ammo for quality assurance. At least, that was how Garcia explained it.

Boredom, agitation, and stress quickly rolled over Harold. Today was the big day, but he was to continue sitting still while others worked. Garcia told him to enjoy the time off, but he had been either relaxing or talking for far too many days. Somehow knowing he would finally have something to do in the afternoon only made the morning that much more maddening. Harold looked around his cabin.

"I need some air," he said to himself.

He showered, dressed, and began his climb up to the top deck. Mid-deck he passed Frank arranging a place setting at the circular table. Harold greeted him and asked that his breakfast be served upstairs.

Harold sat down at the top deck's dining table, looked over the turquoise waters, and let out a long, slow breath. He heard footsteps coming up the stairs. Garcia emerged with two mugs of coffee, and Frank appeared directly behind him with two plates of eggs benedict. Harold said nothing and watched the two men approach.

"I come bearing gifts of food if I might join you," said Garcia.

"Suit yourself," responded Harold curtly.

Garcia took a seat directly across from him and put a coffee in front of himself and Harold. Frank placed the two plates down in front of the men and left.

"A million for your thoughts," joked Garcia.

Harold rolled his eyes. "I'm bored. Bored and irritated."

Garcia made a show of looking over the deck of the yacht. "First world problems?"

"I'm not joking. You've done nothing but keep me in the dark about what we are really doing today. In fact, you've been keeping me in the dark for most of my life."

Garcia's right eyebrow went up slightly. "Me? Who told you this?"

"Who told me doesn't matter. The fact that you aren't denying it just confirms what I found out." Harold took a sip of coffee and a large bite of his eggs benedict. He was in a mood to argue, but he was also hungry.

Garcia's lips curved up. "You would be such a good agent."

Harold waved his empty fork in Garcia's direction. "Forget it. Quit deflecting. We both know what I know. Why didn't you tell me about you, Dad, and Darla?"

"What do you mean?" asked Garcia. "I told you when we met I'd been watching your family."

Harold took another bite of food and let Garcia stare at him while he chewed. Harold pointed to Garcia's plate. "You should eat this before it gets cold. Frank did a great job."

Garcia leaned against the table and hovered just over his plate. "Don't try and play me."

Harold smiled and took a sip of coffee. He put his mug on the table and let loose a satisfied sigh. After wiping his mouth, he said, "I wouldn't try to play you, Agent Hernandez. At least not any more than you've played me. I'm curious though, why didn't you try and stop John's extortion scheme before my father killed himself? From the sounds of it, you and Dad were close enough to help Darla overcome her demons."

"Oh." Garcia began to eat his eggs, followed by a long swallow of coffee. "So, she told you about all of that."

Harold finished his food and coffee without saying a word.

"Okay, I see you want an explanation, and you deserve one," Garcia said. "I did know about John's schemes. That's why I brought Darla and your dad together. She's a good agent, a real good agent. I needed her to see that there were things she could use her talents for besides finding terrorists to bomb."

"But that's not my concern. You knew John was dirty. Why didn't you take care of him?"

Garcia finished off his food and then continued. "I'm surprised you would even ask me that. You know the CIA can't target US citizens. The FBI would have had to get involved."

"Exactly."

Garcia looked him in the eye. "Harold, you may not realize it, but your dad had enemies besides John. All powerful men do."

A small frown formed on Harold's face. "I never thought of my dad as powerful."

"Your father was building nuclear weapons. It doesn't get more powerful than that."

Harold's mouth dropped open slightly and he nodded. His dad never talked about what their weapons could do. He always focused on the business. Harold had been viewing his new role as chairman as a purely business responsibility. If he was honest with himself, he blocked out what their weapons would do to humanity. "It just never occurred to me."

Garcia pushed his chair back and put his napkin on the table. "I know. Ironically, your father's enemies obsessed about the power your company represents, but your dad never thought about his business that way either, and I can tell you learned his lessons well."

"Thanks."

Garcia continued, "If I had pulled in the FBI, then word would have gotten around to certain politicians. I didn't know how deep the conspiracy went at the time. John boxed your father in, and he took the only action he thought he could. I was angry, so I knew I couldn't handle things directly for fear my emotions would cause me to make a dumb mistake somewhere along the way. I knew Darla could get us the evidence without directly involving the CIA. I was right too, at least until John went full psycho. I didn't see that coming, but fortunately, you had that handled."

"You should have seen the local cops when you pushed your way into the house that day. They were none too happy. To be fair to those guys, they're all good people. They were really nice to our family when Dad died."

"It's a territory thing. None of us like it when someone comes over to take a case we think we should solve."

"Even," Harold raised fingers to form air quotes, "the CIA?" He let his arms drop and slapped the table and laughed.

"Yea, yea," said Garcia, rolling his eyes. "Listen, I didn't really come up here to explain myself to you. I need you to be ready for this afternoon."

Harold pushed back his chair, stretched his legs, and crossed his ankles. "Well, since you haven't been telling me anything, I'm sure I'm totally prepared."

Garcia dismissively waved off Harold's verbal jab. "Relax. You're not really doing anything. Chuck may ask you if the boxes of weapons really came from PDS. You're just there to reassure him and validate the transfer."

Harold put his elbow on the table, rested his chin on his hand and fluttered his eyelids. "I think Chuck has a man crush on me since he thinks I saved his life. I could probably tell him a box of water pistols are the smart rifles and he'd believe me."

Garcia moved up to the edge of his seat and leaned in. His tone became urgent. "Harold, listen to me. Chuck is a very dangerous man. Even his friends fear him. He may say you saved his life and now you're best buddies, but he can just as quickly put a bullet in your head."

Harold leaned back in his chair. "Easy. I was only making a joke."

"This is not the time for joking. From this moment until we see Chuck sailing away with his sample boxes, we have our game faces on. And, for the record, Darla is off limits. She is in her cabin talking with Alice via radio finalizing today's events before we all leave."

Harold slapped the table with his large right hand causing the dishes to bounce. "What! She can't go. She has an injured arm."

Garcia glared at Harold. "Never tell me how to take care of my team. Darla knows what she's doing. I already offered to pull her and take one of the Franks along, but she refused. Besides, there shouldn't be any gunplay. We're simply delivering the weapons."

"Really? What about the first two times we met? There was plenty of gunplay then."

"Yes, and Haidar was at the center of it all. He's dead. Nigel isn't exactly the aggressive type."

Harold grunted and went silent for a few seconds. "We're sure they won't find the trackers?"

"Not unless they bring an electrical engineer with a microscope to trace all the circuits, and even then, your engineers confirmed it was impossible."

"Fair enough, I trust my people to do a good job."

Garcia stood. "I'll see you in three hours at the dive deck. Today we're going to put away some very dangerous people."

Harold watched Garcia make his way quickly down the steps. He was a man on a mission, hopefully a successful one.

***

The next three hours were long and restless for Harold. He had eventually made his way back to his small office. He decided to write out a quick impromptu update to his will. He had no idea where the thought came from, but it seemed like the right thing to do. Tom had done something similar when he was deployed while in the military. Tom mailed his will to Harold to avoid upsetting his parents. Harold wanted Joshua to have half of everything, and his lost half-brother, Bill, to have the rest. He folded and slid the paper inside an envelope and then gently laid the envelope on top of the bloodstains on his father's desk.

Finished with his paperwork, he made his way to the main deck a half an hour early. Garcia, Darla, and Frank were busy on the diver's deck prepping the Kodiak and checking communications gear hidden in the small craft.

Garcia pointed at Harold. "You're on time. Have you ever shot a gun?"

"Dad made sure I could safely handle a weapon."

"Good. Do me a favor, grab that hand radio and sound check with Alice. After that, check those small handguns and make sure they're properly loaded. Those are for Darla and me."

Harold strolled over to the coffee table near the ladder leading to the dive deck. He picked up the radio. "Radio check, radio check."

"Five by five," Alice's voice replied. "Why do you have the radio?"

Garcia hollered from below, "No names!"

"I know." Harold pressed the transceiver's button, "I was told to do the radio check,"

"Roger," answered Alice.

Harold put down the radio and checked the Smith and Wesson M&P pistols. Both weapons had full clips.

He carefully placed them back down and hollered to Garcia below, "Everything checks out."

Clattering feet quickly came up the ladder from the dive deck. Garcia hopped up on the main deck with Darla quickly following.

Garcia placed the pistol in a holster and slid it into the small of his back. Darla reached over with her left hand and grabbed her pistol.

"Need a hand?" asked Harold.

Darla's eyes looked cold and serious as she stared into his eyes. "Not today."

To Harold's surprise, Darla slipped a holster out of her sling and holstered the pistol. She slid the holster back into her sling and appeared to shove it into an unseen pocket.

She looked up at Harold, and for a moment her familiar smile returned. "Sorry, game faces." With that, her smile disappeared as though it had never existed.

Harold turned to Garcia. "Why pocket your weapons? You promised me no gun play."

"That doesn't mean we go in unarmed. Chuck will be armed as well. I'm sure of it."

"Darla better not get hurt."

Garcia ignored Harold's warning.

"Let's get boarded. We're on a clock," said Garcia.

The team loaded into the Kodiak and began the rough ride over to the desert island as the yacht turned away and headed far away to safety. Nobody said a word as the Kodiak bounced along. Harold took point as usual. He looked over his shoulder at Darla and Garcia. They were the most serious he had ever seen either of them. For the first time, the demon he held inside seemed small and insignificant. It was clear his compatriots had worked to entrap people of violence before. The look in their eyes told Harold they had seen deals go bad and were working through their options. Harold turned back to the front of the boat and watched the island grow quickly before them.

Garcia beached the craft, and everyone disembarked. The whistle of a breeze blowing left to right gave the empty desert key an eerie feeling. Harold was used to Alice or someone from the team greeting them. Today there was nobody. Two rifle boxes standing three high sat only ten yards from the water. The familiar meeting tent was nowhere to be seen. Near the rifles sat a folding table with four chairs.

"Why four chairs?" Harold asked Garcia. "There's five of us."

"We're not here to chit chat with Chuck and Nigel," he responded. "I doubt they will even get used. I asked Alice to put something down where we could rest if Chuck was delayed."

"He should be coming into view anytime now," Darla said.

The three stood silently and scanned the horizon.

"Why wouldn't he come around from the other side of the island?" asked Harold.

Darla had her eyes shaded as she continued to peer towards the watery horizon. She responded without moving, "Chuck's ship is supposed to meet our cargo vessel about sixty miles out from this direction. We're fairly certain he will remain with his ship after he leaves us, so it stands to reason he'll come from the same direction."

After ten more minutes, Harold went and dropped down into one of the chairs. "I don't understand. He's never been late."

Garcia looked over his shoulder at Harold. "He wasn't technically buying illegal weapons. Today we're exchanging money and guns. Chuck isn't a fool. He'll take every precaution."

Harold replied, "I still say he's coming from…"

The sound of a boat approaching from around the island broke through the rushing wind to their right. Nigel piloted the shallow watercraft while Chuck manned the lone machine gun mounted on the bow of the boat. Nigel pulled the boat up and stopped it just short of the shoreline. Chuck hopped over the craft's side and dropped a small anchor that was tied to a rope into the wet sand.

"Sorry to keep you waiting," said Chuck with a smile. "Even in calm waters, she's a little bumpy, but I don't have to tell you. That Kodiak must be a real bum buster. I can't imagine riding in that thing for very long."

"You get used to it," Garcia replied.

Nigel left the boat with a metal briefcase and stood next to his boss. "Well, let's take a look at those weapons."

"And the money?" asked Darla.

Chuck gave a quick nod towards Nigel. "We'll take care of transferring the funds as soon as we confirm the weapons."

"Let's see what's in the case first," Harold said from his seat.

Chuck looked over at him. "Well, my favorite warrior, it appears you are a man of brawn and brains. Fair enough." Chuck pointed at the table. "Nigel."

Nigel walked over and cracked open the case. A laptop was hooked up to a spare battery with a folding satellite antenna tucked away inside the case.

"Boot it up," said Harold.

"What? You don't trust us, mate?" asked Nigel.

Harold stared at Nigel and said nothing.

Darla interrupted, "Harold's serious when it comes to his company. Don't take it personally."

"Of course not. It's just business. I hook into the bank account, and you open the crates."

Harold gave one nod. Garcia took that as his cue to open the top crates. Chuck walked over with him.

"Let's open them both up."

"We're going to unload both crates?" Garcia's voice sounded a little concerned.

Chuck raised his eyebrow, looked over at Nigel, and back at Garcia. "There's four of us. Your winged dove over there can watch the computer."

Nigel immediately stood and gestured his hand towards the seat for Darla. She stepped over and lowered herself into the chair. Harold and Nigel joined the other men and unstacked the boxes. Garcia grabbed a crowbar and broke the tops off each crate. Chuck and Nigel grabbed one weapon out of each box and placed them on the table.

Nigel looked over at Darla. "I say, lovey, mind if we close that computer and move the two of you? We need this space."

"Everything on the screen appears ready to go. Suit yourself."

Nigel shut the lid, and the computer's power light began to blink on the side. He moved the laptop over and set it on top of the guns in the nearest box.

Chuck pointed to the gun boxes and looked over at Garcia. "If you three wouldn't mind standing over by the other guns, we'd like to examine these unimpeded."

"Of course," said Garcia, and the three of them stood near the laptop.

Chuck and Nigel opened the bolt of each weapon and examined it. They then proceeded to go through the process of breaking down each weapon via the convenient buttons and latches that allowed the owner easy access to clean them. By the time they were halfway through, Harold was beginning to wonder if they were going to have to be there all day while the two examined every weapon.

Harold crossed his arms and looked up into the sky. There was not a cloud to be found or any sign of a drone. He had hoped to spy even a dot the size of a mosquito, but there was nothing nearby in visual or audio range. Anything high enough not to be seen or heard had the possibility of leaving a faint contrail or would sometimes reflect the sun if only for an instant. It would be imperceptible unless you knew how to focus your eyes. There was nothing in the air anywhere near them.

"Looking for something?" asked Chuck.

Harold blinked and looked back down at Chuck. "No, I was just admiring the sky and contemplating how long today will take if you do this to each of these guns."

"I understand. We have a celebration planned as well. Don't worry. These will do. I don't suppose you all would like to join our party. I can promise you, it will be unlike anything you've experienced."

Garcia jumped in, "We can't disappoint our own guests."

"Of course," Chuck responded. "I don't suppose anybody bothered to bring some ammunition."

"Right here." Garcia reached down, opened a lone box and handed Chuck three magazines.

"Where are the rest of my rounds?"

"Out on the cargo ship with the guns."

Harold interjected, "I assumed you weren't going to light up all your ammo on the island. They're expensive after all."

"Always the businessman I see," Chuck said.

"When there's business to be done."

A loud static squawk rose up from the walkie-talkie sitting at the back of the Kodiak.

Chuck cleared his throat. "I thought this handoff was supposed to be unobserved. You assured me that you had gotten the approval from your superiors to run this operation off the books. Why would you need a radio?"

"Come on, Chuck," Darla said. "We all know we both have radios. Would you want to ride in that small thing without one? Besides, I know, and you know, we both have ships out in the ocean somewhere, and judging from your boat, yours is bigger than ours. How do you think they'll know to pick us up without a radio? Stop playing games."

Chuck's eyebrows raised slightly. "Even wounded you're a shrewd woman. I suppose that's why Harold is in love with you."

Harold's body tensed up at Chuck's flirtatious tone.

Chuck let loose a nervous but maniacal laugh.

"What's so funny?" asked Harold.

Chuck gained control of himself. "Your pecs puffed up when I mentioned your girlfriend."

Harold crossed his arms.

Darla stood closer to Harold and patted his arm. "Harold," she said quietly, "in our last meeting, you killed Haidar for shooting me. I believe Chuck thinks you're the jealous type."

Chuck interjected, "I'm sorry, big man. I know you didn't finish off Haidar just for my benefit, but the effort is still appreciated. Your love for one another is obvious to anyone who watches the two of you together." Chuck looked over to Garcia. "I appreciate you letting the two of them work together. Lovers can make powerful allies."

"I know what I'm doing."

"Nigel, go get their radio."

Chuck quickly raised his hand. "Before you protest, I'm not taking it, but I prefer to have it nearby. In case anyone says something on it I should hear."

Nigel brought back the walkie-talkie and put it on the table.

Chuck and Nigel each loaded a magazine. "Back to business."

One by one, they flipped on the targeting system and squeezed off a round in each weapon. Harold wondered if the dummy weapons were on the waiting cargo vessel or if Garcia had lied to the board about his intentions.

Once they laid all the weapons back on the table, Chuck looked back at Nigel. "Did you leave all the sites activated?"

"Absolutely," responded Nigel.

Chuck pointed to their boat. "Go get the scanner."

Garcia started to walk towards the table, but Chuck put his palm up and then pointed to the guns. "We're not done here."

"What are you scanning for?" asked Garcia.

"Why do you care?" asked Chuck.

"I don't want some device running across my hardware and screwing up the electronics."

Harold thought he saw a glint of anger in Chuck's eyes. Chuck's left eye twitched slightly as he looked at Garcia. "Don't worry. I'm not going to break your toys. Besides, if I do, they aren't worth buying." Chuck turned his attention to Harold. In an instant, his eyes changed from a glare to a glint, and a slight smile formed on his newly relaxed face. "Besides, I know you wouldn't sell me junk. We're friends, right, big man?"

Harold gave a cautious nod. He tried to decide if Chuck was psychotic or the world's greatest actor who wanted to keep them on their heels. Nigel walked back up with a gray box about the size of a gauss meter. He put on a pair of headphones, connected them to the device, and began to wave it over the smart sites.

"What's the toy?" asked Harold.

Chuck pointed towards Nigel. "You'll have to ask my genius there. It's something he built himself, and no, he can't work for you."

"Pity."

Nigel finished and motioned for Chuck to follow him. The two walked out of hearing range, and then Nigel whispered in his ear.

"I don't think this is good," mumbled Harold.

"Easy, honey," said Darla.

Garcia murmured, "Be ready, just in case."

Chuck hollered back to the group, "Darla, would you please join us?"

"Why?" asked Garcia.

Harold stepped forward and Chuck did the same, hollering, "Both of you, calm down and stay where you are. Nigel has a question that Darla should be able to answer. Frankly, Garcia, I trust her more than you."

Harold took a step back. His fists clenched at his sides. His voice deepened, and he turned to Garcia. "I don't like this."

"Neither do I."

Harold watched Darla walk over to the table. The two men showed Darla the readings. Her eyes scanned across the weapons, and she said something. Before Harold could blink, Nigel pulled a revolver from the front of his pants, put it against Darla's head, and wrapped his left arm around her neck. Harold immediately ran towards Nigel and Chuck, and Garcia passed him.

"Stop!" Chuck held both arms extended. "Don't move. I would hate to kill such a beautiful woman, but I will."

"Have you lost your mind?" asked Garcia.

"Let her go!" growled Harold as he attempted to keep himself under control.

"You disappoint me, Garcia," Chuck said. "I mean, I'm impressed but disappointed nonetheless. You said you were double-crossing the CIA, but here I find trackers on the guns."

Garcia recovered his poise. He pulled his sunglasses out of the front pocket of his shirt and slipped them on. "I don't know what you're talking about, Chuck."

Chuck frowned, and Harold felt the beast pushing to rise from within. He wanted Chuck to try something, anything. Everyone would die if Darla was harmed. Guns would not stop him. Harold struggled to stay in control, his breaths quick and shallow. He looked at Nigel and saw fear in his eyes while Darla's eyes glinted, almost as if she was happy to be in this predicament. Her breaths were almost imperceptible, even to Harold. Garcia's breath was even and determined. Chuck's breathing carried a faint growl, and Harold saw the rage inside his eyes.

Chuck's voice sounded like a controlled rage was building inside him. "There are GPS trackers embedded in the weapons. Nobody betrays me. You know that."

Garcia's palms pointed to the sky as he raised his arms in a pleading motion. "Chuck, it's me, Garcia. How long have we known each other now? Why would you think I'd ever betray you? Maybe the CIA did it and didn't tell me. Did you think about that? Who's to say they aren't after you and me?"

Chuck crossed his arms, and Harold could see the rage relax slightly, but then it returned. This time his lips twisted into a snarl beyond any micro expression. Chuck's gun came out, and a bullet embedded itself in the sand in front of Garcia before he had a chance to flinch.

"Are you out of your mind?" asked Garcia with a slight quiver in his voice.

Chuck's voice thundered, "One more word and I'll drop you where you stand. The only reason you're breathing is my big friend next to you. Bullets will only make him mad, and I can't have that."

Garcia faced Harold, whose view of the world was quickly turning crimson. His heartbeat grew louder, but Harold could see Chuck's rage disappear as he looked into his eyes.

Chuck spoke calmly and evenly to Harold, "I don't want to kill her, but I will. You can't stop me. Even you aren't faster than a speeding bullet. If you understand me, nod your head."

Harold desperately wanted to feel the hot steel projectiles hit his body and to destroy everyone before him, but something held him back. Darla. He would not let Darla be harmed. His father and Joshua's voices rang inside his mind, *"Protect the village."* Harold's head twitched.

"Don't move," warned Chuck as he waved his gun in Harold's direction.

Harold snorted.

"Good boy," Chuck responded with a wry smile. "Nigel, with me. Darla, you're going for a short boat ride."

Darla attempted to wiggle free, and Nigel let his left fist rise and push against her wound. She twitched, and a small cry rose from her lips. A low growl rumbled from Harold and grew louder until everyone stopped and turned his way.

"No!" hollered Chuck. "Nigel, you hurt that woman, and I'll let Harold tear you limb from limb. Darla, don't resist or Nigel will shoot. If we kill you, we'll unload these weapons into your boyfriend. I don't care how crazy he gets. He won't survive."

Harold looked at Darla. For a moment, he saw defeat and then contentment. "Okay," she muttered.

Nigel slowly started backing up towards their boat.

"Chuck," said Garcia, "don't do this. I'm telling you I didn't know."

Chuck stopped but pointed for Nigel to continue. "If your friends were after both of us, they would have appeared by now. You don't put trackers on something unless you intend to catch someone, and you don't wait when you have your prey. If there are trackers here, I'm sure your ship is loaded with bugged or bogus rifles."

Garcia was silent.

"You'll be hearing from me," said Chuck.

"Not if you hear from me first," Garcia responded.

Chuck gave a wry smile. "You have no idea what you've done. When I don't deliver these weapons, I'll not only be out of business, but it will ruin everything I've built. I am going to have to show my associates I'm still in control if I want to survive. Do yourselves a favor, hide, all of you—your families, friends, everyone. Hide them all, and maybe some will survive. I'm only warning you as a favor to Harold." Chuck turned to

Harold. "I like you. You're a man of your word, not like Garcia. I'd hate to hunt you, but you've been warned. I don't know what rock you hide under, but go there and wait. Find anyone you love and get them there too. Anyone I find in the open is fair game. You'll find your wounded love in the ocean, unharmed. Make sure Garcia monitors for an emergency beacon. If he doesn't, you should kill him."

Chuck turned and ran to the boat. He quickly climbed on board and began working to start the engine. He hollered down to Nigel, "Get the anchor and don't forget our insurance."

Nigel backed to the anchor. Harold walked ten steps closer, and Nigel pressed his pistol against Darla's temple and shook his head once. Harold heard the click of a large rifle bolt and looked up. Chuck stood behind the mounted M240 at the front of the boat. The gun was pointed directly at Harold. Harold stood still, drawing in more air. He could sense it, his moment was coming. Harold's muscles tingled, and his arms and legs flexed in anticipation. He glared at Nigel. The fear in Nigel's eyes made him hungry for battle. He longed to tear him apart but then Darla's eyes caught Harold's.

She looked deeply into his eyes. Her contentment was replaced with the love Harold had gazed into for hours. The beast within stared intently into her face. She gave a slight shake of her head. *What does she mean, no?*

Nigel put his pistol behind his back. Harold looked up at Chuck. He swept the gun from him to Harold's left where Garcia stood out of his sight. Harold knew he wasn't fast enough. His father's voice echoed in his mind once more, *"Protect The Village."* Joshua's voice trailed behind, *"Don't harm your family."*

A smile escaped Darla's lips and then they twisted. She screamed in pain as she forced her sling and arm up and back down hard. Harold watched Nigel's breath escape from his lips and pain fill his face. Darla stomped on his instep and ran towards Harold. Bullets hit the sand around him as he ran for Darla. He grew angrier. *How can he miss?* Harold ran in a straight line, hungry for the feeling of his flesh burning. It didn't matter. He would soon taste the flesh of his enemies.

Harold drifted right to avoid Darla, but she suddenly dove into his path and wrapped her left arm around him.

"Stop!" she screamed.

Harold tried to push her away, but he was unable. He was angry and confused. There was no reason she should be able to hold him, but he could not push her away without injuring her.

"Look at me," yelled Darla as bullets peppered the sand around them.

Harold looked down into her eyes. Tears pooled up in them, and they were sadder than he had ever seen. Darla put her head on his chest. "I can't lose you."

"You stupid cow!" screamed Nigel from beside the anchor.

Darla released Harold, and he watched her quickly pull the pistol from her sling with her left hand. With barely a glance over her shoulder, she shot in Nigel's direction. Harold's face formed a menacing grin as he watched a maroon mist fly into the reddish air out of Nigel's knee. Nigel screamed and collapsed in the shallow water. Chuck's bullets grew closer, and Harold grabbed Darla, spun around, and collapse on the ground with her underneath. He heard her scream in pain as his weight went down on her injured arm.

Soon, thought Harold, *soon the hot metal will finally pierce my flesh, and then my anger will rise and nobody will be able to stop me.* A bullet kicked up the sand at his foot, but then the gunfire stopped raining down on them. Harold could hear gunfire to his left. Round after round, left and right continued.

"Let me up," grunted Darla.

Harold grunted. "Hold still, Mom"

Everything went quiet, and then two more shots came from Garcia's direction. The boat's motors roared and then also fell silent.

"We're even, Harold!" screamed Chuck. Then the motors screamed back to life.

Harold refused to move as he listened to the boat begin to sweep around the island.

CHAPTER 24

"You're crushing me, and what the heck do you mean by *mom?*" moaned Darla.

Harold tried to push himself up, but his body felt heavy, far too heavy to lift on his own. He tried to suck in more oxygen to give himself the strength to get up, but he felt as if he was suffocating. "Help me," he gasped.

Darla's good arm pushed against his shoulder. Both shouted as they rolled him over. Sunlight met his eyes, and Harold covered them with his arm. He sucked in more and more air. With each breath, he could feel the heaviness of his body dissipate.

Garcia's voice broke through his determined breaths, "Are you two okay?"

Harold removed his arm and found Garcia's silhouette blocking the sun. "I'll survive."

Darla's pained voice responded, "I think all the wrinkles are pressed out of me. Thanks, dear."

Harold looked over. "Sorry."

Darla had a familiar twinkle in her eyes, and she responded in a raspy voice. "Don't be sorry. Some women pay a lot of money to have that done."

Darla's face turned back to the sky, and she took determined breaths. After taking in an extra-long breath, Darla asked in a pained voice, "Why did you call me mom?"

Harold took two more long breaths and then answered, "I don't know. I just knew I had to protect my family."

"Do you mean I remind you of your mother?"

Harold looked up at the sky. "No. I mean…I don't know. It's not like I think about her that way."

"Joshua and I may have a little chat," said Darla. A faint smile appeared between breaths and winces of pain.

"Do either of you feel up to moving?" asked Garcia.

Harold turned back towards Garcia's voice, and the sun hit his eyes again. When he shaded his eyes, he found Garcia standing at their feet. "Sorry, yea."

Harold's muscles felt stiff as he forced himself to his feet. He turned to help Darla up. She ignored the gesture and groaned as she got to her feet.

"Where's the radio?" Darla asked. "We need to catch him."

Garcia pointed to the sand near the table. A bullet had pierced all the way through the device. Several guns and Chuck's laptop had taken several rounds as well.

"Let's get to the Kodiak," gasped Darla.

She took one step and stopped. Harold looked over at their craft. The large inflatable craft sat deflated on the beach with multiple bullet holes.

Darla's head drooped. Harold scanned the beach. A blood trail headed towards the water's edge and then disappeared.

"Where's Nigel?" asked Harold.

Garcia crossed his arms. "It was the craziest thing I've ever seen. When the bullets stopped flying, Chuck backed his boat into the small bay dragging the anchor with Nigel holding onto the rope at the waterline. Then Chuck pulled both of them up. Actually, it was almost like he yanked them free of the water. I've never seen strength like that. Present company excluded, of course."

A thought popped into Harold's head. "You don't suppose he's like me, do you?"

Garcia scowled and was silent for a moment. "He's far too controlled. I mean, if he is, and he has that much control, he's deadlier than we thought."

Darla's voice was hesitant. "Do you think, maybe, that's Bill?"

Harold turned to Garcia. "Take off your sunglasses."

"What?"

"Just do it," said Harold. "Take them off and look me in the eye."

Garcia complied.

Harold stared intently into his eyes. "Tell me the truth. Was that my brother?"

He could see the effortlessly calm look in Garcia's eyes. "I promise you, that's not your brother."

"Do you know where he is?" asked Harold.

Garcia put his sunglasses back on. "Not really. We think he's in North Carolina. We know he studied business while in college in New York, but he's no arms dealer. By all accounts, your half-brother has lived a very normal, boring life."

"If he's not Chuck, we need to find him before Chuck does," Darla said.

"Why?" asked Harold.

Darla drew in a slow breath and focused her speech. "Chuck said he needs to show he's in control. He may use your brother to not only pull Garcia into the open, but also other agents who would attempt to capture him. If he kills Garcia and anyone else his buyers would consider high-value targets he might be able to win back their favor."

Garcia spoke up, "Please, don't forget who we are. If the CIA isn't tracking him, I doubt Chuck will be able to dig him up."

"But you could find him, which means Chuck could find him?" asked Harold.

"Sure, we can find anyone given enough time and resources, but you're assuming Chuck even knows he exists. I'm more concerned for Joshua."

A wave of panic hit Harold. "We need off this island now!"

"Easy," said Garcia. "Help should be here in about an hour."

Harold started running up the path. "I'll be back," he shouted over his shoulder.

"There's nothing over there," yelled Garcia, but Harold was not convinced.

Despite his stiffness, Harold forced his legs to move as fast as they were able. Burning pain bit into his calves as he fought the sandy ground. He traveled over the hill to the other side of the island and scanned the horizon, but all he saw was the clear water without so much as a speck. Then he remembered.

Harold traced his steps back, searching for any sign of a trail or broken sawgrass. At last he found what he was searching for—footprints in the soft ground partially hidden by the low grasses. They would have been easy to miss if he hadn't been searching diligently. Harold veered to his right and followed the footsteps to a short drop off. There he found thick bushes sitting against one another. Although they were native to the Caribbean, he thought they seemed a little out of place. Growing up in California, he knew lush plants didn't grow in a desert landscape or rough mountainous terrain without an increase in water and more of the same plants nearby. Yet, here sat a group of lone cocoplums near the seawater's edge without another plant anywhere on the island.

His father had taught him about camouflage as a teenager. Harold would sometimes join his father at a test range to see a weapons test. The secret to finding something that did not belong was to look for it hidden out in the open. He looked closer. In the center of the plants was a bump in the sand. Harold reached down and found a handle. The plastic bush separated from the real vegetation, and the door swung open. A small concrete bunker sat before him. Harold stepped into and then squatted inside the small space. It was little more than a glorified duck blind made from concrete. He felt around, but there was no radio or storage, just a short concrete shelf where Alice likely placed her laptop and perhaps a small radio. Discouraged, Harold pushed and twisted his way free of the hiding place and closed the camouflaged door.

The path back was long and painful. Harold stood at the top of their traditional meeting hill when he heard the buzz of a large drone. High above, a speck in the sky increased in pitch and accelerated straight over the island in the general direction Chuck had gone. Harold started back down the trail. He caught sight of the beach below. Garcia had moved the gun boxes and pieces of the deflated craft to fashion a large arrow in the sand pointing in the direction Chuck had disappeared. Harold made his way towards the beach. Darla was resting in a chair; a small blood stain had formed on her shirt.

"How bad is it?" asked Harold as he approached her.

Darla tried to shrug but then winced. "I think I tore some stitches."

"Do you want me to look at it?" Harold asked as he reached for her shoulder.

Darla pulled back. "No, I'll be okay. Help will be here soon."

"I saw the drone."

Darla's face formed pained expressions as she spoke. "Oh, that isn't the cavalry. That was just a predator drone. I'm sure Alice sent it to see what's going on. I expect they'll be along shortly. Why don't you sit down?"

Harold grabbed a chair that had been knocked over and sat down next to Darla.

"What were you looking for?"

"I don't know. I thought maybe I could see Chuck or maybe he would change his mind and try to double back. I'm worried about Joshua and Maria. Chuck's really gone, and we're stuck here unable to contact anyone."

Darla used her good hand to pull Harold's hand into her lap. He looked into her eyes, and she leaned in to kiss him. He could feel her lips quiver with pain.

Darla released her kiss and said in a determined voice, "Don't worry. If he's within fifty miles of here, and he is, that drone will take care of him."

The still, salt air belied the chaos around them until it was broken by the roar of a fast-moving boat. A Navy riverine cut through the waters with speed and determination and then slowed as it beached. A second craft came into view before the first silenced its engines. The Special Boat Team disembarked and formed a quick perimeter around the beach as the second boat made its landing. A crewman attempted to help Alice out of the small craft, and she slapped his hand away.

Easily clearing the craft's ledge, she made a small splash in the shallow water. Alice pointed at Garcia as she walked up the beach. "You, with me, and take off those ridiculous sunglasses." She then pointed at Darla. "Somebody take a look at her shoulder and stop the bleeding." Lastly, she turned her attention to Harold. "You, don't move. We need to have a chat."

Garcia removed his sunglasses and skulked quietly behind Alice to the normal meeting area and then disappeared over the hill as they continue walking. A medic came over, and Harold moved out of the way. He knew Darla did not need him hovering over her while she was having her shoulder tended to. Harold wandered over to the boxes and noticed the bullet holes. Many of the rifles inside had sustained damage from the barrage but had managed to stop the bullets from penetrating from the other side. Garcia's body imprint firmly packed the sand where he had hidden behind the shallow boxes during the gun battle. Three empty handgun magazines lay in the sand. A single smart rifle lay near the imprint with its magazine still in it. Harold picked it up and ejected the magazine to find it spent of ammo. He dropped both back on the sand at his feet.

Harold looked over at their stricken craft. He was surprised to see bullet holes from this side. One of the Navy crafts sat where Chuck's boat had been earlier. There could not have been any cross fire. It looked as if Garcia had shot at the boat as well as at Chuck. A chilling thought entered Harold's mind, *What if Garcia really is dirty? Darla and I had our heads down. Did Chuck really escape the way Garcia claimed or was it all made up?* Harold walked over near the location Nigel should have been. Unfortunately, in their haste to secure the beach, the Navy crewmen had managed to stomp out any signs of footprints and had even covered the blood trail.

Alice and Garcia appeared back at the top of the hill. Alice followed him partway down the hill, stopped, and hollered, "Harold, I told you not to move."

Darla raised her good arm. "My fault." Her slurred speech told him the medic had given her some pain medicine.

Alice pointed to Harold. "Never mind. Grab two chairs and bring them up here."

He started to acknowledge her, but she had already turned and headed back over the top of the small hill. Garcia walked over to him as he gathered the other two chairs that lay on their sides. Garcia's eyes pierced into Harold's. "I can't believe you did that."

"Did what?" asked Harold. "I've had enough games for one day. What are you talking about?"

"You and Tom went behind my back."

"I don't need your permission to run my company," Harold quipped.

Garcia put on his sunglasses with exaggerated determination. "We'll talk about it later. Alice is not a patient woman."

Harold headed up to Alice with the two chairs.

Alice was waiting just over the ridge. Her foot tapped, and her arms were crossed in front of her.

"Where do you want these?" asked Harold.

Alice pointed directly in front of her. He placed the chairs down.

Alice pointed at an empty chair. "Sit."

Harold complied. There was something about Alice that made him feel like a schoolboy in the principal's office. He sat quietly as Alice glared into his eyes.

Finally, she broke the silence. "Mr. Brown, I want you to know that you have caused me a great deal of trouble."

Harold started to protest, "My company put those trackers in according to your specs."

Alice cut him off, "I'm not talking about the stupid trackers. Don't worry. I know certain computer chip maker I'll be having a conversation with concerning today's fiasco."

"I think it could be Garcia."

She leaned forward. "What about Garcia?"

"I think he could be dirty."

"I know every move Agent Hernandez makes. Nothing gets past me. You can be assured of it. Speaking of which, that's my problem. What made you think you could get around the CIA by going to your political allies?"

Harold did not say a word. He knew he had done nothing wrong, but there was something about Alice's demeanor that made him feel guilty.

She took a breath and leaned back into her chair. In an instant, her expression changed. Her squinting eyes and tight cheek muscles relaxed, and then a smile crossed her face. Harold knew he was well out of his element.

Alice continued talking, "I believe I have a solution that satisfies not only you and your precious company but the CIA and the politicians."

Harold's right eyebrow rose slightly. "Really? I thought you'd kill the merger and bankrupt the company."

Alice gave an icy laugh. "Oh, I thought about it. However, the idea you and Tom are pursuing is not without merit. A larger defense company would have an easier time hiding certain black box research. As I understand it, you want to avoid being involved in fieldwork."

"I'm not equipped for this kind of life."

Alice smirked. "That's obvious. Now, getting back to your company, you'll be happy to know that I want you and Tom to stay in place. Tom's military background and history with the company makes him a great fit. Your family's legacy keeps PDS respectable.

You only need to pursue some R&D in one of your buildings on the agency's behalf. Consider it a skunkworks department. In exchange, I'm willing to deliver to you certain properties I know you desire."

"Those would be?" asked Harold. Inside, he hoped he would hear the words.

"The *Sweet Revenge* and Salvation Key."

Harold kept his expressions in check. "Okay, that might work, although I'm not sure I want that island. I miss Malibu."

Alice raised her arms up and stretched. "Excuse me, that boat ride was a bit tedious." She lowered her arms. "I'm afraid you can't go back home."

"What?" asked Harold in shock.

"No, that came out wrong. You can visit home, after we find Chuck, but you just can't move back home. Mr. Brown, you have made several new friends and powerful enemies. Between the senator's suicide, John's murder—"

Harold cut her off, "That was self-defense."

Alice stopped for a moment and then continued, "John's death, the decimation of your rival companies, and then your backroom greasing to get approval for Maria's marriage, you have left quite a wake behind you. While I can help with some things, interjecting myself or the agency into untoward political matters could cause a lot of unwanted questions and perhaps leak our deep cover work here to the press. I like you, Harold, but not that much."

He crossed his arms. "So what? I'm in some sort of exile? I thought this was America."

"Yes, and you are free to go where you want. However, if you want your plans for the merger to go through, and to receive the compensation for your troubles of relocating, you have to play ball. Technically, your new island is in international waters. Consider your location the ultimate tax shelter. Officially, it places you out of the country, which means you are out of the crosshairs of certain politicians."

"Play ball, huh? Is that what you and Garcia told the late John Richmond?"

Alice's eyes narrowed. "I don't know what you know about that operation, and I don't care. I was not involved with Agent Garcia at the time, but I can assure you, Mr. Brown, I have considerably more sway than Agent Hernandez."

"Wait," Harold's voice turned anxious. "You had me so focused on my company I forgot all about Doc. Where is he? Chuck said he was going after everyone we love."

Alice's face relaxed. "Dr. Zeev appears to be quite busy in North Carolina. It seems he and his friend Dr. Adam are diligently trying to find your brother. Maria also enjoys working at the children's home near Thomasville. I wish we had more people like them in this world."

"How do you know about Bill? Are you helping them find him?"

"Given today's little drama, we don't have a choice but to help Dr. Zeev."

Harold leaned forward. "Wait, how do you know all that?"

Alice smiled and said, "Please."

Harold pointed at her and interrupted, "Don't you dare. Tell me what's going on with Doc right now."

She surprised Harold by taking his hand while it was still extended and held it the way his mother used to. "Harold, they are safe. I had a man shadowing them while they were in North Carolina. We were concerned Chuck might try to find them if things went wrong. As soon as Garcia failed to radio in at the appointed time, we picked them up. They should already be wheels-up out of Concord. Fortunately, race car drivers fly their business jets in and out of that airport all the time, so one more business jet doesn't draw anyone's attention. They are perfectly fine. They should be back at Salvation Key before we get there."

Harold gently pulled back his hand. "So, Doc told the agent this stuff on their way out of town?"

"Not exactly. He protested having to return and said he did not intend to leave until he found your brother. When our agent explained the situation, he and Maria left immediately."

Harold sat back. "Good."

Alice leaned back towards Harold. "So, do we have a deal?"

Harold looked into Alice's eyes. Unlike Garcia's deadpan expressions, her face showed sincerity. "Of course."

"Excellent," she responded.

Harold heard one of the riverine boats start its motor. "We should hurry."

Alice put up her hand. "Slow down. We're going to take the second boat."

"What about Darla?" Harold asked.

"She will meet you at the…excuse me, your is-land."

Harold crossed his arms and scowled.

"There are times I can see why she likes you. Unfortunately, we do need to talk about your relationship."

Harold cut her off, "That's our business. I'm out, remember?"

"Yes, but are you going to have a problem if she continues working with us?"

"I didn't have a problem before."

Alice bent over and rested her elbows on her thighs. She looked at Harold like a concerned aunt. "I know, but after today, after the mess I saw down there, I thought you might have a different opinion."

Harold shook his head. "You weren't here. She shot Nigel in the knee with one of the fastest shots I've ever seen and only with her pistol."

Alice sat up. "You've seen a lot of shooting then?"

Harold shrugged. "Dad would take Tom and me out in the desert to play with some guns. We had a good time. Dad would get prototypes from engineers or companies that hoped they could get Dad to expand into more weaponry."

Alice sat up and crossed her legs. Harold was surprised how quickly she could change her mood. He could still feel a tension between them, but looking at Alice, anyone else would think none existed.

"What sort of prototypes did you shoot?"

"Shouldn't we be going after Chuck?" asked Harold.

The smile momentarily left her face. "Mr. Brown, I can assure you we have this situation is under control. Nothing gets away from our drones. He doesn't have that large a lead on us."

Harold's forehead crinkled. "It's a big ocean."

"It's a big sky," Alice shot back.

Harold unfolded his arms and allowed his shoulders to droop. "Okay, you win."

"Good." Her smile grew larger, and the tension Harold felt eased a little. "I believe we were talking about your shooting experience."

Harold clasped his hands in front of him. "We were talking about Darla."

"Of course, I believe you were telling me you were okay with her remaining in the CIA."

Harold shook his head. "I was trying to tell you I am okay with Darla doing whatever Darla wants to do."

Alice's hand tapped her knee. "Does that include working with the CIA?"

"If that's what she wants."

Her hand stopped. "Good. Now, back to my other question, you said your father would receive gun prototypes. Where did he keep those?"

Harold shrugged his shoulders. "Beats me. I'd assume they're stored somewhere at the company or they were destroyed."

A frown passed across Alice's lips and then just as quickly vanished back into a smile. "Do you mind if my people have a look around to see if we can find them?"

"I do, very much," said Harold. "I'm sure Tom and our people can find them if they still exist."

Alice uncrossed her legs. Her face became serious. "Good. I have one other thing, but it is top secret."

Harold sat up.

Alice continued, "If we're going to be in business together, I want you to call me by my real name. Keep in mind that it's need to know."

"Finally, something I need to know," quipped Harold.

Alice's eyes narrowed a bit. "You don't just accept what you're told very well."

Harold shrugged. "Do you blame me?"

"I suppose not."

"So, let's hear the big secret," joked Harold.

She leaned forward. "You do realize if my name gets out it could mean my death."

"But Darla and Garcia are what, expendable?"

"Some names are more real than others, but they may not be what our parents called us."

"Do you mean Darla's been lying to me?"

Alice patted his knee. "Nothing could be further from the truth. Darla and Garcia's past work were done under other names."

"Then why did you let Chuck know who they are?"

"We had to draw him in. However, not everything found in a personnel database or a birth certificate is always one hundred percent accurate. As you know, my truth is not always the truth."

"I'll never understand how you people do it."

"Yes, well, we all have our talents. Perhaps I should keep my name to myself."

"Tell me or don't. I already assume half of what Garcia tells me is a lie. Why should what you say be any different?"

Alice leaned back. "Of course you do." After a short pause, she said, "My name is Poppy Clark."

A snicker passed from Harold's lips before he could stifle it.

Alice raised her eyebrows. "My name amuses you?"

Harold waved his hand in front of him. "No, no. I mean, it was just unexpected. If I'm honest, I find your demeanor quite stern, for a woman or a man. Poppy is not what I think of when I'm around you."

"That's why it's Alice. The aliases are meant to be generic and believable."

"Good job."

"Oh, one other thing. Don't get used to my name. Unless you are in a meeting with me alone, it's always Alice."

Harold scowled. "That's awfully complicated. I may just stick with Alice."

"If it will stop you from accidently slipping out my real name in public, that's fine."

Alice stood up, and Harold followed her cue.

She pointed at the chairs. "Grab those, please. Our boat is waiting."

They made their way back to the beach. The disaster that had been scattered about was gone. The Kodiak's remains had been pulled onto the shore although nothing was left inside the craft but its shell. All other remnants of the day's events had been erased. Alice moved in front of Harold and pointed to one of the crewmen standing guard around the shallow watercraft. He stepped forward, took the chairs from Harold, and tossed them into the boat. Harold followed Alice into the armed craft.

Without a word, the crewmen boarded the boat, and they departed. Harold looked past the bow into the open water. He had no desire to ever see Crossroads Key again. In the distance, a small dot appeared. He didn't expect to see the yacht this close to the island with Chuck still about. Harold soon realized it was not his yacht, and the craft was much smaller, and closer, than he realized.

The Coast Guard Motor Lifeboat cruised towards their small craft at an equally high rate of speed. Before Harold had time to ask Alice any questions, the crews of both crafts were tying their boats together.

Alice turned, grabbed Harold's hand, and shook it. "This is where we part ways for now. The Coast Guard will get you back home quickly."

"What about my yacht?" asked Harold.

"We are taking her to the naval air station next to Key West. Chuck will be looking for her back at Islamorada, and we don't dare leave her in open waters."

A crewman hollered, "Time to go."

Harold climbed aboard the Coast Guard ship, and the two boats quickly parted ways. He wondered if Darla had made her way back to Salvation Key and if Garcia knew where Chuck was.

CHAPTER 25

The Coast Guard craft cruised up to the dock at Salvation Key. As he disembarked, Harold noticed the fishing boat's ladder had been repaired. Frank and the Coast Guard were busy untying the boat as he hurried up the pier towards the compound. Garcia and Darla came out of the boat shack, and Harold held up.

Darla threw her arm around Harold and buried her face into his shoulder. Her speech was clearer now. "I'm so sorry, darling. I should have never pulled you into this. You've been through so much."

Harold closed his eyes and whispered into her ear, "It isn't your fault. I made my choices, and I would do it again, as long as I have you."

Darla lifted her head, and Harold kissed her. Never had her silky lips felt so welcoming. He could not have cared less about what would happen to Chuck once Alice and her crew found him. He was just thankful to have Darla still alive and in his life. The two finally parted lips and released one another.

Garcia cleared his throat. "I'm afraid I have some bad news."

Harold looked at him and back at Darla.

Garcia continued, "Chuck got away."

Harold had had enough. His large right hand grabbed hold of Garcia's shirt. Garcia's feet tripped and scooted as Harold pulled him in close.

"Harold!" exclaimed Darla, but he ignored her.

"Tell me, Agent Hernandez, how did Chuck get away?" Harold growled.

Fear washed over Garcia's face as he looked at Harold. "I don't know. How could I?"

Harold shoved Garcia away, and he backpedaled, slamming against the boat shack to avoid falling down.

Darla stepped between them. "What are you doing?"

Harold gently moved Darla out and the way. "Ask Garcia about the Kodiak."

Darla stepped in front of Harold again. "I already know. I noticed it while they were cleaning things up."

"And?"

Garcia spoke up from behind Darla, "And as I told Darla, I was blind firing from behind the ammo box once he turned the gun on me. I was aiming away from the beach, and I probably hit the boat. The gunfire was heated, and Chuck had me pinned."

"It couldn't have been too heated," replied Harold from around Darla. "Nigel wouldn't have escaped that easy."

"I told you about that already," responded Garcia.

Harold took a deep breath to calm down. "Okay, for now. So, how could Chuck disappear?"

"We think he had a sub or someone did," Darla said. "The drone found his boat, and it looked empty. We blew it up, just in case they were hiding below."

"But you don't think they were hiding?" asked Harold.

"No." She stepped aside, and Garcia took a step forward. "We believe Chuck would have either tried to shoot down the drone or simply jump overboard. He's a smart guy. He would have known his ship was about to be blown up."

"So, what do we do now?" asked Harold.

"We wait," responded Darla and Garcia in unison.

"What about Doc?" asked Harold.

"He and Maria arrived a short time ago and are waiting at the house. We asked to talk to you first," responded Darla.

"Are they okay?"

"They're fine, although Maria is upset with you for getting yourself in danger."

"I'm going to my bungalow," said Garcia.

"You mean my bungalow," responded Harold.

Garcia's shoulders slumped. "Yes, your bungalow," and he headed down the trail.

"I heard about that from Garcia," Darla said. "Congratulations, dear. Maybe this sandbar will finally become respectable."

"Hopefully not when we're together," joked Harold.

Darla smacked him in the chest. "Boys."

The two began their trek back to the main house.

Joshua and Maria were standing at the front door. Maria ran up and drove her head into Harold's chest as she hugged him.

Joshua casually walked up. "We heard the boat had docked."

Maria let go, and Joshua and Harold hugged one another.

Joshua stepped back. "I'm glad you're safe."

"Are you stupid?" asked Maria as she slugged Harold in the shoulder. "Why would you fight men with guns? You're not bulletproof. I should take you over my knee."

Harold laughed at the image.

Maria crossed her arms. "I'm not joking. That was stupid."

Harold regained control. "I know. I'll try not to do it again. I promise. I've missed both of you so much."

"So, what now, secret agent man?" asked Joshua.

"Whoa, I'm no secret agent." He pointed to Darla. "That's her department. Ask her."

"I'm not sure I'm a secret agent man, but for now we wait," Darla said.

Maria rolled her eyes. "More wasting time. My children need me."

Joshua interjected, "Maria quickly formed a bond with the orphans."

"Is it the way you remember it, Doc?"

"The place looks older. Adam looks older, and I look older."

"Don't we all?" responded Harold.

"I don't," chimed in Darla and Maria.

"Present company excluded," said Harold. "Well, I'm bushed. I have had more than my fair share of arms dealers, butt-busting boats, and spooks. I think I'll go relax upstairs. Darla, would you please join me?"

Darla took his hand, and the two headed inside and upstairs. They settled onto the wooden swing inside the covered breezeway. Harold turned, lying down with his head in Darla's lap. His legs bent upward to fit into the limited space, and he closed his eyes. The cool salty breeze washed over his body.

Darla gently played with his hair. Her voice sounded distant as she said, "Rest, my warrior. Your fight is done."

***

Harold awoke in his bedroom. It was nighttime, and the moonbeams danced along the walls. He could not remember how he got to bed, but he was exhausted. He looked out at the darkness through the French doors as he thought about Darla's hands running through his hair. A sound from the bathroom caught his attention, and he rolled over to see what it was. Harold frowned in disgust as John appeared wearing only a towel and his twisted smile.

"What? Were you hoping I was someone else?" asked John. "Perhaps your girlfriend? You naughty boy." John cackled at his own joke.

Harold sat up and crossed his arms. "I thought we were done."

John came over and sat uncomfortably close to him. His temple no longer had the gun in it or blood pouring out of it. "Harold, you can't get rid of me that easy. So, have you figured out who my partner is?"

"I couldn't care less," replied Harold. "That's the CIA's problem. I'm out, done, finished."

"Uh-huh. Do you think that's what Chuck thinks?" John asked.

"Again, not my problem."

John turned towards Harold. "I'm trying to tell you something, brat. You can't just walk away."

Harold stared into John's dead eyes. "I know that, but I've been told to wait it out, and that's what I'm going to do."

"I don't know how to get through to you."

A voice hissed behind Harold, and a black mist passed around him to hover next to John. "Let me try," said the dark specter.

The smell of sulfur made Harold gag. He didn't need this. He was tired and had been through enough. "Get out of here, Haidar. I told you, I'm not going to feel guilty over your death. You sealed your fate the moment you threw in with those terrorists."

The mist hissed, "Who said I'm Haidar?"

A chill cut through Harold, but then he remembered something his father had taught him. True evil only existed to accuse people of their wrongs and fill them with bitterness and hate. "I know what you are. Do you think I'll cower or cry out? I won't be accused or tormented by the likes of you."

The mist cackled. "Really? Joshua and Maria are in danger, and what about your half-brother? It's all your fault."

Harold reached for the mist, but his hand passed through it. Its yellow eyes turned red, and a cackle filled his bedroom.

"No, none of this is my doing. John started this." Harold turned to John. "I don't blame you. I know you felt slighted by my dad, and then your hate took you and twisted you into the monster you became. You killed my father, but I forgive you."

A hiss filled Harold's room, and the black mist passed through him, pushing him sideways. He caught himself and watched the specter fly from the room, but John still sat there.

"I told you. I'm not done yet. This is my island after all."

Harold leaned close to John's putrid flesh and whispered, "I guess you haven't heard. This is my island now." He sat back up. "All of it. The government gave it to me. Well, it wasn't exactly given. I have to give up moving back home to Malibu, but I can live with that for the time being. Tom will take good care of my home in California. I will outwait my enemies and then be back home one day. That reminds me, your company—it's mine as well. You don't have any reason to stay, John. You're forgiven, and everything you had is gone. You're free to leave. You need to leave."

"Well played. You're smarter than you look, but I may return. You just never know."

"Don't waste your time."

John's specter stared into Harold's eyes as he slowly vanished.

Harold took a breath and walked around his room and bathroom to confirm nothing else was hiding. Once he was satisfied he was alone, he lay back down and drifted off, content in the knowledge that he had defeated his demons.

***

The sun hit Harold's eyelids. He instinctively shielded his tired eyes and sat up. The smell of dirt, wood, leather, and straw filled his nostrils. As his eyes adjusted to the light, he found himself inside his father's longhouse. He knew exactly where he was. Much of his childhood was spent in the Viking village with Joshua. *Doc. This was all Doc's doing,* thought Harold. He stretched and went outside. His father, mother, Joshua, and Maria sat outside the entrance. To his surprise, the entire village stood before the longhouse with them.

"Did I miss something, my Lord?" asked Harold.

"Of course not."

His mother stood and gave him a hug. "We're so proud of you."

"What's the occasion?" asked Harold.

"Saving the village, of course," responded his mother as she returned to her seat.

From within the ranks, came John's familiar voice. He stepped out from the crowd to stand in front of Harold and his family. "This is all for you, brat. You survived, for now. But before you celebrate too much, maybe you should ask mommy and daddy about your half-brother."

The king stood with his battle ax at his side. "Mind your tongue, vermin."

To Harold's surprise, John dropped to his knees and bowed his head. "My apologies, King Richard and Queen Barbara. I was wrong. I was wrong about you and your son, but he has a right to know."

Richard sat back down on his throne. "You may rise."

John stood and a crooked smile formed on his lips. "Actually, your parents may not know everything." John pointed to the other side of Harold's father. "Maybe you should ask Joshua about Bill."

Joshua leapt to his feet and unsheathed his sword. A blinding light filled the sunlit sky and swept through John. As fast as lightning, Joshua had his sword sheathed, and John was gone.

"I don't understand," said Harold.

Harold drew in the salty air and banged his foot on the swing as he sat up.

"What is it?" Darla asked in an alarmed voice.

Harold rubbed his face for a moment. "How long have I been asleep?"

She slid over and grabbed his hand. "Just a few minutes. Are you okay?"

Harold released her grip and kissed her on the cheek. "Yes, I need to talk to Joshua."

He stood up. "Where is he?"

Darla looked up at him confused. "I think he and Maria are sitting by the pool."

Looking over the balcony, Harold saw the two of them sunning themselves in the lounge chairs.

Darla stood. "I'll go with you."

Harold gave her lips a long kiss and then said, "No, honey. I'll explain later because I'm not sure what's going on myself."

She gave Harold a puzzled look and sat back down as he rushed downstairs. Joshua and Maria sat up at the sound of him rushing down the stairs towards the pool.

"What's wrong?" asked Maria.

"I need to talk to Doc."

Joshua looked concerned. "What is it?"

Harold walked over and sat down on the side of the lounge chair next to Joshua. "Doc, it's about Bill. I had another dream. John claimed you haven't told me everything about my brother. Please, I need to know about my half-brother."

"What sort of dream?"

Maria interjected, "You need to tell him what you and Adam talked about."

"What is she talking about, Doc?"

"I'm afraid I owe you an apology."

"Why, Doc? What did you do?"

Joshua sat up and took hold of Harold's hand. "You have no idea how much I love you and your brother. There is a bond that forms during hypnotherapy. Over time, Bill became like a son to me. Then there was you and your family. I never knew a group of people could change my life so much." Tears began to pool in Joshua's eyes.

"Doc, come on, what is it?"

Maria sat up on the edge of her chair and started to rub Joshua's back.

Joshua continued, "When I couldn't find a way to calm your rage, I decided it was safer to keep you and Bill apart and to try and stop you from ever hurting your family."

Harold stood and paced for a moment. "We were already apart. And why would I want to hurt my family?" Harold sat back on the edge of Joshua's chair. "Please, Doc, you're starting to scare me."

Joshua took a long, deep breath. "I put a failsafe in your brain, or rather, I tried to. I tried to compartmentalize your memories of Bill away from everything else. Next, your father and I worked to program your subconscious so your rage would never be directed at your family, but your mind was too strong. You never forgot about Bill, and then you were unable to save your father."

"But, Doc, it did work. I heard your voice when we were being shot at. I saved Darla."

"What about your dad?"

"I couldn't save Dad. I didn't know what to do. As soon as I saw him pull the gun up to his head, my vision went crimson. I hoped he would shoot at me instead, but when he put the gun in his mouth, I didn't know what to do. He pulled the trigger, and I tore the room apart."

Tears trickled down Harold's face, and Joshua hugged him for a moment. "Are you okay?"

"I'm alright, Doc."

Joshua let go. "I gave Adam instructions to attempt the same procedure on Bill in hopes that it would work. I told Adam to not only hide his memories of you, but his memories of me as well. I had promised to come back, but after two years, I knew I would not be returning anytime soon. Adam and I were concerned Bill might regress at the thoughts of me being gone and the realization I was with his brother. Adam was completely successful with Bill. Any memories he has of us are locked away somewhere deep in his subconscious."

Harold took in everything he had heard and was silent for a moment. Then he asked, "Doc, does that mean if you find Bill, he won't remember us?"

"Perhaps. We could trigger those memories just by appearing or if he hears our names repeatedly. We aren't forgotten, but don't expect Bill to know who we are right away."

"Okay, I don't know why you're so upset. It doesn't sound like you damaged us, and you thought you were doing the right thing."

Joshua looked at Maria, and she kissed his forehead. He turned back to Harold. "No, I knew the dangers in what I was doing. I just thought I was smarter than the other experts. I was young and cocky, and I played with your lives. Adam and I reviewed our decisions from that time. We both agree it was a mistake, no matter how well-intentioned. I've been too ashamed to admit it to you until now."

Joshua broke down, and Harold and Maria hugged him.

"Is everything alright down there?"

Harold looked up to see Darla watching from over the balcony.

"Yes," hollered back Harold. "We'll talk later."

Darla pulled her head back, and he heard her walking across the balcony towards the main part of the house.

He turned back to Joshua, who was wiping his face with a handkerchief.

"Doc, let me help you find my brother."

"What can you do to help?" asked Joshua. "You never really knew him."

"He's my brother."

Joshua sniffed, wiped his nose then put away his handkerchief. "Nature over nurture?"

"Something like that. I mean, we may not know each other, but we're bound to have something in common."

"I don't see how, but I can use all the help I can get. Like many orphans, Bill has not had contact with the orphanage since he left it when he turned eighteen. After graduating from Columbia Business School, he took a job on Wall Street. He was there two short years and amassed four million dollars in investment commissions. He left and disappeared after that."

A knowing smile crept across Harold's face. "Take the money and run."

Joshua cocked his head. "Why would you say that?"

"That's what I would do if I had to work on Wall Street. Come on, Doc, nobody wants to live in New York. It's expensive, overcrowded, and dirty. The investment guys grab their commissions and move away to someplace cheaper the first chance they get. Normally they show back up at another investment house in a less expensive city after they blow through their money and do it all over again."

Joshua raised an eyebrow. "How do you know this? You never worked in the stock market."

"Stanford's MBA program. Honestly, Doc. Do you think I didn't have friends when I was away? I shared an apartment with this guy Carl. He had just burned through his first two million and was working on a graduate degree in hopes of moving into a management position and getting off the trading floor when he returned to work."

Maria took Joshua by the shoulders. "You see, I told you and Adam that Harold could help. Boys—"

"We know, we're stupid," finished Joshua and Harold together.

EPILOGUE

Bill and Lori snuggled against one another on the couch. He enjoyed the intoxicating smell of her perfume as he looked out the window, admiring the Charlotte evening skyline that glowed like diamonds on a crown against black velvet.

He let out a sigh. "This must be what heaven feels like."

Lori reached over to slide her fingers through his thick wavy black hair.

He felt a shiver of pleasure at the touch of her fingernails lightly teasing his scalp as she wound her way through his hair. His smile broadened. "Have you ever seen the likes of the light show from the top of these skyscrapers? I tell you what, they never get old."

Lori's soft hand grasped his face, turning his head towards her. She leaned in and gave Bill a long lingering kiss. His head felt light and dizzy. When she released his lips, he allowed his gaze to travel from her eyes, over her lips, and down her hair. She playfully put her finger up to his mouth and then turned to sit back against the couch.

Bill flopped his head back onto the couch and spoke at the ceiling. "I don't know what I like more, the view of Bank of America's colored crown or the thrill of your kisses."

Lori gave his chest a playful slap. "How dare you make such a comparison," she said in a pouty tone.

Bill sat up and gazed into her dark eyes. Her silky lips sent electric shockwaves through his body. When their mouths released again, he could no longer tell if he was sitting or floating. He let a silly grin spread across his face.

Lori sat back. Her dark hair framed her high cheekbones and smooth olive skin. To Bill, she glowed like an angel floating in heaven with the skyline behind her framing her beauty.

The sound of his cellphone destroyed his vision. Bill scowled towards where it rang on the coffee table.

Lori reached over, picked it up, and handed it to him.

"Let it go to voicemail," Bill said, and he pushed the side button to silence the ringing.

"What if it's work?"

"It's 11 p.m.," he protested.

"Not in Asia." Lori reached over and hit the green button.

Bill quickly brought the phone to his ear and said, "Go away." He hung up and tossed the phone back onto the coffee table.

Lori's eyes widened. "Are you crazy?"

Bill winked. "Worried? It's Friday night. All the markets I care about are closed. If it's work, they'll wait until tomorrow."

"What if it was your boss?"

"It's what? Four a.m. in the UK?"

Lori sat back on the couch. "You know what I mean. You're my boss. What if it was work and then it leaks out that we had a date?"

Bill leaned in to kiss her, but Lori turned away. He kissed her cheek instead.

"Look, don't worry."

Bill stood and walked over to the outside wall. Bank of America's corporate center rose up over the other towers. He watched a large group of people mingle with each other on a nearby rooftop club and then stared at the crowned corporate tower. To Bill, it symbolized the stranglehold massive banks held on the world. Still, it held options.

Lori walked up behind him and put her arms around him. "I thought you said you would never work for a major bank." She nestled her lips against his neck, and Bill felt a thrill travel down his spine.

"For me, no. But for someone I love, I'll do anything."

"But what if I don't want to live in New York? That's where Merrill Lynch is."

"Oh, I'm not thinking about working for them. I'm just thinking about the options I'll have when I leave Clark and Company so we can be together."

Lori spun him around, and Bill lost all sense of where he was as she wrapped him up in her arms and kissed him passionately.

The cell phone went off again, and the two of them ignored it. The ringing finally stopped. Bill pulled back and came up for air. "If that thing rings again, I swear I'll throw it off the balcony."

Lori playfully tapped the end of his nose. "If you do, you'll hit someone on the ground and go to jail, and then who will I end up with?"

The phone rang again.

Bill turned. "I swear…"

Lori stopped him mid-sentence by grabbing his arm. She turned him and planted a quick kiss on his lips. "Just answer it so they'll go away."

Bill hurried over and snatched up the phone.

An unfamiliar voice came through the receiver, "Is this Bill Johnson?"

"Speaking, who's this?" grumbled Bill.

"Did you grow up at the Carolina's Chidren's Home?"

"Who's asking?"

The man on the other end sounded relieved, "Oh good. This is Chuck. I'm a friend of your brother."

"Chuck who? I don't have a brother," Bill responded in a clearly annoyed tone.

"Excuse me. Yes, you do. Harold Brown, your brother. You don't know your own half-brother?"

"No," Bill responded emphatically. "If you don't mind, it's very late here, and I'm busy."

"Come on, Billy, your brother who got adopted. Do you care if I call you Billy?"

"It's Bill." He began to pace about the kitchen, impatient for the phone call to end.

"Fine, Bill. I'm telling you that you do have an older brother, but maybe you don't remember him. Perhaps Joshua never told you about him."

Joshua…why do I know that name? He looked over at Lori who was staring in his direction and tracing her partially exposed thigh with her fingernail. He was growing more impatient with each passing moment. He needed to end the phone call now.

"I don't know who you're looking for, but it's not me. I have no family. There are lots of Bills from lots of orphanages. You have the wrong number. Please, don't call back. Good night."

Bill disconnected the call and strolled back to Lori. He tossed the phone towards the table, and it slid off the end of the furniture before plopping onto the hardwood floor.

"Where were we?" he asked with his best sly smile.

Lori stuck out her bottom lip. "That ruined our moment."

He sat down next to her, leaned over, and gently pushed her towards the armrest. She pulled him down with her as she let her body give in to his advance.

He hovered over her face and whispered, "I believe I can fix that."

Lori giggled as Bill went in for a kiss.

Coming Soon

Bill and the Sting of Death